John Peile

Notes on the Nalopåkhyanam

Or, Tale of Nala

John Peile

Notes on the Nalopåkhyanam
Or, Tale of Nala

ISBN/EAN: 9783337074067

Printed in Europe, USA, Canada, Australia, Japan

Cover: Foto ©Andreas Hilbeck / pixelio.de

More available books at **www.hansebooks.com**

NOTES

ON THE

NALOPÀKHYÀNAM

OR

TALE OF NALA,

FOR THE USE OF CLASSICAL STUDENTS.

BY

JOHN PEILE, M.A.

FELLOW AND TUTOR OF CHRIST'S COLLEGE, CAMBRIDGE.

EDITED FOR THE SYNDICS OF THE UNIVERSITY PRESS.

Cambridge:

AT THE UNIVERSITY PRESS.

1881.

PREFACE.

THE 'Story of Nala' has been already so well edited for English students that it may seem necessary to explain why I have chosen to write notes upon it rather than upon some other Sanskrit work. My reasons were two. First, many years ago I made a careful examination of the case-usages in the 'Nala,' to assist me in the comparative study of syntax: it was therefore most convenient to bring the result of this study to bear upon the 'Nala' itself. Secondly, I wished to write for those who were not acquainted with the Sanskrit character, who (at first at least) did not wish to obtain a technical knowledge of Sanskrit grammar with all its minutiæ, but to get such a knowledge of the language as might fit them to commence the study of comparative philology in a more scientific way than is possible without any knowledge of Sanskrit. It was therefore convenient to select a poem which had been already edited in the Roman character: and the Syndics of the University Press kindly agreed to publish these 'Notes' as a companion volume to the text already excellently edited for them with a Vocabulary and a Sketch of Sanskrit Grammar by Professor Jarrett. But the notes may of course be equally well used by those who understand the Devanāgarī character, and have the well-known edition of Prof. Monier Williams; against which it is only possible to bring the unthankful charge that, with the translation of Dean Milman at one side and every word parsed in the

Glossary, it gives only too much grammatical help to a beginner. For the use of those who do not use Prof. Jarrett's text I have made constant reference to the grammars of Prof. Monier Williams and Prof. Max Müller.

As my notes are intended for classical scholars, I have of course given special attention to comparative grammar. I have not entered into any discussion of etymologies, thinking it best in a work of this description to state merely the undoubtedly cognate words, and to refer for further information to Curtius' *Grundzüge* (tr. Wilkins and England). The second part of that work is so full and satisfactory, that it seemed sufficient to refer to it alone, with but slight reference to other writers. In questions of syntax I had no such book to which to refer: I have therefore discussed them at as much length as seemed advisable here: I have sometimes assumed results of which I hope one day to offer proof in a work upon the origins of syntax comparatively treated, which is at present in an inchoate state. I shall be thankful for criticism upon any of the views herein stated.

The practice of joining together many bases into one long compound is so common in Sanskrit that it must occupy the attention even of beginners. I therefore thought it worth while to give a short sketch of the employment of the same principle in other languages, in order thereby to shew more clearly the immensely greater importance which it has in Sanskrit than in any other language, not excluding Greek.

But while I have mainly adhered to my original purpose of simply teaching as much comparative grammar as was possible in the limits of notes, I felt as I progressed in the work that it was undesirable to omit all reference to the Hindū beliefs and customs which occur so plentifully in the 'Nala.' I had constantly felt the want of help on these points when I first read the poem. Fortunately there now exist books which amply supply it: and I have frequently referred to Dowson's 'Classical Dictionary of Hindū Mythology' (Trübner's Oriental Series)—a capital book, giving just the information which a beginner needs, and to Prof. Monier Williams' 'Indian Wisdom,' and to his little work on 'Hinduism,' published by the Society for promoting Christian Knowledge, both of which works seem to me to be admirably executed. Reference has also been often made to the so-called 'Law of Manu'; I shall be glad if by doing so I may cause in any a desire for further acquaintance with that most interesting book. Dr Muir's well-known work is better adapted to the wants of advanced students.

It will be seen that I have followed Prof. Jarrett's method of transliteration. The great peculiarity of this is the employment of the dot to denote long vowels only; short i therefore loses its dot and becomes ı. This is certainly a very simple and reasonable reform: it offers no difficulty whatever to a reader, and it does not require half an hour to learn to write in this way. But the difficulty of printing from a manuscript so written is very great, and I fear that some slips may have escaped my observation, though I have been as careful as I could. Like Prof. Jarrett, I write *c* to represent the English sound *ch:* I do so with some reluctance, but it is an advantage that a single sound should be represented by a single symbol, and that when *h* follows a consonant it should consistently represent the aspirate of that consonant: on the same principle the *sh*-sound is denoted by *ṣ*: and this mark connects it with the cerebral class. The only point where I part company with Prof. Jarrett is in the notation of the palatal sibilant: this he expresses by *ś*: I prefer *ç*, which indicates the origin of the sibilant from an original guttural; and this is of the greatest importance to a philologist: there is much difficulty in keeping distinct in the mind three different sibilants when all denoted by *s* with different diacritical marks—a difficulty which is not found to any great extent with the nasals.

I have to thank Prof. Cowell for some valuable suggestions which will appear in their place. He also kindly revised some of the earlier sheets.

JOHN PEILE.

Feb. 2, 1881.

ADDENDA AND ERRATA.

p. 17, l. 20, *for* "sa-Varṣṇeyo Jivalaḥ" *read* "sa-Várṣṇeya-Jivalaḥ."

p. 18, l. 15, *after* "genitive in Latin," *add* "and mille takes the genitive regularly in Plautus, e.g. 'mille drachumarum,' Trin. 425."

p. 24, l. 24, *add* 21 before sakáçe.

p. 33, l. 7, *for* "Sāvitri" *read* "Sāvitrī."

p. 67, 5 lines from bottom, *for* "çirṣha" *read* "çirṣa."

p. 87, l. 13, *for* "kalántaráviṛttı" *read* "kálántaravṛttı."

p. 157, 11 lines from bottom, *for* "dávana" *read* "dávane."

NOTES

ON THE NALOPÀKHYÀNAM

OR

TALE OF NAḶA.

Nalopàkhyàna = Nala + upàkhyàna, 'the Nala-tale' or 'tale of Nala.' The crasis of *a* + *u* into *o* is one of those euphonic rules, or 'laws of Sandhi,' i. e. collocation (sam + √dhà), which must be fully mastered before a line of Sanskrit can be read. They invariably admit of a physiological explanation: thus *a* and *u* are the extreme points in the series of compound vowels formed by progressively advancing the tongue and rounding the lips (see my 'Intr. to Gr. and Lat. Etym.' pp. 94—97, ed. 3): now *o* lies on the line between *a* and *u*, and is therefore naturally produced in the endeavour to combine the two extremes. These euphonic changes enter into our own daily speech, and if our spelling were phonetic would regularly appear in our written language as well as in Sanskrit.

upàkhyàna = upa + àkhyàna, where *upa* has the same force as 'sub,' i.e. a diminutive. Àkhyàna is formed from à + √khyà 'to tell,' and means a legendary or historical poem; the line between the two is not drawn in India. The tale is in fact an episode in the third book of the enormous epic the Mahābhārata, which "is not so much a poem with a single subject as a vast cyclopaedia or thesaurus of Hindū mythology, legendary history, ethics and philosophy" ('Ind. Wisdom,' p. 371, where a full account of the poem may be found). The third book is called the 'Vana-parvan' or 'forest-section' and describes the enforced residence of the Pāṇḍava princes in the forest; during which this tale of Nala was recited to them by the sage Vṛihadaçva (see line 1), to encourage them by the account of a similar wandering and subsequent restoration to power.

Observe that the title of the tale is not denoted by a derivative from the name of the chief actor, as the 'Οδυσσεία from 'Οδυσσεύς. It is compounded out of two independent bases. This method of composition is so common in Sanskrit, and the traces of it in other languages (Greek, Latin, English) are so numerous, that it is worth while to give a general sketch of the system and to point out the extent to which different languages have employed it. The native division of the Sanskrit compounds may be studied with much profit in Max Müller's Sk. Grammar, c. xxiii, more briefly in Benfey's Sk. Grammar (English), § 195—207; and differently arranged in M. Williams' Grammar, § 733—781, or Wilson's Grammar, § 265—282. A right knowledge of the principles of composition in Sanskrit is important; for the same mental training is given by the analysis of compounds which is given in Greek and Latin by the study of the rules of syntax.

Compounds may be divided into two main classes, (1) where the two (or more) members of the compound are syntactically independent of each other, (2) where one member is dependent on the other by standing to it in the place of an adjective, participle or appositional substantive, a numeral, an indeclinable prefix or a case.

I. Independent Compounds.

These are called in Sanskrit 'Dvandva' (doubling); we may term them 'collective' or 'aggregative' compounds. Each member of the compound is independent of any other, and might stand alone, connected with the rest by a particle, or with the connection only implied by the context. It is in Sanskrit (I think) only that these compounds can be said properly to exist. Two bases (as 'Bráhmaṇa' and 'Kṣatriya') are combined together and declined with dual terminations (as 'Bráhmaṇa-kṣatriyau'): but to express several things of more than one kind, which are either inanimate, or at least not human, the compound is declined in the singular, as 'yánayugyasya' vii 9 'of chariots and horses;' comp. our 'horse and foot' of an army. Often more than two bases are combined and declined with plural terminations (as deva-gandharva-mánuṣ'-oraga-rákṣasán, i 29, an acc. plur. of a compound made up of five bases). These compounds are very common in Sanskrit: and when restricted to proper names, or to a list of different species, are not liable to cause confusion: otherwise one part of the compound might be regarded as syntactically dependent on another, and so the meaning would be uncertain. This is perhaps the reason why these compounds fell out of use in Greek and Latin. Traces of them (but not satisfactory ones, see below at page 5) are to be seen, though very rarely, in derivative words; as in βατραχομυομαχία = 'frog-mouse-fighting' (where the first two bases form a Dvandva); also in Latin in the derivative 'suovetaurilia,' formed from the triple compound base 'su-ovi-tauro' + the suffix *-ili*. One undoubted example is the famous dish-compound beginning λεπαδοτεμαχοσελαχογαλεο... in Aristophanes, Eccl. 1169: but this is obviously a tour-de-force and alien to the genius of the language.

II. Dependent Compounds.

Here we no longer find two or more bases logically coordinate; we find one base expressing an idea subordinate to another, or a base combined with some preposition or indeclinable word, modifying its meaning. The different classes of this kind distinguished by Sanskrit grammarians are three, called respectively, Tat-purusha, Bahu-vrīhi, and Avyayī-bhāva: but, as the Tat-purusha compounds are subdivided into three classes, Tat-purusha proper, Karma-dhāraya, and Dvigu, we may consider the whole number five. The names generally exemplify the nature of the compounds.

(1) Tat-purusha is 'the man of him,' i.e. a compound in which the first member stands as a case to the other, here as a genitive. Such are Virasena-suta, i 1, satya-vádin (truth-speaker), i 3, kha-gama (goer in the sky), i 24, &c.

(2) Karma-dhāraya (i.e. 'object-comprehending') is a compound in which the first member would stand to the second (were the two expressed syntactically) as an adjective or appositional substantive, e.g. vara-nári (excellent woman), i 4, nara-çárdúla (man that is a tiger), i 15, where however the determining base comes last, see note, a. 1.

(3) Dvigu ('two-cow') is the name of compounds where the first member is a numeral; this class is really only a subdivision of the Karma-dhāraya. It is nearly always neuter.

So far these compounds have agreed in this, that they express a complete idea, some person or thing.

(4) The next class (Bahu-vrīhi) differs in that a compound of this sort is no longer a substantive, but is used as an attribute of some other person or thing. Thus áyata-locana (i 13) would mean as a Karma-dhāraya 'a long eye:' but it is there (and regularly) used as a Bahu-vrīhi, 'long-eyed,' an attribute of some person. The name Bahu-vrīhi is itself an instance: it means 'much rice'—but is actually used as an attribute of land 'having much rice.' Just as a Bahu-

vrīhi compound may be based on a possible Karma-dhāraya, so also it may be based on a Tat-purusha. Thus at line i 5 apraja = having no offspring, is based on a possible K. D. aprajā = not offspring, comp. abrāhmaṇa = one who is not a Brāhman, &c.: just so prajākāma (same line) might be a T. P. = desire of offspring, but is there a B. V. = 'having desire of offspring.'

(5) The final class Avyayī-bhāva (i. e. the construction of indeclinables—'avyaya' = ἄπτωτος) is formed by combining a preposition, conjunction, or other indeclinable word with a base, the result being put in the form of an acc. neuter; e. g. anu-rūpaṃ = 'conformably;' yathâ-tatham (iii 2) = 'truthfully.' This last example shews the principle on which these compounds are formed; if the second part has not the termination of a neuter accusative (as anu-rúpam) the final vowel must be altered so as to get a neuter form, e. g. yathâtathâ (= 'in such way, as it is,' i. e. 'truly') becomes yathâtatham. It will suffice however if the second base have a termination which can be regarded as neuter, though the word be masculine or feminine when uncompounded: e. g. anu-Viṣṇu = after Vishṇu; and it is regarded as a neuter acc. used adverbially, because there exist neuter bases in *u*, e. g. madhu. This last class of compounds is much more developed in Sanskrit than in any other language: we may compare ὑπέρμορον in Greek, comminus, eminus, in Latin. But in no other language except Sanskrit could they have been raised into a separate class: and historically considered, their type must have been the neuter of a K. D. compound, to which therefore they should be referred in any attempt to trace the development of these compound words as found in several languages.

Care should be taken in studying these forms to take examples which are true compounds, and not derivatives: e. g. μεγαλόνοια = μεγαλονοο + suffix ια, and is therefore not a K. D. but a derivative of a B. V. μεγαλο-νοο = having a great mind. Similarly biennium is not properly a 'Dvigu,' but is derived from bienni- (which is a B. V. based on a Dvigu) by the further suffix *-o*. We want compounds of two true bases, with no more alteration of the second base than is necessary under the altered circumstances in which it is placed (e. g. sa-bhârya, 'with a wife,' i 8, is compounded of sa, and bhâryâ 'a wife,' but the compound must of course be declined in the masculine, and so the final ā of bhâryâ must be shortened): we must also allow final change for phonetic convenience (e. g. semi-animis, which is altered, like so many other adjectives whose base originally ended in *o*, from semi-animus, which is still found in Lucretius). Where we have an apparent derivative from a compound base (as e.g. in *βατραχομυομαχία*, mentioned above) the history of the word is always uncertain. That compound is not rightly formed to mean 'frog-mouse-fight:' it is not a legitimate T. P. 'battle of frog-mouse,' based on a Dvandva 'frog-mouse,' because *μάχη*, not *-μαχία*, is required; *μαχία* is no word. According to the laws of formation of Greek words, we can call *βατραχομυο-μαχία* only a derivative, with suffix *-ια*, from *βατραχομυο-μαχο-* = frog-mouse-fighter, and such a compound admits of no satisfactory explanation. Very likely the form *-μαχια* obtained currency from common words like *συμμαχία*, which is a perfectly intelligible derivative form *συμμαχο* + *ια* = 'the state of allies;' and then was early used instead of *μάχη*, e.g. in *θεομαχία* (Plato) or even *τειχομαχία* (Herodotus). But in the uncertainty as to their history it is well to reject such real or apparent derivatives, though we may thereby lose good examples of composition.

There are some points about these compounds which require a passing remark: more may be found in the special grammars of each language, and (so far as Greek compounds are concerned) in Curtius' 'Elucidations, &c.,' pp. 164—176 (a most suggestive comment) and in the 'Studien,' esp. G. Meyer's articles in vols. V and VI and Clemm's critique in vol. VII.

1. The forms of the bases when compounded sometimes vary from their original form. We have seen that the final base is liable to be affected, in the same way as any other uncompounded base, by phonetic influence: thus in Latin bi-anno becomes bienni with two merely phonetic changes. But the termination of the first base also frequently differs from that in common use: e.g. we have *τειχο-μαχία* though the base is *τειχες*, or *φαεσ-ί-μβροτος* where a vowel appears which at least has nothing to do with the second base. Here again it seems that euphony is the regulating principle: but its action is (apparently at least) irregular. Thus we might have expected *τειχεσμαχία* as well as *σακέσ-παλος*: but probably the ο is due partly to Dissimilation. Sometimes we must allow for the possibility of variant stems, e.g. *χερ-* in *χέρνιψ*, *χερο-* or *χειρο-* in *χειροήθης*. The *ι* in *φαεσίμβροτος* (and in the very numerous similar forms) has been commonly explained as a 'connecting vowel,' i.e. an inorganic sound produced by the desire for euphony. I should acquiesce in this explanation myself: but among the latest gram-

marians some (as Meyer) prefer to regard it as the remnant of a fuller base (see 'Studien,' v 61, &c.), or, as Clemm (vii 13, &c.), refuse to regard the vowel as *consciously* employed to facilitate the combination of difficult consonants, but *unconsciously* produced in connection with those consonants, which, (as λ, μ, ν, ρ, ϝ) by their continuous character, and also by being sonant, are favourable to the production of a parasitic vowel sound[1].

2. Sometimes the first part of a compound belonging to the T. P. class is found in the actual case-form, not in the base: e.g. iuris-consultus, not ius-consultus; Πυλοι-γενής, a loc. compound, 'born at Pylos,' and formed with the locative case and not the base, so also ναυσί-κλυτος, &c.; divas-pati, 'lord of heaven' (see our 'doomsday,' &c.), and we may compare our inverted compounds such as 'man-of-war.' But here again there is reason to think that the number of these compounds has been somewhat exaggerated: e.g. ἁλι in ἁλί-τρυτος need not (as formerly) be explained as a real locative, but only a weaker form of a base ἁλο-, co-existent with ἁλ-. Still many are genuine; but their character is exceptional: e.g. manaso-ruj, 'pain of mind,' for mano-ruj, Çakuntalā, st. 57: and, rather often in this poem, accusatives (or apparent accusatives) occur, as paraṃ-tapa x 19, sagaraṃ-gama xii 36, vihaṃ-ga xii 41, arin-dama vii 10, &c. For other exx. see M. M. Gr. § 514. As a class, they must be regarded as the product of a later period than the true compounds.

3. As a rule where one part of the compound stands in the relation of a case, that part comes first; e.g. θεό-δματος, θυμοβόρος, paricida, brow-beat, &c. Yet there is a considerable class of compounds (especially developed in Greek) where the reverse is the rule, e.g. ἀρχέκακος, πείθαρχος, λυσίπονος, ταμεσίχρως, &c.

There are parallel forms in Vedic Sanskrit (see Meyer, 'Stud.' v 26) such as 'tarad-dveṣas' = 'enemy-conquering,' an epithet of Indra, in which the weak participial base 'tarad' comes first. The explanation seems to be rightly given by Meyer. 'Compounds must date from the earliest period of the Indo-European language: in fact the verb itself, e.g. bhara-ti, 'he bears,' is nothing but a compound = 'bearer-he;' though the second base has been corrupted. Now in that stage of the language, before the case-suffixes had any existence, it was only possible to distinguish in a sentence subject from object by position: the base which expressed the subject would come before

[1] For regular Sanskrit variations in form, see M. M. Gr. §§ 516, 520, 528, 531.

the verb; that which expressed the object, afterwards. The same rule would hold at first for compounds: where one base had a verbal force, the other base, at least when expressing the object, would naturally come second. Afterwards—long indeed before the separation of the languages—when the case-forms were established, the reason for the order ceased, and the governed base could stand either first or second. That this is a true account of the matter is rendered probable by the history of the compounds both in Sanskrit and in Greek: in Sanskrit those in which the governing base precedes occur only in the Vedic hymns—except a few which are found in later times crystallised into proper names, e.g. Jamad-agni 'honouring Agni.'

As to form the Greek compounds of this character are well divided by Clemm ('Studien,' VII 63, &c.) into those in which the first base shews a σ, and those where it does not. In this latter class there is a great similarity observable between the base and the corresponding verbal present base; e.g. in the forms ἐχέ-φρων, ἐπιχαιρέ-κακος, πείθ-αρχος, &c. Of the 'sigmatic' class by far the commonest type is that in which the first base resembles a verbal noun in σι, e.g. λυσί-πονος, ἑλκεσί-πεπλος, ῥαψ-ῳδός: here the explanation is doubtful, and probably no one will suit all cases: Clemm (*ib.* p. 51) mentions no less than six: the one which appears to me to suit most passages is that which regards the σι as weakened from τι, which was used to form a verbal noun of the agent (cf. μάν-τι-ς, πόσις for πο-τι-ς, Sanskrit 'pa-ti', and in Latin 'hos-ti-s,' &c. In later usage this suffix chiefly formed feminine nouns denoting operation: but there is sufficient evidence for the older masculine forms. Fuller details may be found in the articles by Clemm and Meyer.

4. There is a tendency, especially as a language ages and loses its original freedom, to add on to a genuine compound a suffix, apparently meaningless, which assimilates it to a derivative; it is not really a derivative, for the suffix introduces no change of meaning. Thus in classical Sanskrit the suffix *-ka* is often added: e.g. at ii 24, sâgnika = sa + Agni + ka, and xii 13, vyûḍhoraska, 'broad-chested,' from vyûḍha + uras + ka: for special rules respecting this suffix, see M. M. Gr. § 528. 18—21. Just so in English we add *ed*, as though the words were past participles—e.g. 'barefoot-ed,' 'lion-heart-ed,' 'pale-face-d;' nay, we have turned 'shame-fast' into 'shame-faced.' In Greek this is not so common: yet in the Hesiodic ἀβούτης = ἀ + βοϝο + τα we see an instance of this affection for some common formation.

5. Not uncommonly one of the bases in a compound (generally the last) is not found separately existent. Thus we have ἀγχέμαχος, ἀγχίμολος, &c. in Greek; but no bases μαχο- or μολο-; we have in Latin 'incola,' 'paricida,' and very many others of the sort, but no 'cola' or 'cida.' It might therefore be maintained that these were not compounds in the strict sense, but derivatives. But there are no such roots as ἀγχεμαχ or 'paricid' from which to form the corresponding nouns by the suffixes *o* and *a*. We must therefore refer such compounds to a creative period in language (such a period as our own Elizabethan age), in which they were consciously modelled on the analogy of genuine compounds. In Latin the greater part are demonstrably old, for they are formed by the suffix *a*—not *o*, the later and almost universal form of the same suffix. Others (also a numerous class) such as 'merobiba,' are doubtless the coinage of the dramatists.

I give here a scheme of compound nouns, as found in Sanskrit, Greek, Latin, and English. It is arranged so as to shew the development of the compound in two ways.

I. When read horizontally, it will shew (1) the compound containing an idea complete in itself; (2) the compound expressing an idea referred to something else—the Sanskrit Bahu-vrîhi compound; (3) that compound referred to some one person or place only, and so crystallised into a proper name.

II. When read vertically, it will shew the progress from the loosest to the closest combination of the parts. Naturally those compounds of which one part is not found alone appear low down in the list. Those compounds which are appositional in character stand at the top, whether the first member be an adjective or a substantive: in these there is the least necessary connection. The compounds where the first part is a numeral or any indeclinable word come in the middle; though the indeclinables might have claimed the lowest place. But it is practically more convenient to take them with the numerals; and the numerals come most naturally after the nouns. Not seldom it is possible to analyse a compound in more ways than one: thus 'vineyard' might come under the case-compounds, as 'a yard (i.e. garden) of' or 'for vines.' I may add that the frequency of every kind of compound must not be inferred from the number of examples given: in general I have given only one in each language, except when it seemed desirable to give more because of some difference of form.

SCHEME OF DEPENDENT COMPOSITION OF NOUN-BASES.

			1. Idea completely contained in the compound:	2. transferred (generally) to any other person or thing:	3. restricted to one person only.
First part of compound appositional.	Adjective.	*Sk.*	vara-nārī	mahā-bāhu, bahu-vrīhi	
		Gr.	ἀκρόπολις, ὠμογέρων, ἀληθόμαντις, κακογείτων	κακογείτων, μελαγχίτων, πολύχρυσος	Ἐτεοκλέης
		Lat.	sacriportus	multigena, flexipes	Ahenobarbus
		Eng.	midsummer, goodman, ill-will, halfpenny	barefoot	Hotspur, Longshanks
	Participle.	*Sk.*		saṃyat-endriya, bṛihad-bhānu (Vedic)	Vṛihad-açva
		Gr.			
		Lat.			
		Eng.			
	Substantive.	*Sk.*	rājarsi, naraçārdūla (spec. var.)	dhyāna-para, ghana-çyāma	
		Gr.	ἱππαλεκτρύων, οἰνοπέδον	ἀελλόπους, μελίγηρυς, ῥοδοδάκτυλος	Ἀνδροκλέης
		Lat.	caprificus	anguimanus	
		Eng.	midsummer-day, steel-pen, wer-wolf, vineyard	clay-cold, blood-red	Ironside
First part indeclinable.	Numeral.	*Sk.*	chaturyugam, trirātram	dvipad	
		Gr.	πένταθλον	πενταέτης	
		Lat.	decemviri	bipennis	
		Eng.	fortnight	twofold	
	Indeclinable particle.	*Sk.*	a-brāhmaṇa, duḥ-kha, saṃ-kalpa, prati-pāṇa	apraja, suhṛid, sabhārya, atigiri	
		Gr.	ἀδώτης, δυσ-αριστοτόκεια, ἄλοχος, ἀμφιθέατρον	ἄπαις, εὐκλέης, ὁμότεχνος, ὑπερβόρεος, ἀμφικύπελλος	Περικλέης
		Lat.	nefas, sem-uncia, con-iux, abavus, advena	innumerus, semianimus, consors, excors, declivis	
		Eng.	unfaith, mistrust, forefather, overcoat	untrue, sam-blind, well-bred, overbold, downcast	
One part in case-relation.	Case (other than acc.).	*Sk.*	dhanyārtha, yupadāru, rājapuruṣa	prajā-kāma	Yudhi-ṣṭhira
		Gr.	χαμαιλέων, ἱστοδόκη, ἀστυγείτων	θεόδματος, ἀρχέκακος, πείθαρχος, ἀξιολόγος, ἰσόθεος	Ἀλκιμέδων, Ἀργειφόντης
		Lat.	tubicen, manceps, terrigena, manupretium	multi-fidus, altitonans, armipotens, montivagus	
		Eng.	ink-pot, wine-bin, self-murder, fish-net	sea-sick, fire-proof, shame-fast, sea-faring	
	Acc. of object.	*Sk.*	vasudhā	veda-vid, loka-kṛit, satya-vādin	Jamad-agni
		Gr.	φωσφόρος, αἰπόλος, φερέ-οικος	πλήξιππος, λυσίπονος, περσέπολις, δακέθυμος	Λυσι-κλέης
		Lat.	merobiba, caussidicus, paricida, vitisator	frugifer, flexanimus	
		Eng.	dare-devil, wagtail, pickpocket	ear-piercing, life-giving	Lack-land

CANTO I.

Vṛihadaçva for Vṛihadaçvas, the *s* falling out after short *a* before any other vowel: M. W. Gr. § 66. M. M. § 85.

uvâca, 3 sing. perf. of √vac, = √VAK, whence voc-o, vox, &c., Gr. ἔπος, &c. The form is irregular: it is corrupted from va-vâc-a, in which the *a* of the root (standing between consonants of which the last is not compound, M. W. Gr. § 375. M. M. § 327) is lengthened regularly. But the reduplicated syllable *va* is weakened to *u*, as generally happens when the verb begins with *v*. (M. W. § 375, c. M. M. § 328. 2.) Sometimes the root itself is weakened, as in the indecl. participle uktvâ, *infra* i 32: cf. uṣita from √vas, ix 10.

These two words are hypermetrical, and are generally found at the beginning of each Canto to mark the teller of the tale. They are also found sometimes (as in Canto II) in the middle of the Canto, in order that the words of some speaker may be kept in the direct statement. The Sanskrit did not develop the mysteries of the *oratio obliqua:* see note on i 32.

---

1 **âsid** for âsit, irregular 3 sing. imperf. of √as 'to be.' M. W. Gr. § 584. M. M. App. no. 173.

nâma, accusative of closer definition. So Xenophon, Anab. 1. 2. 23, ποταμὸς Κύδνος ὄνομα, and a few other accusatives are so employed; but this use of the case was naturally limited; others were employed for it, because they gave the sense more plainly. In Latin it is almost confined to parts of the body, e. g. palo pectus tundor, Plaut. Rud. 5. 2. 3. Nâma is often so found in Sanskrit, but generally it has lost its primary sense, and serves merely as a strengthening particle. See xi 4 and note.

upapanno, p.p. of upa + √pad (M. W. Gr. § 540, M. M. § 442): often used, as here, = 'provided with,' 'possessed of'; a peculiar extension of meaning as the verb = 'to arrive at,' 'attain to.' Sampanna has the same force, i 13.

guṇair iṣṭai, rûpavân = guṇais iṣṭais, rûpavân. The final *s* of the instrumental iṣṭais would become *r* before a soft letter; but that soft letter being also *r*, the first *r* is dropped; M. W. Gr. § 65 a. M. M. § 86. Iṣṭa is p. p. of √iṣ 'to wish,' of which the present base iccha occurs ix 32. It = 'desired' or 'desirable,' 'choice.' For the root (originally √IS) see Curt. Gr. Et. no. 617. It occurs in Greek ἰότης and ἵμερος, where the rough breathing seems to arise from the misplaced *s*, as in ἡμεῖς from 'asmes.'

kovidaḥ = 'very knowing.' *Ko* is an intensive prefix, as in komala, 'very soft.' It may be identical with the interrogative pronominal root *ka:* and the compounds such as 'kiṃpuruṣa' (= 'a bad man,' apparently condensed from 'what? a man!': see for exx. Hitop. 1033) give some colour to the supposition. But the form is peculiar. It occurs again, xx 19.

2. **atiṣṭhad.** M. W. Gr. § 269.

manujendrâṇâṃ, a T. P. compound, 'king of men.' **Manuja** 'man' (Manu + ja from √jan orig. √GAN whence γένος, gigno &c.) is literally 'born of Manu' the progenitor of the human race—or rather one of the fourteen so-called Manus, either the first (the mythical legislator), or the seventh, also called Vaivaswata, the Manu of the present age, in whose time the flood took place which left him as the sole occupant of the earth which was again peopled from him. See Dowson, Class. Dict. s.v. Manu: and for a translation of part of the story of the flood from the Çatapatha Brâhmaṇa, see M. Williams, 'Indian Wisdom,' p. 32.

Indra, the name of the Sky God, the chief deity of the older Hindū mythology, see note on ii 13. The word is used here as often in compounds = 'king': i.e. pârthivendra v 40, gajendra xii 54: cp. mahendraṃ sarvadevânâm, iv 11.

mûrdhni, 'at the top of,' locative of mûrdhan 'head,' the *a* being lost in the weak cases of the singular, as in nâman, M. M. Gr. § 191. This locative sense 'upon' is a natural development of the primary sense 'in,' but is not a very common one. In Greek we have the dative-locative in this sense, e.g. Il. 5. 32, ἄγρια πάντα τά τε τρέφει οὔρεσιν ὕλη; and in Latin the same, e.g. Verg. Aen. I 501 fert umero pharetram. But the somewhat metaphorical sense which the case bears here is probably not found in Greek or Latin; except perhaps in some prepositions which were originally the locative cases of nouns now lost, such as * ὕπερι (implied by ὑπείρ and ὑπέρ) which points back to original * superi, a locative of a lost noun meaning 'height.' Similarly, if the other cases of mûrdhan had died out, we should have called the surviving mûrdhni a preposition and translated it 'above.'

upari, 'above'; it *may* be the same as super and ὑπέρ, but the absence of the *s* is peculiar. See Curt. Gr. Et. no. 392. Note the reduplication in 'upary upari.' Comp. punaḥ punaḥ x 3, muhur muhuḥ xi 20, dvâri dvâri xxv 7, &c.

tejasâ, instrumental of tejas, 'brightness,' 'splendour.' See iv 26 note.

3. **brahmaṇya**, 'fit for a Brahman,' and so 'pious.'

vedavic chûro, i.e. veda-vid çûro, 'learned in the Veda, heroic.' For the Vedas see note on vi 9. **çûra** is probably connected with Greek κῦρος and κύριος (see Curt. G. E. no. 82) and is not to be confounded with sura, a God, ii 13 note. It should be carefully remembered by young philologists that this palatal ç in Sanskrit is regularly a corruption of *k*. Thus √çi to lie is the Greek √κι in κεῖμαι, çvan 'a dog' is κύων, √çru 'to hear' is √κλυ in κλύω, &c. The gutturals have been more corrupted in Sanskrit than in the classical languages. By the side of this corruption, and of occasional cases of Labialism (e.g. √lap = Gr. λακεῖν, Lat. loqu-i, see vii 16 note), we have the peculiar Sanskrit weakening of k into c (our *ch*-sound which arose in the same way, as in 'church' from 'kirk'), e.g. catur = quattuor, regularly found in reduplicated tenses, e.g. cakâra, perfect of √kar; also the parallel change of *g* into *j* as in √jan for orig. √GAN mentioned above.

akṣapriyaḥ 'a lover of dice,' a genitively dependent T. P. compound. Gambling was a favourite, albeit unlawful, amusement of the heroes of the Hindū Epics. It is prohibited in the Mānava dharma-çāstra (commonly called the 'Law of Manu'); e.g. ix 221, where the king is ordered to exclude all gaming from his kingdom, because it causes the destruction of princes; and *inf.* 225 "gamesters, public singers and dancers, revilers of scripture, open heretics, men who perform not the duties of their several classes, and sellers of spirituous liquors, let the king instantly banish from the town." It may be suspected that what was a vicious habit in the lower orders was no vice when practised occasionally in a palace. At xiv 20 skill at the dice is mentioned as one of the accomplishments of king Ṛituparṇa. Yudhishṭhira himself the chief of the Pāṇḍava princes gambles away all his money, land, and even Draupadī, the common wife of the five brothers: in consequence of which they are obliged to give up the kingdom to Duryodhana for twelve years and to live in the Kāmyaka forest. The story of Nala is similar: hence that tale, as told to Yudhishṭhira, naturally recounts Nala's taste for dice among his other high qualities.

satya-vádi, 'truth-speaking.' Vádin is a derivative of váda 'statement,' formed by adding the suffix *-in*, a common formative element in Sanskrit, but not in other languages. So in line 1 balin is formed from bala 'strength.' See M. W. Gr. § 85 vi: a useful list of Sanskrit formative suffixes is given §§ 80—87, and should be carefully read: the suffixes common to other languages should also be studied in Schleicher, 'Compendium,' §§ 215—236.

akṣauhiṇi, 'a complete army,' from akṣa (axle, axi-s, ἄξων, also used of the whole car, not the same as akṣa, dice), and úhini 'an assemblage,' perhaps from √úh = √vah 'to bear,' and with *vi* 'to arrange.'

4. **ipsito**, p. p. of ipsa, irregular desiderative (M. W. § 503) of √áp 'to get' (apiscor, &c.), = 'to desire:' comp. abh'-ips-u, v 2. 'Desired of noble women.' Vara = 'better' from √vṛi 'to choose' iii 6 note; it is 'best' i 30, or 'excellent' as it might be rendered here: as a subst. it comes below, i 8. Note the genitive of the agent, so called, really only an extension of the subjective genitive. It is frequent in this poem with the perf. part., v 17 me Niṣadho vṛitaḥ, ix 29 bhiṣajám matam, xiii 40 me pápakṛitam kṛitam, xvi 12 iṣṭaṃ samasta-lokasya, ib. 32 bhrátur iṣṭaṃ dvijottamam, xvii 41 tan naṣṭam ubhayaṃ tava, xxiv 3 parikṣito me Váhukaḥ: less frequent with the fut. part.; i 20 hantavyas te, xii 29 ko nu me vá 'tha praṣṭavyaḥ, xix 15 pralabdhavyá na te vayam. Compare the English 'seen of me;' but the origin of this use may be different. In Greek the genitive is no longer so used alone, but helped out by ὑπό for the sake of clearness: probably it represents an original ablative. Generally in Sanskrit the instrumental is used to represent the agent (about 145 times in this poem), not distinguished, except by the sense, from the same case used of the instrument (about 135 times in this poem). In Latin the ablative had originally both functions (either borrowed from the instrumental, or pure ablative denoting the origin of the action): but, as is well known, the agent-ablative was almost universally distinguished from the instrument-ablative by the addition of *ab*. See note on hṛidá i 18, and, generally, 'Primer of Philology,' c. v §§ 45, 46.

saṃyatendriyaḥ, 'sense-restrained.' Saṃyata, p. p. of sam + √yam v 27 and xxv 22 notes. Indriya, an organ of sense, including the five organs of perception, eye, ear, nose, tongue, skin, and the five organs of action, voice, hand, feet, anus, penis; an eleventh, 'manas' or mind is internal, the others being external, and is an organ both of perception and of action: see Manu ii 89—92. It is the subjugation of sense, i.e. the abstinence, so far as possible, from either passion or action, which is the chief help along the road which leads each man through different lives upon earth to the final felicity of Brāhmanism, absorption into the Supreme Being: see M. W. 'Hinduism,' pp. 49—52. In Manu ii 98, 99 we find "He must be considered as really triumphant over his senses, who, on hearing and touching, on seeing and tasting and smelling, neither greatly rejoices nor greatly repines. But when one among his organs fails, by that single failure his knowledge of God passes away as water flows through one hole in a leathern bottle." This restraint is the duty alike of all; but, perhaps because of his greater opportunity for indulgence, it is specially enjoined on the Kshatriya, or man of the second caste (see ib. pp. 34, 57, &c.), from which kings were chosen. Thus in Manu i 87—91, where the special duty (dharma) of each caste is laid down, the duties of the Kshatriya are summed up as 'defence of the people, almsgiving, sacrifice, and reading of the Veda (cf. veda-vid, line 3), and *absence of attachment to objects of sense* (viṣayeṣu aprasakti).'

rakṣitâ, nom. of rakṣitṛ (√rakṣ iii 10, &c., orig. √ARKS, secondary of √ARK, ἀλέξω, where ε is auxiliary, Curt. G. E. no. 581; cf. √vakṣ, Gr. αὐξ, formed from simpler √aug in augeo, ib. p. 67) 'the protector,' i.e. of the people. See last note.

dhanvinâm, formed from dhanu 'a bow' by suffix *-in*, see note on vâdin, last line.

çreṣṭaḥ, 'best,' superlative of çreyas 'better' (see x 10), has no corresponding positive; but is connected with Çrī, the deity of plenty.

sâkṣâd, &c., 'in appearance like Manu himself,' see note on line 2. Sâkṣât must be regarded as the abl. of a compound sâkṣa (though no other case is found)—not as compounded of sa and akṣât. A similar compound is sakâça (i 21, Damayanti-sakâçe = in the presence of Damayanti); also sârddham (ix 7 note), samakṣam, 'in presence of,' where the parts of the compound are the same as in sâkṣât, but a different case is used. Akṣa 'an eye' (oc-ulu-s) may be the same word as akṣa, 'a die.' Other ablatives used as adverbs are samantát xii 39, na-cirát ii 22, xvii 24: also samipatas vi 4, see note.

5. **parákramaḥ**, 'prowess,' pará + krama from √kram, 'to go,' ix 6 note. Pará is an interesting form: it is the old instrumental of para, ii 2 note, (pareṇa also is found in the same adverbial use), and like Greek παρά meant at first 'by the side of,' and then received a variety of secondary meanings: here it apparently = 'beyond,' cf. παρὰ δύναμιν, &c.: but most commonly it gives the word a bad sense, just as the identical *ver-* in German (verkehren, verlegen, &c.) and O. English *for* in forego, foredone, forspent, &c. See Curt. Gr. Et. no. 346. Cf. parásu, xi 38 note: also paras in parokṣa, xx 12.

sarvaguṇair = sarvair guṇaiḥ—a good instance of the Sanskrit love of compounds.

yuktaḥ, 'joined to,' and then 'endowed with,' much like upapanna above. It is p. p. of √yuj, orig √YUG (ζεύγνυμι, iungo): but in Sanskrit the range of secondary meanings of the compounds (esp. with *ni* and *pra*) is much greater than in the other languages.

prajá-kámaḥ, 'offspring-desire,' used as a B. V. 'having desire, &c.' káma is from √kam (amo), see note on kán-kṣanti ii 23.

sa, often inserted thus in the final clause of a sentence; it reminds us of the Latin ille (e.g. Aen. 7. 805); but it has not the same emphatic force, being indeed often redundant. Observe that sas, the nominative of sa, drops the final consonant before all consonants. M. W. Gr. § 67, M. M. Gr. § 87.

6. **prajá-'rthe**, 'for the sake of' (lit. 'in the matter of) offspring,' the locative of artha used adverbially, but generally artham is found in this sense. For the general force of artha see note on iii 7.

The desire for offspring—especially for a son—was almost as strong in a Hindū as in a Jew, though for a different reason. An important part of Brahmanism is the daily worship of departed ancestors (pitṛi-yajña) required from every 'twice-born' man: hence the need of offspring to perform the so-called Çrāddha ceremonies (for which see M. W. 'Hinduism,' 66—68, comp. also 29 note), whereby the progress of the deceased through the intermediate stages between different lives is accelerated. This efficacy of a son appears in different parts of the Mánava code: e.g. iii 37, where the son of a wife married by the Brāhma, or most approved, marriage-form is said to redeem from sin ten ancestors, ten descendants, and himself: again at vi 37 it is said that if a Brāhman have not read the Veda, not begotten a son, and not performed sacrifices, yet shall aim at final beatitude, he shall sink to a place of degradation. Compare also the fanciful derivation of putra 'a son,' given Manu ix 138, "since the son delivers (trâyate) the father from the hell called 'put' (see note on vi 13) he was therefore called 'puttra' by Brahmâ." Hence we frequently find mention of great sacrifices performed by kings to the gods, or great penances undertaken for the sake of offspring.

akarot, 3 sing. imperf. of √kṛi 'to make' (orig. √KAR, creo), M. W. Gr. §§ 355 and 682. **yatnam**, see note on xv 4.

susamâhitaḥ, p. p. of sam + â + √dhâ (√DHA, τίθημι, con-do, &c.). The prefix *sam* intensifies, just as *con* does in Latin: *ā* gives the sense of 'intent,' 'set upon' a thing: so xxii 2, Hitop. 2307. Samâdhi and samâdhâna = 'abstraction.' Hita (alone) = 'friendly' viii 4, ix 20, &c. Avahita has the same force as âhita Megh. 98: compare Latin 'deditus.' For vi + hita see v 19 note.

abhyagacchad, 3 sing. imp. of abhi + √gam. The present base gaccha- probably = βα-σκο-: see Curt. G. E. vol. 2, p. 365 (Eng. tr.).

brahmarṣir, i.e. brahma (for brahman) + ṛiṣi, a sage of the priestly class, such as Vasishṭha. For the Rājarshi (or sage of the royal class—inferior to the Brahmarshi) see M. Williams, note on Çak. p. 38: such were Purūravas and Viçvāmitra. The devarshi (see ii 13 note) is higher than either. The Maharshis, 'great sages' are produced by the ten Prajāpatis, Manu i 36.

7. **toṣayâmâsa**, 'made glad,' from √tuṣ 'to be glad:' note this peculiar periphrastic perfect of verbs declined in the 10th class (including causals), see M. W. Gr. § 490. M. M. Gr. § 342. It is made up of two originally separate words, the √as 'to be' and the acc. of a verbal noun. For the acc. so used cf. the Homeric ἀκὴν ἔσαν; the use of 'uenum ire,' 'pessum ire' in Latin is somewhat similar, but less strange.

dharmavid, i.e. knowing the duty of giving presents (to a Brahman), see i 4 note. For the general idea of dharma see x 24 note.

mahiṣyâ, 'with his queen'; the sociative use of the instrumental case, but helped out by saha (= sa). It is found alone about 23 times in this poem, and 22 times with a preposition, saha or sârdhaṃ: see vi 2 note. Mahiṣa and mahiṣi are properly the buffalo (as at xii 9), but used to express size and dignity. This comparison of men with beasts is not uncommon: e.g. Nala at i 15 is called 'the tiger among men' (nara-çârdûla).

râjendra, note on i 2. These vocatives frequently occur; cf.

viçâm pate, i 31, 32; they are addresses to Yudhishṭhira, first of the Pāṇḍavas—also called Kaunteya (i 17) i.e. son of Kunti, Bhârata (i 6) i.e. descendant of Bharata: and they merely fill up the line, often weakly.

suvarcasam, acc. of suvarcas, M. M. § 165. Varcas = 'brightness,' 'splendour,' but (Vedic) 'energy,' 'activity.' It agrees with taṃ, though it stands so far away from it. Possibly the order may be intentional, 'with hospitality as being very glorious' i.e. 'according to his glory.' But we do not find in Sanskrit epics the nice arrangement of the words which we have in Homer and Vergil.

8. **prasanno**, p. p. of pra + √sad (sedeo, ἕδος) = 'settled down': it = 'clear' (of water) xii 112, nadiṃ ramyâṃ prasanna-salilâṃ: here it = 'calm,' 'propitious,' 'well disposed to,' in which sense the verb also occurs xii 130, no...Maṇibhadraḥ prasidatu. Prasâda = 'favour' xvii 39, Hitop. 1190. For √sad with ni see x 5; with â, x 7 note.

sabhâryâya, 'with his wife,' dative agreeing with tasmai. Sabhârya is a B. V. compound of sa and bhâryâ 'a wife,' and must of course be declined in the masculine. It is as though we could say in Greek ἀνὴρ ἁμάγυνος or in Latin 'vir conuxor.' So xv 8 sa-Varṣṇeyo Jivalaḥ, 'having V. and J. with him.'

dadau, M. W. § 373, M. M. § 329. **varaṃ**, 'a boon,' as v 34, = 'a thing to be chosen,' from the first meaning 'choice' (√vṛi).

kumârâṃç ca, i.e. kumârân ca, by Sandhi. M. W. § 53, M. M. § 74.

mahâyaçâḥ, 'of great splendour.' Note that mahat in K. D. or B. V. compounds becomes mahâ: M. W. § 778, M. M. § 517. Yaças (decus) is from √DAK (δοκέω, δόξα) and is equivalent to δόξα in meaning: see next line where it occurs twice, once as the quality of the person, once as the external repute. Daças is another form. In yaças the *y* is parasitic and has expelled the *d*. Curt. Gr. Et. no. 15.

10. **tejasâ**, 'by her brilliance': so at iii 13 she by her 'tejas' surpasses the moon. See note on iv 26 for further meanings.

çriyâ, instr. of çri 'beauty' (M. W. § 123, M. M. § 220). The word has commonly a secondary sense of 'wealth,' 'prosperity,' and is often used of the goddess thereof, personified, infra i 13. There seems little distinction in the use of the epithets in this line.

saubhâgyena, 'prosperity' but also 'charm,' 'attractiveness.' Secondary noun formed from subhâga by vṛiddhi of *u* and new suffix *ya*. For bhâga see x 14 note.

lokeṣu, 'among the folk,' a colloquial use of loka 'place,' 'world.' So inf. i 15: compare also loke, xix 6.

11. **vayasi prápte**, 'when the period of life was come,' a locative absolute, the commonest construction in Sanskrit, about 36 instances occurring in this poem. See my 'Primer of Philology,' c. v § 47. Prápta, p. p. of pra + √áp 'to get,' has this secondary force at iii 20, v 1, xxiii 18 amanyata Nalaṃ práptaṃ; perhaps too xii 49, krama-práptaṃ pituḥ...rájyaṃ = 'his father's kingdom arrived in due course,' though the earlier meaning 'obtained' (cf. adeptus, also from √AP) would do equally well; see also v 15. The common Av. B. compound 'práptakálaṃ,' 'at the right time' (e.g. v 15, &c.) can also be explained either way.

çataṃ dásinám, 'a hundred of slaves,' a partitive use with numerals unlike the Greek and Latin idiom; though the plural neuters can take the genitive in Latin. Dási, fem. of dása, *perhaps* seen in δεσπότης i.e. dása-pati, see Curt. no. 377. Comp. dásatva xxvi 21.

samalaṃkṛitaṃ, p. p. of sam + alam + √kṛi. Alam = 'enough,' and is often (though not in this poem) used with an instrumental e.g. alam upadeçena 'enough of advice!' The sense of alam with √kṛi is to 'adorn.' √Kṛi and √bhú are frequently thus compounded with adverbs or prepositions e.g. pari(ṣ)kṛi (i 19), puras-kṛi, viná-kṛi (xiii 25), see M. W. Gr. § 787; also with nouns as namas-kṛi 'to salute' (iv 1 note), whence namaskára (v 16); cf. satkára (i 7), 'good treatment,' 'hospitality.'

paryupásac Chacim, i.e. paryupásat Çacim. Çaci is Indra's queen. Paryupásat, 3 sing. imperf. of pari + upa + √ás to sit (√ÁS ἧμαι, ἧσται) = sit round beneath: comp. xxvi 33 upásitum. For √ás with anu, see vii 3 note. Ásana = 'seat' or 'sitting' ii 4, iii 15, &c. The whole sentence = 'A hundred female slaves splendidly adorned, and a hundred female friends attended on her round about, as though she were Çaci.'

12. **sma rájate**, 'shone.' The particle sma has the peculiar effect of turning a present tense into a past. Thus at xii 117 prahasanti sma táṃ kecit, 'some laughed at her,' comes among several past tenses in the same connection: probably also at vii 9 dyúte jiyate sma Nalas tadá, the force is the same. At iii 18, v 5, xxi 20 and 22, the particle is practically meaningless. It does not seem to have this special force in the Rig-veda (see Grassmann, Dict. s.v.): there it follows a noun or pronoun as often as a verb. It is doubtless con-

nected with sama, being probably (so Benfey) an old instrumental (like parâ i 5) with the final *a* shortened, as ἄμα, κάρτα, &c. If it originally meant 'together,' 'at once,' we can understand its later force on the verb, as connecting it with the preceding statement so closely that the operation described by the second verb might be regarded as already done in the past. We may perhaps infer that the original use of the augment was something of this sort: there can be no doubt that it was at first an independent word, just like 'sma': and possibly it was the instrumental of a pronoun 'a.' But while 'a' established itself fully, 'sma' has been one of the failures of language.

sarvâbharaṇabhûṣitâ, 'adorned with every ornament': a T. P. compound of sarvâbharaṇa (instrumentally dependent) and bhûṣitâ: while sarvâbharaṇa is itself a K. D. compound of sarva and âbharaṇa (√bhar, fero, φέρω).

sakhimadhye, 'in the middle of her mates': so 'medio montium,' Tacitus, where 'medio' is a locative ablative. Cf. tasyâḥ samipe i 16; Damayanti-sakâçe i 21; Damayantyâs...antike i 23.

anavady-ângi, 'with faultless limbs,' x 32. Avadya (= a, neg. + vadya from √vad) is equivalent to ἄρρητος, 'unmentionable,' 'bad' (but generally as a noun, = 'blame'): then an-avadya = unblameable.

vidyut saudâmini. Each word means 'lightning': perhaps the second is adjectival here. Vidyut is from vi + √dyut 'to shine': saudâmini is formed from sudâman 'a cloud,' lit. 'one that gives good.'

13. **ativa**, 'exceedingly' = ati + iva 'beyond as it were.' Ati is doubtless Greek ἔτι, Latin et. It *may* mean 'going' (i.e. continuation) from a root at 'to go,' but this is perfectly uncertain. See Curt. G. E. no. 209.

âyata-locanâ, 'long-eyed.' Âyata is p. p. from â + √yam (i 4) 'to restrain.' The preposition â in compounds has a negative force. Thus âyata = 'unrestrained': so also √gam = 'to go,' â + √gam = 'to come,' i 32, iii 3, ix 16: √yâ = 'to go,' â + √yâ = 'to come,' x 27: √dâ = 'to give,' â + √dâ = 'to take,' ix 14. This effect of the preposition is not easy to explain: and it has another equally strange. It is apparently the same as Latin 'ad' = 'to': and as such we might look to find it with an accusative. Yet it is regularly used with an ablative: e.g. â Kailâsât = 'to Mount Kailāsa,' Megh. 11. The history of the phrase *may* have been this: the ablative had its proper force and meant 'on the line *from* Kailāsa': and then â gave the contrary sense 'on that line from K., *up to it*.' This is of course a mere guess: but it would explain the almost equally puzzling construction of the genitive in Greek with ἐπὶ = towards a place; and with ἰθύ in older Greek; where the genitive is probably ablatival.

locana, 'an eye,' from √lok ('seeing'), a variation of original LUK ('brightness'), just as √λευκ (λεύσσω) is in Greek. The simple root takes in Sanskrit the form √ruc with two phonetic changes, see iv 28 note. In Greek it is seen in ἀμφι-λύκ-η (Iliad 7. 433), Latin luceo, lux, &c., our 'light.'

na deveṣu, &c., 'not among the Gods, not among the Yakshas, further (not) anywhere among men, besides was any maid so beautiful seen before or heard of, disturbing the minds even of the Gods.' The Yakshas are an order of superhuman beings, generally described as the attendants of Kuvera the Hindū god of wealth, but of negative character, and at least inoffensive. They have a 'loka' or world of their own. See Dowson, s. v. loka: also ii 13 note.

tádṛg, i.e. tádṛk from tádṛç (M. M. Gr. § 126) = tad + dṛç 'that like,' 'so,' used adverbially with rúpavati; cf. idṛça iii 8. √Dṛç is orig. √DARK (δέρκομαι, δράκων, δόρκας), and meant specially 'to flash,' but then (like so many others) reached the general sense of seeing, Curt. Gr. Et. Bk. I § 13. It is noticeable that no present base is formed from it in Sanskrit, paçya from √paç (orig. √SPAK, σκέπτομαι, σκοπός, -specio, spy) being used instead—probably because its special sense, of looking fixedly, adapted it better for a present base; see v 9. Even in Greek δέδορκα is used rather than δέρκομαι.

14. **anyeṣu,** used here just like ἄλλος: οὔτε ἐν τοῖς θεοῖς οὔτε ἐν τοῖς ἄλλοις ἀνθρώποις. For the locative compare rájasu xxvi 37.

dṛṣṭa-púrvá, an irregular compound, called T. P. by Pāṇini (6. 2. 22), but probably really a K. D., with the natural order changed. It seems most like compounds with antara, i.e. janmántara, 'another birth,' where antara stands last. M. W. Gr. § 777 b. Comp. also rájápasada. xxvi 21, perhaps also xxvi 32. Sometimes púrva has little force at the end of a compound, e.g. smita-púrva iii 19, ib. § 777 c. But see note on mṛdupúrva, xi 34.

átha vá. Atha marks something consecutive, 'then,' 'thereupon'; see e.g. xvii 35. It commonly stands at the beginning of a sentence, as at v 1, sometimes even at the end, v 10, sometimes medial, iii 1, &c. It often marks a question, e.g. xxii 10, 13 (something like Greek μέν) with no special meaning: neither has it any before vá, here or at xxiv 4, &c.

cittapramáthini devánáṃ. Here we might have had as usual a compound beginning with deva: but devánáṃ is used in order that api may follow. Pramáthin is from √math 'to churn': hence the common epithet Manmatha, 'mind-churner,' for Love ii 28, &c.: also Greek μόθος. For the interesting explanation of the Prometheus legend, given by Sk. pramantha, 'the fire-stick,' from this root, see Curt. Gr. Et. no. 476.

15. **nara-çárdúlaḥ,** 'man-tiger,' a K. D. compound, in which çárdúla should logically have come first. But in these compounds, where a comparison is said to hold good throughout, the name of the thing with which comparison is made stands last. So Benfey, short Sk. Gr. § 201. Cf. puruṣa-vyághra v 7, puruṣa-çárdúla xii 126.

apratimo, 'having no equal'—pratimá, lit. 'copy,' from prati + √má to measure, orig. MA, μέ-τρον, μι-μέ-ομαι, ma-nus, me-tior, Curt. Gr. Et. no. 461. For mátra see note on ix 10.

bhuvi. M. W. Gr. § 125 a. M. M. § 220.

Kandarpa (for Kandarpas, *s* being lost after *ă* before *i*), another name for the Hindū Eros or Cupid, called Kāma, or Kāmadeva. "He is usually represented as a handsome youth riding on a parrot, and attended by nymphs, one of whom bears his banner, displaying the Makara or a fish on a red ground." Dowson, Cl. Dict. s. v.

svayam, 'self,' 'very,' the original sense of this pronoun which afterwards in some languages (notably Latin) became only a reflexive pronoun. But in Sanskrit and Zend it never lost its old sense, of which many traces are still visible in old Greek. See Windisch's most valuable article 'Relativpronomen' in Curt. 'Studien,' vol. 2. Observe the form, which corresponds to agham and tvam, the pronouns of the first and second person: and see note on viii 3.

samipe, 'in the presence of,' sam + √áp weakened to ip (cf. ipsita i 4), just as in Latin compounds we find *i*, e.g. inquiro from quaero, &c. For samipam, similarly used, see ii 24 and vii 4 note.

16. **praçaçaṃsuḥ,** 3 pers. plur. perf. of pra + √çaṃs, 'to speak of,' 'laud,' orig. KAS, whence Latin Ca(s)-mena, Carmenta and carmen (for cas-men), which has therefore nothing to do with √KAR to make, despite the tempting analogy of ποίημα); probably also censor, censeo, &c.

kutúhalát, 'eagerly,' xiii 48, ablative of attendant circumstance, derived from the primary sense of external cause, which is common: but this derived use is uncommon.

17. 'There was a passion for an unseen object of these two constantly hearing (each other's) virtues.' **tayoḥ** is dual gen. of tat. **adṛṣṭa-káma** is a genitively dependent T. P. **abhút**, aorist of √bhú. **çṛṇvatoḥ** is dual gen. pres. part. of √çru (i 3 note) a verb of the 5th class, which therefore adds *nu* to the root to form the present base, and changes *u* of the root to *i* by dissimilation.

anyo-'nyaṃ, i.e. anyo (nominative) anyaṃ 'the one towards the other.' We should certainly have expected a compound here like Greek ἀλλήλω. It is however rather an anomalous compound resembling ἔστιν οἵ. Compare parasparatas, v 33.

vyavardhata, 3 sing. imperf. middle of vi + √vṛdh: the perf. vavṛdhe iii 14, and p. p. vṛddha xxvi 9: for root see viii 14 note.

hṛcchayaḥ, 'heart-lier,' i.e. 'love,' from hṛd (καρδ-ια, cord-, heart)—observe the rare and irregular substitution in Sanskrit of *h* for *k*. This is not uncommon when the original sound was the aspirate *gh*; so that Latin and Sanskrit correspond, e.g. haṃsa, χήν, hanser; hima, χεῖμα, hiemps; √há, √χα in χάος, χάσκω, hi-sco. The second base, çaya, is from √çi 'to lie,' orig. KI in κεῖμαι, &c.—Note that d (or t) + ç = cch. M. M. §§ 62 and 92.

Kaunteya, i 7 note.

18. **açaknuvan**, 'unable,' pres. part. of a + √çak (5th class, inserting *nu*), a verb with no obvious connections. Benfey thinks queo may be for que(c-i)o, which would not be a greater change than that of aio from agh-io, which seems certain. Note the composition: we have *a(n)*—negative—with the participle, just like Latin impotens: but * a-çak is as impossible as * im-possum. Similarly in Greek we can have ἀδύνατος, and hence ἀδυνατέω, but no * ἀδύναμαι.

dhárayitum, inf. of dháraya, causal of √dhṛ (DHAR, perhaps θρᾶνος and θρόνος, fretus, frenum: so Curt. no. 316) a very common root in Sanskrit. The causal and simple verb have nearly the same meaning, 'to bear,' 'maintain,' 'endure': see iii 14.

hṛdá, instrumental where we should expect a locative: so Cicero used 'animo' instead of the older 'animi.' Any part of a man can be regarded as instrumental: so one use is almost as natural as the other.

antaḥpura-samipa-sthe vane, 'in a wood situated in the neighbourhood of the private apartments,' a locatively dependent compound of antaḥpurasamipa and stha, which the Indian grammarians regard as a derivative of sthá 'to stand,' formed by dropping final *ā* and adding *ā*. Antaḥpurasamipa is a genitively dependent T. P.—'the presence of the inner apartment': and antaḥpura itself is a K. D. formed of the indeclinable antar, 'within' (inter), and pura (√pṛi, orig. PAR, whence πόλις, plenus, &c.), 'the within-building,' generally applied to the women's apartments, but sometimes used, as here, in a wider sense.

raho gataḥ, 'gone secretly.' Rahas is an acc. used adverbially, comp. xviii 14. It is from √rah: aspirates in Sanskrit often pass into *h* at the end of a root, e.g. √sah for SAGH (ἔχω, ἔ-σχ-ον), √vah for VAGH (Fεχ-ω, Foχος, &c., veho), √grah for GRABH i 19, &c. Note that the same change is found, though very rarely, in Latin, in veh-o, trah-o. The original RADH is Gr. √λαθ, whence λᾶθος (Theok. 23. 24) parallel to rahas in form but not in meaning.

19. **haṃsán.** This is a frequent bird in epic poetry, the wild grey goose (χὴν, hanser, goose—but the nasal survives in 'gander'). Dean Milman wrongly translates 'swan.'

játarúpa, 'gold,' but why 'born-form' should mean this is not clear: perhaps originally = naked (so P. W.), then 'unalloyed' (metal). Játavedas, the Vedic epithet of Agni is described as the 'knower of the essence' (játa), Grassmann, Dict. s.v.

pariṣkṛitán, 'adorned,' supra i 11 note. Perhaps the *s* represents an older form of √kṛi, i.e. SKAR, cf. saṃskṛita, saṃskára, avaskára, &c.

vane, &c., 'one of those birds as they were wandering in the grove he caught.' **vicaratám**, gen. plural of vi + √car 'to go in different ways'; comp. xxiv 59. Vi, a very frequent element in composition = (d)vi, = δις for δFι-ς (where the *v* is lost, not the *d*), Lat. bis (comp. the change from duonus to bonus, &c.) our twy-(form), &c. For √car see v 9 and vi 8. **jagráha**, perf. of √grah: grahitum, infinitive, i 24. The Vedic form is the original GRABH, to which our slang word 'grab' corresponds more exactly than 'gripe' does: *p* however is found in all the Low German dialects (see Skeat, Lex. s. v.), and H. German shews the *f* in greifen: so perhaps the original letter was *b*, changed to *bh* in Sanskrit alone. The *g* at the beginning of the word is retained in all the Teutonic languages because *r* follows: in roots beginning with two consonants Grimm's Law generally fails because of the assimilation. Derivatives in Sanskrit are gráha, 'a serpent,' lit. 'a seizer' xi 21, and garbha, 'an embryo," 'that which is conceived' = βρέφος, where labialism has taken place, see also xvi 16.

20. **antarikṣa-go**, 'sky-goer,' 'bird,' a loc. dep. T. P. Antar-ikṣa = 'that which can be seen within' or 'into,' from antar (i 18), and √ikṣ, 'to look,' a weakened form of √aks (whence akṣa, 'an eye,' i 4), a secondary root from AK (oc-ulu-s, ὀπ-ωπ-α, labialised.)

vácaṃ vyájahára, 'uttered a speech,' and so as being equivalent to 'addressed' it takes the accusative Nalam. So jitvá rájyaṃ Nalam, vii 5, where see note; uváca Naiṣadhaṃ vacaḥ, ix 25, Ṛituparṇaṃ vaco brúhi, xviii 23, &c. It is common enough in Greek, e.g. Herod. i 68 θώυμα ποιεύμενοι τὴν ἐργασίην. Vyájahára is perf. of vi + á + √hṛi, 'to take,' weakened from GHAR, χερ- in χειρ, &c., Curt. no. 189 (an interesting comment). With these two prepositions it = 'to utter'; comp. xxvi 18: for its uses with á alone, see xi 29 note on áhára.

hantavyo te, 'to be slain of thee'; for the genitive, see note on i 4. Hantavya is fut. pass. part. of √han, and is both in form and in its use here identical with Gr. -τεο. See notes on xix 16, xxiv 20. The derivation of √han is perplexing: there seem to have been no fewer than three different roots meaning to 'strike' or 'kill,' from any one of which √han might come, (1) GHAN, seen in the base ghna (e.g. çatru-ghna, 'enemy-slayer,' xii 18), also in ghátaya, the causal of √han; (2) DHAN, whence θάνατος, θείνω, &c., and nidhana, ii 18, see note; (3) BHAN, = φεν whence φόνος, &c., Curt. no. 410: the Lat. -fendo could also come from any one of these three forms.

sakáçe, 'in the presence of' (see i 12 note), a noun formed from √káç, a special Sk. root for which see xvii 5, note on san-káça.

yathá maṃsyati: so with yat in xviii 20 we find a future—tvayá hi me bahu kṛitaṃ...yad bhartrá 'yaṃ sameṣyámi. But generally after yathá in the final sense the optative is found, just as with ὅπως, though in Greek also there are still remnants of the indicative future. Compare for the Sanskrit use v 21, xii 107, 121, xiv 14, xv 6, xvii 40, xviii 16.

tvad anyaṃ, 'other than thee.' So xi 38 Naiṣadhád anyaṃ. The same ablative occurs Hor. Epp. 1. 16. 20 neue putes alium sapiente bonoque beatum. In Greek we have the genitive (doubtless for the abl.) after ἄλλος (ἄλλα τῶν δικαίων, Xen. Mem. 1. 2. 37), ἕτερος, διάφορος, &c. It is the regular construction in Sanskrit as in Latin: comp. duḥkhád duḥkham abhyadhikaṃ, xi 16, and note there.

22. **utsasarja**, 'let go,' perf. of ut + √sṛij v 27 note, orig. SARJ which is seen in the perfect. The vowel ṛi is really nothing but a weakened

ar, as may be clearly seen by comparison of the numerous words in which it occurs with the corresponding forms in other languages: e.g. hṛd = καρδ-, see i 17 note, dṛç = δρακ for δαρκ.

samutpatya, 'having flown up,' indecl. part. of sam + ut + √pat (PAT, πέτομαι and πίπ(ε)τω, peto, feather). The two senses to 'fly' and to 'fall' (Curt. no. 214) are found in Sanskrit as well as in Greek; see nipetuḥ (next line). Although samutpatya is the indecl. part., yet logically it agrees here with haṃsâḥ. The construction of these so-called participles seems often loose in Sanskrit, and thereby we are reminded of their origin. Sometimes, as here, they agree with a noun in sense though not in form: sometimes they are thrown in at random with no noun to which they can be referred, except loosely from the context. Thus in Hitop. 18 mitralâbhaḥ...pancatantrât tathânyasmâd granthâd âkṛṣya likhyate, i.e. 'the getting of friends is described (by some one) having extracted it from the Panchatantra and other sources'; comp. xx 24. Often they become mere prepositions, e.g. ix 21 samatikramya parvataṃ, 'beyond (lit. having crossed) the mountain.' There can be little doubt that both forms of this participle, that in *-tvā* and that in *-ya*, are alike old instrumentals of verbal nouns ending in *-tu* and *i* respectively. Viewed in this way their apparently loose construction is seen to be natural. Thus in the passage quoted above âkṛṣya is 'by the taking it,' an instrumental of *âkṛṣi, i.e. â + √kṛṣ + i. Compare the use of kṛtvâ, x 10 note, and the passages quoted at viii 22.

agamaṃs tataḥ for agaman tataḥ: cf. khagamâṃs tvaramâṇâ, i 24, = khagamân tvaramâṇâ. M. M. Gr. § 74, M. W. § 53. In either case the *s may* represent a lost final letter of the word, retained under these circumstances because euphonically useful, but not elsewhere. Thus agamans may be for agamant(i), the *i* having changed *t* to *s*; khagamâns may be the older full form of the acc. plural, like the Cretan τόνς and τάνς.

23. **nipetuḥ,** 3 plur. perf. of ni + √pat, see samutpatya, above. For the change of *a* to *e* see M. W. Gr. § 375 a, M. M. Gr. § 328. 1. NI is a common prefix meaning 'down': it has no clear cognate in other languages. Curtius conjectures (no. 425 note) that it = ani and so = Gr. ἐνί, and has got the secondary meaning 'down' like ἔνεροι 'those within' the earth and so below it: he also compares H. German 'ni-der,' our 'nether,' which is very probable. For the cognate form 'nis' see ix 6 note. San-ni-pâtita, the p. p. of the causal, occurs iv 3. Ut + √pat, the opposite of ni + √pat, occurs ix 15.

24. **adbhuta-rûpán**, 'of exceeding beauty': adbhuta is prob., as Bopp suggested, a corruption of atıbhuta.

vaı, intensive, prob. of the preceding word alone: so below i 28 with tasya, and very often thus with a pronoun; ke vaı, iii 2, eṣa vaı xxvi 5, &c.: with a verb at ix 8, &c. See vii 4 note.

hṛıṣṭá, p. p. of √hṛıṣ orig. HARS (horrere, where the second *r* is due to assimilation) 'to be stiff or erect.' In Sanskrit it expresses 'delight'—the state in which the hair over the body is erect: hence harṣa = delight, x 2: comp. also xxvi 32. Hṛıṣṭa occurs again, ii 25, v 30, &c.: hṛıṣıta 'erect' of flowers (with inserted *i*) v 24, xxiii 17; the perf. jahṛıṣe, xxv 8. In Latin the meaning is, of course, opposite.

khagamán(s), 'sky-goers,' like antarikṣaga above i 20: the shorter form kha-ga occurs ix 15.

tvaramáná, 'in haste,' middle participle of √tvar v 2 note.

upacakrame, perf. mid. of upa + √kram ix 6 note. Grahıtum upacakrame is a parallel construction to the Latin ire with the supine —as though it were 'subiit captum.'

25. **vısasṛıpuḥ**, 'went this way and that': 3 plur. perf. of vı + √sṛıp (SARP, ἕρπω, serpo). Observe that the vowel ṛı is gunated in the singular (as in sasarja from √sṛıj, i 22) but not in the dual or plural: M. W. Gr. 364 b.

pramadá-vane, 'in the women's grove.' Pramadá is from √mad 'to be excited' (MAD, madeo, madidus, μαδάω, Curt. no. 456). The participle pramattá = careless, unobservant, xxiii 20, Meghadûta 1: with ud, it has an intensified sense ii 3, viii 1, &c. and with sam, vii 10. Mada occurs vii 10 = madness; xiii 7 (where it comes nearer to the primary sense, as shewn by the Latin) = the juice which flows from the elephant's temples when rutting.

ekaıkaças, i.e. eka + eka + ças (-κις), 'one by one.' So sarvaças ii 22, x 9, &c. bahuças = πολλάκις, &c. The history of the suffix is not clear, but it attaches itself to numerals.

samupádravan, 3 plur. imperf. of sam + upa + √dru, 'came running up together.' Dru (a special Sanskrit form) seems to belong to the same family as DRA in δι-δρά-σκω, √δραμ in ἔδραμον, and √δραπ in δραπ-έτη-ς: it may be a weakening of DRA, or a formative with *u* from an older DAR (daru, dru; comp. TAR, τ(α)ρυ in Greek).

26. 'But the goose which D. ran close up to, took a human voice and spake thereupon to her.' Note the attraction of haṃsaṃ to the relative yaṃ: it is like the well-known 'urbem quam statuo vestrast' of Vergil: but in Sanskrit it is one of the commonest forms of the

relative construction to put the noun into the relative clause which precedes (as here) see iv 3 note: so that the attraction is natural.

samupâdhâvad, from sam + upa + â + √dhâv a lengthened form of Vedic √dhav = θεϝ in θέω.

antike, lit. 'in the neighbourhood,' as i 23 above. The word is mainly used adverbially like ἄντα, ἄντην, ἀντί in Greek. In Manu ix 174 mâtâpitror...antikât = 'from the presence of (i.e. away from) mother and father.' The history of this family of words is obscure. Curt. no. 204.

giraṃ, 'speech,' in plural = 'words' xi 6.

27. **Açvinoḥ sadṛço**, 'like the Açvins, cf. tâdṛç, i 13. The genitive, here and with samâḥ in this same line, is parallel to the Latin genitive with similis, found in old Latin; but the dative in the Augustan age. The Açvins, i.e. 'the horsemen,' are the Castor and Pollux of Indian mythology. They are Vedic deities, and the object of enthusiastic worship. They have healing power, wherein they resemble Apollo Paian, and like him they are light-gods. See Dowson, Dict. s. v.

28. 'If thou shouldst become *his* (tasya *vai*) wife, O very fair lady, fruitful would be this thy high birth and beauty, O shapely maid.' **varavarṇini** is from vara + varṇin: for vara see i 4: varṇin is a derivative of varṇa 'colour,' cf. pâṇḍu-varṇa ii 3, and vi-varṇa ii 2, but also the term for 'caste,' as originally dependent on colour—see M. Williams, 'Indian Wisdom,' 218 note. The compound is sometimes used in the literal sense (as a derivative) 'having a beautiful colour' (see P. W. s. v.): but varṇini (literally, 'belonging to a varṇa or caste') has got a secondary sense of 'woman'—and so the compound = 'fair woman.' **bhavethâ** = bhavethâs, 2 sing. optative middle, but with no different sense; the active bhavet occurs in the apodosis. Note the form of the conditional sentence: it corresponds with the simplest Greek form, εἰ γένοιο...γένοιτο (ἄν), except that nothing answers to the ἄν; which is however no essential part of the construction (as is shewn by the epic usage), but is added to make it more clear. At xii 126 we have the imperative in the apodosis, yadi jânitha nṛpatiṃ...çaṃsata me. Sometimes a participle occurs with asmi understood, as at xiii 68, xiv 24. The indicative future is found with yadi quite as often as the optative; e.g. iv 4 yadi na pratyâkhyâsyasi...viṣam âsthâsye = 'if thou shalt not reply...I will, &c.': here again we have Greek and Latin analogy as well as our own. This use of the indicative is the oldest and most natural, as is plain

when we consider that the conditional and final particles are nothing but locatives of pronouns: thus yad-ı is 'in which (case)' an old locative of yat (yad), the relative base; just as ut (uti, cuti) is the locative of the corresponding base kat (quod), and ὅπως is the ablative of the same base labialised: εἰ and si are also presumably locatives from svai (which occurs in Oscan) loc. of base sva: see Curtius no. 601.

saphalaṃ, 'fruitful,' lit. 'having fruit with it,' a B. V. compound. For phala see ix 11 note.

29. 'We have seen the Gods, the Gandharvas, men, the Nāgas and Rākshasas; and yet by us no one of such a kind has been seen before.' Supply smas with dṛṣṭavantaḥ, the past active participle of √dṛıç (i 13 note), formed from the base of the passive past participle by the suffix -vat; cf. kṛıtavantaḥ ix 9, kṛıtavàn xi 17. The same suffix (in the form Ϝοτ) is used in Greek, but added to the perfect base as in πε-φευγ-(Ϝ)οτ: corresponding to the Sanskrit forms in -vas, e.g. x 9 upeyıvàn (from upeyıvas), where see note. The Gandharvas have been identified (as to name) with the Κένταυροι: if so either there is a double Sanskrit weakening, or the Greeks have tried to get some etymology (however fruitlessly) for a foreign word and so altered its form: however there is no resemblance in function, the Gandharvas being in Epic poetry the minstrels of the world of Indra: in the older Sanskrit their work is not clear, but in the Veda they prepare the soma-juice for the Gods. See Dowson, s. v. In the P. W. it is suggested that the primary Gandharva may have been the genius of the Moon: hence the connection with Soma. **Uraga**, 'serpent' (from uras 'chest' xxiv 45 and ga 'goer') v 5, xi 27. These serpents, the Nāgas, as they were specially called, had human faces and dwelt beneath the earth: see note on Bhogavati v 7. The name also belongs to a non-Aryan race, see Dowson, s. v. **Ràkṣasa** is the name of a race of evil spirits, specially occupied in hindering the devotions of holy men. Thus in Sakuntalà, act 3, end (where they are called 'pıçıtàçanàḥ,' 'feeders on raw flesh), their shadows 'sandhyà-payoda-kapıçàḥ' 'red as the evening clouds' are said to be cast upon the altar of sacrifice, hindering the worshippers. Like the Dasyus, they may have been historic. "It is thought that the Rākshasas of the epic poems were the rude barbarian races of India who were subdued by the Āryans," Dowson, s. v. The combination of classes, beginning with the Gods, seems strange. But it must be remembered that the Gods were themselves mortal at first, and only attained immortality by sacrifice and austerities: see the curious passage in the Çatapatha-

brāhmaṇa, translated by M. Williams, 'Hinduism,' p. 35, and that from the Aitareya Brāhmaṇa (trans. Haug) quoted in 'Ind. Wisdom,' pp. 31, 32. The physical character of many of the deities (such as Indra and Agni) is transparent, and must have always been so. Eternity belonged only to the great self-existent cause (Svayambhū).

hı (ii 19, viii 18, ix 6, 16, 34, &c.) generally goes in a clause which gives directly or indirectly the reason of an action or statement. Thus here the connection is 'It is *because* we have seen the Gods, &c. that we know that there is no one like Nala': in ii 19, the link is still plainer. It corresponds throughout to γάρ (see esp. xii 119, xxvi 25), including the 'inceptive' use at the beginning of a narrative (e.g. iv 20), where the idea of causality is certainly latent. Sometimes it seems little more than γε. At xxii 2 and 5 it seems completely otiose.

tathàvıdha, comp. of tathà and vıdhà 'form,' 'manner,' from vı + √dhà, notes on iv 17 and 19. Vıdhà must not be confused as to form (though very parallel in use) with Greek -ειδης from √VID.

30. **varaḥ**, i 4 note.

vıçıṣṭàyà, for vıçıṣṭàyàs, genitive of p. p. of vı + √çıṣ 'to separate,' a very common Sanskrit root, but not obviously found in other languages: Benfey compares quaeso, which would do as to form but the meaning is not close. Vıçeṣa = 'difference,' iv 16 'excellence' (cf. the Greek use of διαφέρω); and often at the end of a compound = the best; vıçeṣeṇa is used adverbially, ii 23 = especially; vıçeṣatas, xi 5, adverbial ablative = 'conspicuously.' Açeṣa viii 20 = 'non-division' i.e. 'entirety.' Çıṣṭa (alone) occurs ix 2: avaçıṣṭa = left, forsaken, viii 5; çeṣa iv 31 note.

vıçıṣṭena, sociative use of the instrumental, vi 2 note. 'The union of the illustrious (Damayanti) with the illustrious (Nala) will be excellent.' Note the independent use of the potential 'bhavet,' or optative, as it is perhaps better called, to bring it into comparison with other languages: bhavet = bhava + ı + t, where *i* is the mood-sign, just as in Greek φυο + ι + (τι), cf. Latin sim, velim, edim, &c. This form corresponds however in use to the conjunctive as well as to the optative. There can be no doubt that the independent use of both moods is older than the dependent: it still exists in Epic Greek; e.g. οὐ γάρ πω τοίους ϝίδον ἀνέρας οὐδὲ ϝίδωμαι, A 261; Πατρόκλῳ ἥρωι κομὴν ὀπάσαιμι φέρεσθαι, Ψ. 151: and it has survived in certain well-known constructions in later Greek and Latin, e.g. in the 'conjunctivus deliberativus.' Just as in Greek, the further back

we go, the commoner do we find the independent use, so also do we
find in Sanskrit. So in Rigveda 5. 4. 7 vayaṃ te, Agna, ukthaır
vıdbema, 'we will serve thee, Agni, with prayers,' where the optative
is nothing more in use than an indefinite future : and this construction is very common. But in this poem, belonging to the later
Sanskrit literature, it is in conditional sentences (e.g. i 29) or final
clauses (e.g. v 21, xii 107, &c.) that the optative is chiefly found :
though it is also found independently, as here, viii 6, 18, &c.: and see
my notes on ix 35 and xix 4[1].

31.　　viçáṃ pate, 'lord of the people,' the uncompounded form, to
which the Vedic compound Vıçpatı corresponds. Weber, 'Indian Literature,' p. 38 (Eng. tr.), speaking of the state of society to which the
Vedic poems bear witness, writes "There are no castes as yet : the
people is still one united whole and bears but one name, that of
'vıças' 'settlers.' The prince who was probably elected was called
Vıçpatı, a title still preserved in Lithuanian." Later on, the 'vıças'
developed into the 'Vaıçyas,' the third class, the agriculturists settled
on the land ; the name, though of different origin, has the same sense
as Latin 'assiduus' : it comes from VIK, Sk. √vıç, 'to enter in' or
'upon,' (vicus, οἶκος, wick), a root which has taken to itself curiously
different associations in different languages, e.g. in the Sanskrit, in the
Greek from the special use of ἱκνέομαι, ἱκέτης, and in the Norse,
through the derivative Vik-ing. In this title, vıçáṃ patı, there is
doubtless a survival of the old general meaning. The king is the lord
of the people, not specially of the Vaıçya class, though Benfey rather
fancifully explains it so (Dict. s. v.) inasmuch as the Brāhmans are
the king's superiors, the Kshatriyas are his equals, the Vaıçyas
therefore are left to be his subjects, the Çūdras (or 4th class) being
too base to be taken into account. For the Vaıçyas see also M.
Williams, 'Indian Wisdom,' pp. 234, 235.

　　abravit, 'spoke' : the verb √brū (2nd class) inserts irregularly i
between the base and the terminations in the 1, 2, 3 sing. pres., the
2, 3 sing. imperf. and 3 sing. imperat. See M. W. Gr. § 649.

　　tvam apy evaṃ Nale vada, 'so then speak *thou* to Nala.'
Apı is the Greek ἐπί, and is very frequent both as a strengthening
particle, as a conjunction, and (in composition) as a preposition. In

---

[1] Full proof of the originally independent use of the conj. and opt. moods,
and of the origin of their dependent use out of loose parataxis, must be reserved
for a larger work (now in preparation) on the origins of syntax comparatively
treated.

the first use it corresponds to Greek γε, qualifying generally the word before it, as here (tvam apı = σύγε) also ii 25 vayam apı, iii 4 ayam apı (οὗτός γε), &c. Sometimes it is rather like καὶ or etiam, viii 18, vınaçed apı 'he might even die.' At ix 19 it = ultro, vâso 'py apaharantı me 'they are actually taking away my robe.' At xi 35 it introduces a new subject, much like ἀλλά; Damayanty apı...prajıjvâl' eva manyunâ: comp. xxiv 44, xxv 8, &c. At viii 6 it begins a sentence, 'apı no bhâgadeyaṃ syât,' rather like 'ergo.' All these meanings are deducible from the primary adverbial force 'over and above'; further than which the history of the word can hardly be carried. That sense is well seen in the Greek adverbial use, e.g. Soph. O. T. 183, ἐν δ' ἄλοχοι πολιαί τ' ἔπι ματέρες.

Nale, the locative, a common Sanskrit construction with verbs of speaking, e.g. ii 6, viii 21, xviii 15, where in other languages we should find a dative. Similarly at ix 8 a locative is used with â + √sthâ 'to help' (lit. 'stand to'); at xxvi 23 with â + √dhâ; often with √krı followed by an acc. e.g. prıyam mâyı kartum 'to do a kindness to me.' The connection in form between the dative and locative is close, and the meanings also play easily one into the other. This is best seen in Greek, where the so-called datives of the consonantal class of nouns (e.g. Ἑλλάδι, ἰχθύ-ι, πόλε-ι) are really locatives in form, and very often so in sense. It is a very plausible conjecture that the dative is only a differentiated form of the locative *ai* instead of *ĭ*: and this differentiation may have been at first only the change from short to long *i*: then in progress of time this *ī* may have changed into *ai* phonetically, just as in England the ī sound has regularly changed into *ai* e.g. in words like 'pride' 'desire' 'mine': see a paper by Mr Brandreth in 'Trans. Phil. Soc. Lond.' 1873, 4, p. 279.

32. **tathety uktvâ**, i.e. tathâ ıtı uktvâ = '**having said** *so* (i.e. *yes*).' This very common use of 'ıtı' is one of the greatest peculiarities of Sanskrit syntax. It follows, and marks, the word or words spoken, when we should use inverted commas; 'so' (ıtı) having said. By this simple device Sanskrit could dispense with all the refinements of the 'oratio obliqua' in other languages: and it thus lost a great incentive to the development of the conjunctive and optative moods: because the indicative mood alone could suffice, the reported words being left in 'oratio recta.' Itı can mark a thought as well as a speech: thus at xiv 14 we have 'mayâ te 'ntarhıtaṃ rûpaṃ na tvâṃ vıdyur janâ ıtı,' literally "by me thy form has been changed 'lest people should know thee' (thinking)." It is found in Vedic very much as

in later Sanskrit. Its origin is uncertain : it is commonly supposed
to be connected with the demonstrative base *i*: but it does not appear
what case it is to be. It stands at the end of each canto of the
poem, as just below 'ıtı Nalopákhyàne prathamaḥ sargaḥ' 'here ends
the first canto in the Tale of Nala.' There it seems to begin a sentence : in reality it joins on to all that has gone before : 'àsid...nya-
vedayat' (ıtı) = the first canto : comp. also xix 9, where it is the first
word. For its use with apparently dependent clauses, see ix 35 note.

uktvà, indecl. part. of √vac. M. W. Gr. § 650 and 375 c : M.
M. § 311.

aṇḍajaḥ, 'egg-born,' a good periphrasis for a bird.

àgamya, i 13 note.

nyavedayat, causal of nı + √vıd = 'made to know' i.e. 'told':
so ii 6, &c. But it has not the accusative of the person as it ought to
have; just as our 'certify' is commonly used with the acc. of the
thing not of the person.

1. **tacchrutvâ**, 'having heard this,' i.e. tat çrutvâ, see i 17 notes.

tataḥ prabhṛtı, 'thenceforward.' Prabhṛtı, a noun, = 'bearing forward,' from √bhṛı (BHAR, φέρω, fero, bear), but only used in classical Sanskrit as the second word of an adverbial phrase, generally either with the common ablative or the older ablative in *-tas*, as here: but also adya-prabhṛtı, Sāvıtri ii 23, 'from to-day onward.' For form cf. ataḥ param ix 23, ato-nımıttam ix 34, where atas is similarly an ablative. It is also used (like âdı, see iii 5 note) at the end of a compound to signify 'et cetera,' so in the Indralokâgamanam (ed. Bopp) ii 18 Vıçvâvasu-prabhṛtıbhır Gandharvaıḥ = 'with the Gandharvas, having Vıçvâvasu first' = 'the Gandharvas, viz. Vıçvâvasu, &c.' The construction here is noteworthy; it is not neuter in form, for prabhṛtı is feminine; yet it is used as a neuter. The phrase is practically an Av. B. compound; and at the end of these compounds a word of any gender can be used, provided its termination is not inconsistent with the neuter, so that the whole compound may be regarded as neuter: e.g. â-muktı, 'up to deliverance,' &c. See M. M. Gr. § 529, and supra, page 4.

svasthâ, 'her own self,' 'under her own command': the negative asvastha ii 5, and atı-svastha ii 7. Stha has lost its radical force here, as often: compare samipastha i 18 = 'being in the neighbourhood,' vanastha xxiv 18, and pra + √sthâ = 'set out,' i.e. actual motion, because of the 'pra,' xii 1: compare also nı-bha (xi 32) 'like,' from nı + √bhâ 'to shine,' but there only 'to be'; âbha (xiii 63), sabhâ (iii 5) where see notes: so consisto, exsisto in Latin, where the simple verb denotes no more than 'being.' If -stha had survived alone, the root √sthâ and all its other derivatives having perished, we should have called it a 'formative suffix,' like *ka*, *ra*, *la*, &c., and should have been equally uncertain about its origin.

2. **çıntâparâ**, 'sunk in thought.' There is a double-formed root, √cıt and √cınt (10th class) 'to think,' ii 7, &c., whence cıntâ here, and cetana ii 3, cetas xi 24. It is perhaps a secondary of √cı (v 15), orig. KI, probably τί-ω, τιμή Curt. no. 649: and see note on ketu xii 58. Para, originally = other (cf. perendie, lit. 'the other day,' perhaps parumper), then 'other than common,' 'distinguished,' 'prominent'; so here, 'having thought prominent,' a B. V. compound; cf. dhyânaparâ, next line. (By a parallel way ἄλλος in Greek sometimes meant 'other than right,' i.e. 'wrong': compare perhaps Latin 'perperam.') Para also = 'hostile,' i.e. other than a friend vii 6, x 19, xii 30. Parama follows the simpler meaning of para, = 'pre-eminent,' 'best,' here and iii 15, v 22, &c.

dînâ, 'miserable,' p. p. of √di, 'to waste,' distinct from the Vedic roots √di, 'to shine,' (akin to the common √dıv and dip iii 12, xi 13), and √di, 'to fly.' At ii 27 we have adin'-âtmâ, 'with happy mind.'

krıçâ, 'thin,' of uncertain origin, connected by Bopp with 'parcus,' but that is probably from √SPAR, whence our 'spare.' Curtius (no. 67) connects the rare word κολεκάνος, and Lat. gracilis.

vadana, 'face,' but properly 'mouth' (cf. Latin os), i.e. 'the speaking instrument' (comp. ânana, iv 28), from √vad = Gr. υδ, comp. καὶ τὰ μὲν ὡς ὑδέονται, Ap. Rhod. ii 530: the forms ἀείδω, ἀοιδός are probably cognate, Curt. no. 298.

nıḥçvâsa-paramâ, a compound like cıntâpara. Nıḥ-çvâsa, 'sighing,' from nıḥ ('out,' and oftener = 'not,' perhaps = ἄνις, Doric form corresponding to ἄνευ from ana, the negative prefix, Curt. no. 420), and çvâsa from √çvas, 'to breathe,' = √ques in questus, querella, not improbably identical with A. S. hweosan, 'to wheeze,' see Benfey, Dict. s. v.

3. **ûrdhva-drıṣṭır**, 'with up-cast look,' a B. V. compound.

unmatta, i 25 note.

kṣaṇena, 'instantly,' 'in a moment,' instr. of kṣaṇa, 'a moment,' v 1: plausibly supposed to be corrupted from ikṣaṇa from √ikṣ, i 20 note; comp. German 'augenblicklich'; see note on abhikṣṇam, ix 34.

hrıcchay'-âvıṣṭa-cetanâ, 'having her mind entered by love,' a B. V. compound, of which the first part, hrıcchaya + âvıṣṭa, is itself an instrumental T. P. Âvıṣṭa, p. p. of â + √vıç, i 31 note: whence veça and veçman, 'a house,' iii 10, xxi 16, &c.; the â is redundant, as vi is in vi-viç-âte, 'the two entered' ii 14: at iii 10 pra with veṣṭum has no additional force.

These two lines seem to be patchwork: the last half of 2 could be well spared, and perhaps the last half of 3: the repetitions are obvious and weak.

4. 'Neither in lying nor in sitting nor in eating (a regular Dvandva compound) findeth she pleasure at any time; not through the night and not by day doth she lie down, wailing 'Ah me, ah me' again and again.' **çayyâ**, from √çi, i 17 note: **âsana**, from √âs i 11 note; comp. Lat. āra (i.e. ās-a) the base or seat of the 'raised' part (altare): **bhoga**, from √bhuj, Latin fungor, 'to eat,' as xiii 68, 'to enjoy,' iv 8: distinct from the other √bhuj, 'to bend' (φεύγω, fugio, bow); this second is not so common in Sanskrit. **ratim**, from √ram, vi 10 note. **vindati**, from √vid 'to find,' which is conjugated in the sixth class, and inserts a nasal in the present base, as many others do: M. M. app. no. 107, M. W. Gr. § 281. It is distinct from √vid 'to see' or 'know,' of the second class: see ix 18, &c.; at vi 6 avindata = 'she has taken (in marriage).' The p. p. vitta is very common = 'riches,' xxvi 4. In the passive voice the verb means little more than 'to be': see ix 29, xiii 40, xvii 5, xxvi 5.

karhicit, indefinite from karhi, 'when,' interrogative. The form ka-rhi is curious; cf. tarhi, which Benfey (s. v.) explains as tatra-hi, rather plausibly. Karhicit is nearly always used in negative sentences, like Latin quisquam, because the idea 'any at all' is rarely needed in a positive sentence: it can come however in an interrogative sentence, e.g. xxiv 22, kathaṃ...karhicit?

divâ, 'by day,' instrumental of div, used as a noun: so kaiçcid ahorâtraiḥ xii 89, ekâhnâ xix 2. In Latin die is for diei, a locative. Observe the change from naktaṃ, accusative. The true Latin parallel (there is no Greek one) is the instrumental ablative of continued time, which (though little recognised by grammarians) appears constantly on tombs, e.g. vixit annis xx. It is 'by the space of 20 years'; the time is regarded as instrumental to the result.

çete. M. W. Gr. § 315. **rudati**, fem. part. pres. of √rud, x 20 note.

5. **tad-âkârâm**, 'having these external signs,' a B. V. compound, based on a K. D.—not a T. P. the class in which tat is most commonly found. Âkâra has this special sense, 'the bodily sign of an

inward feeling,' e.g. paleness: so in Hitop. 1084. 5 we find

> âkârair ingitair gatyâ ceṣṭayâ bhâṣaṇena ca
> netra-vaktra-vikâreṇa lakṣyate 'ntargataṃ manaḥ,

i.e. 'by the features, gestures, gait, action and speech, by change of eye and mouth is seen the inward mind.' The simple sense of the word is 'form,' 'make': see v 5: comp. vikṛtâkâra xiii 26.

jajñur, 3 plur. perf. of √jñâ, 'to know' (GNA, γι-γνώ-σκω, gnarus, gno-sco). See iii 1 note for its meaning with different prepositions. For form see M. W. Gr. § 373.

ingitaiḥ, p. p. of √ing, a denominative of inga, 'movement'—with the same meaning; but commonly meaning 'gesture' or 'hint.'

6. **nareçvare,** locative, see i 31 note.

sakhi-jana, 'companion-folk.' For jana, so used, see ix 27 note. Sakhî is feminine of sakhi = socius, √SAK, in Sanskrit √sac and √sap, the latter corresponding to ἕπ-ο-μαι, Latin sequor.

sakhigaṇât. Note the ablative with a verb of hearing. As in Latin the ablative also is used (though helped out by the preposition ab), it is probable that the Greek genitive in the same construction represents an original ablative.

7. **cintayâmâsa,** 'he thought this matter very great with regard to his daughter.' This verb has several constructions, the acc., the dat., the loc., and as here acc. with prati; see P. W. s. v.: and for the last construction cf. v 15 çaraṇaṃ prati devânâṃ prâptakâlam amanyata: xii 41 giri-râjam imaṃ tâvat pṛcchâmi nṛ-patiṃ prati.

kâryaṃ, originally fut. part. pass. of √kṛ (as it is in line 8), 'a thing to be done,'—but commonly used = 'business,' 'affair.' Similarly kriyâ is used regularly of an act of devotion; compare our 'service.'

nâtisvastheva, i.e. na atisvasthâ iva, 'not as one fully herself': iva = ὡς. For ati, see i 13 note.

lakṣyate, pres. passive of √lakṣ (iv 27, v 14, &c.—probably, as Benfey suggests, a denominative from lakṣa, 'a mark') formed, as usual, with suffix *ya*. M. W. Gr. 461, M. M. Gr. § 397, &c. See esp. § 401, "The *ya* of the passive is treated like one of the conjugational marks, which are retained in the special tenses only [pres. imperf. opt. imperat.], and it differs thereby from the derivative syllables of causal, desiderative and intensive verbs, which, with certain exceptions, remain throughout both in the special and in the general tenses." The Sanskrit middle and passive are therefore the same in their other tenses (exc. 3 sing. aor.): so that Greek and Sanskrit are almost exactly opposed in regard to the passive, the Greek distinguishing where the Sanskrit confounds, and confounding where the Sanskrit distinguishes. The reason is given in the quotation above. The Greek passive is only the middle voice developed: 'I do a thing to myself,' 'I have a thing done to myself,' 'I am done to.' But in Sanskrit the special passive tenses are formed by *ya*, and we may fairly suppose that this *ya* was the verb 'to go' on the analogy of the Latin infinitive 'amatum iri,' and the verbs 'uenum eo,' &c. 'To go to a state' is a natural way of expressing the getting or being brought into that state: cf. iv 7 martyo mṛtyum ṛcchati, 'a man goes to death,' i.e. dies, and other exx. at ii 18: we might compare our slang phrase 'he is gone dead.' When *ya* was once established in this use with verbs expressing a state, it could be employed (in the less natural way) with verbs expressing action.

prâpta-yauvanaṃ. Compare vayasi prâpte, i 11.

8. **apaçyad**, 'he saw (i 13 note, and v 9) that Damayanti's self-choosing must be held by him (Bhima).' **âtman** is regularly used with this reflexive meaning in Sanskrit, the pronoun sva not having been differentiated into that sense, see i 15 note: for âtman see note on line 13.

svayaṃ-vara is the 'self-choosing' by a maid of a husband, a custom found more than once in the Epics, but elsewhere unknown. It nowhere occurs in the Mânava Dharmaçâstra—unless it be at ix 90—92: but that is probably an interpolation. Indeed it is contrary to the whole spirit of that code, which inculcates the entire submission of women: see the beginning of chapter ix, e.g. line 3,

> pitâ rakṣati kaumâre, bhartâ rakṣati yauvane,
> rakṣanti sthâvire putrâ, na stri svâtantryam arhati,

i.e. 'a father protects in childhood, in youth a husband, sons protect in age: a woman is not fit for independence.' As this code represents an older stage of social usage than the Epics, and as modern custom agrees with it, it is not plain how the greater freedom of women, which is certainly observable in the Epics, should have arisen. See M. Williams, 'Indian Wisdom,' p. 438. He says (ib. note), "the Svayaṃvara seems to have been something exceptional, and only to have been allowed in the case of the daughters of kings or Kshatriyas." Compare Athenaeus, xiii 575.

9. **sannimantrayàmàsa**, 'he caused greeting to be sent,' perf. of sam + ni + √mantr (10th class—hence the periphrastic perfect), a denominative verb from mantra, 'advice'; a term which in the older Sanskrit is used for the Vedic hymns.

anubhùyatàm, 'let this svayaṃvara be attended.' √bhù with anu = 'to take part in a thing,' v 39.

prabho, voc. of prabhu 'lord,' pra + √bhù. Yudhishṭhira is addressed. Comp. vibhu ii 15, and vibhùti 'power' xvii 7.

10. **abhijagmus**, cf. jajñur, ii 5.

Bhimaçàsanàt, 'by the command of Bhima': abl. of origin of action. Comp. Nalaçàsanàt, viii 5 and 10: na te bhayaṃ...bhavità mat-prasàdàt ('by reason of my favour') xiv 18: Vidarbhàdhipater niyogàt 'by the order of Bhima,' xvii 35, &c. But more frequently the instrumental case is employed—the two uses being closely akin. In Latin the two uses are combined in the ablative, which has taken most of the work of the lost instrumental. But the true ablative-use (i.e. origin) is plain in such phrases as Cic. de fin. I 13 gubernatoris ars utilitate non arte laudatur. In Greek it is doubtful whether any genitive represents the ablative so used: though a gen. of place, from which motion takes place, is found, e.g. *βάθρων ἵστασθε*, Soph. O. T. 142; but nearly always this use requires a preposition to explain it.

11. **hastyaçvarathaghoṣeṇa**, 'with the din of elephants, horses, and cars,' a genitival T. P., of which the first part is a Dvandva. **hastin** is 'the beast with a hand': compare karin (xiii 9) and Macaulay's 'beast that hath between his eyes a serpent for a-hand.' Hasta (xxiii 16) may be formed by dissimilation from √ghad, whence *χανδάνω* and prehendo. **ratha**, 'a chariot,' xix 20: in composition at xii 44 mahàratha is a 'great chariot man' or 'chief': dvairatha (xxvi 3) is 'combat from a chariot.' **ghoṣa** is from √ghuṣ, 'to speak loudly,' 'proclaim,' ix 8: xii 6 nikuñjàn parisaṃghuṣṭàn, 'thickets ringing all round'; xii 113 pra + ud + ghuṣṭa.

pùrayanto, pres. part. of pùraya, i.e. √pṛi declined in the 10th class: or it might be called the causal of pṛi, but there is no difference in meaning; M. W. Gr. § 640. The p. p. pùrṇa occurs xi 32; sampùrṇa v 7.

vasuṃdharàm, 'the wealth-holder,' i.e. earth. For the *m*, see page 6. The truer form vasu-dharà occurs v 47, and vasumati Çak. i 25. Vasu is neuter; so that the *m* has no place, even in an irregular compound. It is just possible that it may be phonetic.

7

balaır, &c., 'together with armies (sociative use) wearing as ornaments varied garlands, conspicuous, and adorned full well.' **målya**, 'a garland,' from the simpler form mâlâ, comp. mâlın xxv 6. **åbharaṇa**, from â + √bhṛı, ii 1 note. **dṛıçya** = spectandus.

12. **yathârhaṃ**, 'as was fitting': an Av. B. compound, see page 4. This class very frequently begins with yathâ, e.g. yathâvṛıttaṃ, 'as it happened' i.e. 'exactly,' iv 31, xi 31; yathâkâmaṃ, 'pleasurably,' v 41; yathâgatam, 'as it was come (by them)' v 39; yathâvıdhı, 'according to rule.' A still stranger one is yathâtathaṃ, iii 2, 'truly,' lit. 'as (it is), so,' tathâ being changed into tathaṃ, because (as already explained) it is necessary that the last member must look like an acc. neuter: so yathâ kâmaḥ has to become yathâkâmaṃ, but yathâvıdhı is unchanged because it looks like the vârı-class. Obviously each of these compounds is originally a compressed sentence.

akarot pûjâm = pûjayâmâsa (see iii 16, ix 36), 'did honour to.'

te 'vasaṃs tatra, i.e. te avasan tatra, i 22 note. **avasan** is 3 plur. imperf. of √vas, orig. VAS, whence are formed ἄστυ, ἑστία, Vesta, verna, &c., Curt. no. 206. The indecl. part. uṣya occurs v 41.

13. **etasmınn**, for nn see M. W. Gr. § 52, M. M. Gr. § 71. 'At that very time those best of the sages, mighty-minded, as they wandered, having gone from here to Indra's heaven, Nârada and Parvata, great in knowledge, very holy, entered the abode of the king of the gods, held in high honour.'

sura is 'a god,' perhaps shortened from 'asura,' Zend 'ahura' 'existent,' √as 'to be'.[1] Here therefore surâṇâṃ ṛısı-sattamau is equivalent to devarṣiṇâṃ sattamau: a 'devarṣı' is even higher in the scale than a 'brahmarṣı,' i 6. Sattama does not imply that this pair is actually 'the best'—only that they are excellent: uttama is used in the same way, e.g. ii 24, 31, &c. It is only in Manu (i 34) that Nārada is included in the list of 'great sages,' the direct offspring of Brahmâ. The list however varies: there are sometimes seven (the seven Rishis of the seven stars of the great Bear,' see M. Müller, 'Lectures,' II 364), sometimes nine, and ten in Manu, Nārada himself being the tenth. At Bhag. Gita x 26 he stands *first* of the Devarshis. Some of the Vedic hymns are ascribed to him—the special function of the Rishis being to communicate orally these hymns, which were handed down afterwards by the Brāhmans: see Dowson, s. v. Ṛishi and Nārada: see also 'Ind. Wisdom,' p. 7.

[1] See however note on √svar, xviii 26.

aṭamânau, 'going purposelessly,' x 4: from √aṭ, whence aṭanam, Hit. 571, 'gadding about' of women. At viii 24, the sense seems to be more general, 'going'; just as ἕρπω meant first to 'creep' (serpo), then 'to go.'

mahâtmânau, 'of great soul.' Âtman is here used in the full sense 'spirit'; like 'spiritus,' it was originally 'breath.' But by far its commonest use is 'self' (as ii 8, xi 8 darçay' âtmânam, 'shew thyself'); thus it does the work of the 3rd person reflexive.

Indraloka, also called Svarga, 'the abode of the inferior gods and beatified mortals, supposed to be situated on Mount Meru,' Dowson, s. v. Swarga. There are several different lists of the 'lokas,' or worlds, which are seven or eight in number: but in all 'Indra's world' occupies a middle place between the abodes of the higher (i.e. newer) deities, and those of men (bhur-loka) and beings like the Yakshas and Gandharvas: Dowson, s. v. loka. A simpler division into three (tri-loka or trailokya, xiii 16, xxiv 35) includes heaven, earth, and the space between the earth: which in later times was also divided into Pātālas (see v 7, note) corresponding in number to the upper spaces.

Indra (who gives his name to the Indraloka) is at the head of the gods of that division, i.e. the atmosphere. He fights against the Asuras or demons, who personify the storms and tempests: hence his epithets Bala-Vṛitra-han ii 17, Bala-bhid, &c. In the Vedic hymns his primary elemental character is very clear: see Weber, 'Ind. Lit.' p. 40: "He is the mighty Lord of the thunderbolt, with which he rends asunder the dark clouds, so that the heavenly rays and waters may descend to bless and fertilise the earth. A great number of the hymns are devoted to the battle that is fought, because the malicious demon will not give up his booty; to the description of the thunderstorm generally, which with its flashing lightnings, its rolling thunders, and its furious blasts made a tremendous impression upon the simple mind of the people." A full account of Indra is given by Dr Muir, Sanskrit Texts, vol. 5, pp. 77—139. See also P. W., s. v.: "Indra is originally not the highest, but is the national and favourite god of the Aryan peoples of India, a type of heroic strength active for noble ends; and with the gradual obscuration of Varuṇa, he became ever more prominent. In the mixed theological system of the later times, into which the three great gods [Brahmā, Vishṇu, Çiva] were received, Indra is certainly subordinated to that Trinity, but has still remained the head of his own heaven." For his attributes and epithets, such as Maghavan (next line), Çakra (ii 20 &c.), &c., see Dowson s. v. The correspondence of Indra in function, though not in name, to Zeus and Juppiter (Dyauṣpitar) is obvious.

14. **mahâprâjñau**, from mahat and prâjña, a secondary noun formed from pra-jñâ by vṛiddhi of *a* and substitution of *ă* for *ā*.

mahâvratau, lit. 'possessors of great austerities,' which, when accumulated, constituted holiness; and so the compound = 'very holy.' Vrata is probably (as Benfey s. v. gives it) an old p. p. of √var, the original form of √vṛi, 'to choose'; and so meant at first 'a chosen' or 'voluntary act,' e.g. Damayantī's choice of Nala, v 20: then specially applied to some act of devotion, any peculiarly difficult vow or course of austerities (also called 'tapas,' x 19 note), such as fasting, burying oneself in the ground, sitting between fires in the summer months exposed to the burning heat of the sun, keeping the limbs in the same posture till the nails grow through the back of the hands, and such like: for which see 'Ind. Wisdom,' 104—106. "According to the Hindū theory, the performance of austerities of various kinds was like making deposits in the bank of Heaven. By degrees an enormous credit was accumulated, which enabled the depositor to draw to the amount of his savings without fear of his drafts being refused payment. The merit and power thus gained by weak mortals was so enormous that gods as well as men were equally at the mercy of these omnipotent ascetics. Hence both Ṛishis and Rākshasas and even gods, especially Çiva, are described as engaging in self-inflicted austerities in order to set mere human beings an example, or perhaps not to be supplanted by them, or else not to be outdone in aiming at re-absorption into Brahma." Ib. p. 344 note. The second is doubtless the true reason. This belief in acquisition by austerities of supernatural power, so as to be able to dethrone even the gods, is one of the most curious phenomena of Hindū religious thought, and parallel in a way to Fetichism. Hence the further remarkable belief that the gods were obliged to interfere with extreme devotion in men, and so thwart their austerities, when they had been carried to such an extent as to threaten the divine power: a belief also in a way like that of the Greeks in the *φθόνος θεῶν*, yet different in its operation.

bhavanaṃ, 'a place of being,' from √bhû, i.e. 'an abode.' Comp. bhuvana 'the world' xxiv 33. **viviçâte**, ii 3 note.

15. **arcayitvâ**, 'having honoured,' from √arc (10th class, so arcayâmâsa xviii 19). This verb, which is rather rare in later Sanskrit, is common in Vedic in the two senses of 'being bright' and 'singing praise.' The meaning 'to honour' may be either a causal of the first, or a development of the second sense. From ARK, the original form, comes arka 'the sun,' xvi 16. It seems to be the Greek √αλκ in ἤλεκτρον, ἠλέκτωρ, and the proper name Ἠλέκτρα. Curt. G. E. no. 24. Abhy-arcana, 'honouring,' occurs xii 78.

Maghavâ. Maghavan, 'the mighty,' a title of Indra. Magha is from √mah, or rather from √magh, which is weakened from the original form MAG, whence magnus, μέγας, might, &c. See my 'Gr. and Lat. Etymology,' p. 365, ed. 3.

kuçalaṃ, &c., 'asked them of their indestructible prosperity (specially in religious exercises) and of their all-concerning health,' i.e. their health with which that of the world is bound up. Note the Indian tendency to high-flown compliment. **kuçalaṃ**, see viii 4 note, and also xii 70 for the special meaning of the question. **avyayaṃ** is compounded of a + vyaya, 'destruction,' from vi + √i, 'to go.' **anâmayaṃ**, 'health,' lit. as an adj. (xxvi 31) 'free from sickness,'—âmaya, from a Vedic √am, 'to be sick,' possibly found in ἀνία, but hardly elsewhere out of Sanskrit. **sarva-gatam**, 'all-pervading,' like sarvatra-gatam in the next line. **papraccha**, xi 31 note.

16. 'The good health of us two, O divine king, is all-pervading, and in all the world, O all-present Indra, the kings are well.' **kṛitsna**, a peculiar word, without affinities, occurs again iv 9.

17. **Bala-Vṛitra-hâ**, see note on ii 14. **bala** also means 'strength': compare the Aeschylean personification of Κράτος and Βία. So in Hitop. 1684 âtmanaç ca pareṣâṃ ca...balâbalaṃ (i.e. bala-abalaṃ), 'the strength and weakness of himself and others.' Bala was an 'army' at ii 11.

tyakta-jivita-yodhinaḥ, 'life-abandoned (i.e. desperate) fighters'—an intelligible, though not perfectly regular compound: tyakta-jivita stands logically to yodhinaḥ as an adjective to a substantive, therefore the compound must be regarded as a K. D.: unless we should consider tyaktajivita as a locative absolute, and so regard the compound as a locative T. P. **tyakta** is p. p. of √tyaj, 'to leave,' a very common and specially Sanskrit root, which we may very fairly regard (with Pott) as formed from ati, 'beyond,' and √aj, which is for AG (ago, ἄγω): the g is seen in tyâga (x 9), and parityâga (x 10), 'abandonment.' **jivita**, used as a noun, = 'life,' prop. p. p. of √jiv, 'to live,' orig. GVI and GVIV, whence βίος, vivo, quick (apparently by reduplication), Curt. G. E. no. 640. **yodhin** from √yudh, 'to join (battle),' secondary of YU, Gr. ὑσμίνη.

18. **çastreṇa,** 'who at the proper time meet death by the sword with face unaverted.' Çastra, 'a sword' or weapon in general, from √çaṃs, see xi 10 note. **nidhanam,** i 20 note; Curt. Gr. Et. no. 311. For the construction nidhanaṃ gacchanti, cf. iv 7 mṛtyum ṛcchati, ix 8 gacched badhyatām, and the common phrase 'pancatāṃ gata,' 'he went to the state of five,' i.e. 'into the five elements,' i.e. 'he died and was resolved': see also note on the passive form above ii 7.

aparān·mukhāh = a + parāñc + mukha: parāñc, 'sideways,' is from parā ('beyond,' 'on one side,' i 15 note) + √añc, to 'go,' or 'bend': the p. p. añcita, 'bent,' or 'curved,' is found xii 45. For the declension of this and cognate words, which are excessively troublesome, see M. M. Gr. § 180. As to the composition, the base used is the weak one parāc, not parāñc: then final *c* passes by the general rule into *k*, and *k* passes into guttural *n·* (not palatal *ñ*) before *m*.

akṣayas, 'indestructible,' from √kṣi, 'to destroy.' It seems to be weakened, through the middle form *kti, from orig. KTA (κτά-μεναι, &c.), but generally occurring as KTAN, in Greek κτείνω or κτεν-ιω, and in Sk. √kṣaṇ, p. p. kṣata, whence a-vi-kṣata, xiii 21, in which the older form really appears.

kāmadhuk, nom. of kāmaduh, i.e. kāma-dugh: but the *h* is transferred to the beginning of the syllable exactly as in θρίξ from τριχ-, and the *s* of the nom. first hardens *g* to *k*, and then falls out—herein unlike the Greek. The word means 'yielding (objects) of desire (like milk),' from √duh = to milk: but the cognate θυγάτηρ and 'daughter' point to DHUG (or DHUGH) as the original form. In this compound the verb seems to have the middle, not the active, sense. It is used absolutely (without dhenu, 'a cow'); sometimes Kāma-dhenu is found. This mystical 'cow of plenty' (corresponding somewhat to the 'cornucopia') belonged to the Ṛishi Vasishṭha. It rose from the bottom of the sea of milk when churned by the gods and demons, as told in the Vishṇu-Purāṇa: see the translation given in Dowson s. v. amṛta; this was the occasion of the second incarnation of Vishṇu; see 'Ind. Wisdom,' p. 329. The cow created hordes of barbarians to aid Vasishṭha in his contest with the Kshatriya Viçvāmitra: ib. p. 363.

19. **çúrá**, i 3 note. **hı**, i 29 note. **dayıtán**, 'my loved guests': so viii 19 dayıtán açván, xvi 28, &c. The √day must be secondary from DA 'to divide' (δα-ίω, δαὶς εἴση)—it has the same original meaning (acc. to P. W.)—then to take share in a thing, have a fellow-feeling, with it—just like the Homeric δαίεται ἦτορ, α 48: see also Curt. Gr. Et. no. 256. Dayá = 'pity' (xii 117), and is frequent in compounds, such as nır-daya, 'unpitying.'

20. **Çakreṇa**, epithet of Indra, 'the strong,' from çak i 18.

çṛıṇu, i 17 note.

mahi-kṣıtaḥ, 'lords of earth (mahi)': kṣıt at the end of a compound = 'lord': so pṛthıvi-kṣıt v 4: and kṣıtı-patıs = 'lord of earth' xii 44: kṣıtı alone at xiii 8. It must belong to a √kṣı = 'to dwell (in a settled fashion)'—and so 'to rule' (alone and compounded): see Grassmann s. v. (for the *-t* see note on -jı-t, vii 5). This root is of course distinct from √kṣı just mentioned. The sense leads us to connect it with √κτι in κτίζω, εὐ-κτί-μενος, &c. Curt. G. E. no. 78: and κτάο-μαι is certainly cognate: the oldest Sk. form seems to have been *kṣa whence kṣatra and kṣatrıya: and so the orig. form would be KTA-, identical with the verb 'to destroy': which is awkward: the Greeks differentiated them by vowel change to some extent.

21. **Damayanti 'ti vıçrutá**, 'renowned, "it is Damayanti," as people say': note the very expressive use of ıtı, and compare xii 33 and 48: see also note on i 32.

rúpeṇa, 'by her beauty she excels all women on the earth.'

samatıkrántá, p. p. of sam + atı + √kram, 'to go.' Note the use of the passive participle in an active sense: so also vıkránta, xii 54: see note on prápta i 11; comp. pravıṣṭa iii 24, also iv 25; prapanná viii 17, &c. It is almost confined to neuter verbs: still it should not have been allowed in Sanskrit, which had perfect active participles: it is excusable in the so-called Latin deponents—really middle verbs.

yoṣıtaḥ: yoṣıt is a peculiar form: the *-it* may be a weakening of a participial ending: and so Benfey takes it. He supposes that the root was √juṣ, 'to enjoy,' xii 65 note, and that the word was originally *joṣat. But it may be from √yuj, cf. con-iux in Latin, and perhaps (y)ux-or: see however Corssen I 171, for the latter word.

22. **nacırád**, i 4 and 16 notes. **sarvaçaḥ**, i 25 note.

23. 'Wooing her, the pearl of the earth, the lords of earth eagerly seek after her.' **bhútám**, the p. p. of √bhú, is redundant after ratna: it is not a regular compound, because the final *a* of ratna

should have been changed into ī, as from sajja, 'ready,' is formed sajji-bhū, 'to be ready.' M. W. Gr. § 788. **prârthayanto**, from pra + √arth (10th cl.), i.e. a denominative verb formed from artha, 'object,' 'aim,' 'matter,' 'business' = Latin res, iii 7 note. **sma**, i 7 note: it has no force here unless it be intensive.

kân·kṣanti, a common epic verb, perhaps an irregular desiderative of √kam (Lat. am-o, perhaps κάσις): the noun kân·kṣâ, xvi 2 and 18. **viçeṣeṇa**, i 30 note.

niṣûdana, 'destroyer,' from ni + √sûd, 'to kill': Benfey compares πασ-συδ-ίη: but the connection of meaning seems hardly sufficient, and the δ there is probably parasitic. Sûdana occurs xii 126.

24. **etasmin kathyamâne**, loc. abs., see i 11 note. **sâgnikâh**, 'together with Agni,' from sa + agni (cf. sabhârya, i 8) + ka, a suffix without value, except to make a more convenient form: see page 7.

lokapâlâs, 'the guardian deities, who preside over the eight points of the compass, i.e. the four cardinal and four intermediate points of the compass:—(1) Indra, east; (2) Agni, south-east; (3) Yama, south; (4) Sūrya, south-west; (5) Varuṇa, west; (6) Vāyu, north-west; (7) Kuvera, north; (8) Soma, north-east.' Dowson s. v. lokapāla. Here apparently only four appear: Indra, Agni, Varuṇa, and Yama.

âjagmur (like jajñuḥ, ii 5 note), from â + √gam, i 13 note.

25. **hṛṣṭâh**, i 24 note. **uta**, perhaps 'also,' much like *api* (for which see i 31 note). At xii 120 utâho, i.e. uta + âho, = 'or' in a double question, like Latin an; and so with vâ in the Rigveda: but there the copulative meaning is most frequent. It is perhaps a weakened instrumental of a pronominal stem *u*, which is not fully declined in any language: it seems to occur in asau (xiii 26 note); also in ἀ-υ-το, and ὁ-υ-το: see Windisch in Curt. 'Studien' ii 266, &c.

26. **sahavâhanâḥ**, 'with their carriages,' √vah, orig. VAGH, whence ὄχος and veh-i-culum.

27. **adina**, ii 2 note. **anuvratâḥ**, 'devoted to,' x 12, xiii 56, &c. For vrata see note on ii 14: it is often used at the end of a compound, as there mahâ-vrata; ii 3 satya-vrata, 'devoted to truth,' 'truthful'; pati-vrata, 'devoted to her husband,' &c. Note the acc. Damayantīṃ after anuvrata; so ix 31 tyaktu-kâmas tvâṃ, 'having a desire to leave thee.' A few well-known examples survive in Greek, e.g. Aesch. Choeph. 21 χοὰς πρόπομπος, Supp. 588 τὸ πᾶν μῆχαρ οὔριος Ζεύς. Historically there is no more reason to be sur-

prised at these constructions than there is to wonder at an accusative following a participle—which is nothing but a noun—though a noun in which the idea of action comes out strongly. And whenever that sense is strong, an adjective could take an accusative: e.g. v 2, Damayantim abh-ipsavaḥ, where the desiderative adjective 'ipsu' seems to lie between an adjective and a participle, and xxi 24 abhivádaka. The use after substantives (e.g. Naiṣadham mṛigayánena xviii 2, or hanc tactio in Plautus) seems stranger. But the distinction between substantive and adjective is one of use, not of form: the suffixes were originally the same for both, and only by degrees were differentiated to some extent: and use rarely became so fixed in language as not to allow relics of older and freer constructions.

Perhaps the construction here is facilitated by the fact that anu is one of the three Sanskrit prepositions which govern a case—all the rest being found in composition only. Anu generally governs an accusative, and follows its case as Gan-gám anu, Yamunám anu, 'up,' or 'along the Ganges,' or 'Yamuna.' The others are (1) á, with the abl., for which see note on i 13; (2) prati, see ii 7, x 11 note.

28. **pathi**, 'on the road,' locative, as though from base path: the base pathin to which it is referred is heteroclite: M. W. Gr. § 162, M. M. § 195. At the end of a compound patha is used as a base, so ix 21 dakṣiná-patham. It is Latin pon(t)-s, probably πόντος, and πάτος, Curt. no. 359.

bhútale, 'on the earth surface,' = mahi-tala x 5; comp. nabhastala ii 30, çilá-tala xii 12, prásáda-tala xiii 51. In most of these compounds tala is redundant. It may be cognate to Lat. tellus, as Bopp suggests, which is 'the bearer' (Corssen II 149) from √TAL, see iv 6 note.

múrtyá, instrumental of múrti, expressing the material cause, while **sampadá** is more general. 'Standing like Manmatha visibly seen in the body, by reason of the excellence of his beauty.' Comp. i 16 Kandarpa iva rúpeṇa múrtiman. For the epithet Manmatha, see i 14 note: we should rather have expected mano-matha, however: other names are Mano-ja, Manasi-ja, 'mind-born': and compare hṛicchaya i 17. **sampad** from sam + √pad, 'to go,' is often used for 'success,' 'prosperity,' and so in compounds 'perfection,' as here, 'of form,' i.e. beauty. Sam appears to be used with implication of 'good,' like Latin con in contingo, 'good luck,' as opposed to accido, 'bad luck,' Sk. á-pad, Manu ii 40, &c.

29. **bhrâjamânam**, 'shining like the sun,' pres. part. middle of √bhrâj (orig. BHRAG, whence φλέγω, fulgeo, Curt. no. 161).

vigata-samkalpâ, 'with purpose gone,' so iv 29. Saṃkalpa is "the resolution formed in the mind, and then the wish, or will, arising therefrom." P. W. The opposite word is vi-kalpa, 'doubt.' So ix 26 tava saṃkalpaṃ...cintayantyâḥ, 'thinking of thy purpose.' It = 'wish' at Çak. iii 58. And in jâta-saṃkalpa (iii 8) either meaning would do. The Sk. root is √kḷp, which points to orig. KALP, which however has been unproductive in other languages. Benfey assigns Lat. corpus to it.

vi-smitâ, 'amazed,' from vi + √smi 'to smile': which last is app. a secondary of the simple root SMI, whence (s)mi-rus, miror (with the sense of the compound in Sanskrit), perhaps μεί-δ-ημα and μειδιάω—see Curtius no. 463. Vismaya occurs xii 73.

30. 'Then the sky-housers (caelicolae) after staying their cars in mid-air spake to Nala after descending from cloud-land.' The gods leave Indra's heaven and pass from the nabhas-tala through the inferior loka (antarikṣa) the abode of Yakshas, Gandharvas, &c. **divaukas** from diva and okas, 'a house,' apparently from UK, the original form of √uc, 'to be accustomed to,' whence p. p. ucita xv 18—see note there.

viṣṭabhya, from vi + √stambh, a secondary of STA (whence στέμφ-υλο-ν, ἀ-στεμφής, and our 'stamp,' Curt. Gr. Et. no. 219), but the Sanskrit verb has the secondary notion of 'supporting,' derived not very obviously from the primary notion of 'pressing upon.' **vimâna**, 'a chariot,' but specially Indra's chariot, see Indr. i 32. The P. W. gives us the primary meaning, 'stretching right through' (from vi + √mâ), in which sense it is only Vedic, and is used as an epithet of a chariot, 'rajaso vimânam sapta-cakraṃ rathaṃ,' Ṛigv. 2. 40. Afterwards, as often, the epithet has become a sort of proper name; like Maghavan and Çakra of Indra himself.

avatirya, from ava (down) + √tṛi (orig. TAR, whence τέρμα, terminus, intrare, trans, through, Curt. G. E. no. 238). Hence the well-known word Avatāra, or Avatār, literally 'descent,' but applied to the incarnation of a deity, especially Vishṇu: for a full account of the different Avatārs see Dowson s. v., and 'Ind. Wisdom,' p. 329, &c. Ud + tṛi, used of crossing a river, xii 112.

nabhas, identical in form with νέφος. The old derivation na + √bhâs, 'not shining,' is amusing. It is not however simply 'a cloud,' but the 'cloud region' the atmosphere. So vyabhre nabhasi xvii 11, 'in the sky when free from cloud.'

31. **bhavân, &c.**, 'your majesty is truthful.' The full sentence would of course be 'bhavân astı satya-vrataḥ,' bhavat being the 'pronoun of respect' of the 2nd person, lit. 'the existing one,' see M. W. Gr. § 233, and for its declension ib. § 143, M. M. Gr. § 188. Cf. iii 2, ke vaı bhavantaḥ ? 'who are ye ?' and iv 11, 28, 31, vii 5, &c. The Greek φώ(τ)ς is doubtless the same word, by attraction from φαϝοτ-ς: but there is nothing analogous in its use.

sâhâyyaṃ, 'help,' formed by vṛıddhı of first syllable, suffix ya, and loss of final a, from sahâya, 'a companion' (vi 2), which is from saha + √yâ, 'to go.'

dûto, 'messenger,' a word of uncertain origin: according to the P. W. of the same family as dúra 'far.'

1. **pratijñâya**, 'having promised,' so Hitop. 1186: at xix 10, Sâv. i 15, it is 'assent to': pratijñâ is 'a promise,' Hitop. 848. √Jñâ with prepositions has many meanings, which rarely correspond to those of other languages. Thus anu + √jñâ is 'to permit' xxiv 5, Hitop. 1130, and with sam, vi 7 samanujñâte; also 'to dismiss' xvii 19, xviii 5, xxiv 4, with sam, v 41, viii 22; this is a special form of 'permission.' Abhi + jñâ = 'to recognise,' v 11. Ava + √jñâ, lit. 'to know down' = 'to despise,' Hit. 1161; καταγιγνώσκω is some way parallel. Pra + jñâ = 'to understand and know,' cf. prâjña ii 14, prâjñâyata xvii 3: vi + √jñâ is 'to discern,' xiii 55 (di-gnosco). Âjñâ is 'a command,' xix 11, Hit. 1098.

kṛitâñjalir, 'having made the añjali,' i.e. the hollows of the hand put together: the raising the hands so joined to the forehead is a mark of respect and submission. Prâñjali (i.e. pra + añjali), iii 7, has the same meaning.

upasthitaḥ, 'standing near'; with acc. xii 47 tvâm upasthitâm, and so the verb upatasthe viii 25, 'he waited upon Rituparṇa, comp. xv 7; so upa + √i, lit. 'to go under,' = 'come near' (iii 7), as Lat. subire: cp. ὑποστῆναι 'to stand under' an engagement.

2. 'Who are ye? (ii 31 note), and who is this whose welcome (lit. 'desired,' i 4) messenger I am?' desired as being his messenger, a complimentary phrase. Or we may take yasya as a dative (see xiii 32 note), 'he to whom I am to go as a messenger.' For asau see xiii 25.

yathâtatham, 'truly,' ii 12 note. At xvi 39 âcaṣṭe yathâtatham, it is used like a substantive 'the truth.'

3. 'It having been thus spoken by Nala,' abl. abs.; but at 7, evam uktaḥ sa Çakreṇa Nalaḥ. Either construction is equally permissible. **abhyabhâṣata**, 'spoke to him,' so iii 10 and 16: not 'replied': for √bhâṣ, see viii 4 note. **vai**, see vii 4, and i 24.

Damayanty-artham, 'because of D.' So parârtham iii 8; and prajâ + arthe i 6; either case is frequently used in this prepositional sense, like Latin 'caussa': for the acc. compare δίκην, τρόπον, &c. For artha, see note on 7. **âgatân**, i 13 note.

4. **Agniç.** Agni (igni-s) is the most transparent of the older gods, and the numerous hymns addressed to him plainly shew his nature. "He is the messenger from men to gods [hence his names such as Huta-vaha and Havya-vâhana xxiii 12, i.e. 'offering-bearer'], the mediator between them, who with his far-shining flame summons the gods to the sacrifice, however distant they may be. He is for the rest adored essentially as earthly sacrificial fire, and not as an elemental force." Weber, 'Ind. Lit.' p. 40: see also Muir 'Sanskrit Texts,' vol. v, pp. 99—203, Dowson s. v. His worship is therefore very unlike the fire-worship of the Persians, which seems a different development of an earlier and less ceremonial conception.

tathaiva = tathâ eva, 'even so,' 'moreover,' in which sense it often occurs, e.g. v 1; and tathâ alone, iv 8, viii 20, xix 37.

Apâṃ patiḥ, 'the lord of waters,' i.e. Varuṇa = Οὐρανός, 'the coverer' (from √var, see iii 6), the all-embracer; and certainly at first the sky-god, though there is no similarity between his functions or character and those of Οὐρανός. In the hymns "he is king of the universe, king of gods and men, possessor of illimitable knowledge, the supreme deity to whom especial honour is due." Dowson s. v. Varuṇa: see the whole article, or Dr Muir's fuller account v 58—76. The well-known hymn (Atharva-Veda, iv 16) which celebrates the omniscience of Varuṇa has often been translated—by M. Müller (see the extremely interesting collection given by him 'Chips,' I 39—45) and by Muir, v, p. 63: the curious parallelism of some passages to the Psalms is noted by both writers: e.g. in the following stanzas (as translated by Muir):

"Wherever two together plot, and deem they are alone,
King Varuṇa is there a third, and all their schemes are known.
The earth is his, to him belong those vast and boundless skies;
Both seas within him rest, and yet in that small pool he lies.
Whoever far beyond the sky should seek his way to wing,
He could not there elude the grasp of Varuṇa, the king.

....

Whate'er exists in heaven and earth, whate'er beyond the skies,
Before the eyes of Varuṇa, the king, unfolded lies."

Later (doubtless in consequence of the rise of Indra, see ii 13 note) he descended into the character of a sea and river god; hence his names Apâṃ-pati, as here, Jala-pati, &c.

çarir-ânta-karo, 'body-end-maker of men': comp. cittapramâthini devânâṃ, i 14. Çarira might come from a √çṛi (çar) 'to lean': and so the P. W. (referring to a fanciful derivation in Manu i 17). But the connection is not obvious. Çaraṇa, 'refuge,' v 15, would be derived from the same root. Others refer it to √çṛi 'to break.'

Yama is a less clear figure in Hindū religion. He appears in the Vedic poems, sometimes as Death personified, sometimes as the first man who died, Muir v 301, &c. But in the Epic poems he certainly appears as a judge, see Dowson s. v., also 'Ind. Wisdom,' pp. 20—22. It is not unnatural that the belief in a future state should have varied in the long time covered by Sanskrit literature: we can recall a parallel variation in Greek literature, e.g. between the Epic and the Pindaric view of future existence. It seems undeniable that in the Vedic hymns there is little or nothing of that distaste for life, and that desire for ultimate emancipation from personal existence, which is a distinguishing feature of Brāhmanism.

5. **Mahendrâdyâḥ**, 'having great Indra first,' 'headed by great Indra,' 'Indra, &c.'; a B. V. compound, in which âdya is used for the commoner form âdi (açvamedh'-âdi, xii 14): which meant at first 'beginning,' 'origin': e.g. Bhag. Gīta, ii 28 avyaktâdini bhûtâni, 'mortal beings are of unseen origin.' But it is commonly found (in the sense of 'first') at the end of a compound to express that there is a series of things of which this one is first: and so is practically equivalent to our 'et cetera'; like 'prabhṛti,' ii 1. It is often used with 'iti' in the Hitopadeça (e. g. l. 469) at the beginning of a paragraph following a speech (which is indicated by iti), = 'so, and more to the same effect.' Similarly at xiii 43 it is used with evam, 'evam-âdini' = 'thus, and more of the same sort.'

sabhâ is 'an assembly' and 'hall for such assembling,' and 'a palace': at x 5 it is used for a dwelling in a wood, and presumably a small one. Here it would seem that the phrase sabhâṃ yânti might mean either 'go to the palace,' or 'go to assembly,' i.e. 'are assembling': see note on ii 7. The word is probably derived from sa + √bhâ, the verb having lost its primary meaning of 'shining,' and serving merely to float the 'sa,' see note on svastha ii 1.

didṛikṣavaḥ, 'desirous of seeing thee,' formed by adding *u* to didṛikṣa, the desiderative of √dṛiç, 'to see.' Comp. abhipsu v 2, jihirṣu ix 16, paripreṗsu xviii 11.

6. **anyatamaṃ**, 'one,' or rather 'the other out of many.' So

katara means 'which of two?' and katama, 'which of many?' In Greek πότερος, and in Latin uter (for cutero-) corresponds to katara, but katama has no equivalent. C. Dickens (in 'Our mutual friend') plagiarised unconsciously when he struck out the strained phrase 't'otherest.'

patitve, 'choose one god out of all these in wedlock.' It is 'the state of a husband,' 'husbandship,' and the loc. expresses 'for him to be to thee in the position of a husband.' The locative is often thus used to give the purpose of an action, e.g. patitve vṛitaḥ, v 17; vratam ârabdham Nalasy' ârâdhane, v 20; Damayantyâ visarjane, x 15; Nalasy' ânayane yata (strive for the bringing here of Nala) xvii 29, &c. This is the origin of the use of the infinitive in Greek and Latin, whether that case was a dative or locative.

varayasva, imperat. of varaya, irregular for vâraya, which may be regarded either as causal of √vṛi, or as that root inflected in the 10th class. It is also conjugated in the 5th class (vṛi-ṇo-ti) and in the 9th (as a middle verb vṛiṇe iv 14, vṛi-ṇi-te iv 28). It has also several meanings, 'to cover,' which is probably the oldest one, 'to hinder' (iii 24, also nivâraṇa, vii 10), and 'to choose,' as here, iv 7 and 9, &c., also vara, i 4 and 8. The different conjugations and meanings do not exactly correspond. The verb is said to be conjugated in the ninth when it means 'to choose,' and in the fifth when it means 'to cover': but here the distinction is expressed by 'varaya' and 'vâraya.' The root in the sense of 'choosing' has its cognates in volo, βούλομαι, will; see Curt. no. 659: the idea of 'covering' is probably seen in ἔριον, vellus, wool; and if it arose from an older sense of 'turning' we should have to compare volvo, εἰλύω, &c., Curt. no. 527. But more probably the primary idea is to 'lay hands upon,' from which all the others naturally flow.

7. 'Deign not to send me who am come on one (and the same) business' (as yourselves, the gods).

artha (as already noted) has most of the uses of the Latin 'res.' At viii 4, sarv'-ârtha-kuçala, it has the primary sense, 'good at all things'; also at xviii 15. At xii 90, ko nu me jîviten' ârthaḥ = 'what have I to do with life?' i.e. what good is life to me? Artha-kâma, xviii 47, = 'desirous of wealth.' At xxiii 10, Ṛituparṇasya... arthâya = 'for the use of R.'; and we have already seen that arthe (i 7) and artham (iii 3) = because of; at iii 25, etad-artham = 'on this business': but aty-artham, xi 20 = 'exceedingly.' A very frequent compound is samartha = 'capable'; used (alone) of horses = 'powerful,' xix 13, or with an infinitive, samartho gantuṃ, 'capable of going,' xxiv 30. From this we have the derivative sàmarthya (M. W. Gr. § 80, x), 'capability,' 'power,' as v 23 sàmarthyaṃ liṅga-dhàraṇe: at Bhag. Gīta ii 36 it is used absolutely = 'courage,' 'fortitude.' Arthin is one who has an artha or object: and so 'seeking,' xiii 11, 50. Similarly pràrthaya is 'to woo,' xiii 69, and pràrthayitṛ is 'a wooer.' Kṛtàrtha = 'one who has got his object,' xvi 10. Arthitavyam, from arthaya the verb, occurs xxvi 9.

preṣayitum, infin. of preṣaya, causal of pra + √iṣ, 'to go' (4th class), distinct from √iṣ, 'to wish,' with pres. base iccha, iii 6, p. p. iṣṭa, i 1. For the irregular Sandhi see M. W. 38, g. Böhtlingk and Roth (P. W.) give as the original meaning 'setting into motion,' and refer both meanings to the same root with different present-bases, iṣya and iccha. If so, the causal and simple verb have the same meaning. Anu + √iṣ, 'to go after,' 'seek,' occurs xii 10; and anveṣana xiii 70.

arhatha. The verb arh is frequently thus used in 2 pers. sing. or plur. with an infinitive, as a polite form of a request: 'ye think it right not to send,' i.e. 'do not send me.' So vi 15, sàhàyyaṃ kartum arhasi; xiv 7 tràtum arhati màm bhavàn = tràtum arha; xxv 12, &c. The derived adjective arha = 'worthy,' so at ix 10, sat-kàra + arha = 'worthy of hospitality.' Arhanà, xxv 4, = 'respect.' The original root = ARGH, whence ἄρχομαι, Curt. no. 165: in ὑπάρχω, and in the sacrificial terms, ἀπάρχομαι and κατάρχομαι, a similar loss of the primary sense is seen. What that sense was is doubtful: the Greek use is not parallel: that of ἀξιόω is more analogous. Benfey (s. v.) compares the use of 'dignor' with the infinitive.

8. 'How can a man with desire' (or 'purpose,' ii 29 note) 'already born in him endure to speak to a woman in this wise for another's sake? Let the lords of earth excuse this.' Note the double acc. after √vac, just as in Greek and Latin after verbs of speaking.

idṛçaṃ, cf. tàdṛç i 13. **utsahate** (iv 15, vi 14, &c.) from ud + √sah (whence utsàha, 'power,' xix 37), orig. SAGH (σ)έ-χω, Curt. no. 170: from the noun sahas, 'power,' comes the instr. sahasà, which is often used adverbially = 'suddenly' (i.e. 'vigorously') v 28, x 7. The verb takes a contained accusative, iv 15 svàrtham utsahe. **kṣamantu**, 'content,' 'endurance,' 'forgiveness,' are the meanings of this verb: vii 8 na cakṣame ràjà samàhvànaṃ 'the king endured not the challenge': and kṣamà = endurance. At xxv 12, tàṃ tvaṃ kṣantum arhasi, the use is the same as here, 'forgive.' For the curious connection of kṣamâ with χθών, see Curt. no. 183. At xxv 9 is the causal kṣamaya.

9. **saṃçrutya**, 'having promised': prati + √çru in the same sense iv 16, comp. prati-jñâ iii 1: polliceor shews the same preposition; see Curt. no. 381. **vraja**, see viii 5 note.

mâciraṃ, 'with no delay': mâ (Greek μή) is so used in compounds; and also with the aorist conjunctive, just like the Greek, xii 73, mâ çucaḥ, 'weep not'; xiv 3, mâ bhair iti; xiv 23 mâ sma çoke manaḥkṛitâḥ: see notes on each passage.

10. **su-rakṣitâni**, 'well guarded,' p. p. of su + √rakṣ i 4 note; **veçmâni**, ii 12 note; also ni-veç-ana, next line.

12. **dedipyamânâṃ**, pres. part. middle of dedipya, frequentative of √dip, 'to shine,' xi 12 note.

vapuṣâ, 'by her beauty,' or 'with her body.' The word (which is of doubtful origin) means (1) 'wonderful' (adj.), or 'a wonder' (subst.): the P. W. compares the Vedic 'vapuṣe,' 'for a wonder,' with the Homeric θαῦμα ἰδέσθαι: then (2) any 'wondrous appearance,' 'beauty,' &c. = and finally 'shape,' 'body.' So Manu ii 232 dipyamânaḥ svavapuṣâ devavad divi modate, 'shining with his own body he is happy like a god in heaven.' It occurs again xiii 52, xvii 8, xix 28. **çriyâ**, i 10 note.

13. **sukumârâṅ·giṃ**, 'with very soft limbs.' **kumâra** = 'a boy,' and kumâri, 'a girl'; hence the secondary meaning of 'youthful,' 'tender.' But this is closely akin to the primary one, if the word be really derived (as in the P. W.) from ku, the depreciatory prefix (see note on kovida, i 1), and mâra, 'death,' and so meant (as applied to a new-born infant) that which might die as easily as live. **aṅ·ga**, 'a limb,' also 'a part of anything,' used especially of the 'supplementary parts' of the Veda, the Aṅ·gas and Upāṅ·gas, as they were called (see xii 17 and 81 notes). It is constantly found in compounds, such as anavadyâṅ·ga i 12, iii 20, xi 32, &c. From it comes the fuller form aṅ·ganâ, iii 15 and 18, &c. = a woman: but, first, a woman's chamber (so P. W.), then (in polite conversation) its occupant.

âkṣipantim, 'throwing shame on the brilliance of the moon by her brightness.' √kṣip is to 'sling' or 'throw,' a somewhat isolated root: with â, as here, it = to throw at, 'scoff,' 'mock.' So Manu iv 141 hinâṅ·gân atiriktâṅ·gân...nâkṣipet, 'a man is not to insult those who have a limb wanting or limbs in excess.' With sam, iv 9 = 'grasp'; with ni, viii 20 = 'deposit,' xx 29 = 'compensation.'

çaçınaḥ, a name of the moon 'he who has the hare,' from a fancy that the spots on the moon resembled a hare. See Hitop. 2. Other similar names are çaça-bhṛıt, çaça-dhara.

14. tâṃ, probably acc. after dṛıṣṭvâ, 'the desire of him having just seen that sweet smiling girl was increased,' see note on samut-patya, i 22. Otherwise it must be taken after kâmas, the acc. of the object, with tasya as the gen. of the subject. câruhâsınıṃ. Câru (v 6, xii 26 and 45, &c.) has been identified with the problematical τηλυ in τηλύγετος, &c., so that c in Sanskrit and τ in Greek should come from original k. Hâsın from hâsa, 'laughter,' from √has, 'to laugh,' iv 1, &c. : with pra at ix 2, xii 117 = 'to mock': at ix 8 parıhâsa = 'jest.'

cıkirṣamânas, pres. part. mid. of cıkirṣa, desiderative of √kṛı, 'desirous to do': again at viii 3. Final ṛı is changed to îr in these verbs, when no i is inserted before the sa (cp. jıhirṣu, ix 16), except when a labial precedes, which assimilates the vowel to û, as from smṛı comes susmûrṣa. dhârayâmâsa, i 18 note.

15. sambhrântâḥ, 'amazed,' from √bhram, 'to whirl,' or 'to wander': see xv 14, xvi 30, and vı + √bhram, ib. xv 16. It is the same as the Latin fremo in form: and this cannot be separated in meaning from βρέμω (comp. βροντή and fremitus, Lucr. v 1193 fulmina grando et rapidi fremitus et murmura magna minarum) —so that the β in Greek is irregular. The development of meaning from the original sense (as seen in Sanskrit) is interesting: see Kuhn Zeitschrift VI 152, and Curt. G. E. p. 519 (II 143 Eng. tr.). samutpetuḥ, i 22 note.

dharṣıtâḥ, p. p. of dharṣaya, causal of √dhṛṣ, orig. DHARS (θάρσος, &c.). The simple verb = 'to be bold,' and p. p. dhṛṣṭa = θρασύς. The causal = 'to lay hands on,' 'overpower': see x 14, xi 36 : and so here in the participle. The compound durdharṣa, 'not to be handled,' 'terrible,' occurs xi 8.

16. praçaçaṃsuḥ, i 16 note. vısmaya, ii 29 note. anvıtâḥ, p. p. of anu + √ı, like upeta, i.e. upa + ıta, vi 8, &c. = 'approached,' or 'entered by,' 'pervaded.' abhyapûjayan, ii 12 note.

17. dhaıryaṃ, 'majesty,' 'firmness,' from dhira = firm (√dhṛı, i 17). bhavıṣyatı, 'will this be?' a not uncommon use of the future to express doubt. So xix 31 n' âyaṃ Nalo mahâviryas, tadvıdyâçca bhavıṣyatı, '(if) this be not Nala, I suppose it will be one with his knowledge.' The Greek and Latin are wiser iu restricting this sense to the 'conjunctivus deliberativus.'

18. **çaknuvanti**, i 18 note. **sma**, i 12 note. **vyâhartuṃ**, i 20 note.
lajjâvatyo, 'modest,' from lajjâ (xvii 33) with suffix -vat, fem. -vati. √lajj (6th cl.) = raj-ya, according to Benfey. The participle, vilajjamâna, occurs v 27.

19. **smita-pûrvâ**, i 14 note.

20. **hṛicchaya-vardhana**, 'love-increaser.' Vardhana is from √vṛidh i 17, viii 14 note.

21. 'How is thy coming here (brought to pass)? And how art thou not seen? For well guarded is my dwelling, and my father is cruel in his commands.' **iha**, perhaps the pronominal root i, with ha for *dha, as Benfey suggests. **ugra** = 'strong,' √uj, which however does not occur; the derivative ojas, 'strength,' is found v 34, &c.; orig. VAG, whence vegeo vegetus; also UG, whence augeo, ὑγιής, &c.; a widely spread root, Curt. no. 159.

çâsana is from √çâs, 'to correct,' 'govern' (comp. sam + anu + çâs, xii 49, pra + çâs xii 94, where the meaning is the same), 'teach.' This is the order of the P. W.: Benfey reverses it. It is probably (so Benfey) short for çaças a reduplicated form of √çaṃs (i 16 note) or rather of a simpler form ças: the irregular base çis would be for çiças, and rather supports the view. Hence comes the common word çâstra, 'a rule,' e.g. in dharma-çâstra, 'duty-rule,' i.e. a code of law: and anuçâsana, 'precept,' xiii 39.

22. **kalyâṇi**, voc. of kalyâṇi, fem. of kalyâṇa, 'illustrious,' xii 15, &c.: the simpler form is kalya, Greek καλός: the varying quantity of the first syllable of that word shews the lost spirant; Curt. no. 31.

23. **varaya**, iii 6 note: note that the active is used here, the middle there, with exactly the same context. The nicety of the Sanskrit in such matters is much inferior to that of the Greek.

24. **avârayat**, imperf. of vâraya, 'to hinder,' perhaps causal of √vṛi, 'to cover,' iii 6 note.

25. **bhadre**, 'good lady,' also used as a subst. in the common salutation 'bhadraṃ te,' xv 5, xxvi 6, 'may it be good to thee,' 'may it please thee.'

buddhiṃ prakuruṣva, 'resolve': kuruṣva is the mid. imperat. of √kṛi formed from the irregular base kuru, M. W. Gr. § 355, M. M. Gr. App. no. 152. The verb is unaltered in meaning by the preposition, but prakṛiti, the noun, is very common = 'the nature or constitution of anything'—with different derived meanings. See vii 13 note. Prakâra (xiii 15) = 'operation,' 'manner.'

çubhe, 'bright lady,' from √çubh (no analogues), whence çobhane (same sense), iii 23.

1. **namas-kṛtya**, 'having done homage to.' Namas is from √nam, 'to bend'; causal passive nâmyatâm (dhanuḥ), 'let the bow be bent,' xxvi 10: with pra, 'to bow down to,' xii 43; ana + nata xii 68; vi + namate xxiii 9. That this is Gr. νέμω is probable from the form: but the difficulty in connecting the meanings is great; see Curt. no. 431: and numerus, Numa, nemus, which go fairly naturally with the Greek family, do not throw any light on the Sanskrit. If they are all cognate, it would seem that 'bending' must be the primary idea: Curtius thinks 'allotting' for Gr. Ital. family. √kṛ is commonly used with adverbs: see note on alam-kṛ i 11. For *s* instead of visarga before *k*, see M. M. Gr. § 89 II. **prahasya**, iii 14, &c.

praṇayasva, 'give me thy affection faithfully' (M. W. gloss.)—and so certainly praṇaya is used in the next line: 'pledge to me thy faith,' Milman. 'Disclose thy inclination,' P. W., which is probably right, though this sense seems not very common, and the simpler one 'lead forward,' would, I think, do here.

yathâçraddham, 'faithfully' ii 12 note. çraddhâ = çrad-dhâ = cre(d)-do. The two words are separate in Vedic. See Curt. no. 309.

karavâṇi, *first* person imperative, a form and use unknown in Greek and Latin: 'Let me do for thee what?' Or if the form is to be regarded (as by Delbrück, 'der Gebrauch des Çonj. und Opt. im Sk. und Gr.,' p. 186, &c.) as equivalent to a conjunctive, we must then compare instances like τί πάθω (§ 465). At xii 69 we have 'brûhi, kim karavâmahai?' Delb. (p. 187) cites from the Çat. Brâhmaṇa 1, 4, 1, 17, sa ho'vâca Videgho Mâthavaḥ 'kvâ 'ham bhavâni' 'ti.

2. **yac c' ânyan**, i.e. yat ca anyad. **vasu** = 'property,' 'wealth'; hence the name for the earth, vasu-dhâ, 'wealth holder,' v 47. Benfey and others connect ἐύς, εὖ, with this word: but it smees better to make it ἐ(σ)υ from √as 'to be,' like sat-ya, ἐτεός, &c. For

yat...kimcana, comp. ix 1 and note there, also xiii 21 ye...kecid, ib. 69 yadi kaçcid, xxiii 3 yadà kimcit, xxvi 9 yena kenâpy upâyena.

viçrabdham, 'without hesitation.' The word is referred to a √çrambh, 'to be careless'—which occurs in hardly any other form.

3. **haṃsánâm, &c.** = anserum vox quae, ea me inflammat. The position of the relative differs; otherwise the construction resembles the Greek and Latin usage, and is regular in Sanskrit: e.g. iv 6, v 12, xiii 38, xiv 16, &c. Another common arrangement is to put the antecedent clause first, but with no demonstrative pronoun, and then the relative clause: e.g. çreyo dâsyâmi, yat param, 'I will give thee happiness which is excessive.' Not unfrequently we find 'yat' with a noun coming first, followed by 'tat,' with a synonymous noun, or alone, as at xii 31: sometimes 'tat,' with the noun, stands first, followed by 'yat,' with a synonymous noun.

kṛite, 'because of,' see ix 19; and comp. ṛite iv 26, for the construction.

sannipâtitâḥ, p. p. of sam + ni + causal of √pat (i 23), 'caused to meet together.'

4. 'If thou shalt repulse me thus reverencing thee, I will undergo for thy sake poison, fire, drowning, hanging.' For the future in the hypothetical clause, see i 32 note. â + √khyâ = 'tell,' prati + âkhyâ = 'to tell back,' 'refuse,' 'repulse,' xiii 42. **mâna-da**, 'honour-giver,' from mâna (√man, mens, μένος, &c.), 'pride,' and then 'honour.' **viṣam** = Ϝι(σ)ον = ἰόν exactly, with the usual phonetic changes in each language—change of *s* to *sh* in Sanskrit, loss of *v* and *s* in Greek. In 'virus' the suffix is different (*as* not *a*) but that word also illustrates the peculiar Latin change of *s* into *r*. **jala**, see Curt. no. 123 and 627. H. Weber's view (given at no. 123), which refers jala to GAL 'to be bright,' whence γαλήνη, γελάω, gelu, &c., and probably γαλα(κτ), lac(t), seems to me on the whole better than Curtius' own, which derives jala from GAL, 'to throw,' whence by labialism βάλλω, &c. Comp. note on √jval xi 35. **rajju** = 'rope,' 'noose'; derivation uncertain. The point of the line seems to be that if Nala wishes to reject her, she will prove by any ordeal that they are plighted to each other, through the agency of the goose in Canto 1. For the ordeal, see Manu viii 114, where it is provided that a judge may make a man hold fire in his hands or dive under water, and "he whom the blazing fire burns not, whom the waters force not up, and who meets with no speedy misfortune, he must be

held pure upon his oath." There are in all ten forms of trial by ordeal: see 'Indian Wisdom,' p. 276 note. But it must be allowed that 'the rope' is not one of these forms: and it may be simpler to understand the line as a threat that she will kill herself some way or other. **tava kâraṇât** = tui caussa, i 4 note. **âsthâsye,** see xviii 24 note.

6. 'Those world-creators, mighty lords, with the dust of whose feet I am not to be weighed in the balance, let thy mind dwell on them.' **loka-kṛi-t-âṃ,** vii 5 note. **tulya** = 'equal,' v 10, &c., atula = 'unequalled,' xii 61; each is from tulâ, 'a balance,' from √tul. The original form is TAL, seen in τάλαντον; and (in the earlier sense of 'lifting,' 'bearing') in tollo, τλάω, &c. The *u* however appears in 'tuli,' and may be older than the separation of the languages, as we have in Gothic 'thulan,' old English 'thole,' in the same sense.

7. 'Mortal man doing what is displeasing to the gods, goeth unto death.' **vipriya** = vi + priya, 'dear,' prob. not = φιλο-, which is rather for σφι-λο- from σφέ. The root is PRI (Sk. pri), whence πρᾷ-ος, &c., friend. **âcaran,** pres. p. of â + √car. **ṛicchati,** pres. base of √ṛi, orig. AR, whence ἔρχομαι = ἔρ-σκο-μαι. For construction, see ii 7 and 18 notes. For p. p. ṛita see xxi 13 note.

trâhi, 'save me,' from √trâ (2nd cl. act.): the other form √trai is 4th cl. mid. It is a secondary from √TAR, to make to cross over, see ii 30 note.

8. **vâsâṃsi,** plur. of vâsas (neuter) from √vas, 'to clothe,' ix 6 note. 'Robes unstained by dust' (rajas), a secondary meaning of the word, which is primarily the atmosphere, or cloud circle, beyond which is the clear ether, like ἀήρ opposed to αἰθήρ. But it is best known as the name of one of the three Guṇas of the Sānkhya philosophy, the three 'cords' or fetters of the soul in mundane existence, i.e. (1) sattva, 'goodness,' which is "alleviating, enlightening, attended with pleasure and happiness, and virtue predominates in it," Colebrooke, 'On the philosophy of the Hindūs'; (2) rajas "foulness or passion. It is active, urgent, and variable, attended with evil and misery. In living beings it is the cause of vice"; (3) tamas, 'darkness.' "It is heavy and obstructive, attended with sorrow, dulness, and illusion... the cause of stolidity," ib. For a short account, see M. Williams' 'Hinduism,' p. 194.

srajas, 'garlands.' Sraj is the older form of the √sṛij (v 27 note) used as a feminine noun without a suffix.

tathâ, iii 4 note.

mukhyâni, 'chief,' 'foremost,' derived from mukha the mouth, v 6, &c.: comp. mukhyaças viii 21, also xii 81 note.

bhun-kṣva, 2 sing. imperat. midd. of √bhuj, 'enjoy' (7th cl.), ii 4 note. Bhuñj (i.e. bhu-na-j) is changed into bhun-k before *s*.

9\. **kṛtsnâṃ**, ii 16. **saṃkṣipya**, iii 13 note.

grasate, 'devours,' from √gras, see xi 21 note: whence prob. Lat. gra(s)men and γράω, Curt. no. 643; p. p. grasta xi 27, xvi 14.

Hutâçaṃ, epithet of Agni, 'sacrifice-devourer,' = Hutâçana v 36, from huta + √aç, 'to eat,' 9th cl., whence prâçya xxiii 22: another √aç or the same conjugated in cl. 5 = 'obtain,' see note on aṃça, xxvi 24. Compare havya-vâhana, xxiii 12. **huta** is p. p. of √hu, 'to sacrifice,' orig. GHU, whence χυ in χέω, &c., futis, futilis, &c., Curt. no. 203: √hû or √hve, 'to call' (â-juhâva, v 1) is to be kept distinct.

10\. **daṇḍa**, 'a rod' (here of course Yama's), from √dam = δαμάω, zähme, tame, Curt. no. 260: it was apparently at first dam + tra then dantra, then dandra, then daṇḍa. These 'cerebral' or 'lingual' sounds commonly represent a lost *r*. Daṇḍin (iv 25) = 'a rod bearer,' 'warden,' comp. σκηπτοῦχος. Kodaṇḍa is 'a bow,' Hitop. 726. There is a denominative verb daṇḍaya, whence the fut. part. daṇḍya xiii 69. **bhûta-grâmâḥ**, 'the masses of living beings.' Grâma is 'a village': cf. grâmaṃ nagara-sammitaṃ, 'a village like a town,' xvi 4 and xvii 49: but at the end of a compound it is 'a collection,' 'mass.'

anurudhyanti, 'observe duty.' √rudh is 'to check in motion' (P. W.), and commonly means 'to hinder' (so with sam, xiii 10, and upa, Çak. i 16), but with anu = 'approve,' 'love,' apparently from the idea of sticking on to a thing without moving. Viruddha (Hitop. 1216) = 'troublesome,' from the primary sense of 'opposed,' 'opposite,' 'perverse.'

11\. **Daitya-dânava-mardanaṃ**, Indra 'the crusher of the Daityas and Dānavas,' the demons who make war on the gods, offspring of Diti and Danu, respectively, by the Rishi Kaçyapa: see Dowson s. v. Kaçyapa. Mardana is from MARD, the original form of √mṛd, a secondary of MAR; see M. Müller, 'Lectures &c.,' vol. II, c. 7. **Mahendraṃ**, i 2 note.

12\. **aviçan-kena**, 'without doubt.' Vi increases the force of √çan-k, viii 3 note. It = Latin cunc-tor, and (with loss of orig. *k*) ὄκνος, Curt. G. E. p. 698 (II 375 Eng. tr.), apparently our 'hang.' 'Let it be done with undoubting heart, if thou thinkest of Varuṇa out of the gods.' **lokapâlânâṃ**, partitive genitive. Others take avıçan-kena adverbially, and join manasâ with manyase, not so well.

13. 'With eyes all overflowed thereupon by moisture sorrow-born.' √plu, same as orig. PLU, whence pluo, πλέϜω, flow. The p. p. sampluta occurs xi 22: âpluta at xviii 11.

netra is 'an eye' from √ni, 'to lead,' whence â + nayya, viii 5: note. **çoka** is from √çuc, 'to grieve for,' 'lament.' Bopp compares κωκύω, which has rather the look of a reduplicated verb, perhaps onomatopoetic.

14. **namaskṛtya**, iv 1 note. **vṛṇe**, iii 6 note.

15. 'Having come by reason of messengership (i.e. because I am a messenger), how can I here do my own business?' **svârtham utsahe**, iii 8 note. **dautya**, from dûta, ii 31: by vṛddhı of *u*, and suffix *ya*.

16. **pratıçrutya**, iii 9 note. It governs the genitive: see v 38 note. **vıçeṣatas**, i 30 note.

ârabhya, 'having undertaken work on another's account.' √rabh = orig. ARBH (ἀλφεῖν, labor, arbeit), Curt. no. 398, originally meant 'to lay hold of,' in Sanskrit 'to take'; with â, as here, 'to undertake'; p. p. ârabdha, v 20, with passive sense; active at xiv 12. With sam (xiii 14) it = 'to confuse': and saṃrambha = 'anger,' xiii 31. Comp. su-saṃrabdhaḥ, xxvi 3.

17. 'This is duty: if after that there shall come on the business of me too, my own business will I perform: thus, good lady, let the arrangement be.' vı + √dhâ = 'arrange,' 'direct,' see v 19 note; hence vıdhı, 'rule,' 'ceremony' (xvii 26), 'pre-arranged event' or 'chance' (xii 98, &c.): comp. vıdha, 'kind,' i 29 note. Nıdhı = 'a treasury,' xxiv 37: san-nıdhı = 'nearness,' 'presence,' iv 2. For the change of vowel from dhâ to the passive dhiya, see M. W. Gr. § 465. It is found in the six commonest roots in â, viz. dâ, dhâ, sthâ, mâ, pâ, and hâ.

18. **âkulâm**, 'confused,' from â + √kṛi, Benfey, 'to scatter' or 'cover,' p. p. â-kirṇa, 'filled with,' xii 2: it is distinct from kṛı: comp. vanaṃ...samâkulaṃ, 'a wood covered (with trees),' xii 4, and saṃkula, xii 112. **çucı-smıtâ**, 'with sweet smile': çucı is 'white,' 'clear,' from √çuc, 'to shine,' a Vedic root distinct from √çuc, the root of çoka, iv 13. **pratyâharanti**, i 20 note.

çanakaır, 'by degrees,' 'gradually,' 'gently,' instr. plur. of çanaka, which is not used. A parallel form çanaıḥ is used in the same sense, especially reduplicated (e.g. Hit. 175), çanaıḥ çanaıḥ, 'little by little'; derivation uncertain.

19.   'This harmless way is perceived by me.' upáya, 'plan,' xix 4, and apáya, 'harm,' 'fraud,' are two of the numerous compounds of áya from √ı. Ny-áya = 'fitness.' Áya (alone) = income, Hit. 1269, cf. πρόσ-οδος, red-*itus*, in-*come*.

20.   hı, i 29 note. Indra-purogamáḥ, 'headed by Indra,' parallel to Mahendrádyáḥ, iii 5. Puro-gama = puras (πάρος, before) + gama = 'fore-goer.'

21.   sannıdhau, iv 17 note, comp. v 19. doṣo, x 15 note.

23.   'They asked him the whole of that occurrence,' double acc. after √prach, see i 20 note: for the verb see xi 31 note. vṛıttánta = 'history' or 'event,' lit. 'the end of the matter': vṛıtta is p. p. of √vṛıt, vi 4 note.

24.   kaccıd = ecquid, and equally redundant.

naḥ sarván, apparently acc. after vada, 'tell,' though this use is rare: P. W. It can hardly go with abravit, 'spake she of us all' (Milman): for √brú with acc. = 'speak to': e.g. Manu i 60 : see P. W.

25.   bhavadbhır, ii 31 note. ádıṣṭo, p. p. of á + √dıç (DIK, whence dic-io, dico, δείκνυμι) 'appointed to,' 'commissioned': comp. xx 22 ekadeçaṃ samádıṣṭam, 'one appointed portion': xvii 21 yáṇam ádıçu, 'order the carriage.' At Hit. 1287 ádeça = 'a rule,' 'maxim'; upa-deça = 'instruction': the verb with upa = 'point out' ix 32. Deça = a region, v 27, &c.

sumahákakṣam, 'the very great gate'—so M. Williams, who takes it as a K. D. compound. But kakṣa means not 'a gate' but 'a wall,' and that which the wall encloses. So at xxi 17, Rıtu-parṇa is mounted on a chariot 'madhyamakakṣáyáṃ,' 'in the mid court': and at Manu vii 224, the king at the end of the day, after doing all public business, is to go with his women to a kákṣántara ('different chamber') in the inner part of the palace to eat his supper. Doubtless the word here means 'with a great court,' and is a B. V. agreeing with nıveçanam. The word has many other mean-ings, for which see P. W.: one is 'the arm pit,' and in this sense it is identified with 'coxa' by Curt. no. 70, and with κοχώνη. He thinks the primary sense was 'a hiding place.' pravıṣṭaḥ, ii 21 note. dandıbhıḥ, iv 10 note.

sthavıraıḥ, 'old,' originally 'fixed,' 'stable': again at v 14, xii 123 : perhaps from √sthú, see note on sthávara, xiv 7.

26.   dṛıṣṭaván, i 29 note. rıte, 'except,' literally 'it being gone,'

a locative absolute of the p. p. of √ṛi, 'to go,' iv 7 note. It is used as a preposition with an acc. xii 90, xxiv 11, 30, 38: or an abl., Manu ii 172.

tejasá, 'by your power,' a further sense of tejas, which we have had twice before = 'brilliance,' i 10, iii 13. It = 'geistige und moralische auch magische Kraft,' P. W. So in Manu ix 303, the king is to follow after the tejo-vṛittam, the brilliant course of activity of the gods. At xix 13 it is applied to horses 'tejo-bala-samáyuktán. The primary meaning of the word is 'sharpness' from √tij (comp. tikṣṇa xx 30), orig. STIG, whence στίζω, stinguo: hence it passes on to the brightness of fire, then the external brightness and brilliance of any object, then the internal strength and energy. In the mythological reason given to shew that the five Pāṇḍava princes are all but portions of the essence of Indra, and so although five are yet but one, and therefore may lawfully marry Draupadī, Yudhishṭhira, the eldest and most stately of the five, represents Indra's 'tejas,' but Bhīma, the second and most vigorous, represents his 'bala' or strength: see 'Ind. Wisdom,' p. 388 note.

27. **vibudha**, 'omniscient one,' i.e. a god, so v 18.

28. **varṇyamáneṣu**, 'being described,' from √varṇ (10th cl.) a denominative of varṇa, 'colour,' i 28 note. So varṇitavat, p. p. act. 'having related,' Hitop. 533.

ruciránaná, 'bright-faced.' Rucira is from √ruc, 'to be bright,' orig. RUK, whence by change of *r* into *l* comes √luk in luceo, λευκός, light. By a natural transition from 'brightness' to 'pleasure' the verb means next 'to please' (comp. the history of DIV); hence ruci, 'desire,' Hitop. 221. Ánana, 'a face,' is from √AN, to breathe, whence animus, ἄνεμος, &c.; and the second part of the compounds ὑπ-ήνη (under-face), ἀπ-ηνής, with face averted, 'harsh,' πρηνής, &c.

gata-saṃkalpá, ii 29 note.

29. **sahitáḥ**, 'all together,' derived from saha with suffix -ita, not a compound of saha and ita from √i, which must have been saheta.

31. **yatháv ṛittam**, ii 12 note. **udáhṛitam**, i 20 note.

çeṣe, 'in the remainder,' 'for the rest,' 'henceforth,' from çeṣa, √çiṣ, i 30 note.

pramáṇam, 'you are the authority,' i.e. you must decide. It comes from √má, 'to measure,' and means (1) 'measure,' 'standard'; so átmaupamyena puruṣaḥ pramáṇam adhigacchati, Hitop. 163, i.e. 'by self-comparison man obtains a standard': (2) 'authority,' as here, and xviii 13, pramâṇam bhavati: comp. Çak. i 22, pramâṇam antaḥ-karaṇa-pravṛittayaḥ, 'the inclinations of the heart are the authority to be followed': (3) proof, xix 33.

tridaçeçvarâḥ, 'lords of the gods,' literally 'of the three times ten' (tri-daçan). The whole number however of the (inferior) deities is given as thirty-three: i.e. 12 Âdityas, 8 Vasus, 11 Rudras, and 2 Açvins. Nevertheless the word must mean 'a god' here. Benfey gives 'heaven': but this is not recognised in the P. W.

CANTO V.

1. **prâpte,** i 11 note. **çubhe,** 'bright' (iii 25 note), and so 'happy,' 'auspicious.'

puṇye tithau, 'on a propitious day and moment likewise' to be fixed by the rules of astrology. "A superstitious belief in the importance of choosing auspicious days and lucky moments for the performance of rites and ceremonies, whether public or domestic, began to shew itself very early in India, and it grew and strengthened simultaneously with the growth of priestcraft, and the elaboration of a complex ritual." M. Williams 'Ind. Wisdom,' p. 181. So also Weber ('Ind. Lit.,' p. 29). "Astronomical observations—though at first these were only of the rudest description—were necessarily required for the regulation of the solemn sacrifices; in the first place of those offered in the morning and evening, then of these at the new and full moon, and finally of those at the commencement of each of the three seasons...... Thus we find in the later portions of the Vājasaneyi-Saṃhitā express mention made of 'observers of the stars,' and the 'science of astronomy:' and in particular the knowledge of the twenty seven (twenty-eight) lunar mansions was early diffused.[1]" These 'lunar mansions' (nakṣatrâṇi, see note on v 6) are the divisions of the zodiac through which the moon successively passes: the word first means 'a star,' then 'a group of stars,' and so is specially applied to those which lie on or about the moon's path. **tithi,** is a lunar day—the 30th portion of a lunar month. A day is divided into thirty muhūrtas (see xi 7) or hours of forty-eight minutes each. **puṇyau,** comp. 'puṇyâha-vâcane,' 'on the proclamation of a holy day' xvi 7: see also note on xii 37 çiloccayam puṇyam.

tathâ, 'and also,' so iii 4, where see note.

[1] See also Weber, p. 246, &c.

âjuhâva, 3 sing. perf. of â + √hve, M. W. Gr. § 379, M. M. App. no. 103; the perf. really comes from the Vedic form hû (iv 9 note). The derivation is uncertain: the original form should be GHU; Benfey connects βοή, βοάω, which agree in meaning, but point to original GU: we may therefore have here a Sanskrit corruption of *g* into *gh*, i 19 note. From √hve comes the compound sam + â + hvâna, 'a challenge,' vii 8.

svayaṃvare; for the case see iii 6 note.

2. **pîḍitâḥ**, 'opprest,' p. p. of pîḍaya, prob. causal of Vedic pîḍ, to be pressed: â + pîḍita xii 102: âpîḍa (xii 103) is a 'chaplet.' Grassmann (s. v.) makes it = pyaḍ, and compares Greek πιέζω, suggesting that the *ḍ* is due to the influence of the *y*. But it may = √pisd a secondary of √pis, which would account for the cerebral even better. From orig. PIS comes Sk. √piṣ, to 'grind,' 'pound,' and pistor, pinso, pisum, Gr. πίσος pease. See Curtius, no. 365 b. √pîḍ in this sense is very common, both simple and compounded: compare ix 11.

tvaritâḥ, 'hurried,' p. p. of √tvar: the middle participle tvaramâna occurs xi 27 and i 24: tvaryamâna (pass.) xix 12. The Vedic form is √tur, whence tura, the 'swift,' 'eager,' an epithet of Indra and the Maruts (Grassmann s. v.): and comp. tûrṇa xx 23. This form corresponds with tur-ma, and also with the secondary Latin √turb in turba and turbo, Curt. Gr. E. no. 250: he suggests that the Teutonic cognates, dorf (Germ.), thorp (Eng.) may be of this family, with the primary sense of 'a meeting together.'

abhîpsu, from abhi + îpsu (desid. of √âp, to get, i 4 note) + suffix *u*: see iii 5 note.

3. 'The kings entered the scene made brilliant by the archway, resplendent with gold pillars, like great lions enter on the mountain.' **stambha** (= Eng. stump) = a 'pillar.' For the forms of these pillars—curiously unlike those of European buildings, and also widely differing from those of the early Aryans as seen at Persepolis—see the illustrations throughout Fergusson's 'History of Indian and Eastern architecture.' **toraṇa** = 'arch' or 'gateway' (acc. to Bopp from √tur, see last line; but this is doubtful). These elaborate gateways are a special feature in Indian architecture: they were sometimes covered with sculptures. See the engraving (from a photograph) of that of the tope at Sanchi (Fergusson ib., p. 96). Their style clearly indicates that they were originally worked in wood, instead of which stone was afterwards used; but the character of the

details remained unchanged: this appears very plainly in the photograph above mentioned. Just so the origin of many of the details of our Norman cathedrals may be seen in the carving of the wood churches of Norway. The word is also applied to temporary arches erected at festivals. **virâjitam**, made to shine, p. p. of râjaya, causal of √râj, to shine: pres. part. vi + râjat, occurs xii 37. **acala**, 'the immoveable' (√cal, to move), hence 'a mountain,' see note on cacâla, v 9.

4. **âsinâḥ**, p. part. mid. of âs, to 'sit' (M. W. Gr. § 526 a), i 11 note.

pṛithivikshitaḥ, ii 20 note.

surabhi, 'sweet,' from su + √rabh + i, apparently = very much be seized. See note on √rabh. iv 16.

pramṛiṣṭa-maṇi-kuṇḍalâḥ,='polished-gem-earringed,' a B. V., of which the second part is a K. D.

pramṛiṣṭa, from √mṛij='to rub' or 'wipe,' orig. √MARG (ἀμέλγω, mulgeo, 'milk'). The p. p. mṛiṣṭa occurs xii 36, mṛiṣṭa-salilâm, 'with clear water:' and amârjita, 'uncleansed,' p. p. of the causal, at xiii 46: also su-mṛiṣṭa (applied to flowers) xxv 6, 'delicate,' 'fine.'

maṇi, 'pearl,' or any jewel; comp. Gr. μαννος, Lat. monile.

kuṇḍala, 'a ring,' as xiv 3, nâgarâjânaṃ...kuṇḍalikṛitam (coiled into a ring), here an earring.

5. **sma**, i 12 note.

pinâ, 'strong,' p. p. of √pyai, to 'swell;' which in its original form was probably √PI, whence this participle, and pivara, 'fat,' Gr. πίειρα, Curt. Gr. Et. no. 363: â + pyâyaya (the causal) = 'refresh;' whence âpyâyitâ (perf. part.) xxiv 52.

parigha-upama, 'like a club' of iron: **parigha** (not = πέλεκυς, of which the Sk equivalent is paraçu) is probably from √gha, an older form of √ghan, whence √han, to strike, kill; see i 20 note. It is also used for the bolt of a door.

âkâra-varṇa-suçlakṣṇâḥ, 'very delicate in form and colour,' a T. P. compound (locatively, or instrumentally dependent): the first member is of course a Dvandva. **âkâra** = 'make,' 'form,' see note on ii 5, and compare âkṛiti v 10, xii 20; also Çak. i 20.

panca-çirṣa, 'five-headed.' pancan, and the other numerals ending in *n*, drop the *n* in composition: çirṣha (like çiras) = the head, Gr. κάρα (but in form κέρας); cf. Lat. cere-brum, &c. Excess of heads (and still more of arms) is a well-known eccentricity of Hindū mythology. Thus Brahmā, the Creator, has four faces; Kārttikeya, the god of war, has six heads; and so on.

uragâh, 'serpents,' see i 29 note. Ura (for uras) must be distinguished from ura = 'wool' in different compounds. Curt. G. E. no. 496.

6. 'With fair locks, delicate, with beautiful nose, eyes, and brows, shine the faces of the kings like the stars in the sky.'

keça = 'hair;' the longer form kesara = Lat. caesaries.

câru, iii 14 note. **bhrû** = (eye) 'brow,' and ὀφρύς: the longer from bhruva (bhrû + *a*) is used as more convenient to end the compound. **nakṣatra**, 'a star,' is probably connected (though in an obscure way) with 'nakta,' which (with the regular modifications is found in nearly every Ind. Eur. language = 'night.' See Curt. no. 94. The primary meaning of nakta is doubtless 'the baneful time' (cf. Sk. √naç, and Latin neco, noceo): witness also the peculiarly Greek euphemism in the name εὐφρονή. For the further uses of the word nakṣatra, see note on v 1, also 'Ind. Wisdom,' p. 183, and 'Hinduism,' p. 180. Against the derivation from √nak must be put the fact that in the earliest usage the word is used of the sun as well as of the stars; also the difficulty in the form of the word. On the other hand √nakṣ, which is regular in Vedic = 'approach to,' 'attain,' though satisfactory in form gives no satisfactory sense. Perhaps there has been a change of form to suit a supposed derivation from nakṣ.

7. **nâgair bhogavatim iva.** The Nāgas—a race of beings half serpent, half man—"inhabit the Pātālas or regions under the earth, which, with the seven superincumbent worlds, are supposed to rest on the thousand heads of the serpent Çesha, who typifies infinity." M. Williams 'Indian Wisdom,' p. 430. "The serpent-race, who inhabit these lower regions which are not to be confounded with the narakas or hells [Nala vi 13 note], are sometimes regarded as belonging to only one of the seven, viz. Pātāla, or to a portion of it called Nāga-loka, of which the capital is Bhogavatī," ib. note. The name bhoga, a 'serpent,' whence the adjective bhoga-vat, is from √bhuj, to bend, ii 4 note. Nāgas and serpents are distinguished in Bhag. Gîta, x 28.

sampûrṇâm, p. p. of √pṛ with *sam*; see ii 11 note.

puruṣavyâghrair, 'man-tiger,' but = 'a tiger-like man.' See i 15 note.

giriguhâm, 'a mountain cave:' guhâ from √guh, 'to cover,' p. p. gûḍha, xxii 15: the *g* has been weakened from original *k*, and *h* from *dh*; see note on i 13. The primary form is KUDH, accurately kept in Greek κεύθω, κευθμών &c., and closely in our 'hide,' probably in Lat. custo(d)s, whence the *dh* has passed through *d* into *s* before *t*, compare claus-trum, &c. See Curt. no. 321. The corruption which the original form of this word has undergone in Sk. is a good indication that that language does not always preserve the original sounds the most truly: see note on i 3.

8. **mushṇanti**, pres. part. of √mush (9 cl.), to carry off. The original MUS is traced by Curtius (Gr. Et. no. 480) into musca and μυ-ῖα, and also to Lat. mus, Sk. mûṣa, mûṣıka, 'the thief' (ib. no. 483); "so that the fly would be among insects what the mouse was amongst mammals" so far as its name is concerned. The root is found in the compound dhṛtı-muṣ = 'firmness-stealing,' applied to the 'dṛṣṭıvânâḥ' or 'arrow-glances' of women, Hitop. 828.

cakṣûṃṣı, acc. plur. of cakṣus, from √cakṣ, viii 5, with which Benfey ingeniously compares παπταίνω: but he is wrong in also connecting ὀπιπεύω, &c., which must belong to √οπ, orig. AK.

9. 'On her limbs fell the eyes of those great-souled kings:' note the locative. So also x 15, 'tasya buddhır Damayantyâṃ nyavartata.' **gâtra** = 'means of going,' i.e. limb; again at x 5. It may come from GA, the older form of GAM, seen in the labialised *βέ-βα-α*.

saktâ bhûn = saktâ abhût. Sakta, 'stuck to,' 'attached; comp. saṃsakta xiii 21, p. p. of √sañj: the original form SAG is doubtless seen in Latin sig-num, sig-illum—which last has preserved the original sense of 'sticking to,' Curt. Gr. Et. I 133, Eng. trans. The Greek words σάττω, σάκος, &c. are dubious from the variation of the guttural. Comp. Hitop. 1248 vânarâḥ phala-saktâ babhûvuḥ, 'the monkeys became engaged upon the fruit.'

cacâla, perf. of √cal, to move, but rather with the sense of 'shaking' or 'trembling,' thus slightly differentiated in use from √car, though the difference at first was probably phonetic only: it is very old; comp. the same in *βου-κόλ-ος* but *αἰγι-κόρ-εις*: the original KAL is still found in Sanskrit = 'drive,' but not KAR, which would have been liable to be confounded with √kṛ, 'to do.' A frequent derivative of √cal is acala, the 'unshaken' = 'a mountain,' e.g. v 3, xii 6, 42, 51: cala, 'shaken,' 'variable,' occurs xix 6. Vı + cal occurs xiv 7. For vı + √car see note on v 15.

paçyatâm, gen. plur. of present participle of √paç = orig. SPAK—used for the present, imperfect, imperative, and optative of the verb 'to see,' the other tenses being supplied by √dṛç; see note on dṛç; i 13. It is the root whence come "Sk. spaça-s, Gr. σκόπος, 'spy'

Lat. specula, 'place of espial;' O. H. G. spĕh-ô-m, 'I espy'" (Curt. Gr. Et. I. p. 123 Eng. trans.); and the primary sense is that of 'fixed,' and not momentary, vision.

10. **saṃkirtyamâneṣu**, 'being proclaimed.' Kirtaya is given as from √krit (10 class). But it is probably as Benfey suggests, a denominative verb from kirti, 'glory.'

tulyâkṛitin, 'of like form:' tulya, iv 6 note.

11. **sandehât**, 'from her doubt:' sam + √dih, 'to smear;' p. p. digdha xxiv 46, and saṃdigdha xii 100, 'indistinct.' Original form of root was DHIGH: the Sk. Gr. and Lat. languages do away each with one aspirate—√θιγ in θιγγάνω, √fig in *fingo*: Goth. √dig is regular; Curt. Gr. Et. no 145: the primary meaning being to touch or work with the hand. The ablative denotes the 'circumstance' of the action; as iv 10, daṇḍabhayât: see i 4 and 16 notes.

abhyajânât, see iii 1 note.

12. **yaṃ yam** = quemquem, just as in Latin. But Latin has no *sam-sam* (eum-eum) to answer to taṃ tam. Compare yathâ yathâ... tathâ tathâ, viii 14.

mene, perf. of √man: comp. nipetuḥ, i 23 note.

tarkayâmâsa, 'thought out, 'considered,' used in next line with acc. of thing, and with acc. of person, xi 36. At xvi 9 we have tarkayâmâsa 'Bhaimi' 'ti, kâraṇair upapâdayan, "he concluded 'it is Bhima's daughter,' coming to this result by reasons:" so also xxi 35. It is from √tark (10) which apparently = Lat. torqueo, τρέπω, ἀ-τρεκ-ής, ἄτρακ-τος—so that the verb meant first to 'turn over' in the mind. In the Nyāya system of philosophy 'tarka' denotes logic, or rather logical reasoning.

kathaṃ jâniyâm, for the mood see note on xix 4.

13. **bhṛiça-duḥkhitâ**, 'much afflicted:' bhṛiça is possibly as Aufrecht suggests, from BHRAK, whence farcio and φράσσω, Curt. no. 413. Comp. bhṛiça-dâruṇaṃ vanam xii 88.

deva-lin.gâni; the marks whereby the different gods are known. Cf. xxii 16, na svâni lin.gâni Nalaḥ çaṃsati. Thus Yama "is represented as of a green colour, and clothed with red. He rides upon a buffalo, and is armed with a ponderous mace, and a noose to secure his victims," Dowson, cl. dict. s. v., p. 374. "Varuṇa in the Purāṇas is sovereign of the waters, and one of his accompaniments is a noose, which the Vedic deity also carried for binding offenders... He also possesses an umbrella impermeable to water formed of the hood of a cobra, and called Âbhoga," ib. p. 338. "Indra is represented as a fair man riding upon a white horse or an elephant, and bearing the vajra or thunderbolt in his hand," ib. p. 126. Agni's representations are sufficiently shewn by his different epithets, "abja-hasta, 'lotus in hand;' dhūma-ketu, 'whose sign is smoke;'... rohitāçva, 'having red horses;' Chāga-ratha, 'ram-rider;'...sapta jihva, 'seven-tongued;' tomara-dhara, 'javelin-bearer,'" ib. p. 8. See also 'Ind. Wisdom,' p. 429.

14. 'The marks of the gods which were heard by me from the aged (iv 25), these marks I see belonging to not even (api) one of these as they stand on the earth here.'

15. **viniççitya**: vi + nis + √ci, 'having thought over.' √ci (see note on ii 2) is one of doubtful development; see Benf. ii 232, Curt. no. 649. It probably meant 'to arrange orderly.' At xvii 8 sam + ā + √ci = 'to heap up,' 'cover.' At xix 9 it occurs with nis alone—meaning as here. At xx 11 pra + √ci seems to mean 'to collect,' or perhaps in an extended sense 'to gather,' as fruits, &c.

vicārya, indec. part. of cāraya, causal of √car, to go = to think over. Vicāranā = 'investigation,' xiii 27. Vicārita = 'hesitation,' Sāv. iii 13. Vicāra = 'discrimination,' Hitop. 1068. 'Thought the time arrived with respect to taking refuge with the gods.' **prati**, see ii 7 note: **prāptakālam**, i 11 note.

çaraṇa from √çri, 'to go;' in the same sense āçraya, Hitop. 678. bhavad-āçrayaḥ...mayā prāptaḥ = your protection has been obtained by me. From the same verb comes pratiçraya, dwelling, xxiv 8. The verb itself occurs vi 8 āçrayeta Nalaṃ, in the middle voice: and the p. p. in āçrita xii 12, ucchrita (i.e. ud + çrita) = high, xii 37. The original root would be KRI, which is probably the origin of √κλι in κλίνω, incline, or 'lean,' though Curtius doubts it, no. 60.

16. **namaskāram**, i 11 note: **prayujya**, 'having performed.' √yuj in this compound (as √dā, dhā, &c.) loses its primary sense. So also prayojanam, xxiv 21 = business (in primary sense), purpose, or use.

prāñjalir. So kritāñjali, iii 1. Note the formation of what is (in effect) a verb—prāñjalir bhū—by the help of the substantive verb. This is necessary when there is no independent verb, as there is none here: but sometimes hardly required—e.g. in saktā abhūt, sup. l. 9.

vepamānā, 'shaking,' iv 15, from √vep, prob. causal of √vi, Benf. s. v. He seems to have read udvepayate at ix 26 (al. *udvejate*) as he refers to that line. The noun vepathu occurs Bhag. G. i 29.

17. **patitve vṛitaḥ**, 'chosen for lordship,' i.e. chosen to be my husband: see iii 6 note.

pradiçantu: iv 25 note.

tena satyena, 'by virtue of that truth,' a simple development of the primary instrumental sense. The Latin (which has lost the distinctive case-form) needs a preposition (per) to adjure with.

18. **abhicarámi**, 'transgress:' the root metaphor is the same in both. Vyabhicárin occurs Hit. 45.

vibudhás, iv 27 note.

19. **vihito** = vi + hita, √ p. p. of √dhá, i 6 note: it occurs at xi 7, and rather more generally, at xiii 26. √dhá with vi = 'arrange,' 'appoint,' 'fix' (as here), at iv 17, xii 121, xxiv 4, with *sam.* It often only = 'make,' e.g. Hit. 138, pravṛittiḥ na vidheyaḥ = the attempt is not to be made.

20. **árabdham**, iv 16 note. **árádhane**, for the winning of Nala. Comp. what Damayanti says at iv 3: it is the locative of purpose as patitve above. It might possibly mean 'for the honouring of Nala:' árádhayitṛi is a worshipper or lover, Çak. 3. 74 (p. 125 ed. M. W.) and árádhya = venerate, pay respect to, Megh. 46. Dean Milman's translation is wrong here. √rádh is of uncertain connection. With apa it means 'injure,' p. p. aparáddham xxiv 12.

vrata, ii 14 note.

21. **yathá...abhijániyám**, i 21 note.

22. **niçamya**, 'having perceived,' viii 9, xxiii 6: so also with *vi*, Indr. v. 62: and çánti is 'satisfaction' obtained by duelling at xxvi 6. But the simple verb = 'to be calm,' and 'to cease:' çánta = 'calm,' of water, xii 112: and çama = tranquillity of mind, vi 10, &c.; cf. çántvayan, viii 12 note. Root apparently = KAM, whence *κάμνω*; and Benfey thinks 'weariness' is the root meaning. But the Homeric use of *κάμνω*, to work out, acquire (Δ 187 Σ 34), is against this, as Curtius points out Gr. Et. vol. 1, p. 130 (Eng. trans.). 'To obtain by effort,' would apparently give all the derived senses.

paridevitam, 'lamentation,' √div (1 and 10) = to lament (xiii 30 note) distinct from √div (4) to play. At xxiv 25 it seems = querella. Compare the striking line of the Bhag. Gīta (ii 28)

> avyaktádini bhútáni, vyaktamadhyáni, Bhárata,
> avyaktanidhanány eva; tatra ká paridevaná?

'where is room for lamentation'?

nıçcayaṃ, 'decision.' It means 'certainty,' xix 8. It is from nıs + √cı, sup. l. 15.

tathyam, 'truth,' tathà + suffix *ya*.

anuràgam, 'devotion,' from √rañj (1 and 4), 'to colour,' and 'to attach oneself to.' Rakta xxiv 16, and àrakta occur in the primary sense, Hit. 712, àraktàkṣaḥ...çùkaraḥ, 'a red-eyed boar.' Anurakta, 'devoted,' viii 4, x 11, xxii 18. The verb = ῥέζω, 'to dye,' with the others of the same family, also the Homeric ῥήγεα σιγαλόεντα: Curt. no. 154. The secondary sense seems to be metaphorical —mental colour. At Hit. 712 the word is used in the general sense of 'passion,' vitaràga = with passions gone. For the construction of Naısadhe comp. viii 14 dyùte ràga, 'devotion to playing:' xiii 57 prasan·go devane; xxiv 41 Damayantyàṃ vıçan·kà; xxvi 24 mama pritıs tvayı. Similarly we have a locative with a substantive alone in v 35 pratyakṣadarçanaṃ yajñe, and v 37 dharme paramà sthıtı: but such constructions are comparatively rare, being more naturally expressed by composition. For the same use with adjectives, see viii 1 note.

23. **vıçuddhım**, 'purity' from √çudh, viii 17 note: p. p. çuddha, xix 14, used of horses, çuddhamatı = pure-minded, Hit. 417: atıçuddha = immaculate, ib. 853.

bhaktıṃ, 'faith,' or 'personal attachment' from √bhaj, (1) to portion out, and (middle sense) to have apportioned to one, possess, enjoy = Gr. φαγεῖν, to get one's share, eat. See inf. l. 30, bhajası, 'takest for thy lot:' bhàga, portion, lot, viii 6; and x 14 mahàbhàga. The p. p. bhakta, 'devoted to,' occurs x 14, xiii 57. Bhaktı was an important conception in later Hindu theology; see M. Williams, 'Indian Wisdom,' p. 137, &c. At Hit. 68 we have 'keçavabhakti' = faith in Keçava, i.e. Kṛishṇa, the 8th avatàra of Vishnu. On the other hand 'Bhākta' is the name of a sect of the Çaivists. See however M. Williams 'Hinduism,' p. 136.

yath'oktam, ii 12 note.

sàmarthyaṃ, iii 7 note. **lın·ga-dhàraṇa** seems to go with sàmarthyam alone, as in l. 22.

24. **asvedàn**, 'without sweat,' √svıd, whence sudor and ἱδρώς: the English word is curiously unchanged from the original. "All the omniscient gods she saw without stain of sweat, with eyes unmoved, with fresh crowns, without speck of dust, standing, yet not touching earth." Note how the gods are described as unaffected by

the heat of India. The 'unwinking eyes' are the one mark of those who have by austerities risen from humanity to divinity, as the gods themselves did, according to some forms of Hindu thought.

hṛiṣita, p. p. of √hṛiṣ = horrere (where the second *r* is due to assimilation), to be stiff or erect: the shorter form hṛiṣṭa occurs below l. 30, also i 24, where see note.

rajohinán, 'destitute of dust:' hina (xii 52, &c.) is the p. p. (irregular) of √há, to leave, ix 14 note, and is often used at the end of a compound, e.g. dhana-hina = moneyless. It means 'worthless' at xix 14. Vihina = hina, at x 11, xvii 20. The whole compound **hṛiṣitasrag-rajohina**, might be differently analysed as a locatively dependent T.P., 'dustless *on* their fresh crowns.' But it is best taken as a Dvandva made up of hṛiṣitasraj + rajohina, where hṛiṣita-sraj is a B. V. Certainly 'mlána-sraj' in the next line is in favour of taking it so. Comp. perhaps Arist. *Clouds*, 332 σφραγιδονυχ-αργοκομήτης.

25. **cháyá-dvitiyo**, 'doubled by his shadow; instrumental T. P: *Ch* in Sk. often represents original *sk*: hence Curtius deduces, by the help of Hesychius, σκοιά, an original skayā, whence Gr. σκιά, and our 'sky' and 'shade' (Gr. Et. no. 112); σκηνή, σκότος are of course from the same root, SKA, with a secondary SKAD = Sk. √chad, 'to cover:' whence chada, 'a wing,' ix 12, and p. p. saṃchanna xii 3, xvii 5: prachanna xix 32.

mlána-srag, 'with garland withered.' mlána is p. p. of √mlai, originally mlá, a secondary of √mal, orig. MAR, whence μαλακός and mollis.

nimeṣeṇa, 'by winking the eyes,' from √miṣ (6). The connection of meaning with μύω, nicto, and mico is rendered uncertain by the phonetic difficulties. Bopp ingeniously conjectured that nicto = ni-micto, which however is also difficult. See Curt. Gr. Et. no. 478.

súcitaḥ, 'pointed out,' xvii 9, from √súc (10), probably as Benfey suggests a denominative of súci, 'a needle.' Abhisúcita occurs in the same sense xxiii 18.

26. **dharmeṇa**: for the instrumental similarly used alone to express the manner of an action; so xiii 8 vegena, 'with haste;' xi 26 javena, ib.; xii 76 vistareṇa, 'at full length;' krameṇa, xvi 31; tattvena, 'truly,' xvi 38; perhaps iv 15, dautyena ágatya, 'having come on a message,' and sárathyena upayayau viii 25. The Latin ablatives of the manner are probably independent developments.

vilajjamáná, see iii 18 note.

vastrânte, 'by the end (or 'hem') of his garment.' The locative in this use is intelligible ('she laid hold *on* the hem of the garment'), but not parallel to either the Greek (genitive) or the Latin (ablative).

âyata, 'long,' from â + √yam. From YAM to 'hold in,' 'restrain,' come ζημία. Curt. Gr. Et. II 610 (p. 261, Eng. tr.). For pra + √yam, see xxv 26 note. The *á* seems to have the usual negative force here (long = unrestrained) as it has in â + √gam, i 32, &c.

skandhadeçe, 'on the shoulder-parts.' The *n* of skandha has passed into *l* in Teutonic. For deça iv 25 note.

asṛjat, 'she placed.' √sṛj is very common in Sk., but seems to have vanished in Latin and Greek. It = to let loose, and to make. With ut, it = to leave, ix 27, x 28; or to let go, i 22, xxiii 27 (vâṣpam utsṛṣṭavân): with ava, to remit, xxv 23: with vi (causal) = 'make loose,' 'lose,' xiii 59: at xxi 27 it means to 'dismiss.' Sarga (which is a derivative) is a canto or chapter of a poem: ut-sarga = leaving, departure x 12.

28. 'Then a sound, "alas, alas," was all at once uttered by the kings.' √muc (6) to let loose (cf. Latin 'emittere uocem'), xi 24 çâpân muktaḥ, 'loosed from the curse,' and xi 29 mokṣayitvâ: see also xxiv 32 muñcatu mama prâṇân. We find pra + muc, xiii 11. The original MUK is seen in Lat. mucus, and weakened in mungo, also in Greek μυκ-τήρ and μύσσω. The meaning is curiously restricted in the European languages. See Curtius, Gr. Et. no. 92; where he ingeniously suggests that Μυκ-άλη may have meant a 'little snout,' like the Norse names in *-naes*, our *ness* and *naze*. In Sanskrit mokṣa is the term which expresses the final letting loose of soul from its successive bodies and consequent beatitude.

sahasâ, iii 8 note.

çabda, 'a sound,' or 'word;' perhaps from √çap + da: niḥçabda, 'voiceless,' xiii 6. √çap is to 'speak;' but specially in the sense of cursing: so vi 11, xx 34; and çâpa is a curse, xi 24; also abhiçâpa xi 16.

29. **sâdhu**, 'good,' from √sâdh, to 'accomplish:' used adverbially at ix 3, xxii 6; somewhat like εὖγε.

iritaḥ, p. p. of √ir, 'to raise oneself' 'excite:' see Curt. Gr. Et. no. 500 and 661. It is probably contracted from iy-ar the reduplicated form of √ar, and corresponds exactly with ἰ-άλ-λω, to send, or shoot, the ι being the regular reduplicated syllable as in ἵημι, ἰαύω, λάπτω, and the original *r* being changed into *l*. The root is that which regularly appears as 'or' in ὄρ-νυ-μι, orior, &c.

praçaṃsadbhır, i 16 note.

30. **açvásayat**, imperf. of açvásaya, causal of √çvas, 'to breathe:' lit. 'made to breathe again,' 'consoled;' so xi 10, &c.: √çvás presupposes original √KVAS, for which see ii 2 note.

varárohám, see note on viii 19.

31. **bhajası**, see 23 note.

pumáṃsaṃ, M. W. Gr. § 169. M. M. § 212.

devasannıdhau, 'in the presence of the gods.' sannıdhı (xxi 3) is 'proximity,' from sam + nı + √dhá, iv 17 note.

32. **dehe**, 'in my body,' said to be from √dıh, sup. 11 note, apparently 'a thing moulded' or 'formed.'

práṇá, 'breath,' 'life' (plur.), from pra + √an, to breathe. It occurs ix 18, xviii 9 práṇán dhárayanti (causal of dhṛı): and comp. práṇeçvara (xiii 63), 'lord of my life'.

ratam, p. p. of √ram, see vi 10 note.

tvayı bhavışyámı, another locative use strange to classical readers, i.e. the loc. in a person—'I will be ever in thee.' Cf. vi. 14 Nale vatsyámı, 'I will dwell in Nala;' xx 35, avasaṃ tvayı rájendra, 'I abode in thee, O King:' at xiii 65, vasasva mayı, and xv 7, vasa mayı = 'dwell under my protection,' i.e. in my sphere of action: also xvii 18. The locative expressing *on* a person has been noted at v. 9.

In all these constructions the Greek and the Latin would employ prepositions, e.g. ἐν σοί.

33. **abhınandya**, indecl. part. of the causal (nandayámı) of abhı + √nand, identical in form with that of the simple verb = 'having caused to be glad.' √nand is of obscure relationship. In Zend √nad = to despise, and this has been connected with ὄνομαι. In Sanskrit √nad is 'to make a noise,' see xii 1, whence the common word nadi, a river. Benfey conjectures plausibly that nand = nanad, the reduplicated form of this √nad. The form is against any connection with ὀνίνημι. At viii 17 abhınandatı = takes kindly, gives heed to. Perhaps the line is an insertion.

parasparataḥ, 2nd abl. of paraspara, xiii 13; for the case cf. sákshát i 14. It seems to me that *s* is probably the nominative sign, so that paraspara is an irregular compound of a full noun and a base: compare anyo 'nyam i 17, and also the phrase αὐτὸς αὑτοῦ, used practically as one word. The *s* is retained instead of passing into visarga before the *p*, as in vâcas-pati, divas-pati, &c. See M. M. Gr. § 89.

Agnipurogama, 'having Agni as leader,' a B. V., cf. Indrapurogama, iv 20.

çaraṇam, sup. 15. For construction comp. çaraṇaṃ tvâm prapannâ 'smi, viii 18: it seems to be akin to i 20, vâcaṃ vyâjahâra Nalam: for çaraṇam is a contained accusative with jagmatuḥ, almost as close as vâcaṃ vyâjahâra. Then the simple idea contained in the two words is followed by the accusative of the person affected. See also note on vii 5. For form jagmatuḥ, see M. W. Gr. § 376, M. M. 328. 3: medial *a* is dropped.

34. **vṛite Naiṣadhe**, i 11 note.

mahaujasaḥ, 'of great might,' from mahâ for mahat and ojas, 'strength,' from √uj; see note on ugra, iii 21.

daduḥ, M. W. Gr. § 373: comp. jajnuḥ ii 5, jagmuḥ ii 10.

35. **pratyakṣadarçanaṃ**, 'the seeing (the invisible) as present to the eye.' Pratyakṣa, 'before the eyes,' 'visible,' is a very common word (as a subst.) in Hindu philosophy to denote 'perception by the senses,' one of the 4 (according to the Nyâya, or 3 according to the Sânkhya) processes by which the mind attains knowledge. See 'Indian Wisdom,' p. 72.

gatiṃ ca, &c., 'a gait firm and noble,' Milman. **anuttama** = 'qui altissimum non habet, i.q. qui altissimus est,' Bopp. It is a curious inversion of the apparent meaning 'not highest,' which would be a natural and proper K. D. compound, but is thus turned into a B. V.

The combination of the two gifts is curious: still more the two gifts of Yama, and the garlands given by Varuṇa.

36. **âtmabhavam**, 'own essence,' i.e. fire. So at xxiii 2, Nala (concealed in the form of Vāhuka) holds up grass, which is at once consumed by fire.

vâñchati, 'wishes'—the same word: the connection is well seen through German, 'wünschen.' The *ch* comes from *sk*, see note on 25: so that the original form would be van-sk or vân-sk, and would correspond with Gr. *εὔχομαι* for *εὐ-σκο-μαι*, √va: for the letter-changes see Gr. Et. II, p. 366 (Engl. transl.). Again at xxvi 8.

lokân: is this the 'trailokyam' (xiii 16), heaven, earth, and the parts below the earth,' or the seven worlds corresponding to the seven pātālas? v 7 note. Probably it means simply 'space,' 'the world.'

Schlegel (quoted by Bopp in his note on Indr. i 37) thought that it was used in the sense of 'people,' as at i 15, and translated it 'feurige Krieger,' which is very improbable.

átmaprabhán: Bopp (ut supr.) translated this 'self-bright,' 'lightened by themselves.' But átman doubtless refers to Agni: the sentence is merely a repetition of the previous one in different words.

Hutáçanaḥ = Hutáça, iv 9; but this is prob. a B. V., 'having fire as food;' that a T. P. 'fire-devourer.'

37. 'Yama gave taste in food, and supreme stedfastness in duty.' In canto xxiii the disguised Nala prepares food, and is at once detected by its flavour. **anna**, p. p. of √ad, to 'eat,' Lat. 'ed-o.' **rasa**, 'taste:' this is a common meaning of the word, which primarily = 'price,' and sometimes the essence of a thing, and so Benf. takes it here, 'the essential properties of food,' i.e. the knowledge of them. Curtius suggests that the word may have lost a *v*, and be connected with varṣa, ἐέρση, and ros (roris), Gr. Et. no. 497: see note on vii 3.

sthiti, so xii 10, sthityá parayá yutá.

38. **uttama-gandáḍhyáḥ**, 'rich in the highest fragrance.' Áḍhya (xxv 6) of course has nothing to with ádi, iii 16. In canto xxiii 16 Nala takes flowers in his hands, and they at once blossom all the more.

mithunam, perhaps = 'a pair of gifts,' as each does give two. But the word is used generally of living beings: and probably means here (as at xxiii 23, where no other word is used) the two children mentioned l. 46. The gods gave the other gifts, '*and* (ca) all joined in giving children'—the greatest gift of all. Dean Milman translates differently.

pradáya asya: note the genitive. This case is rather a dwindling one in Sanskrit, never having had the work thrown upon it which it has to perform in the European languages (esp. the Greek) from the loss of other cases. It is used with the p. p. to express the agent as we saw at i 4. It is also used, as here, with several verbs, where, according to classical usage, we should expect a dative. It is found with √dá, xvii 15, xx 27, xxiii 4 (but the dative at xx 30, xxiii 4, xxv 17), with nivedaya (causal of √vid), xviii 13, with á + √khyá, xxiii 5: with sam + á + √dhá, xxiii 12: with √kṣam, xxv 13: with √bhi, xii 11. Other uses are more like Greek or Latin, e.g. the gen. with √çru (κλύω), xii 76, xviii 14 (in each of these passages however there is a neut. pronoun as well, and the gen. might go with that); with smṛi, xv 10 and 15: but the accusative goes with anu + smṛi, xv 20.

tridivam, 'Heaven,' 'the third most holy heaven' (Benfey): but probably Svarga is meant (so in the P. W.) the heaven of Indra; see ii 13 note.

39. **anubhûya**, 'after being present at,' ii 9 note. For the use of the ind. part. with a case, see note on viii 22.

vivâham, 'marriage,' vi + √vah. For the different forms of marriage, see Manu iii 20, &c.

yathâgatam, see note on iii 2.

muditâh, p. p. of √mud, 'to be glad:' perf. mumude, xix 36. The root is used as a fem. noun, xix 37.

41. **uṣya**, indecl. part. of √vas, 'to dwell,' ii 12 note. For the form see i 1 note.

samanujñâto, iii 1 note. **svakam**, i.e. sva + ka, which marks the pronoun more plainly as adjectival: see note on viii. 3. Again at xxv 4.

43. **aṃçumân**, 'the rayed one' = the sun. The root is probably AK, nasalised: and the suffix is *-u*. See note on tigmâṃçu xxiv 33.

arañjayat, 'he caused to be attached to himself,' imperfect causal of √rañj, see sup. 22 note.

prajâ = prajâs (acc. plur.) = Lat. progenies, but used of the whole people. The king is conceived of as the father of his people, like the 'pater Romanus' of Vergil (Aen. ix 449), and like Odysseus who πατὴρ ὣς ἤπιος ἦεν (Od. ii 47).

paripâlayan, 'protecting,' from pâlaya described as a causal of √pâ, but not different in sense.

44. **ije**, perf. mid. of √yaj. M. W. Gr. § 375 e, M. M. App. 99. 'He sacrificed with the horse-sacrifice,' a natural use of the instrumental rather than the contained accusative, just as in Lat. we find 'ire via' as well as 'ire viam,' and the 'cognate instrumental' in Lithuanian is even more exactly parallel, see note on ix 14. The 'horse sacrifice' is often mentioned as the greatest of all Hindu sacrifices; it is old, two of the hymns in the first book of the Ṛig Veda relating to it. In later times it was believed that any one who performed this sacrifice a hundred times could depose Indra, comp. note on ii 14. In the 14th book of the Mahābhārata, the ceremony is performed by Yudhishṭhira after his victory over the Kauravas. Daçaratha's horse-sacrifice in the Rāmāyana is minutely described in 'Ind. Wisdom,' note to p. 343.

Yayâtı, son of Nahusha, fifth king of the lunar race—father of Puru, the founder of the line of the Pauravas. For the different accounts of him given in the Purānas, see Dowson Dict. s. v. The horse-sacrifice is not mentioned there.

kratubhıs, 'with sacrifices which have fit gifts' (for Brahmans). Cf. xii 14, 45, 81, at all of which passages Damayantī invokes her husband by the piety shewn specially in such sacrifices and offerings to the sacrificing priests. The prominence of sacrifice in the Hindu ritual and the corresponding exaltation of the Brahmanic caste are well commented upon by M. Williams, 'Hinduism,' pp. 38—41. The word kratu = 'strength' in Vedic—it is from KRA, the secondary of KAR, whence come *κράτος*, *κρείων*, creo, &c. See Gr. Et., no. 73. **dakṣıṇa** = Lat. dexter, the right side; and by a natural transition of meaning to the 'right thing' to be done, comes to mean a gift to a priest. Dâkṣıṇya (Hit. 468) apparently means 'straight-forwardness,' though elsewhere it = 'politeness.'

45. **upavaneṣu**, a sort of diminutive of vana. Cf. Lat. use of *sub*.

47. **vıharaṃç ca**, i.e. vıharan (pres. part of vı + √hṛı) + ca. The ç is euphonic.

rarakṣa, perf. of √rakṣ, see i 4 note.

vasudhâ = the 'wealth-holder,' i.e. earth, see iv 2 note. The alliteration of the last line is noteworthy.

CANTO VI.

1. **Kalınâ.** Kali is the Kali-yuga (see Dowson, s.v. *yuga*) personified. "There are properly four yugas or ages in every Mahâyuga [great yuga, or cycle, of which 2000 make up a Kalpa or aeon] viz. Kṛta, Treta, Dvāpara and Kali, named from the marks on dice—the Kṛta being the best throw, of four points, and the Kali the worst, of one point." 'Ind. Wisd.' 188 note. This system of chronology was fully developed in the Mahābhārata, though unknown in the Ṛigveda. It is parallel to the metal ages of Greek mythology: the first being the age of perfect righteousness, happiness and plenty, the last the opposite when unrighteousness prevails and the lives of men are shortened down to their present span. But in the Kali-yuga, the evil which prevails is of course evil according to the Brahmanic standard. There is no knowledge of the Veda, no *dharma*, no sacrifices: and the outward manifestation consists in passion and different emotions which delay the final emancipation of the soul from being born again. Dvāpara is the personification of the third age, as Kali is of the fourth.

2. **sahâyena,** 'with D. as companion'; sociative use of the instrumental: see note on i 7. So ii 11, vii 4, divya Nalena, 'play with Nala'; xxvi 15, devana asuhṛıdganaıḥ, 'play with those who are not friends'; xxiv 30, gantum açvaıḥ, 'to go with horses'; xx 41, &c.: but most commonly of inanimate things, e.g. xxvi 19,

eka-pâṇena vireṇa Nalena sa paràjıtaḥ
sa ratnakoṣanıcayaıḥ prâṇena paṇıto 'pı ca.

'By one throw was he overcome by the hero Nala, together with his stores of jewels and treasure, and even his very life, was he won.' But very frequently we find a preposition, such as *saha* i 7, v 45, vi 1 and 15, &c., or *sàrddham* ix 7, xv 7, xvii 3, xxvi 30: or with a verb or participle compounded with *sa* or *sam*, e.g. xviii 20 bhartà sameṣyàmi; comp. xxv 3 Nalena sahita. If I have counted rightly, there are in these poems out of 50 instances of the pure sociative, 23 with no preposition, 22 with a preposition, and 5 with some compound word.

The traces of this usage are very plain in Greek and Latin, though (except in the -φι form in old Greek and the rarer α-form) the external mark of the case has perished. But the dative is found in Homer combined with the -φι-case in such a way as to leave no doubt of the origin of the use. Compare θεόφιν μήστωρ ἀτάλαντος, Od. iii 110, with the common phrase ἵπποις καὶ ὄχεσφι, and ἀλώμενος...νηί τε καὶ ἑτάροισι: and regularly with nouns of multitude, Jelf § 604. Very commonly the construction is marked by αὐτός, e.g. αὐτοῖσι ὄχεσφι, Il. viii 290: and, with this word, which practically does the duty of a preposition, the case survived into Attic Greek. In Latin there is no sociative (or instrumental) case-form (for the -bi and -bis in the pronouns have no such meaning): but the work of the case has been taken completely by the ablative: and some examples of the pure sociative use are unmistakable: e.g. Caesar, B. G. v 9, illi equitatu atque essedis ad flumen progressi (but vii 54 *cum* omni equitatu profectum), Ovid, Am. II xvi 13, si medius Polluce et Castore ponar, where 'medius' does something to help out the construction. In Lithuanian the sociative use is quite regular. It is also used like the Lat. abl. of description, see xii 37 note.

There is no doubt that the sociative use was a primitive one, but it wanted distinctness because of the original confusion of the two case-forms, ā and bhi, and perhaps from other causes. Consequently prepositions were needed in each language to help the usage out. But these prepositions differ so much among the different peoples that their use was probably not established before the division of the languages. Thus in Sk. we find *saha*, *sàrddham* and *sàkam*; also *vinà* in the peculiar Sanskrit *disjunctive* use of the case, e.g. xvi 19, bhartà nàma param nàryà bhùṣaṇam bhùṣaṇair *vinà*, i.e. 'a husband is a wife's highest ornament, *without* (other) ornaments.' See note on xiii 34. In Greek we have ξύν (Lat. cum), ἅμα (Sk. sam) (ἅμ' ἠοῖ φαινομένηφι, Il. ix 682) μετά (Germ. mit) (μετὰ πνοιῇς ἀνέμοιο, Il. xxiii 367): these few usages therefore are found each in two languages.

3. **varayiṣve**, 2 fut. middle of varaya, see iii 6 and 24 notes.

4. **nivṛittam**, 'finished,' 'done with,' from ni + √vṛit, a very common verb, equivalent in form, and (when compounded) in meaning, to Lat. vertor and sometimes versor. Thus e.g. at x 15, tasya buddhir Damayantyâṃ nyavartata, but with something also of the sense of 'returning' found at x 20, nivṛittahṛidayaḥ = 'with heart turned back,' Hit. 235, sa vyâḍho nivṛittaḥ. In Bh. Gita xvi 7, nivṛitti is cessation from action, i.e. beatitude, as opposed to pravṛitti = 'progress,' 'activity'; and pra + √vṛit is found ix 2, xii 14. In Pāṇini's grammar, nivṛitti marks that some general rule (adhikâra) which is implied in all the following sūtras ceases to operate any longer. The simple root is seen in vartate xiii 71, vartin viii 15, vṛitta 'conduct' xii 46, 'an event' Sāv. vi 8, vartaṇa 'maintenance' Hit. 272 &c.

samipataḥ, 'in presence of.' See note on vii 4. These forms in *-tas* are used (as here) without much feeling of their original sense in the different languages;—for they were at first ablatives as tatás, ii 1, atas ix 23, &c., çatrutas xiv 18, where see note. But ἐντός and ἐκτός, intus and caelitus, and Sk. kutaḥ, mukhataḥ (xi 28), ekataḥ (xii 17), dharmataḥ vi 9, pṛiṣṭhataḥ ix 7, vâhyataḥ ix 7, vegataḥ xi 27, agrataḥ xxiv 14, have only a general locative sense. Çak. p. 5 prasâdanatas = prasâdât (Prakrit).

5. **krodha**, 'wrath,' from √krudh, see note on xviii 9.

âmantrya, 'having addressed,' generally with the idea of taking leave; e.g. viii 24, xxvi 1. For the simple root see note on ii. 9.

6. 'For that she has taken as husband a man in the midst of gods, therefore be her bearing of punishment fitting and great.' **yat** = quod: comp. xi 10, viii 17, xiii 39, xviii 10, xxiii 14, xxiv 17. **avindata**, ii 4 note. **nyâyyaṃ**, derivative of nyâya + suffix *ya*: nyâya = 'method,' 'manner'; whence came the name of one of the chief philosophical 'methods' of the Hindus—the Nyāya of Gotama (acc. to M. Williams, however, Nyâya is analysis, as opposed to Sânkhyâ, synthesis).

vipulaṃ, 'full,' 'large,' ix 6; probably one of the large family of words belonging to √PAR, Gr. √πλα, Lat. 'ple.' **daṇḍa**, iv 10 note.

7. **divaukasaḥ**, ii 30 note.

samanujñâte, 'consent being given by us': iii 1 note.

8. **âçrayeta**, v 15 note. It is the optative expressing a question, like the Gr. and Lat. conjunctive.

upetam, 'endowed with,' p. p. of upa + √i; comp. upapanna, i 1.

akhilân, 'entire,' 'whole,' from khila = 'a remainder.'

carita-vrata, 'with his vows duly performed,' p. p. of √car, for which see note on câritra xviii 9: and vicarita = 'wandering' xxiv 49; it is used as a noun = 'doings' xxiii 2: for vrata see ii 14, note.

9. "He who reads the four Vedas entire, together with the Purâṇas (? the whole eighteen) as a fifth." These Purāṇas, however, or legendary histories of the Gods, are not only much later than the Vedas, but also than the mass of the Mahābhārata: so that either these lines are a late insertion by some Brahmanic reviser of the poem (which is quite possible from the tone of the passage); or else the ākhyāna must be understood generally as 'tradition,' referring not to the Purāṇas but to some older Itihāsa, or legendary poem, wherein the actors are still men and have not been deified as in the later accounts[1]. "The Purāṇas and Tantras...are sometimes called a fifth Veda especially designed for the masses of the people, and for women." M. W. 'Hinduism,' p. 116. The four Vedas are the Ṛig-veda—a large collection of hymns to the elemental powers, and not arranged for sacrificial purposes: the Yajur-veda, hymns arranged for sacrifice: the Sāma-veda, most of the hymns of which are found in the Ṛig-veda, but they are adapted here for the Soma-offerings: and the Atharva-veda, which is considerably later in time and contains incantations, &c., due according to Prof. Whitney rather to popular than to priestly sources. Each of these collections of hymns, &c. (called Mantras, see note on ii 9) is accompanied by one or more Brāhmaṇas: these are "written in prose and contain liturgical and ritualistic glosses, explanations, and applications of the hymns, illustrated by numerous legends. To the Brāhmaṇas are added the Āraṇyakas and the Upanishads, mystical treatises in prose and verse which speculate upon the nature of spirit and of God, and exhibit a freedom of thought and speculation which was the beginning of Hindu philosophy." Dowson, s. v. *Veda*. The whole of this collection of Mantras Brāhmaṇas and Upanishads is included under the general term *Vedas*.

[1] Thus Weber, 'Ind. Lit.' p. 45, writing of the Aitareya (probably the oldest) and the Kaushītaki-Brāhmana, says 'Both presuppose literary compositions of some sort as having preceded them. Thus mention is made of the 'ākhyāna-vidas,' 'those versed in tradition.'

âkhyâna-pancamân is a B. V. 'which have the âkhyâna as a fifth.' It is something like the Greek method of reckoning πέμπτος αὐτός.

adhite, middle of adhi + √i, to 'go over' = 'read.'

tṛptâ, 'pleased,' p. p. of √tṛp orig. TARP, whence τέρπω, &c.

10. 'He who delights in doing no harm, who is truth-speaking, firm in his vows.' **dṛḍha**, see xxiii 7 note.

ahiṃsâ = not hurting, from √hiṃs, to hurt, possibly (as Benfey suggests) a desiderative of √han, to kill. Among the things from which a Brahma-chârin (i.e. a Brahman in the first stage of his career) must abstain is 'prâṇinâṃ caiva hiṃsanam,' 'injury to any animate things,' Manu ii 177, comp. vi 28 &c.

nirata, p. p. of ni + √ram, possibly found in Gk. ἠρέμα, see Curt. Gr. Et., no. 454—who makes 'comfortable rest' the underlying notion of the somewhat different forms. Rata (alone) occurs v 31 : rati 'rest' at ii 4.

tapaḥ, ii 13, x 19 notes.

çaucaṃ, from çuci, pure, iv 18 & 24, xxiii 7, by vṛiddhi of *u* and suffix *a*, and loss of final *i*. It = cleansing, vii 3, xxiv 48.

çamaḥ, v 22 note.

11. **dhruvâṇi**, 'firm,' 'steady,' 'sure' (as xxvi 11, druvam âtmajayam matvâ) : = Germ. treu : used adverbially xiii 27. The primary root is DHAR, i 17 note, whence dh(a)r-u is secondary.

kâmayec chapitum, i. e. kâmayet çapitum 'desire to curse': for √çap see v 28 note.

12. **mûḍho**, 'fool,' p. p. of √muh (4) to be disturbed in mind; here, and at xviii 10, Hit. 881, 986 &c. : another form is mugdha : mohita the part. of mohaya (causal) to 'infatuate,' occurs vii 16, xix 4 ; and to 'bewilder' xix 24. Hence moha 'delusion,' Hit. 204 'lobhân mohaç ca nâçaç ca' = 'from covetousness (comes) delusion and destruction.' It is hardly possible that μῶρος should be from this root (Bopp, s. v.).

âtmânam âtmanâ, a not uncommon alliteration (see xii 57, xviii 8). We may compare idioms like the Latin 'suo sibi gladio hunc iugulo.'

13. 'Let him be plunged (or 'he is to be plunged') in wretched hell in the mighty bottomless lake.' **kṛicchra** (of uncertain derivation) is 'difficult,' 'painful'; e. g. xv 17 vane, xxiv 18 çâpena. It is frequently used as a neuter subst. = 'difficulty,' e. g. artha-kṛicchreṣu, xv 3 : also xi 30 : Hit. 1062 kṛicchrâgataḥ = reduced to difficulties; ib. 1275, Brâhmaṇas siddham api arthaṃ kṛicchreṇa api na

yacchati = a Brahman gives up money, even though due, not even on pressure.

naraka, 'hell': 21 of these are enumerated in Manu (iv 88), where Naraka is the name of one only (see 'Indian Wisdom,' 66 note 2). According to the common Hindu belief the soul, after each life, goes either to one of the heavens or one of the hells, whence it returns again into a body in order that it may fully work out the results of former existence.

majjet, opt. of √majj (6) = Lat. √merg: the p. p. magna is frequent, Hit. 133, 783, 864 &c.

agáḍha, = a (neg) and gáḍha, p. p. of √gáh, to dive into: the original form was probably GADH, recognisable (after labialism) in βαθύς, ἄ-βυσσος &c; Gr. Et. no. 635.

hrada, a 'lake,' 'piece of water'; whence hradini 'a river,' xii 112.

14. **utsahe**, iii 8 note. **kopam**, 'anger,' see note on xix 15.

vatsyámi, fut. of √vas, to dwell: the *t* is euphonic, M. W. Gr. § 304 *a*, M. M. § 132.

Nale, for the locative see v 32 note.

15. **bhraṃçayiṣyámi**, fut. of causal of √bhraṃç, 'to fall'; whence xx 2 bhraṣṭa, xviii 10 paribhraṣṭa.

tvam &c.—'Do *thou* (*api* here like Greek γε), having entered into the dice, think well to join company with me,' or 'help me' (as viii 13). **sáháyya**, formed regularly from saháya vi 2 note, see ii 31.

arhasi, iii 7 note.

Dvápara, as being one throw of the dice—the worst but one—is naturally conceived of as becoming embodied in them.

1. **samayaṃ kṛtvâ**, 'having made agreement': samaya from sam + √i has also many other meanings, e.g. 'condition,' as at xiii 67, samayena utsahe vastuṃ tvayi, i.e. 'on a certain condition I am able to dwell in thy power,' Sâv. iv 17 &c.: it also = 'time,' xiii 6, ârddha-râtra-samaye = at midnight (half-night-time): and other meanings, for which see the P. W.

tatra, yatra, tatra (partly because of the subsequent yatra) is used here = 'thither,' just as we use 'there' in that sense. For the general form of the sentence, see note on xiii 30.

2. **antara-prepsur** = 'eager to get an opportunity': prepsu = pra + ipsu, compare abhipsu v 2, &c. Antara as an adj. = 'other'; and is frequently found at the end of a K. D. compound; e.g. janmântara, 'another birth,' xiii 33, kalântarâvṛitti, 'the revolution of time,' Hit. 894: and so is akin to Sk. an-ya, other, * Goth. anthar, and prob. Gk. ἔν-ιοι: which shew the *n* form instead of the *l* seen in ἄλλος, al-ius, and Gothic alis, alya, &c. But antara occurs also as a neut. substantive, meaning the 'inner part,' in which sense the word must be connected with ἐνί, ἐντός, ἔν-εροι, &c., in-ter, Goth. inna, &c. So at xii 103 vanântare = in the depths of the wood: xxi 10 bâhvor...antaraṃ = the space between the arms: and loc. antare = in the interval, e.g. Hit. 94. So by a natural transition it takes the sense 'occasion,' as xiii 59, 'opportunity,' as here. Curtius discusses this, and the words quoted above under nos. 425, 426, and 524: he would separate them into three groups, but he does not take account of the different meanings of antara, which would bring it under both his first and his second group.

varṣe, 'year' (so xxiv 51), literally 'rain' (from √vṛiṣ, whence vṛiṣa line 6, and vṛiṣṭi, xxiv 40), = Gr. ἐέρση (for ἐ-Fερση). In the plur. it denoted the rainy season—one of the Indian six of two months each—i.e. Grīshma, Varshā, Çarad, Hemanta, Çiçira, and Vasanta. This use of one important or descriptive period of the year instead of the year itself is not unknown with us, e.g. a man of seventy winters; and in Wordsworth's 'Two April Mornings,' "Nine summers had she scarcely seen, the pride of all the vale." Comp. xxvi 25, saṅjiva çaradaḥ çatam.

3. **upaspṛçya** = 'having rinsed the mouth with water' (Benf.), 'having sipped water' (M. W.), literally 'having slightly touched.' Orig. form √SPARK, found in Lat. spargo, to touch with water, &c. This upasparça is necessary after evacuation as part of the ceremonial purification: this therefore Nala performs; but he neglects to wash his feet, another part of the process. At Manu v 138 foot-washing is not mentioned: kṛtvâ mûtraṃ puriṣaṃ vâ khâny âcânta upaspṛçet, 'he is to sprinkle the cavities of the body (mouth, nose, &c.) after having rinsed his mouth' (p.p. (in active sense) of â + √cam, the technical word). This gives a good illustration of the extreme minuteness of the ceremonial law. Comp. Manu iv 93:

> utthâya, avaçyakaṃ kṛtvâ, kṛtaçaucaḥ, samâhitaḥ
> purvâṃ sandhyâṃ japaṃs tiṣṭhet, svakâle c'âparâṃ ciram,

i.e. 'having arisen, having done what is necessary, having purified himself, with his attention fixed let him stand praying the morning prayer, and at the proper time the other in the evening, for a long while.'

sandhyâm anuâsta = 'sat down to the (evening) meditation.' âsta from √âs, to sit, i 11 note, ἧς-ται: anu = 'after,' and seems therefore scarcely to give the sense required: perhaps the meaning may come as in Greek compounds with μετά—e.g. μετελθεῖν, to go *after*, i e. to find, a person. Anu seems to be from the same origin as Greek ἀνά and Gothic ana, and Latin *an* (in anhelo, &c.): but of all these the sense is 'up.' **sandhyâ**, 'meditation,' used for the morning, noon, and evening observance: it is from √dhyai, 'to think,' doubtless a shortened form of adhi and √yâ, the secondary form of √i. The accusative is governed by the transitive sense which the compound has acquired—just as insidere, insilire, &c. come to be transitive in Latin.

âviçat, imp. of â + √viç, with same meaning as simple verb, i 31 note.

4. **samipam** goes with **Puṣkarasya**, like sakâçam, sâkshât, and

other adverbs when used prepositionally it goes with a genitive—naturally—from the strong substantival sense which remains. So also samipe i 16 takes the genitive: samipataḥ (vi 4) was in composition with the base asmat. See further i 14 note. Puṣkara is the brother of Nala.

àha, 'spoke'; only found in this tense, and of that only in the sing. 2 (àttha, ix 30) and 3, dual 2, 3, plur. 3. The primary root is √AGH, found in the equally defective Lat. verb aio; but the guttural survives in ad-ag-ium. It is also found in the Homeric ἦ, and the Platonic ἦν δὲ ἐγώ, ἦ δὲ ὅς.

divya Nalena, vii 2 note: √dıv (4 d.) lengthens the root-vowel before ya. M. W. § 275.

vaı strengthens a whole sentence, as here, and perhaps ix 8, ghoṣayàmàsa vaı pure: or one word, e.g. adbhutarùpàn vaı, i 24; xxvi 5, eṣa vaı mama sannyàsas; iii 5, tvaṃ vaı; vi 11, yo vaı—and so very often with a pronoun. It may be the loc. of a pronominal stem *va*; see note on vata xi 10: and if so, may be compared to the Homeric αὔτως (e.g. παῖς ἔτι νήπιος αὔτως, Od. xii 284), and also to οὕτως.

5. **dyùte**, 'in the game,' apparently = dıv + ta, the vowels and semivowels exchanging to avoid the meeting of *v* and *t*. So dyutı, 'brightness,' for dıv + tı, xii 15.

jetà = 3 pers. sing. fut. of √jı (to conquer) = orig. GI, whence βία, &c. by labialism; Gr. Et. no. 639. It often occurs at the end of a compound, with suffix (of auxiliary letter) *t*, as xii 77, saṃgràma-jıt: compare the *t* in mahikṣı-t ii 20, loka-kṛı-t iv 6, &c.: and see Curt. 'Studien,' v 104.

bhavàn, ii 31 note.

pratıpadyasva, √pad (4) with pratı (middle voice) = 'go to,' or 'obtain' (as here and xiv 25), or 'learn,' as xviii 16, yathà na nṛıpatır Bhimaḥ pratıpadyeta me matım. Orig. PAD is seen in πέδ-ον and pe(d)-s (Gr. Et. no. 291): Curtius is probably right in keeping √PAT distinct—whence πέτομαι, πίπτω, peto, &c. (ib. no. 214, and see i 22 note): 'treading' is the primary meaning of the first: 'quick movement' (whether flying or falling) of the second.

jıtvà ràjyaṃ Nalaṃ, a clear double acc.; though probably the use arose from the acc. of the thing being combined with the verb so as to denote but one idea (here 'despoil') which then takes an acc. of the person. See notes on i 20, v 33.

6. **abhyayàt**, imperf. of abhı + √yà. M. W. § 644.

vṛiṣo gavàm = the principal die in some game of dice: 'the cows' being the rest.

àsàdya, 'having reached,' from √sad, to 'sink down': in several derived uses of the verb helplessness is the common idea. It = Lat. sed-eo, Gr. ἕζομαι, where no such change of meaning is found. The simple verb + à is used in the same sense as here at x 18, àsasàda khadgam. But generally the sense is given by the causal, or (if the causal sense be not apparent) by declining the verb in the 10th conjugation: àsàdya = à + sàd(aya) + ya. Ni + sad = 'sink down in despair' at x 5. But in pra + sad (= to be propitious, xii 130) we seem to have only the simple idea of 'bending toward' in sign of assent: Benfey well compares the Latin 'propensus' and the German 'geneigt': we might add Lat. annuo (ad + nuo), and the nod of Olympian Zeus.

7. **paravirahà,** 'slayer of foemen': para = other (than a friend), see ii 2 note. Hà is the nominative of han (i 20) used here as a noun without suffix: comp. 'Balavṛitrahà,' ii 17.

8. **cakṣame,** perf. mid. of √kṣam, iii 8 note.

samàhvànam, v 1 note.

Vaidharbhyàḥ, &c., 'although the princess of Vidharba was looking on (whose presence should have restrained him) he thought it time for play.' The construction is a gen. absolute, which is rare: comp. paçyatas te, xx 15. **paṇa,** xxvi 6, from √paṇ (1 atm.): the *ṇ* indicates a lost *r*, which gives *par-n; and this (compared with πέρ-νη-μι) leaves no doubt that the original root was PAR, and that it was originally declined in the ninth conjugation—whence the *ṇ*. Paṇa also = 'a price.' Pàṇa likewise occurs, and pratipàṇa, ix 2—where see note.

9. **hiraṇyasya,** 'of wealth,' 'gold,' connected with harit, and doubtless therefore deriving its name from its colour: comp. argentum and ἄργυρος, which however perhaps imply brightness only. **suvarṇa** (of good colour) also = 'gold': probably hiranya is the more general word.

yàna-yugyasya, 'of carriage and beast.' A collective Dvandva, of the kind called 'samàhàra,' M. M. Gr. § 521, and therefore declined in the singular neuter. yàna = 'going' at xviii 6, as here xvii 21: yugya is fut. part. of √yuj, i.e. 'that which may be yoked,' and so can be used either of a carriage (comp. yugya-stha, 'standing in a car,' Manu viii 294) or beast of burden, as here: comp. ζύγιος. The genitives are curious: there seems no reason why they should go with jiyate: we have 'jito rājyam vasūni ca,' xii 83: at xxvi 6 the genitive is used of the stake in a game: 'paṇena ekena bhadram te, prāṇayoç ca paṇāvahe': but there the case seems natural with *paṇ*, as at ix 3, Damayantyāḥ paṇa. Perhaps therefore they are better taken with dyūte, 'the game for wealth, &c.,' though this is forced.

jiyate, final *i* and *u* are lengthened in forming the base of passive verbs.

10. **akṣa**, &c., 'maddened with dice-madness.' **mada**, as at i 24 (see note), xiii 7, &c.

arindama: for form see page 6. **ari**, 'an enemy' (xii 47, 50, &c.) is of doubtful origin; ἔρι-ς agrees in form, but not sufficiently in meaning: and it is not likely to have anything to do with Ἄρης. Curt. no. 488 note.

nivāraṇe, 'for the hindering,' i.e. 'to hinder'; from ni + √vṛi, in the sense of 'covering': see iii 24 note. The loc. of verbal nouns in *-ana* is often used thus precisely like the Greek infinitives in *-εναι* and *-μεναι*: see examples at iii 6 note on patitve. **chakto** = çakto, 'capable,' p. p. of √çak, to be able, i 18 note. The verb (in the passive voice) and participle are both remarkable for being used in a passive sense with an infinitive; as at xx 5 āhartum çakyate, x 13 çaktā dharṣayitum, 'capable of being harmed': also çakya at xvi 4 and xxvi 15.

11. **paurajanāh**, 'townsfolk': but paura alone = 'a citizen' (from pura, a city), so that jana (as often) is superfluous. **draṣṭum**, inf. of √driç, coming nearer to the orig. root √drak, or √dark. Cf. future drakṣyāmi. **āturam**, 'full of desire,' but, apparently, only of an unhealthy sort: cf. xi 36 'pradharṣayitum āturam.'

12. **kāryavān**, 'having business': = kārya (fut. part. of √kṛi) and *-vat*: formed like the perf. act. participle, i 29 note.

13. 'Let it be told to the king of Niṣadha, "all thy subjects are standing, not brooking well the calamity (or perhaps 'fault') of their duty-observing king".' Observe that no *iti* is used in the quotation here, which is left in orat. recta, entirely undistinguished.

prakṛiti, a most common word in Hindu philosophy, but in a very different sense; i.e. the everlasting essence out of which existing things are evolved, see 'Hinduism,' p. 194 &c. Yet our word 'subject' has had a somewhat similar history.

amṛiṣyamāṇā, from √mṛiṣ (4) to 'endure,' whence marṣaṇa 'endurance,' and amarṣaṇa 'impatient,' xii 54. It seems to have no equivalent in Greek or Latin, and must be distinguished from √mṛiç to 'touch,' 'stroke' (whence parâ + mṛiç, 'to disturb,' xvi 15, and vi + mṛiç, 'to consider,' xvi 27): of which the orig. form is MARK, Latin mulc-eo, to touch gently: the opposite kind of touching is seen in the rarer verb mulco, e.g. Plaut. Mil. 163 ni ad mortem male mulcassitis. We must also distinguish √mṛij, whence mṛiṣṭa, v 4 note.

vyaçanam, from *vi* + √aç 'to throw,' xii 11 &c.; whence both senses given above come naturally. It is 'vice,' Çak. 2. 39—something like Lat. perdo, perditus. At Hit. 221 vyasanaṃ çrutau = intense study of Scripture, app. = abandonment of all else for this study; something, again, like 'perditus in quadam' in Latin.

dharma-artha, the artha is redundant: for its general sense, see iii 7 note.

14. **vâṣpa-kalayâ**, 'indistinct by reason of tears.' Kala may be from √kal, to drive, whence κέλομαι, κελεύω, celer; Curt. G. E. no. 48: this root he separates from another KAL, whence καλέω, calendae &c., hail.

karṣitâ, 'distressed,' p. p. of karṣaya, causal of √kṛiṣ 'to drag'; again at xx 31. Benfey compares 'accerso.' At ix 11 it is used of plucking flowers; at xxiv 41 vyapâkarṣad = 'swept away'; at ix 33 apakṛiṣṭa = 'distracted:' at x 26 avakṛiṣ is 'to drag away,' and âkṛiṣ is 'to draw to,' or 'back.'

çoka, 'grief,' iv 13 note.

15. **bhakti**, v 23 note.

puras-kritaḥ, 'put forward,' i.e. brought by their loyalty. So at Hitop. 1205 it is used of putting forward a combatant. But it often has the derivative sense of 'putting in the first place,' 'honouring,' and M. Williams translates here 'adorned by': according to the P. W. it need not mean more than upapanna 'possessed of.'

16. **rucirâpân-gim**, 'with bright corners of the eye' (apân-ga = off-member). For rucira see note on iv 28.

vilapantiṃ, 'making moan'; from vi + √lap = Gr. λακ, and Lat. loquor; x 27, xi 10, xxi 16: pra + lap xxvi 17. It takes a contained accusative—evamâdini—at xiii 43.

17. **nâyam asti** = 'this is not he,' i.e. he is possessed by an evil spirit.

duḥkhârttâ, 'afflicted with misery.' ârtta is p. p. of √ard to 'hurt' or 'vex,' so viii 24, ix 24 &c.; another form—ardita—at xii

106. Bopp conjectures that it is the same as Lat. ardere: and that too great heat may be the radical meaning of the word.

vriḍitá, 'ashamed': from √vriḍ, which however hardly occurs except in this participle; which may therefore have been formed from vridá 'shame,' a common word: then the verb would arise from the supposed participle. It occurs Sáv. i 34 'sá abhivádya pituḥ pádau vriḍiteva tapasvini.'

álayán, 'abodes,' from a + √li 'to stick to.' Comp. áliyate, xi 14. Probably 'to melt' is the primary idea both of this root and of the secondary √lib; Curt. no. 541. The simple form is seen in po-li-o, li-no, and perhaps de-le-o. The word álaya is familiar to us in the compound Himálaya = the abode of snow.

18. **másán**, 'months.' mása = mens-i-s = μήν: Sk. & Gr. have both compensation in the lengthened vowel for the loss of the nasal in Sk., of the sibilant in Greek. The Aeolic μῆννος (for μηνσ-ο-ς) shews it in Greek, as Curtius points out, Gr. Et. no. 571.

1. **unmattavad anunmattá** = ὥσπερ μαινόμενον οὐ μαινομένη : for √mad see i 24 note.

devane gatacetasam = 'mind-lost in play': the locative is used with an adjective as here, at xii 70 dharmeṣu anagha, xii 83 devane kuçala, xx 26 san·khyáne visárada; it does not essentially differ from the use with a participle, v 31 vacane rata, xv 2 açvánáṃ vahane yukta, xx 25 tvarito gamane, xxii 12 sáṅthye bhojane ca vṛta, xv 3 arthakṛcchreṣu prastavya. The uses with a substantive are given at v 22 anurágaṃ ca Naiṣadhe, &c. They all express more or less fully the purpose of an action, and as such are more commonly found with verbs than nouns. For the use with verbs and verbals see iii 6 note.

2. *b.* almost = ii 7 *a.*

3. **çan·kamáná**, iv 12, note: 'hesitating thought' is the primary idea: comp. ix 31 'kim-artham, bhiru, çan·kase,' almost = 'why dost thou *fear*, timid!' and xii 32, 'vrajámy enam açan·kitá,' 'I go to him (the tiger) without hesitation.' With pari it = 'to think all round,' i.e. suspect; so xxiv 26, na mám arhasi, kalyáṇa, doṣeṇa parican·ki-tum: but with an abl. at xxiii 28.

tat-pápam = 'the ill of (or 'to') him,' Nala—a Tat-purusha, just like the very name of the compound which = 'the man of him.' So tat-priyam = 'what is pleasant to him.' Comp. tava priyam i 20.

cikirṣanti, fem. pres. part. of the desiderative of √kṛi. See iii 14 note.

pápa, 'bad' (xii 94), connected by Bopp with κακός and pecco (as √pac with √πεπ and Lat. √coc). But the double labialism required makes the identification dubious. It might be supported by the Aeolic πέμπε 'five,' if we take the usual view that 'kankan' was the original form of the word. But the commoner opinion is now that 'pankan' was the form, and that the initial guttural in Latin is due to assimilation. See Curt. Gr. Et. no. 629.

hṛtasarvasvam, 'with all his property reft,' a B. V. **sva** has its primary sense of 'own': like suus, it is the adjective, and means 'belonging to self'—se, which is the substantive. Compare the use of suus in old Latin, e.g. Plaut. Men. 19, 'ita forma simili pueri ut mater sua (their *own* mother) non posset internosse.' At first sight it seems as though the forms had been interchanged in Sanskrit (the fuller svayam corresponding to se, and the simpler sva to suus—originally souos). But svayam must be connected with aham and tvam, and not regarded as the neuter form of a *svaya. See note on i 15. There is another adjectival form sva-ka at v 41, xxv 4, &c.

upalabhya, 'having perceived,' xi 34 &c.; a common sense of upa + √labh = to get: the compound has the simple sense at xiii 66, bhartáram upalapsyase. We might compare our 'understand' and, except for the preposition, 'percipere.' √labh = Gr. √λαβ; and is not to be confounded with √lamb = Lat. lāb-i; which with vi = delay, xx 16.

4. **atiyaçám**, an irregular compound of ati and yaças, i 10.

dhátrim, 'nurse,' from √dhá. It is generally derived from √dhe, to suck, but there can be little doubt that dhe is only a modified form of dhá. Cf. θε and θᾱ (θη) in Greek, Curt. no. 307.

paricárikám, 'attendant' (= paricáraka xxvi 30), from pari + √car, see v 9 note. There is the same root and prep. in the Attic περίπολοι: but the corresponding sense is given by ἀμφίπολος. Comp. note on upacárya, xxi 30. Paricaryá = service xxv 4.

hitám, i 6 note.

sarvártha-kuçalam, 'skilled in all things': used with devane 'in play,' xii 83; kuçala is commonly used as a substantive = weal, happiness, e.g. ii 16; esp. of success in devotion, e.g. xii 71: see note there. Hence comes the adj. kuçalin, ii 16. Kuçala as an adj. also means 'happy' (ii 16), but is commonly used either alone or, as here, at the end of a compound, in the sense of 'prosperous (i.e. dexterous) in some matter.' Compare xix 19, tvam eva hayatattvajñaḥ, kuçalo hy asi, Váhuka.

anuraktam, v 22 note.

subháṣitám, 'of good speech': √bháṣ ('to speak,' xii 19 &c., pra + bháṣ xiii 68), like √bhás (to shine), are alike secondary forms of orig. BHA 'to shine,' see xii 103: which in Greek (√φα, φημί), by the same natural transition as in Sanskrit, reached the meaning of 'speaking,' i.e. making clear: while the primary meaning remained in the secondaries √φαν, φαίνω, and √φαϝ, φάος. See Curt. no. 407, where he traces beautifully the development of the primary root into five secondaries, *bhan*, *bhav*, *bhas*, *bhak* (Lat. fac-ie-s, fac-etus, fac-s) and *bhad* (in Celtic). I may say here that in speaking of primary and secondary roots I do not hold with Curtius that the secondaries were universally developed at a later period of time than the primaries—a view to which weighty objections have been urged by Max Müller ('Chips' &c. vol. IV ch. 1). But for purposes of analysis the terms are convenient, and need not mislead if it be understood that by 'primary' no more is necessarily meant than the shortest and simplest form of such groups as this: which form was also, no doubt, in many cases also the oldest. In other respects I think Curtius' 'Chronology' both probable and important.

5. **vraja**, 'go,' sup. iii 9; √vraj = √VARG, ἔργον, 'work.' In Sanskrit alone the work is limited to motion, generally motion for a particular purpose.

amátyán, 'counsellors' (xxvi 32), from amá, together, with suffix *-tya*. Amá must not be identified with Greek ἅμα, which is the shortened form of an old instrumental from sama.

ánáyya (xxv. 9), indecl. part. of á + náyaya, causal of √ni 'to lead,' p. p. nita xvii 20, a very common root in Sanskrit, but there alone; hence netra 'an eye' at iv 13, &c.; netṛ 'a leader' xii 128; for vi + √ni, see note on xii 68.

Nala-çásanát, ii 10 note.

ácakṣva, 'report,' xvi 38, from á + √cakṣ, 'to see,' whence cakṣus, 'an eye,' v 8. Both the simple verb and all compounds of it shew the same transition of sense.

yad dhṛtam, i.e. yad hṛtam, 'what part is taken.'

dravyam, 'property,' curiously unlike in meaning to √dru, 'to run,' of which, so far as the form goes, it might be the fut. participle. For its use in this sense comp. Hit. 1276, dravye niyukta = employed in pecuniary matters: and dravina, 'wealth,' 'property,' xiii 17, xvii 27. In the Vaiçeshika philosophy it stands for 'substance,' the first of the seven categories. If we could hold with Benfey that the word is connected with *dru* (a tree), there would be a curious (though unprofitable) parallel between this use of it, and the Aristotelian use of ὕλη.

avaçiṣṭam, i 30 note.

6. 'It may be our portion belike': for **api** see i 31: **bhágadheyam** from bhága, 'portion,' 'lot': see v 23 note: dheya = fut. part. of √dhá, 'to be assigned.' The compound may be a T. P. = 'to be

assigned as a lot,' or a K. D., where the adjectival part follows, like janmántara, note on vii 2.

7. **prakṛitayo**, vii 13. **samupasthitá**, 'having approached': so ὑπό and *sub* are used of coming beneath some place. At 10 it = 'near,' 'impending' (without sam). **pratyanandata**, 'saluted,' xxiv 14; from prati + √nand, see v 33 note.

8. **praviveça ha**, 'entered indeed'—if **ha** has really any force here. Benfey (Lex. s. v.) notes that it often follows a reduplicated perfect. So at xi 26, xii 14, xv 15, xvii 31, xix 37, xxiii 25, xxiv 40, xxv 18, xxvi 27. It is, no doubt, from original (Vedic) gha, and so equals Greek γε. But that word is not associated with any particular tense in Greek. Benfey compares the Teutonic *ga* or *ge*, which is found at the beginning of a perfect. If this be so, we might give as parallel the use of sma after a present, e.g. i 12. Ha is found with a present, samanuçásti at xii 49, and the time referred to is certainly past: it seems therefore as though it might be used there like sma.

9. **niçamya**, v 22 note. **satatam**, 'constantly,' from sa + tata, p. p. of √tan: comp. Latin continuo. **parán-mukhán**, ii 18 note.

11. 'Caused Várṣṇeya to be brought by means of trustworthy men': the instrumental use, not the sociative, 'together with.' **ápta-kárin** = 'doing fit things.' Note the irregular causal, nayaya for náyaya.

12. **çántvayan**, 'soothing,' pres. part. of çántvaya, see x 3, xi 34: which is referred to a √çántv, but is almost certainly a denominative verb from çántva, 'mildness' (√çam, v 22 note). I have followed Benfey in writing the first letter *ç*; it is commonly written *s*, into which *ç* sometimes passes, and may have done so here.

çlakṣṇayá, v 5.

práptakálam, 'at the proper season,' i 11 note.

aninditá, 'unblamed,' common title of respect, like ἀμύμων in Homer. It is p. p. of √nind (simpler form √nid, whence perhaps ὄνειδος): but rarely found except in the participles.

13. **jániṣe**, 2 sing. mid. of √jñá (9): the radical *n* is lost for euphony, leaving jáni, not jñá-ni.

samyagvṛittaḥ, 'altogether resting on thee.' Samyak is neut. of samyañc, 'going together' from sama + √añc, see ii 18 note on paráñc: the final *a* of sama is changed into *i*, and then into *y* before *a*. Samyak = 'together,' ix 8; = 'fully,' 'duly,' xi 6, xxiv 29; Çak i 29.

tvayı, locative; see above note on line 1.

vışamasthasya, 'standing on difficult ground': vışama (= vı + sama) is used literally at xiii 14: metaphorically here, and x 1. In the same sense the derivative vaışamya occurs ix 20, xviii 8.

sâhâyyam, &c., ii 31 note.

14. **yathâ yathâ...tathâ tathâ**: comp. yaṃ yaṃ...taṃ taṃ, v 12, and note there.

dyûte râgo, v 22 note.

bhûyo, 'more'; at xviii 19 it is used as an adj. with vasu: at ix 2, xii 94, xxiii 2, xxiv 2 it is used of time = 'again.' It is the neuter of bhûyaṃs, compar. of bahu, i.e. bahu + iyas, Gr. -ιον as in βέλτ-ιον, Lat. ius (ios) in mel-ius.

abhıvardhate, 'grows,' pres. mid. of abhı + √vṛdh, orig. VARDH, whence √βλαθ for ϝλαθ, seen in βλάστη, βλαστάνω, &c. by change of θ into σ (comp. λέλησμαι from √λαθ) which however remains in βλωθρός, though not in βλο-συρό-ς: we have the same root in ϝρόδον, ϝρίζα, &c. See Curt. no. 658. It is probably also seen in English 'weald,' Benfey Lex. s. v. We had the verb at iii 14, and with vı at i 17: also the verbal form vardhana at iii 20, and vıvardhana (in the same sense) occurs at ix 6, x 2. Vṛddha = 'grown up,' 'old,' xxvi 9.

15. **vaçavartınaḥ**, 'waiting on the will of Pushkara': comp. xvii 34: vaça from √vaç, orig. VAK, whence ἑκών, and Lat. inuitus = in-uic-tus: Gr. Et. no. 19. Vartın, see vi 4 note.

vıparyayas, 'change,' generally for the worse. So at xix 34 there is seen in Nala, disguised as the deformed Vâhuka, 'rûpeṇa vıparyayaḥ': but it may mean simply 'contrariety,' 'difference.' At Hit. 1291 'karmavıparyaya' is explained by Benfey (Lex. s. v.) as 'wrong doing,' i.e. 'change of conduct for the worse' (Johnson ad l. however takes it as 'change of office'). At Hit. 1073 gurutvaṃ vıparitatâṃ vâ = 'respectability or the opposite state.' So here vıparyaya (from vı + parı + √ı + a) = 'the opposite to good luck,' and vıparita (i.e. vı + parı + √ı + ta) is 'adverse,' 'unlucky,' xiii 24.

ca...ca. Note the archaic construction—the co-ordination of clauses by particles of general meaning, preserved together with the later pronominal adverbs. Just so in Epic Greek we have τε...τε. It dates from a time when the 'relative' pronoun had not yet been clearly differentiated from the mass of demonstratives.

16. **abhınandatı**, v 33 note.

mohitaḥ, vi 12 note.

17. **nûnam**, a fuller form of nû (or nu), which corresponds to Greek νύ, νῦν, and νυνί, Lat. num. It is found in almost all the Indo-Eur. languages, see Curt. no. 441. In use it = Lat. profecto, 'of a surety, I deem, it is not the fault, &c.' or we might translate by the same word 'now, I feel sure, &c.': but 'now' is rather used by us in an argument, to indicate a strong point, much as in Greek ἤδη (but not νυν). Nu is common, especially when preceded by an interrogative, just as νυ is used in Homer. Thus 'kiṃ nu me syât?' (x 10) is curiously parallel to the Homeric τί νύ μοι μήκιστα γένηται; Compare also kathaṃ nu, xi 12.

manye, pres. mid. of √man (4)—used here parenthetically, as often. So Greek οἶμαι.

yat tu: yat = quod, as vi 6, or rather as xiii 40. But the *tu* following it is strange. Even 'δέ in apodosi' is never found, I think, with ὅ = quod. Benfey apparently read 'yatra,' as he refers to this line s. v.

18. **çaraṇaṃ tvâṃ prapannâ**, for construction, see v 33 note. Prapanna, p. p. of pra + √pad = 'to go': see note on samatikrântâ, ii 21.

sârathe, 'charioteer,' formed from saratha, *id.* (i. e. sa + ratha, 'a chariot'), by vṛiddhi of first vowel and suffix *i*—rather a rare formation.

na hi, &c. 'For my being (or 'condition') is not cleared (of emotion),' i. e. therefore I am unable to think or act for myself. **bhâva** is 'being,' 'state,' and is used much as φύσις in Greek: so x 15 'Kalinâ duṣṭa-bhâvena,' 'by Kali whose state (or 'nature') is bad,' 'φύσει κακός.' It has many further extensions of meaning, such as 'purpose,' &c. It might be construed here 'mind' or 'reason'; but there seems no reason in translation to limit, further than in the original, a general word whose meaning is defined by the context. 'Being' is perhaps as clear here as in Tennyson, 'Locksley Hall,' "Trust me, cousin, all the current of my being sets to thee": where no doubt it might be more accurately replaced by 'nature,' 'reason,' or what not.

çudhyate, pass. of √çudh, 'to clear': hence p. p. çuddha, 'clear,' 'bright,' v 33 note: causal çodhaya, xvii 10. The analogy of καθαρός and castus (for cad-tus) seems to leave no doubt that the original root was KADH, from which Sanskrit shews a double weakening, ç from *k* (i 3 note) and (less usual) *u* from *a*. **hi**, ii 19 note.

kadâcid, &c., 'at some time or other he may even perish.' **vinaçet**, a good illustration of the primary use of the optative form, which has so nearly perished in Greek: seen, however, in ῥεῖα θεός γ' ἐθέλων καὶ τηλόθεν ἄνδρα σάωσαι, &c., see note on i 30. The root of the verb is √naç, orig. NAK, whence νέκυς, νεκρός, neco, &c. &c., Gr. Et. no. 93. The p. p. naṣṭa occurs xiii 10, xvii 41, and in compounds at x 29, xxii 15: praṇaṣṭa xxiv 17, and sam-praṇaṣṭa xx 40.

19. **dayitân**, ii 19 note.

manojavân = 'thought-speed' = 'swift as thought.' java, 'speed' (comp. java-yukta xix 20, and the adj. javana xx 41) is apparently from √jû, 'to push on,' which Benfey connects with γηθέω, gaudeo, &c. But γηθέω must be from a root GA (not GU), from which a secondary √gav will give all that is wanted in Greek or Latin.

idam, &c., 'having caused this pair (of children) to mount (the car).' **ropaya** is an irregular causal from √ruh, comp. xiii 51 note: rohaya is also found: √ruh = 'to grow': with â = to grow to, i.e. 'ascend,' 'mount': as here xiii 14, xix 21, and Hit. 790 vṛkṣâgram ârûḍha = 'perched on the top of a tree,' and Megh. 8: also = 'to overcome,' Hit. 142. Hence comes âroha, 'growth,' 'stature'—but generally applied to the waist of the body: varârohâ, as at v 30, x 22, &c.: the *p* of the causal seems to refer the common word rûpa, 'form' to the same root. The original form is RUDH, whence Latin rudis, A. S. rōda. Gr. Et. no. 515 note.

20. **jñâtiṣu**, 'relations': jñâ-ti, from √jan—or possibly from GNĀ, before that root had got differentiated into the sense 'know,' when it was merely a secondary form of GAN with no distinct meaning: the existence of such a time seems to be indicated by the Latin *gnatus* and Gr. γνήσιος.

nikṣipya, iii 13 note, and again at xxii 14: nikṣepa xx 29.
tathâ, iv 8.

21. **açeṣeṇa**, 'entirely': a + çeṣa, from √çiṣ, i 28 note.

mukhyaçaḥ, 'principally,' from mukhya, 'chief,' iv 8, xii 81, &c. M. Williams takes it as = mukhyeṣu, which seems impossible. 'She told them especially, without distinction among them.'

22. **sametya**, the indeclinable participle of sam + √i goes with **taiḥ**: compare xii 83, xiii 15; at i 22 (where see note) and v 39 it goes with the nom. plural. At xiv 10 it goes with the acc., tam...âsâdya: at xvi 21 with a gen. dṛṣṭvâ mama. Generally however it is found with the nom. singular; that is to say, the person whose operation is described by this instrumental case (for such the participle originally

was, see i 22 note) is the same as the subject of the main verb: which might have been expected.

vıniçcıtya, v 14 note. **samanujnáto**, iii 1 note.

våhınå, 'with that car,' sociative case, like ὄχεσφι, see vi 2 note. We should have expected våhın to mean 'he who carries,' as at xvii 22: våhana (ii 26, &c.) is generally used for 'a vehicle.'

23. **rathavara**, 'choice car,' the adj. vara following the subst. ratha, like janmântara, xiii 33; kratu-mukhya, xii 81.

24. **årttaḥ**, vii 17 note.

çocan, pres. part. of √çuc. The bases of these participles end in *t* alone, varying herein from the corresponding bases in Greek and Latin, e.g. λεγοντ, legent. They are therefore declined like other bases in *-at*, with this important exception, that in the nom. masc. the vowel is not lengthened, as in Greek λέγων (λεγοντ-ς), in compensation for the loss of *ts*. Thus we find çocan, not çocån. This might seem to be the natural result of the original weakening of the base; if *t* alone were combined with *s* to form the nominative, the loss of one of these letters would not lead to any compensatory lengthening; we find none, e.g. in harıt + *s* = harı̆t, or in χαριτ + ς = χάρῐς. But on the other hand is the fact that firmly fixed in the consciousness of the language remained the recollection that the suffix was originally *-ant*, not *at*; for the *n* actually appears in the nominative, and the acc. ends in *-antam*. Reduplicated verbs (and a few others) have the further peculiarity that the masc. singular ends in *t* not in *n*: e.g. from √då the masc. participle is dadat, not dadan. Perhaps for the same reason—a wish to lighten as far as possible the termination of a word overburdened at the beginning—we find the *nt* entirely lost in Greek verbs of this class: τίθεις, δίδους, ἱεις, a practice afterwards followed by the remaining verbs of the -μι form. The Latin (as usually) consistently adopts one form.

aṭamånas, ii 13 note.

25. **upatasthe**, middle perf. of upa + √sthå, note on iii 1. Greek and Sanskrit differ in their principle of reduplication of these verbs beginning with two consonants. Thus Sanskrit takes the second, e.g. tısṭhåmı, tasthau: Greek the first, *σίστημι whence ἵστημι.

bhṛıtım (from √bhṛı ii 1 note—used as here, in the middle voice, xv 4) = 'nourishment,' then 'wages'—and so (as here) = 'service.'

upayayau, perf. of upa + √yå, 'underwent,' or (as we say) 'undertook,' 'entered upon.' Verbs ending in ā, drop the ā in the perfect, and substitute *au* for the regular *a*-termination of the 1st and 3rd person singular: so dadau i 8, &c. This seems to have no analogy in Greek or Latin.

sârathyena, 'by reason of his charioteering,' or 'on the score of it': comp. 'dautyen' âgamya' iv 15; and v 26 note.

1. **divyataḥ**, vii 4 note.

yac ca, 'and what other property soever (he had)'—fuller at iv 2, mam' ástı. Note that the two pronominal stems are used, yat and kım; for similar instances see iv 2 note. Latin employs but one—used twice or thrice—quicquid, or quod-cum-que. Greek has the two in ὅ τι: τι is a dentalised form of *kı*. It might almost be said that Greek has three distinct stems in ὁτι(δή)πο-τε: for πο (though derived (by labialism) from KA the older form of kı) is yet quite distinct in use from τι.

2. **prahasan**, iii 14 note. **dyútam**, vii 5 note. **pravartatám**, 3rd sing. imperative of pra + √vṛıt (1), declined in middle voice: for √vṛıt see vi 4 note. **bhúyaḥ**, viii 14 note.

pratıpáṇo (from √paṇ vii 8 note), 'a stake,' apparently with no additional sense given by *pratı*. But at xxvi 7, pratıpáṇa = 'the counter-game,' 'revenge at play.'

3. **çıṣṭá**, i 30 note. **sarvam anyat**, singular, where the Latin would employ the plural cuncta alia, and the Greek τἆλλα πάντα: the Greek gain from the article is considerable.

Damayantyáḥ paṇaḥ, 'the game for Damayanti'; for the genitive see note on vii 9. **sádhu**, v 29 note.

4. **manyuná**, 'by grief' (as xi 13) or 'by anger'—or perhaps by their combination, for manyu shades between the two. It corresponds exactly to Greek μῆνις; compare also μαίνομαι. In the next line, parama-manyumat = 'full of the highest scorn.' For the history of the important root MAN, see Curtius, no. 429.

vyadiryata, 'was torn asunder' (xix 3), from vı + √dṛi 'to tear'; our word corresponds in form and meaning; from orig. DAR, whence δέρω &c. in the physical sense; as also dari xii 6: √dal 'to split' seems cognate, to which perhaps δηλέομαι (Benf. s. v. dṛi) is akin. There is less doubt about δῆρις—'strife,' 'division.'

5. **ut-sṛıȷya**, 'having stripped off'; see v 27 note. **gátrebhyo**, v 9 note.

6. **ekavásá hy asaṃvitaḥ**, 'for (he went) with one garment, not (fully) covered.' **hı** here is used as γάρ is sometimes in Greek, not giving the exact reason of what precedes: e.g. his having one garment is not the reason why he strips off his ornaments: but stripping off his ornaments implies nakedness, and the clause with hı explains how far this idea is correct, see i 29 note. **ekavásas** is a B. V.: vásas, from √vas 'to clothe' = vestis and εἷμα and ἐσθής in meaning; but has not the same suffix as any of these: and another suffix is seen in vastra Hit. 85, so 'vıvastra' naked, x 6, and avastratá 'nakedness' x 16. Vásas seems to be the commonest form in this poem; it occurs iv 8, vii 9, ix 16, 19, x 5, 17, xiv 25, &c., also vı-vásas, ix 17, sa-vásas, ix 16. Vasana (xiii 58) = Greek ἑ-ἄνό-ς (not ἑᾱνός). The root VAS, 'to clothe,' is to be distinguished in use from VAS, 'to dwell,' infra line 7, whence vasatı 'a dwelling,' Megh. 1 and Gr. Fάσ-τυ, see ii 12 note: but Curtius is doubtless right when, in discussing the root 'to clothe' (Gr. Et. no. 565) he says that the common primary notion of the two is 'to surround' so as to 'cover' and 'protect.'

asaṃvitaḥ, again at x 22, from a + sam + √vye: but this root is obviously itself a compound, perhaps of vı + √ı, so that vita = vı + ıta: yet the sense is not clear. Benfey compares the ι in ἱμάτιον; but this presupposes that vı + √ı had coalesced in the sense of 'clothe' before Sanskrit and Greek separated—a principle much employed by Pott, but rightly criticised by Curtius. See my 'Gr. and Lat. Etym.' p. 115. **vıvardhanaḥ**, viii 14 note.

nıçcakráma, 'went out,' perf. of nıs + √kram. **nıs** is here used in its primary sense of '*out*,' as in the well-known term nır-váṇa, lit. 'blowing out': generally it negatives as in nır-jana ix 27: it is a word of very doubtful connection: Curtius suggests Gr. ἄνις 'without' (ἄνευ), so that it should come originally from *ana*, the negative prefix (seen in ἀνά-εδνος, Il. ix 146; ἀνάελπτος, Hesiod, Theog. 660; Gr. Et. no. 420): so that the initial vowel would have fallen off: comp. note on nı (for a-ṇı) i 23. √kram 'to go,' p. p. kránta, whence apa-kránta xi 1, is common in Sanskrit: but not clear in other languages. Benfey connects it with κρέμ-α-μαι, &c. 'to hang.' It may be a secondary of KRA, which is itself a modification of KAR to do, the ideas of 'doing' and 'going' being found united in the same root; compare note on VARG, viii 5.

tyaktvá, 'having left,' indecl. part. of √tyaj, ii 17 note.

suvipulám, i.e. su + vipula, vi 6 note.

7. **pṛṣṭhataḥ**, 'behind,' from pṛṣṭha + tas (vi 4 note). Pṛṣṭha 'the back' is of uncertain derivation; the termination is probably *-stha*: but Benfey's suggestion of 'pra' for the first part, is very unlikely, even if referred to an age when men had tails.

váhyataḥ, 'out of doors,' from váhya, 'outer,' 'foreign,' from vahis or bahis ('outside') + ya.

sárddham, 'with,' xv 7, xvii 3, &c.; see note on vi 2. It is an Av. B. compound of sa + arddha = 'half,' x 3, &c., so that it meant at first 'one half (or part) taken with' (something else).

8. **ghoṣayámása**, 'caused it to be sounded abroad,' ii 11 note. **vai**, ix 8, it seems to emphasise the enormity of the deed; it was a public proclamation to all the city.

samyag, viii 13 note. **átiṣṭhet** = 'stand by,' 'assist,' cf. Latin 'adesse.' **badhyatám** = 'the state (*-tá*) of fitness (*-ya*) to be killed' (√badh or √vadh (P. W.) for which see xi 26 note) = 'let him incur death': for accusative comp. mṛtyum ṛcchati iv 7, vaçam iyiván xi 33, and note on ii 7.

mama, 'at my hands,' or 'from me,' an extension of the subjective genitive, like that of the agent, i 4 note. Or gacched badhyatám may be regarded as logically = a passive, and so *mama* will be strictly a gen. of the agent.

yo...átiṣṭhet, sa gacchet. Here the indefinite future action—which (as I have already pointed out at i 30)—is the primary force of the independent optative is somewhat limited by the relative clause adjoining, This, I think, is the only example within this poem in which we have the pronoun with the optative in the relative clause giving the condition, while the demonstrative with the optative in the main clause gives the result. Perhaps vi 11 may be an exception, but there the main clause may express a wish. The optative with 'yadi' (conjunction) however occurs i 28 (where see note), xiii 67; and some other passages where the main clause contains the fut. part., as xvii 44.

9. **vidveṣaṇena**, 'enmity' ('causing abhorrence,' Benfey, apparently among the people: but this seems improbable). The root is dviṣ, 'to hate' = (ὀ)δυς in 'Οδυσ-εύς, ὠδυσάμην, &c.: Curt. no. 290.

kṛtavanto, comp. dṛṣṭavantaḥ i 29 note.

10. **abhyáse**, 'neighbourhood,' xi 21, from abhi + √ás i 11, or √as (Benfey and P. W.) 'to throw' xii 79. At Hit. 47, anabhyáse

viṣaṃ vidyâ = 'where there is not practice (or 'experience') knowledge is poison': and ib. 7 kṛtâbhyâsa = 'one who has been trained.' Benfey distinguishes the two words by spelling the first with a ç, as though from √aç, see xxvi 24 note: see also P. W. s. v. Perhaps there are three distinct words; that from √aç (which is rare, see P. W.) meaning 'attainment.'

satkârârho, 'worthy of being entertained.' For satkâra see i 7: arha iii 7 note. **uṣito**, p. p. of √vas to dwell, ii 12 note.

jalamâtreṇa vartayan = 'sustaining life (vartaya is causal of √vṛt, vi 4 note) by means of water alone.' This is a common use of **mâtra** at the end of a compound; see xi 39, uktamâtre tu vacane = 'when the word was only spoken,' i.e. 'but just spoken': xvi 5 jñâtamâtre, 'if it be only known': xx 44, rûpamâtra 'nothing but form.' At Hit. 80, 'na garbhacyutimâtreṇa putro bhavati paṇḍitaḥ' = 'not merely by being born does a boy become learned.' It is literally 'measure' = μέτρον, from √mâ, see i 15 note: such a compound is therefore a B. V. = 'having so and so (and no more) for its measure': comp. the common term, 'tan-mâtra,' for an atom or element.

11. **pîḍyamânaḥ**, v 2 note. **kṣudhâ**, instr. of kṣudh, 'hunger,' ix 28; kṣudhâ (fem.) is also found in the next line; also kṣudhita, p. p. of a verb kṣudh, at xi 12, xviii 12.

phalamûlâni, 'fruits and roots': a dvandva. Phala is from √phal, referred by Benfey to original SPAR, of which √sphar and √sphur are Sanskrit forms. Latin flos, Flora, &c. are doubtless cognate. Curtius connects both sets of words with Latin fla-re, Greek √φλα in παφλάζω, &c., our 'blow' &c., Gr. Et. no. 412. It occurs again at xx 9: and at xiii 22 'kasy' edaṃ karmaṇaḥ phalam?' 'of what action is this the fruit?' It bears the common sense of the result of past actions in this life or antecedent lives: see xii 33. Karma-phala is not either retribution for bad actions, nor the reward for good ones: it is (in effect) the transmigration from one terrestrial life to another, "the unavoidable effect of acts of all kinds being to entail repeated births through numberless existences until the attainment of final beatitude," 'Ind. Wisdom,' p. 217: see also pp. 292—4. This doctrine being once granted it is clear that the only wisdom lies in abstinence from all action, good, bad, and indifferent, as the quickest way of gaining freedom from new births and becoming absorbed into the supreme existence.

karṣayan, vii 14 note.

12. **bahutıthe 'hanı** = 'on a very long day': so xiii 2, 'kâle bahutıthe' = 'in long time.' Bahutıtha is formed from bahu by the suffix tıtha, so Pāṇ. 5. 2. 52: it is not a compound of bahu and tıthı (v 1). Yet it seems not impossible that the suffix may be the original noun, with its meaning lost. If so, the phrase would be curiously like the μυριέτης χρόνος of Aeschylus, Prom. Vinct. 94. For ahan see xii 61 note.

çakunân, 'birds,' ix 12: said to be the Indian vulture; but in the P. W. merely 'any great bird,' esp. those that give omens: for the neuter çakuna, see xiii 24.

hıraṇya-sadṛıça-c-chadân, 'having wings like gold': see vii 9, i 27 notes: chada ix 12 note. The *c* is euphonic, see M. W. Gr. § 48 b.

13. **bhakṣyo** = 'food,' fut. part. of √bhakṣ, xii 20, &c., akin to √bhaj, see v 23 note, and so to Gr. φαγεῖν.

14. 'Then he covered them with his clothing, his under garment.' **parıdhâna**, that which is wrapped round the body. **samâvṛıṇot**, imperf. of sam + â + √vṛı (5), M. W. Gr. § 675, iii 6 note.

âdâya, 'having taken,' from â + √dâ, 'to give.' This negative force of *â* in composition has been often already mentioned, see i 13 note.

vıhâyasâ, 'by' or 'through the air': prob. from vı + √hâ, but the suffix is not clear. √hâ (see xxvi 24 note) = Greek χα in χάος, &c. and Latin hisco, &c. Note the instrumental: this case is regularly used of the means of motion, offering herein an interesting parallel to the Lithuanian (see Schleicher, Lith. Gr. I 258); also to the Latin instrumental ablatives, e.g. (ire) via, fluvio, iugis, &c. It seems not unlikely (as Delbrück suggests) that the peculiar genitives in Homer such as πεδίοιο, with verbs of motion like διώκειν, θέειν, &c. (cf. Il. vi 507, xxiii 449) may be the Greek representation of this lost case-usage. See further note at xxvi 6 on paṇena paṇâvahe.

15. **utpatantaḥ**, i 23 note. **khagâ**, i 24 note.

dıgvâsasam, 'clothed with the sky' = naked, a descriptive compound. Compare dıg-ambara (ἀναβολή) the name of a sect of the Jains. Dıg = dıç, 'a quarter' or 'region' (of the sky): the root being used instead of the ordinary derivative deça, iv 25 note.

dinam, ii 2 note. **adhomukham**, 'with downcast face,' from adhas 'under,' which may be = ἔνθεν so far as form is concerned; but the meaning is not close.

16. **jıhirṣavaḥ**, nom. plur. of jıhirṣu, formed by suffix *u* from jıhirṣa, desiderative of √hṛı. For the vowel change cf. cıkirṣa, iii 14.

àgatà, 'arrived,' i 32 note. **hi**, here used exactly as γάρ, giving a parenthetic reason—οὐ γὰρ τὸ ἡμέτερον ἡδὺ πέπρακται.

savàsasi, sup. 6 note: it is locative absolute.

18. 'They by whose wrath I am fallen from my royalty...they, having become these vultures, are now bearing off my garment as well.' This conception of the embodiment of gods, and the inferior orders of supernatural powers in the shape of animals for some particular purpose, runs through all Indian mythology. Thus Vishṇu's first four incarnations were into (1) a fish to save the Manu from the deluge, (2) a tortoise to take part in the 'churning of the ocean of milk' (see note on Kāmaduh ii 18, and 'Indian Wisdom' p. 419) in order to procure the *amṛita*, or drink which gave immortality, &c. (3) a boar, in order to slay the demon Hiraṇyāksha, who had carried the earth down to the depths of the sea, (4) a lion, to kill another demon Hiraṇyakaçipu.

prakopàt, vi 14. **aiçvaryàt**, formed from içvara 'a lord' by vṛiddhi of first syllable, and suffix *ya*. **pracyuto**, p. p. of pra + √cyu 'to move,' or 'fall'; pari-cyuta occurs x 2; vicyuti xiii 34 = 'separation.' Benfey (lex. s. v.) connects A. S. 'scur,' our 'shower': also χέω and iacio: but these are more simply connected otherwise.

pràṇayàtram = 'the going on (i.e. 'support') of life': for pràṇa v 31 note.

vinde, ii 4 note.

19. **yeṣàṃ kṛite** = quorum opere: so mat-kṛite x 11. **mayi**, i 31 note. **te ime** = ii hi, or rather, illi ipsi (te) hi (ime), in *use*, not derivation.

20. **vaiṣamyaṃ**, viii 13 note. **hitam**, i 6 note.

21. 'There go many paths along the south road (or, simply, 'to the south,' patha being redundant, see xi 37 note) beyond Avanti and the mountain Ṛikṣavat.' **dakṣiṇà**, 'south,' because in looking east the right hand (see v 44) lies to the south. The Deccan, i. e. the south of India, still retains the name. Avanti, also called Ujjāyinī, whence the modern name Oujein, lying north of the Vindhya mountains, one of the seven sacred cities of India, capital of Vikramāditya. **Ṛikṣavat**, 'full of bears,' in the Vindhya mountains, the important chain which running east and west, north of the Narbadā forms the southern watershed of the tributaries of the Ganges. The river Payoshṇī rises in the Vindhyas.

samatikramya, so atikramya xxi 25. Here is a good example of an indecl. participle which has come to be nothing more than a prep.: literally it = 'having gone beyond,' but no reference being made to any special person, it is general 'for *all* that having gone beyond,' and so simply = 'beyond.' Just so uddiçya (inf. 24) is properly 'having pointed out,' but is regularly used for 'with reference to,' and simply = 'towards.' See note on i 22.

Latin datives of reference, such as 'descendentibus' (Livy I viii 4), 'intranti,' &c. perhaps appear more parallel than they really are.

22. **mahâçailaḥ**, 'the great mountain.' **çaila** is properly 'the rocky' from çilà 'a rock': comp. çilà-tala, lit. 'rock level' or 'surface,' xii 12, çiloccaya (i. e. çilà + uccaya = 'rock eminence' = 'mountain' ib. 37.

samudra-gâ = 'ocean-goer,' a frequent description of a river. Samudra contains the root of ὕδωρ (wrongly aspirated in Greek) and of unda.

âçramâs, 'abodes of hermits': from â + √çram (4) 'to be wearied,' p. p. çrânta inf. 28, xv 10, comp. xiii 6, probably from the primary idea of 'labour,' seen in çrama; and with *vi* at xxi 27. 'Çramaṇa' is the regular term for a Buddhist ascetic. The Brāhman who goes through the whole of his prescribed course is called in the fourth stage a 'bhīkshu,' i. e. mendicant; but still retains his priestly character: whereas a çramaṇa is in no sense a priest: he is more analogous to a monk. The third stage of the Brahman's life, however, corresponds better with the hermit-life—that in which he is called a 'vāna-prastha,' or dweller in the woods. In the first stage he is a 'Brahmachārin' or pupil; in the second a Gṛihastha or 'house-holder.' Each of these stages is technically called 'āçrama' (see 'Indian Wisdom,' p. 245) in a different sense from that in which the word is used here.

23. 'This is the Vidharba-road'—a rare instance where we should express by a compound that which the Sanskrit denotes by the genitive. Yet it is the simplest idea which the genitive conveys—connexion between two things,—a certain relation which must be explained more fully by the context, for the case does not explain. Thus (to take a well-known example), it is only from the context that we know whether 'hominum timor' means 'the fear felt by the men' (subjective) or 'the fear felt of the men' (objective): the difference in meaning is immense, yet the same genitive will equally express either.

Vidarbha, generally (as here) declined in the plural, is supposed to have been the modern Berar, the capital being Kuṇḍina-pura.

Koçala, generally supposed to be the country of which Ayodhyā (Oudh) was the capital. But it is also applied to places about the Vindhya mountains, and this is the required direction. Oudh lies northwards: whereas all Nala's instruction refers to a southerly journey.

ataḥ paraṃ = 'from thence beyond.' Atas has here the genuine ablative sense. So Hit. 769 'kiṃ nu duḥkham ataḥ paraṃ?' = 'what misery is greater than this?' So also ato 'nyathâ xiii 71. At Bhag. Gîta ii 12, it is used of time = 'henceforward.' Here 'and beyond, there is the region on the south on the southern route.' Comp. tataḥ prabhṛti ii 1.

24. **samâhitaḥ**, 'intent,' 'with his mind fixed thereupon': i 6, where the force is heightened by *su* in composition: the simple âhita = 'fixed,' 'undertaken,' 'determined,' at xiii 69, &c.

asakṛt, 'not once,' 'again and again.' Curtius (Gr. Et. no. 599), groups together words apparently so distinct as sa-kṛt, ἅ-παξ, ἁ-πλόο-ς, sim-plex, sin-guli, as all agreeing in the first part of the compound, *sa*, or *sam*, the second part differing according as it took people's fancy to say that things were 'cut' (√kart, Sk. √kṛt, see x 16 note), or 'folded' (√plic) 'together,' or the like, and so made 'one and undivided.' The word occurs again, xiii 69, xiv 2.

ârtto, vii 17 note. **uddiçya** = 'to': see note on line 21.

25. **uvâca...Naiṣadham...vacaḥ**, for construction see i 20, vii 5 notes.

karuṇaṃ, v 22.

26. **udvejate**, 'trembles,' from √vij (6. in the middle), rarely used alone: with *ut* at xiii 54, governing an ablative: Bh. G. ii 55, udvigna-manas: sam-vigna xiii 30, xix 7, nir-udvigna xiii 74 'undisquieted.' We have the derivative vega, xi 27, xiii 9.

sidanti, irreg. pres. of √sad, M. W. Gr. § 270, 'settle down,' 'sink.'

saṃkalpam, ii 29 note.

27. **tṛiṣâ** (also tṛiṣ, and tṛiṣṇâ, Hit. 497), 'thirst,' from √tṛiṣ, orig. TARS, a root found with great regularity in nearly all the languages, e.g. Gr. τέρσομαι, Lat. torreo and our 'thirst.' Tṛiṣâ = 'insatiability,' Hit. 650. Tṛiṣṇâ is an important word in Buddhist thought; it expresses desire arising from sensation, causing love of the world, and so all misery: see Rhys Davids' 'Buddhism,' p. 106.

utsṛijya, v 27 note. **nirjane**, 'unpeopled,' from nis (ix 6) and jana 'people,' generally collectively, ix 27, janena kliçyate bâlâ, and often at the end of a compound, as sakhi-jana ii 5. It is used with ayam of a single person, like ὅδ' ἀνήρ in Greek. At x 9 it is used alone of one person.

28. **çrántasya**, see note on áçrama, sup. 22. **náçayiṣyámi**, 2 fut. of náçaya, causal of √naç (viii 18) = 'I will do away with thy weariness,' so xi 25. **klama**, xi 1, from √klam, whence p. p. klánta xxi 27. Phonetically the two roots with the same meaning — √klam and √çram—might be identical; but perhaps it is not safe to assume this. Neither has any clear analogues in other languages, for Bopp's comparison of κάμ-νω, and suggestion of lentus (i.e. *clentus) and claudus, are certainly wrong.

29. 'And no medicine is there found, known of physicians, like unto a wife in all miseries.' **vidyate**, from √vind, ii 4 note: observe the loss of the nasal in the passive which is usual, M. W. Gr. § 469. **bhiṣaj**, 'a physician,' almost certainly from abhi + √sañj exactly as our 'bishop' has been mutilated from ἐπίσκοπος. For √sañj, see v 9 note; for the genitive with mata, i 4 note. From bhiṣaj is formed bheṣaja, 'medicine' (next line), and bhaiṣajya 'a drug,' Hit. 559. **auṣadha**, 'medicine,' is formed from oṣadi 'a plant' of very uncertain origin; Benfey suggests √uṣ: according to the P. W. it is contracted from avasa (refreshment) + dhi.

30. **áttha**, from √áh, vii 4 note.

31. **tyaktu-kámas tvám**, 'desirous to leave thee': comp. utsraṣṭu-káma xiv 10, kartukáma xix 5. **tvám** follows tyaktukámas, a B. V. compound (see ii 27 note), just as it might follow a desiderative, such as tityakṣu. The compound is interesting, as shewing the elements of the Latin construction of the supine in *u* with a noun, e.g. 'bonum uisu' (for uisui) 'good for the seeing'; for uisu (i.e. uid-tu) is a noun formed from uid, just as tyak-tu from tyaj.

çan·kase, viii 3 note.

tyajeyam, &c. 'I could leave myself rather than thee.' For this use of the optative, see i 30 note. **na ca**, this (with varam) is an idiomatic use in comparisons, instead of the regular ablative. Sometimes we find a mixture of constructions, e.g. Hit. 37, varam eko guṇi putro, na ca múrkhaçatair api, i.e. 'better one virtuous son than even a thousand fools.' If our 'better than' arises as I suppose from 'better (is A), *then* (B),' we may see how such constructions are naturally developed out of two paratactic clauses.

32. **icchasi**, i 1 note. **samupadiçyate**, iv 25 note.

33. **avaimi**, 'I understand,' ava + √i, lit. 'I come down upon it.'

na tu...tu. Similarly a Greek might express a like disjunction by οὔτε...τε (not οὐδέ...δέ), but of course more idiomatically by μέν...δέ. 'Although thou dost not think fit to leave me, yet with mind distracted thou mightest leave me.'

34. 'Because (*hi*) thou tellest me repeatedly of the way, thou highest of mankind, from this very cause thou makest my sorrow increase, thou who art like a god.' We might almost render *hi*, as 'why,' in our colloquial use—here again it corresponds to Greek γάρ: see i 29 note.

abhikṣṇam, an Av. B. compound of abhi + ikṣṇa, perhaps, as Benfey suggests, shortened from ikṣaṇa 'an eye' found (in different compounds) at xi 27, xii 30, xvi 21. It means 'repeatedly,' but how, is not easy to see. If kṣaṇa be from the same word (ii 3 note)—and kṣaṇena certainly means 'momentarily'—then it would seem that ikṣaṇa had got the sense 'moment,' apparently through the idea of 'a glance of the eye,' like the German 'augenblick.' Then abhikṣṇaṃ would mean literally 'a moment thereupon' (abhi), and so 'each moment,' 'repeatedly.' So we have some Greek adverbs compounded with ἐπί, e.g. ἐπιδέξια, ἐπιπλέον.

ato nimittam, compare tataḥ prabhṛti, ii 1. Nimittam is often used in this redundant way with pronouns, e.g. 'kin-nimittam,' 'why,' literally 'having what as its cause,' i.e. a B. V. compound (cf. the common 'kim-artham,' 'why,' ix 32, xi 23), 'kuto nimittam' = 'whence?' At xiv 19 we have viṣa-nimittâ pidâ, i.e. 'annoyance because of poison.' Nimittam (alone) is found xxiii 5 = 'sign,' 'token.' At Bh. G. i 31, nimittâni viparitâni = 'adverse omens': Arjuna is about to fight with his kindred, and the sight of them drawn up in battle array is a nimittam or 'sign' of evil. In the logic of the Vaiçeshika system 'nimitta-kâraṇa' is the instrumental cause, corresponding (although loosely) to Aristotle's efficient cause: 'Indian Wisdom,' p. 81.

35. 'And if this be thy intention, "she is to go to her kinsfolk."' Observe how briefly the Sanskrit can thus express with *iti* (see i 32 note), what would require in the classical languages a long apposition, or a subordinate clause. It must not be supposed that the mood is here used in the same way in which we should expect a conjunctive or optative in such a dependent clause. It is perfectly independent—'she is to go at some indefinite time'; see note on i 30. But such a construction is wonderfully instructive, as shewing the origin of the mood in really dependent clauses. In these it is

difficult (when the usage is once firmly established) not to suppose that the mood depends on the particle of purpose (ἵνα, ὅπως, or the like) as we call it. Yet nothing can be more certain than that the idea of 'purpose' first developed itself out of the mere collocation of two independent statements, and that the particle was only a sign to denote the closeness of that combination. Then as time went on, the mood which had practically ceased to be used independently, seemed to have a natural fitness to express 'purpose' or the like. Compare xiv 14, and note there.

abhiprâyas, from abhi + pra + √i with suffix *a* = 'purpose,' 'plan,' xxiv 5: comp. Sâv. iii 7.

vrajet, viii 5 note.

36. **pûjayiṣyati**, 'shall honour,' √pûj (10) really a denominative of pûjâ, ii 12.

1. This line seems to mean 'great as is thy father's realm, so great also is mine,' i.e. 'in thy father's realm I can do what I like.' This is parallel to xvii 16,

> yathaiva te pitur geham, tathaiva mama, bhâvini,
> yathaiva ca mam' aiçvaryam, Damayanti, tathâ tava.

Dean Milman construes "Mighty is thy father's kingdom, once was mine as mighty too": but this seems to require âsit or some such past tense, to make the meaning plain. The first interpretation seems also to suit best with the following line 'But I will *not* go there, &c.'

na saṃçayaḥ, 'there is no doubt,' used adverbially here and at xvii 19, xviii 8, xxii 25, like the common asaṃçayaṃ, xiii 70, and niḥ-saṃçayam, x 12: the word is derived from sam + √çi (κεῖμαι), but the connection is not very obvious. Does it mean 'lying close together' and so 'confusion'?

viṣamastha, viii 13 note.

2. **samṛiddho**, 'prosperous,' sam + √ṛidh 'to grow,' orig. ARDH, whence *ἀλθ-αίνω*, &c. in Greek, Curt. Gr. Et. no. 303. It, therefore, properly = 'grown up,' 'increased.' The simple p. p. ṛiddha occurs xii 59, in the sense of happy and giving happiness: samṛiddha, 'wealthy,' xiii 15. The root and its derivative must be separated from VARDH (viii 14) with the same meaning; both roots are found in the derived languages: and we cannot assume either the loss of v in Indo-European times, or that v is the remnant of some lost preposition.

harṣa, i 24 note.

paricyuto, ix 18 note.

3. **çântvayâmâsa**, viii 12 note. **vâsaso 'rddhena**, 'with the half of a garment,' agreeing with our English idiom. Vastr-ârddha (T. P. compound) occurs at x 16.

4.   aṭamánau, ii 13 note. pipásá, 'desire to drink,' 'thirst,'
formed from pipása, desiderative of √pá.

sabhám, 'a dwelling,' see iii 5 note.

upeyathuḥ, 3rd pers. dual of upa + ıyáya, perf. of √ı.   M. W.
Gr. § 645, M. M. App. no. 171.

5.   mahitale = bhútale, ii 28 note.

6.   vivastro, ix 5 note.

vikaṭo, 'without mat' (kaṭa, probably = karta from √kar, Benfey).

malinaḥ, 'muddy,' xii 23, from mala 'mud,' xvi 13, xvii 6 ;
nir-mala, 'clear' (of water), xiii 4. Curtius (Gr. Et. no. 551) connects
the word with μέλας, μολύνω, μολοβρός (Od. xvii 219), and Lat.
malus, &c. (comparing for the latter Horace's line, 'hic niger est,
hunc tu, Romane, caueto.'   Sat. i iv 85).

pámçu-guṇṭhitaḥ, 'dust-covered,' p. p. of √guṇṭh : neither
word seems to have any analogues.

suṣvápa, perf. of √svap = orig. SVAP, whence sopor, ὕπνος, &c.;
the p. p. supta occurs, x 19.

7.   nidrayá, instr. of nidrá, 'sleep,' from √drá or √draı. The
original form must have been DAR; of which dorm-io shews a secondary root : the modified √dra appears in ἔ-δρα-θον, &c.

apahṛitá, 'carried off,' or, as we say, 'surprised by sleep.'
sahasá, v 28 ; iii 8 note.

ásádya, 'having found,' 'lighted upon,' xiii 5, samásádya xxiii
5, from á + sádaya, causal of √sad, 'to settle down,' so puram
ásádayat, xiii 45, also ásasáda, inf. 18, xx 6, and ásáditá, xvii 4. For
√sad see i 8.

8.   sma, i 12 note. unmathita, 'stirred up' from √math, 'to
churn,' see i 14 note.

9.   suhṛit-tyágam, 'desertion of his friends.'   In the next line
occurs janasya parityága. Either suhṛid or janasya might be
'subjective' or 'objective.' The sense seems to fix suhṛid at least
as subjective. On the other hand it is best to take 'janasya' as
objective, 'the forsaking of my people,' i.e. Damayanti, see ix 27,
note, not as a repetition of suhṛittyága. The variation of construction may point in the same direction. For tyága, ii 17, note.

paridhvaṃsam, 'distress,' 'ruin'; from √dhvaṃs, 'to perish,'
see note on xii 115.

cintám, &c., 'he betook himself to thought.'

upeyiván, masc. nom. of upeyivas (the simple form ıyıvas, xi

33), a past active participle of a somewhat rare form. Instead of adding *-vat* to the base of the past passive participle, as in dṛṣṭa-vat i 29 (where see note), kṛta-vat ix 9, práptavat xiii 33, &c., the language forms these by adding *-vas* to the perfect base; e.g. under √vid we get vivid + vas: when that base consists of one syllable only (from contraction or any other reason) an *i* is inserted between it and the suffix; e.g. from √tan we have tenivas, i.e. tatan-i-vas. For the declension of these participles, see M. M. Gr. § 204, 205, M. W. Gr. § 168. The *n* of the nom. sing. du. pl., and acc. sing. dual, is accounted for as an insertion before final *s* which it then ejects; so that the result is upeyiván, not upeyivás as it should be, if the base ends in *as*. But clearly the nominative is formed from the base when ending in the original suffix *-vant*, afterwards weakened into *vat* (cf. Greek Ϝοτ, i 29 note), and into *vas*. The *n* is then perfectly proper. See note on çocan, viii 24.

Note the omission of the verb with the participle: so also at ix 9. The 3rd persons 1 fut. really shew the same omission in regular use: for bhavitá, bhartá, &c. are nothing but nominatives sing. of bhavitṛ, bhartṛ, &c.: 'he shall be' is reached through the idea 'he is one that is,' and so will continue to be: and the dual and plural shew the same omission of the verb; which is found in the other persons, bhavitásmi, i.e. bhavitá + asmi, &c. Exactly parallel (though in the 2nd person) are the Latin 'regi-mini, &c.,' and the archaic singular, as in the XII. Tabb. 'ni it, antestamino,' 'unless he goes, call a witness,' for antestaminos (later *-us*).

10. 'What will become of me if I do it? or what if I do it not?' **kiṃ syát** corresponds to the conjunctivus deliberativus of Greek and Latin, except that the form is optative—as indeed 'sit' (= siet) is in Latin. See i 30 note; and compare v 12, ix 27, and especially **xix** 4, and note. **kṛtvá** is supposed to agree here with me, just as akurvataḥ does in the next clause. But the old sense of the instrumental is here plain—'by the doing of this,' the noun taking an accusative just like the rare examples in Plautus. See note on i 22. For **nu**, see viii 17 note.

akurvat is the pres. part. of √kṛ with negative *a*; see note on açaknuvan i 18.

me must be regarded as genitive because of akurvataḥ, otherwise the dative would have seemed most natural, just as in Greek in the already quoted passage (at viii 17), τί νύ μοι μήκιστα γένηται. But we have already seen that the genitive is frequently used with

Sanskrit verbs, where the dative is found in the classical languages :
see note on v 38.   In Latin, 'quid me fiat,' or 'quid hoc homine
faciatis' (Cic. Verr. i 16), is slightly different : here the ablative
certainly represents the instrumental 'what will be done *with* me,'
just as in the construction with opus and usus, and with fungor,
fruor, utor, uescor.

'Is death for me a better thing, or the forsaking of my people ?'
where 'of' gives the same ambiguity as the Sanskrit genitive ; see
note on last line.

çreyas, a comparative (and superlative, çreṣṭha at i 3, iv 20),
with no regular positive adj.   It is used as a noun, xii 89.   They
are certainly connected with çri = fortune, success, beauty, &c., and,
as good luck embodied, the common title of Lakshmī, the wife of
Vishṇu, who sprang (like Aphrodite) from the ocean of milk, at the
churning thereof (ii 18 note).   The name is often compared with
the Italian Ceres, but without much real analogy : and Ceres is
doubtless formed directly from √ker, orig. KAR, like Cerus, 'the
maker,' in the Carmen Saliare.

11.   anuraktá, v 22 note, both for the word and for the construction.

madvihiná, 'reft of me,' v 24 note.

pratı, one of the few prepositions used regularly in Sanskrit
with—or rather *after*—a noun, see note on anu, ii 27.   It is noteworthy (as shewing the little inclination of Sanskrit to the use of
prepositions), that this is just the one which seems to have been
least required : it denotes 'motion to' or 'reference to' (ii 7 note) :
but 'motion to' is just one of those usages for which all languages
could employ the simple accusative without any preposition at all.
Pratı (= Greek προτί, πρός), was originally the adverb 'forward';
and in the sense 'furthermore,' πρός was used adverbially even in
Greek.

12.   anuvratá, ii 14.   mayı must go with prápsyatı 'will find
in me.'

utsarge, v 27 note.   saṃçayaḥ, 'doubt,' 'possibility,' i.e. of
her faring better, a rather unusual use, I think, of the word—probably because of nıhsaṃçayam, above.

13 a.   = v 15 a.

14.   çaktá, &c., 'capable of being harmed by any person on the
road': for the peculiarity of the construction see vii 10 note.   For
the instrumental, comp. xvi 25, yuktaṃ samáçvásayıtum mayá.

dharṣayitum, iii 15 note. **tejasá**, 'by reason of her splendour,' iv 26 note.

yaçasvini, 'she the illustrious.' Yaças, although not always distinct in use from tejas (they occur together at i 10), has a different original, see i 8 note.

mahábhágá, 'she whose lot is high.' Bhága occurred in the sense of 'lot,' 'portion' at viii 6 (bhágadeya). For the √bhaj, bhakta, and other words, see v 23. Mahábhága is also used for 'eminent in virtue' (xii 63), which would suit the context here very well: comp. mandabhágya, xiii 38, alpabhágya, xv 19. This sense, though apparently analogous to that of bhakti, did not come in the same way: it is the merit obtained in former existences, which determines a man's 'lot' or 'fortune' afterwards.

15. **nyavartata**, vi 4 note. **duṣṭabhávena**, viii 18 note: duṣṭa, 'corrupt,' is p. p. of √duṣ, 'to sin,' 'to be depraved.' Curtius, Gr. Et. no. 279, connects with it the Sanskrit and Greek prefix *dus*, and also √dviṣ, 'to hate,' ix 9; this last is less likely, for duṣ does not seem to be used actively 'to hurt' as Curtius takes it. Doṣa = fault, iv 21, &c.

visarjane. For the case, iii 6, note.

16. **avakartanam**, 'the cutting off,' from √kṛt, orig. KART, whence cort-ex, cult-er (possibly) and probably Gr. κέρτ-ομο-ς: it is a secondary root from KAR, whence κείρω, curtus, &c., Curtius Gr. Et. no. 53. The oldest form was probably SKAR, whence our 'shear' &c.

17. **vikarteyam, na ca budhyeta**: note again the old paratactic form of expression; though the first member gives the main thought, the second only a condition under which it is to be performed. Yet that condition being here of very great importance, it is natural that it should receive equal prominence. In Latin we might also have had, 'quomodo scindam, neque sentiet uxor mea,' but rather 'quo modo ita scindam ut non sentiat.' In English we have the convenient prepositional clause 'without her knowing.' A Greek would probably have kept the two clauses with a μέν and a δέ: perhaps the neatest and clearest way of all.

18. **paridhávann**, i 26 note.

uddeçe, (1) a pointing out, (2) a region, like deça, iv 25.

vikoṣam, 'unsheathed,' from koṣa or koça, 'a sheath': it has many other apparently incongruous meanings, but all apparently give the idea of a covering: at xxvi 19 it = treasure. Benfey connects with κόκκος (Gr. Wörterbuch, ii 159) as though the primary idea were 'roundness.'

khaḍgam, 'a sword,' xxvi 17, but also 'a rhinoceros.' Is it so called from some likeness to the rhinoceros' horn? We have a far-away analogy in the name rhinoceros used for the horn alone in Juvenal. But in the P. W. the meaning 'sword' is given first.

19. **nivasya**, ix 6 note. **paraṃtapaḥ** = 'foe-troubler': for the form of the compound see page 6; for para ii 2 note. Tapa is from √tap, 'to warm,' in the first place; whence tapas 'heat,' and Lat. 'tepeo' &c., Greek τέφρα, 'ashes.' But the secondary sense of tapas (and the commoner) in Sanskrit is 'pain': and hence it is commonly used (e.g. xii 70, 92, &c.) for the mortification by which each man was expected to subdue all desires and passions as the surest way of liberation from the succession of lives on earth: see note on ii 13. Hence come the terms 'tapasvin' xii 67, and 'tapodhana' xii 69 for those who thus mortify themselves; also the derivative 'tâpasa' xii 61.

prâdravad, 'ran away,' from pra + â + √dru 'to run,' see i 25 note.

20. **nivṛitta-hṛidayaḥ**, 'with heart turned back': vi 4 note.

ruroda, 'wept,' from √rud (2 cl.) = Lat. rudo, lifting up the voice being the common meaning. The present is rodimi (xi 11, 14 &c.) where *i* is irregularly inserted. The root is certainly connected, probably as a secondary, with √ru, whence rava 'a cry' and ârâva, id. xiii 16, Greek ὠ-ρύ-ω and possibly ὀ-ρυ-μαγδός: in Latin we have raucus: and rumor may come from either ru or rud. See, generally, Gr. Et. no. 523. The part. rudat occurs frequently, e.g. ii 4.

21. **vâyu**, 'wind,' from √vâ 'to blow,' whence also vâta xix 14, xxii 9, Latin ventus and our own word. An older form is AV which the Greek preserved in αὖρα, and which is also seen without the v in ἄημι, ἀήρ &c.

âdityaḥ, 'sun': the name is formed from Aditi, 'infinity'; or (personified) the mother of the Gods. In the Vedas we find seven, and in later times twelve Âdityas, i.e. the sun conceived of in different characters at different parts of the year. For the primary meaning of the term see M. Müller, Ṛigveda Saṃhitā, vol. 1, pp. 230—249, and Dowson, Cl. Dict. s. v. Vāyu was also personified as one of the oldest deities: but here both vâyu and âditya are used simply as wind and sun. At line 24 however we have the plural 'âdityâḥ.'

anâthavat, 'without protector,' used here adverbially—not in the fem. nominative, anáthavati. Nátha, 'a protector,' 'master,' 'lord,' is of uncertain derivation. It is familiar to us in the name 'Jagannáth' (i. e. lord of the earth—jagat—but commonly spelt Juggernaut) a name of Vishṇu or Kṛishṇa.

22. **saṃvitá**, ix 6 note. **cáruhásini**, iii 14 note. **varároha**, 'of fair waist,' viii 19 note.

buddhvá, 'having wakened,' comp. abudhyata, xi 1; also xiii 19: so used with pra, Hit. 1041.

23. **eká sati** = μόνη οὖσα, 'when she is alone,' comp. ekákini sati xii 25. Sati must not be taken here in the sense which it often bears elsewhere of 'good,' literally 'existent,' and so 'real,' 'genuine,' 'excellent.' The word is well known (under the form Suttee) as applied to the faithful wife who sacrifices herself on her husband's funeral pile. Such sacrifice was barely known in the Epic period—certainly it was not then a custom. Neither is it found in the Mānava code, wherein second marriage is prohibited to a widow: see note on xix 4. See 'Ind. Wisdom,' 315, compare p. 258 note.

mṛiga, 'a deer,' xi 26, 30—also used of any kind of beast (as of a tiger xii 34). It also = 'hunting,' 'search,' as in mṛiga-jivana xi 28; and the denominative verb, mṛigaya, xii 118, xiii 65. It may come (so far as the form goes) from √mṛij, 'to cleanse': but the connection of sense is not obvious. Márjára, 'a cat,' from that root, seems natural enough.

vyála, 'a serpent,' originally an adjective = 'wicked,' and applied to different beasts, but especially to the serpent.

nishevite, 'inhabited by.' This is the commonest meaning of sevita, both alone (xii 2) and with ni. The verb sev has many meanings, e. g. 'to apply oneself to,' 'practise,' 'dwell,' 'observe,' 'honour'—all shades which are found in the unconnected Latin colo. It used to be identified at once with Greek σέβω; which is wrong, for Sanskrit ē can never correspond to Greek ε or Latin ĕ; neither can Sanskrit ō correspond to Greek ο or Latin ŏ: this general rule may guard us from identifications which are so obvious as e.g. of Sanskrit ēkatara with ἑκάτερος, or of Sanskrit lōka with locus. But it is quite possible that sēv may be contracted for sa-sav (compare the regular contraction in the perfect, e.g. ta-tan = ten, perhaps through te-t(a)n, as Latin fecit, compared with Oscan fe-fac-id), and then √sav would correspond rightly to the root of σέβω, σέβας, Lat. severus &c., cf. Curtius, II 218 (Eng. tr.). At Çak. i 29 the verb is used of observing a vow 'vrataṃ nishevitavyam.' Sevá = service, Hit. 641.

24. **Vasavaḥ**. The Vasus, like the Ādityas, are represented as children of Aditi. "They seem to have been in Vedic times personifications of natural phenomena. They are Āpa (water), Dhruva (pole-star), Soma (moon), Dhara (earth), Anila (wind), Anala (fire), Prabhāsa (dawn), and Pratyūsha (light)," Dowson, s. v. In book v of the Mahābhārata, they with the Ādityas, Açvins, Maruts, &c. are all manifested from the body of Kṛishṇa, who thus represents the eternal principle of all life: see 'Ind. Wisdom,' p. 400, and compare the 'viçvarūpadarçana,' or 'manifestation of all form' by Kṛishṇa to Arjuna in the 11th chapter of the Bhagavad-Gītā.

Rudrā. Rudra in the Ṛig-Veda is the storm-god, and when he is pluralized as here, we probably have only an extension of his attributes. In later mythology he is identified with the god Çiva, chiefly in his destructive aspect. This constant identification of deities is a source of much difficulty. "There can be no doubt that a change of name in Hindu mythology does not necessarily imply the creation of a new Deity. Indra, Vāyu, the Maruts and Rudras, appear to have been all forms and modifications of each other, and these with different names in the later mythology were gathered into the one personification Çiva. Similarly Sūrya, the sun, had various forms such as the Ādityas." M. Williams, 'Hinduism,' p. 25. These companies of semi-deities still are objects of the Hindu worship; "the ten Viçva-devas; the eight Vasus; the eleven Rudras; the twelve Ādityas; the Sādhyas, celestial beings of peculiar purity; the Siddhas, semidivine beings of great perfection." Ib. p. 167.

Açvinau, i 27 note. **samarudgaṇau**, a B. V. compound agreeing with Açvinau, 'having with them the company of the Maruts.' The Maruts or storm-gods are plural even in the Vedic hymns, many of which are addressed to them (see M. Müller's Ṛig-veda-saṃhitā, Vol. 1). "Various origins are assigned to them; they are sons of Rudra, sons and brothers of Indra, sons of the ocean, sons of heaven, sons of earth": Dowson, s. v. A full account of the Vedic character of all these deities will be found in Vol. v of Dr Muir's Sanskrit Texts.

dharmeṇa, 'by thy own virtue art thou thoroughly guarded.' Dharma may be rendered 'virtue' here, and is often rendered 'duty.' Yet neither word conveys the exact meaning. Dharma is the exact performance of the duties of each particular caste. Thus there is no one dharma alike for all men: the dharma of the Brāhman differed from the dharma of a Kshatriya, see note on dharmavid i 7. For the duties incumbent on every Brāhman see M. Williams, 'Hinduism,' pp. 59—68. The performance of these duties constituted 'merit,' which is also called dharma. The 'strīṇāṃ dharmás' or 'duties of women' are described in Manu v 146—166: the essence of them is dependence on a husband.

25. **apratımám**, i 15 note. **bhuvı**, 'on the earth,' loc. of bhú, i 15 note.

udyataḥ, 'eager,' 'hurriedly': p. p. of ud + √yam, 'to lift up'; and so the p. p. 'uplifted,' 'intent,' 'ready.'

26. **muhuḥ**, 'for a moment,' perhaps xi 14; whence muhúrta, xi 7: often (doubled) = 'repeatedly,' xi 20: and apparently in that sense here and xi 19. Origin unknown.

ákṛıṣyamáṇaḥ, pres. pass. part. of á + √kṛıṣ, vii 14 note, = 'torn away,' lit. 'dragged by Kali *to* himself.' **avakṛıṣyate**, 'he is drawn back (or, more exactly 'down') by his affection.'

27. **dvıdhá** = δίχα (in meaning at least), 'in two ways,' 'asunder.'

dolá, 'a swing': there is a root dul probably weakened from √tul 'to lift' (whence tulá, a balance), iv 6 note.

áyátı, 'comes,' i 13 note.

28. **vılapya**, vii 17 note.

29. **naṣṭ-átmá**, 'his very soul destroyed': so naṣṭa-rúpa, xxii 15; naṣṭa is p. p. of √naç, viii 18: vı-naṣṭa occurs xi 3: sam-pra-naṣṭa xx 40. 'Átman' is much wider than 'manas': from which it is always to be distinguished. Manas is an internal organ of perception, distinct from, but correlative to the five organs of sense, and the five organs of action; see note on ındrıya, i 4. The soul on the other hand is universally diffused, though it acts and feels only in the body to which it belongs.

vıgaṇayan, 'counting over,' 'thinking on,' xxi 23, from vı + √gaṇ (10) 'to count,' alone at xiv 11, xx 13. Probably, as Benfey suggests, it is a denominative verb from gaṇa, a multitude, ii 6 &c.

çúṇye, 'empty,' xii 1 &c., = κενός, or more nearly the Ion. κενεός, where ε corresponds to Sk. *y*. But the reason of the Sk. *u* is not clear. Comp. √çudh, viii 18, for the same weakening.

1. **apakrànte**, ix 6 note. **gata-klamà**, ix 28 note.
abudhyata, 'awoke,' so buddhvà, x 22.
sam-trastà = 'con-territa': again at xiii 19; vitràsita (causal), xvi 15. It is the p. p. of sam + tras, orig. TRAS, whence Gr. √τρες in τρέω (but best seen in aor. τρέσ-σα, Il. xi 546, &c.), τρήρων, &c.; terreo, terror: we have tràsa, 'fear,' Hit. 539. It is of course distinct from the root TRAS, to be dry, ix 27.

2. **pràkroçàd**, 'cried aloud,' here with acc. Naiṣadham. The root is kruç, apparently original KRUK; whence κραυγή, 'a cry,' might come by weakening of *k* to *g*; and κρώζω seems to be akin. It is used intransitively at xxiii 22, xxiv 43: the perfect pra-cakruçuḥ, xii 116. Hence anukroça, xvii 42.
uccaiḥ, 'shrilly,' = instr. plur. of ucca, 'high'; acc. to Benfey, from ud + √añc, like nica, 'low' (xxi 14), from ni + √añc.

3. **jahàsi**, from hà (3 cl.): M. W. Gr. § 665, M. M. App. no. 196.
vinaṣṭa, x 29 note.

4. **nanu nàma**: a strong interrogative, 'art thou not surely'; no doubt first of all literally 'in thy very name.' It is used as here with nanu (xii 19), with api (Çak. i 22), with ka (Hit. 558), and even alone as xxiv 10: 'pùrvaṃ dṛṣṭas tvayà kaçcid dharmajño *nàma*, Vàhuka, suptàm utsṛjya vipine gato yaḥ puruṣaḥ striyam?' Benfey compares quis-nam, &c. in Latin: this would be a very interesting coincidence of use, but *o* must in all probability have been established in this word instead of *ā* in Graeco-Italian times: though the *ā* is still seen in gnā-ru-s.
uktvà satyam, not in the common sense 'having said a true thing'; but equivalent to satyavàc in the previous half-line. 'How then art thou one that hast spoken truth (i.e. truthful) in that thou hast left me asleep and gone?'

5. **dakṣâm**, 'fit,' 'suitable,' the simpler form of dakṣiṇa = δεξιός and dexter. Cf. Hit. 832, 'sâ bhâryâ, yâ gṛhe dakṣâ.'

viçeṣato, &c., 'there being especially no wrong done (by her), but there being wrong done by another,' i.e. Pushkara. For **viçeṣatas**, see i 30 note. **Apa** + √kṛi = 'take away,' and so 'harm,' 'injure'; so also with *ni*, xiv 15, xix 5. **sati**, redundant with apakṛite, comp. xvi 37, evaṃgatâ sati.

6. **samyak**, viii 13 note. Here with √kṛi it seems to mean 'to make good.'

7. 'At one fit time (lit. not at a wrong time) is appointed the death of mortal men: inasmuch as thy loved one, forsaken by thee, lives even for an hour,' i.e. were it not fated that she must live her due time, she could not have lived even an hour after her desertion: she must have died at once. **vihito**, see v 19 note. **yatra** = 'where': but indirectly gives the reason here, as though = '*in* which state of things.' The use of ἵνα, though that is an old instrumental, not locative, is somewhat parallel in phrases like ἵν' ἦν τυφλός τε καὶ κλύων μηδέν, Oed. Tyr. 1389: 'in which case I were (would have been) blind or dumb': comp. the use of ὡς (old ablative) ib. 1392. But the usage with the *past* tenses of the indicative is peculiar to the Greek language, I think. **muhûrtaṃ**: see v 1: again at xvii 12.

8. 'Sufficient is thy sport, up to this point,' i.e. go no farther. **âpta**, the p. p. of √âp, to get, has the same sense as Lat. aptus, i.e. 'fit.' Comp. âpta-kârin, viii 11: and so with pari = sufficient, complete.

parihâsa, from √has, see iii 14 note. **etâvân**, from etad + vat.

atidurdharṣa, 'reckless king'; lit. 'exceedingly difficult to crush,' from √dṛiṣ, iii 15 note.

9. **gulmair**, 'in the bushes,' or rather, 'having hidden thyself *by* the bushes' (instrumental): for gulma see xiii 12.

10. 'O king, injurious in sooth, because that thou comest not to me in this stress, and comfortest me not.' **nṛi-çaṃsa** = 'man-injuring'; çaṃsa from √ças: if the original meaning be 'to cut' (Grassmann, s.v.), Benfey is doubtless right in comparing Lat. castrare. We have viçasya, xi 28, and çastra, a sword, ii 18. This root is obscure. The same compound occurs in the sense 'wicked,' xix 5: see also xvii 43. **vata**, an intensifying particle, perhaps = *va* + *ta*, *va* being the base from which comes *vai* used in the same way, vii 4, &c.

yat = quod, see vi 6 note. **âçvâsayasi**, xi 10 note, and ii 2.

11. **rodimi**, 'I wail,' from √rud (x 20 note). This verb of the

2nd class is exceptional in inserting an ı (euphonic) before the consonantal terminations except *y*. (M. W. Gr. § 326, M. M. App. 176.) As it also regularly gunates before the P terminations (M. W. Gr. § 244), the present singular is rod-ı-mı, rod-ı-ṣı, rod-ı-tı (xi 14), rud-ı-vas, &c.

12. **tṛṣıtaḥ, kṣudhıtaḥ**, ix 27.

sàyàhne, 'at the evening,' so xiii 45. Sàya, alone, expresses the same thing; see xv 9, 'sàyaṃ sàyam' = 'evening by evening': ahne (from ahna, used in compounds instead of ahan, a day) is redundant. **vṛıkṣa-mûleṣu**, 'among the roots of the trees': for mùla, see ix 11. **vṛıkṣa**, perhaps from √vṛh, a weakened Sanskrit form of vṛdh, viii 14.

13. **tivra**, 'sharp,' 'violent': so tivra-roṣa, xi 35: commonly with çoka, e.g. xxiv 8: connected by Benfey with √tıj, whence tejas, &c., see x 14. **manyunà**, ix 4 note. **pradiptà**, 'lit up,' 'enflamed,' from pra + √dip, 'to shine,' p. p. dipta, xi 36; intensive, dedipyamàna, iii 12: a rather common Sanskrit secondary of √dị, which is Vedic: see note on dina, ii 2.

14. **vıhvalà**, 'agitated,' xii 55: from √hval, 'to shake,' of doubtful origin.

àliyate, 'she sinks helpless,' 'faints,' from à + √li, to melt. See note on vii 17.

16. **abhıçàpàd**, 'curse': see v 28 note.

abhyadhıkam, 'in excess, over and above,' abhi being redundant: comp. datà abhyadhıkaḥ, xxi 14. adhıka, at xvi 9, = 'excessively': it is frequently so used with the ablative of comparison, which here shews its primary signification, 'setting out from our sorrow, a sorrow in excess.' See note on tvad-anya, i 21. The simple form occurs at xvii 19, 'sukhàt sukhataro vàsaḥ.' For adhıka as used in numeration see xx 9.

bhavet is here doubtless optative in sense: compare vi 11. We have the imperative **jivatu** in the same connection of thought in the next line.

17. **kṛıtavàn**, i 29 note.

18. **anveṣàṃànà**, 'seeking after,' from anu + √ıṣ, to go, iii 7 note.

çvàpada, a wild beast, xv 19. çvapad is also found: the apparent derivation 'dog-foot' seems to imply speed.

19. **dhàvatı**, i 26 note. Below at 23, anu-dhàvası.

20. **krandamàṇàm**, 'crying miserably,' from √krand, probably a nasalised form of √krad, which is Vedic. It occurs with à, xi 26.

They are doubtless of the same family as √kruç (sup. line 2): and κρώζω (there quoted) may be for *krad-yo*. Benfey (Lex. s.v.) compares κ-έ-λαδος, which is probable enough: but κρήνη and κρουνός are much less likely: κρήνη is connected by Curtius with κάρα = the head of the stream.

atyartham, 'exceedingly'; iii 7 note.

kurarim, 'an osprey,' xii 113, where the cry seems to be regarded as agreeable: and it is probably only meant to express loudness here.

vâçatim, 'screaming,' pres. part. of √vâç (or √vâs), to scream: Megh. 43. If the ç be the true spelling, then it may be a variant of VAK, whence the common √vâc, 'speak.'

muhur muhuḥ, x 26 note.

21. **abhyâsa**, ix 10 note. **parivartinim**; pari merely increases the general force of √vṛit, vi 4 note.

jagrâha, perf. of √grah, 'to seize': see i 19 note.

ajagaro, 'a boa constrictor' = 'goat swallower,' from aja, a goat (αἴξ, &c.), and gara, from √gṛi (6 cl.), orig. GAR, whence this base and √βορ (by labialism) in βορά, βιβρώσκω, &c.: also in Lat. gula, gur-gul-io (where the *u* marks the Graeco-Italian *gu*), and also uoro, &c., where the *g* has itself disappeared. The root gras in grasyamânâ (next line) may, as Curtius suggests (Gr. Et. no. 643), be a secondary of this: it means 'to swallow,' or 'devour,' as at iv 9, where see note. But here, and inf. 27, it only means to seize, doubtless with the intention of eating.

22. **pariplutâ**, 'overflowed,' iv 13 note.

24. **anusmṛitya**, from anu + √smṛi, orig. SMAR. The initial *s* is shewn in no language but the Sanskrit—not in Greek μέρ-ιμνα, &c., Lat. me-mor, Goth. mēr-jan. The German 'schmerz' (referred by Bopp to this root) more probably belongs to SMARD, Lat. mordeo, our 'smart.' The root is found with sam, xiv 24, and with anu+sam, xv 16.

muktaḥ, v 28 note.

25. **pariglânasya**, 'exhausted,' p. p. from pari + √glai, of uncertain origin. **nâçayiṣyati**, ix 28 note.

26. **vyâdho**, 'a hunter,' from √vyadh, to pierce; p. p. viddha, Hit. 968, 'nâkâle mriyate jantur viddhaḥ çaraçatair api.' The root is probably compound, according to Benfey (Gr. W. Lex. i 252) = vi + adh, in which compound adh = Gr. οθ in ὄθη, ὄθομαι, ὠθέω, &c.: he thinks the long form √vâdh = ava + adh. Curtius takes √vadh as a simple

root = οθ (Gr. Et. no. 324); which is simpler, so far as √vadh is concerned; and also the Homeric compounds ἐνν-οσί-γαιος, εἰν-οσί-φυλλος, which are probably from √οθ, shew apparent traces of a lost Ϝ. But Curtius leaves √vyadh unexplained. From √vâdh (or bâdh) comes bâdhâ, 'annoyance,' and the compound abâdha (xii 104) = free from annoyance.

javena, 'with haste,' from java, viii 19 note: for the case compare 'vegena,' xiii 8; 'vistareṇa,' xii 76; and the plural instrumentals, such as 'uçcaih,' sup. 2, çanaiḥ çanaiḥ, Hit. 175.

abhisasâra, 'ran up,' perf. of abhi + √sṛi (whence sṛitvâ, xvii 35), from orig. SAR, apparently = 'to flow'; whence sarit, a river, and Gr. ὀρ-μή, &c. (Gr. Et. no. 502); probably also σάλος, salum: but these Curtius separates (no. 556), regarding the original idea as 'tossing motion.' There is a very large number of words in the different languages which both by sound and meaning might plausibly come under this root, but we find on following the different lines of meaning that at last we run into other roots with which each of our strings of words might be equally well connected.

27. **urageṇa**, v 5 note. **âyatekṣaṇâm**, 'long-eyed.' **âyata**, v 27, and i 13 notes. **ikṣaṇa**, ix 34 note. **tvaramâṇo**, v 2 note. **vegataḥ**, ix 26 note: for suffix *tas*, see vi 4 note.

28. **pâṭayâmâsa**, perf. of √paṭ (10), 'to split,' divide.' **çastreṇa** is translated 'an arrow' here: but it would rather seem that he cut the serpent in two with a sword, which is the regular meaning of çastra. It comes from √çaṃs, sup. 10. It occurs ii 18.

niçitena, p. p. of √çi, 'to sharpen'—or, as the grammarians give it, √ço (4 class), present çyâmi. Benfey thinks that the original form was aç-yâmi from √aç, whence açva, açman, açra, &c. = orig. AK, to be sharp. Curtius (Gr. Et. no. 57) connects çi with κίω and Lat. cio, cieo—less probably, I think.

ca: inexplicable except on metrical grounds.

nirviceṣṭam, 'motionless,' from nis (negative), and vi + √ceṣṭ, 'to struggle' (xiii 11), a doubtful root. The verb occurs (with ati) Hit. 756, 'vṛittyartham na aticeṣṭeta,' 'a man should not struggle too much for the sake of subsistence.' The p. p. ceṣṭita = 'conduct,' at xxiii 18, and ceṣṭâ (ib.): also vi-ceṣṭitam, xxiii 3, and the pres. part. middle of sam + √çeṣṭ, ib.—all with same meaning.

viçasya, sup. 10 note. **mṛigajivanaḥ**, 'having his living by the chase,' see x 23 note; a B. V. based on a T. P.

29. **mokṣayitvâ**, indecl. part. of mokṣaya, causal of √muc, v 28 note.

prakṣâlya, 'having washed,' from pra + √kṣal (10), again at xxiii 23. Prakṣâlana occurs Hit. 764, prakṣâlanâd dhi pan-kasya dûrâd asparsanaṃ varam, i.e. 'better the not being touched by mud than the washing it off': also at xxiii 11, prakṣâlanârthâya, 'for the sake of cleansing.'

samâçvâsya, ii 2 note.

kṛitâhârâṃ, 'having taken food.' âhâra, xii 62, from â + √hṛi, which has the same meaning M. B. iii 54 (Benf.). But it has many others; e.g. xx 5, âhartum = to get back: at xxvi 7 parasvam âhṛitya = 'having taken another's property from him': and probably 'to give' at xxv 14, where see note. It also = to perform a sacrifice, in which sense the verbal noun âhartṛi occurs xii 45. For vi + â + √hṛi see i 20 note.

30. **mṛigasâvâkṣi**, 'thou that hast the eyes of the young of a deer.' Akṣi is a variant form of akṣa, the eye, and much used in compounds. It corresponds closely with * ὀκι, found in the dual ὄσσε (= ὀκι-ε). **sâva**, 'the young of any creature,' from √su, whence υἱός (i.e. su-yo-s), compare Gothic su-nu, where the suffix differs, but the Indo-European word snusa (see xii 43) seems to preserve it: Gr. Et. no. 605.

kṛicchraṃ, vi 13 note.

31. **pṛicchyamânâ**, pres. part. pers. of √prach (6 cl.), present base pṛiccha, apparently by mere weakening before two consonants, as from √bhrajj + ya comes bhṛijja, M. W. Gr. § 282. The perf. papraccha occurred ii 15, iii 1, &c.: apṛicchan iv 23: fut. part. praṣṭavya at xv 3. The original root must have been PRAK, to which an *s* has been added in Sanskrit. It is seen in Lat. precor, procus, procax, &c., and in Gothic 'fragan,' but it does not seem to occur at all in Greek.

yathâvṛittam, ii 12 note. **âcacakṣe 'sya**, for construction see v 38 note.

32. **pina**, v 5 note.

çroṇi = cluni-s. Gr. Et. no. 61.

payodhara = breast, from payas = 'fluid,' whence payo-da, 'a cloud,' payo-dhi, 'the ocean': and comp. Payoṣṇi, a river, at ix 22: then (in a limited sense) 'milk.'

sukumârânavadyân-gim (comp. iii 13), 'having very tender faultless limbs.'

avadya = blame (hence an-avadya = blameless): see i 12 note. On the other hand vâc-ya = to be spoken of as bad, and vacaniyatâ = blame (Hit. 1153). The whole word is a B. V. based on a K. D., of which the first member is a Dvandva.

pûrṇacandranıbhânanâm, 'having a face like the full moon.' **pûrṇa,** p. p. of √pṛi (i 18 note), 'to fill.' The *u* seems to be due to the labial, as regularly roots in *ri* change to *ir* before *na.* M. W. Gr. § 534. **nıbha,** 'like,' from nı + bha, from √bhâ, to shine, which has lost its special meaning, ii 1 note. If we analyse the compound we shall find that pûrṇa + candra = a K. D.; and pûrṇacandra + nıbha = a genitively dependent T. P.; and pûrṇacandranıbha + ânana = a B. V. It occurs again xvi 26. Comp. pûrṇendu-vadana, id. xii 8.

33. **arâla,** 'curved.' But the word is also specially applied to the curve of the arm = Gr. ὠλένη, Lat. ulna, Gothic aleina, and our 'el-bow': Gr. Et. no. 563. It is to be observed that here Sanskrit keeps the *r*, whereas all the European languages shew *l*: see Curtius Gr. Et. II p. 176 (Eng. tr.).

pakṣman (pakṣma in composition) = 'eyelash.' Pakṣa, 'a wing,' seems akin. The first member of the compound, arâla-pakṣman, is a K. D., and the whole a sociatively dependent T. P., which is here used (as any T. P. can be) in the sense of a B. V.

lakṣayıtvâ, ii 7 note.

kâmasya, &c., 'he came into the power of love': for **iyıvân** see note on upeyıvân x 9, and for the accusative see note on ix 8.

34. **çlakṣṇayâ,** v 5 note.

mṛıdu-pûrvayâ, 'mild at first,' a K. D. compound, with pûrva placed last instead of at the beginning; so dṛıṣṭapûrva, i 29 note. At xxv 12 buddhı-pûrva = 'with understanding first,' that is, 'intentional': that may be a B. V. compound. But in a K. D. pûrva when second has generally ceased to be much more than a mere suffix: and even mṛıdu-pûrvam at xxii 2 = 'blandly.' **mṛıdu** = mollis (i.e. mol(d)u-i-s) from √mṛıd, orig. MARD, iv 11.

lubdhako, 'a hunter'—but also = desirous, covetous: and it does not seem clear that that is not the sense here. It is formed by suffix *ka* from lubdha, p. p. of LUBH, to desire, whence lobha, 'desire,' xx 24; also Lat. lub-et, lub-ido, &c., our 'lief' (the proper change acc. to Grimm's law not having taken place, as sometimes happens at the end of a word, but Gothic has 'liub'), Gr. λίπτομαι, λελιμμένος, Curt. no. 545. For a very convincing argument that ἐλεύθερος (which is commonly compared) has nothing to do with this root, see ib., Vol. II pp. 102—4 (Eng. tr.).

çântvayámása, viii 12 note.

35. **duṣṭam,** x 15 note. **upalabhya,** viii 3 note.

'However' (the usual sense of apı, 'even,' will not do here: see note on i 31) 'Damayanti, when she understood the evil one, she that was constant to her lord, filled with sharp wrath, blazed forth as it were with indignation.' **tivra,** sup. line 13. **roṣa,** from √ruṣ, whence, by change of *r* to *l*, Greek λύσσα, λυσσάω, &c. **saṃâvıṣṭá,** 'thoroughly entered,' and so = filled: comp. samupeta, &c.

prajajvála, from pra + √jval, 'to blaze,' one of many roots which seem referable to an original GAL: to which Curtius, Gr. Et. no. 637, refers the Sk. √gal, and jala, 'water' (iv 4 note), and also the common Greek verb βάλλω, calling attention to the many times in which it is used of water; he takes the original meaning to be 'fall, glide,' passing to 'slip away, let slip, let fly' an arrow, &c.; and so from this special sense he thinks that the extended use in Greek might arise. He connects also the Teutonic family, the A. S. cwellan, German 'Quelle,' and our 'well.' The Greek and Teutonic would therefore point to a secondary √gval, from which Sk. √jval might come: probably also Greek ζάλη—which Curtius (Gr. Et. 567) connects with YAS, Gr. ζέσ, to seethe—much less naturally on phonetic grounds; though ζῆλος may belong to that root: Benfey connects it with √jval. There is however this difficulty in connecting jval with GAL: if GAL have the primary meaning 'to fall' it is very unlikely that this should pass into that of 'blazing' in Sanskrit. If on the other hand we could assume that 'bubbling' was the primary notion, we can easily understand how it should pass into both meanings, if we compare the parallel history of BHUR or BHRU: whence come both the verb to 'burn,' and the noun 'burn,' a brook; and φρέαρ, a well (from the same root, = φρεϝ-ατ), shews the one sense, while the Homeric πόρφυρε has, I think, that of being hot, burning, in the well-known phrase πολλὰ δὲ ϝοὶ κραδίη πόρφυρε κίοντι: which was afterwards misunderstood by the Alexandrians, and turned into an active verb 'to meditate': see Ap. Rhod. iii 456, οἴσσατο πορφύρουσα. The family is much restricted by Curtius, Gr. Et. no. 412. The verb jval is used of 'brightness,' 'brilliance,' e.g. Sāv. i 23, where Sāvitri is described as 'jvalantim ıva tejasá.'

36. **kṣudraḥ,** 'small,' 'mean,' xix 5: doubtless connected with the verb √kṣud, 'to pound,' of which the history is doubtful. Benfey

compares Lat. cudo; but the initial change in Sanskrit is not clear.

pradharṣayıtum, iii 15 note. **áturaḥ**, vii 11 note. **tarkayámása**, v 12 note.

agnıçikhám, 'like a crest of fire.' Çıkhá is a 'point,' 'crest,' but also used of flame itself. Benfey translates 'as hot as fire' (Lex. s. v.): çıkhara, xii 41 = a peak.

37. **vınákṛıtá**, 'deprived of'—lit. 'made without,' p.p. of a compound like alaṃ-kṛı, i 11, &c.

atita, &c., literally, 'time having speech-way past,' locative absolute. **atita** = atı + ıta, p. p. of √ı. **vák-pathe** is a good instance how a word may lose its distinctive meaning, and become no more than a suffix. Patha is 'a road'; then it is merely redundant as here, and in dṛıkpatha, i. e. drıç + patha = sight (Benf. Lex. s. v.): sometimes however it gives an adjectival force, such as 'giving room for,' 'admitting of,' 'fit': our 'way' in 'lengthways,' 'likewise,' &c. shews a somewhat parallel use. M. Williams (Gloss. s. v.) seems to take it in this second way here: but then we must surely read atite vákpatha-kále.

38. **Naıṣadhád anyam**, i 20 note. **manasá 'pı na cıntaye** = 'ne mente quidem teneo.'

parásur, 'breathless,' lit. 'with the breath driven the wrong way,' from asu (√as, to breathe, whence = to be), and pará, old instrumental of para, 'otherwise,' i.e. by the wrong way, i 5 note. Vy-asu, next line, has the same meaning.

39. **uktamátre**, ix 10 note.

medınyám, loc. of medıni, 'the earth' (xvi 23), of doubtful origin. Benfey conj. = mṛıdhıni (see note on geha, xvii 16).

dagdho, p. p. of √dah, to burn, of which the original form must have been √dagh, of the same family as √δαϝ in δαίω, &c.—but not the same secondary root.

1. **nihatya**, indecl. part. of ni + √han, i 20. **pratasthe**, ii 1 note, comp. prasthitam, xii 28, 'going forward.'

kamalekṣaṇâ, 'with lotus eyes,' a very common comparison: so padma-nibh'-ekṣanâ, xii 30. The flower is more fully brought out in the compound kamala-garbh'-âbha, xiii 63, 'bright as the calyx of the lotus.'

pratibhayam, 'fearful,' prati + bhaya, 'fear,' from √bhi: there is no doubt that φοβέω is reduplicated from the same root, but the β should rather have come first. See Curt. no. 409. The verb in Sanskrit is of the 3rd class (bibheti) and takes an ablative of the source of the fear. So also the noun, bhayaṃ daṃṣṭribhyaḥ çatruto 'pi vâ, xiv 18, 'fear from tusked creatures or enemies.' Sometimes it takes a genitive, as xii 11.

çûnyâm, x 29 note. The 'emptiness' must be only of men, or rather of good men, for bad ones are there.

jhillikâ-gaṇa-nâditam, 'made to ring with swarms of crickets.' nâdita (comp. nâdayan, xxi 2) is p. p. of the causal of √nad (perf. neduh, xxiv 40), which appears in Greek in several river names Νέδ-η, Νέδ-ων, Νέσ-τος (Curt. no. 287 b): comp. Sanskrit nadi, the general term, xii 7.

2. Note the convenient Dvandvas in this and the following lines. It is tempting to connect **siṃha**, 'a lion,' with σίνις. **dvipin**, 'the ounce,' is apparently the beast with spots, for dvipa = an island. **vyâghra**, 'tiger,' may come from vi + â + √ghrâ, 'to smell.' **mahiṣa**, see i 7. **ṛikṣa** is ἄρκτος, perhaps from an orig. ARK seen in ὀλ(έ)κ-ω. Curt. G. E. no. 3.

yutam, p. p. of √yu, the simplest form of the family, √yuj, √yudh, &c. It is primarily 'joined to,' then 'full of,' as here, or 'endowed with,' xii 10: comp. â + yuta, in the same collocation, xii 39.

nâná, 'different,' often used at the beginning of a compound. Bopp regarded it as the pronominal root *na* reduplicated. Perhaps it is the negative particle ná (= νή), and so resembling in use οὐδεὶς οὐ.

ákirṇa, iv 18 note.

mleccha: "aboriginal tribes, who occupied the hills and outlying districts, who were called Mlecchas, as constituting those more barbarous and uncultivated communities who stood aloof, and would not amalgamate with the Aryans." 'Ind. Wisd.,' p. 236 note.

taskara, 'a robber,' connected by Grassmann with Vedic √taṃs (a secondary formed with *s* from √tan, 'to stretch'), to 'pull,' or 'drag,' so that the word should mean originally 'dragging-causer.' This is preferable to Pott's (a)tas-kara, 'hence-doer.'

sevitam, x 23 note.

3. "The Çal-tree is the *shorea robusta*, which yields a resinous exudation: the Dhava is the *grislea tomentosa*; the Açvattha is the *ficus religiosa* or holy fig-tree, also called Pippala... The Ingudī commonly called Ingua or Jiyaputa is a tree, from the fruit of which necklaces of a supposed prolific efficacy were made (Jīvaputraka)... The Kiṃçuka is the *Butea frondosa*, a tree bearing beautiful red blossoms." M. Williams, Glossary. In the Bhagavad Gītā, x 26, where Krishṇa is describing himself as the best of every kind of thing, he calls himself 'açvatthaḥ sarvavṛkṣāṇám,' 'the açvattha among all trees.' **veṇu** is the bamboo; **tinduka**, the ebon. The whole line must be regarded as a sociative instrumental.

ariṣṭa is the nimb-tree. **saṃchanna**, v 25 note.

syandanaiçca, &c., 'together with Syandanas having the silk-cotton trees with them,' apparently an attempt to vary the monotony of the list by a B. V. compound.

4. "Crowded with the Jambu or rose-apple, the Mango-tree, the Lodh (*Symplocos racemosa*), the bark of which is used in dyeing, the Khadira or Catechu tree, the exudation of which is used in medicine, the Çāl-tree, the cane or ratan." M. W., Glossary. **samákulam**, iv 18 note. In the next half-line the Udumbara is another fig-tree, the *ficus glomerata*, ib.

5. The Vadarī is the jujube, and the Vilva the Bel-tree. The Nyágrodha is the *ficus Indica* or banyan-tree. The Tála is the palm, and the Kharjúra the date-tree.

6. **dhàtu**, 'a mineral,' perhaps short for giri-dhatu, 'the constituent part (of a mountain)'—for this is the first meaning of dhàtu. In grammar it stands for a 'root.'

naddhàn, 'full of,' lit. 'tied up with,' p. p. of √nah, corrupted from NADH, whence νήθω, 'net' and 'needle.' The simpler form of the root is seen in νέ-ω and ne-o: another secondary is seen in nec-to. See Curt. Gr. Et. no. 436. **acalàn**, v 9 note.

vividhàn, see note on tathà-vidha, i 29. **parisaṃghuṣṭàn**, ii 11 note.

dariç, 'caves,' from √dṛi, ix 4 note.

7. **vapiç**, 'lakes,' of uncertain derivation: according to the P. W. from √vap, 'to sow,' which is traced back to another sense of 'laying down'—in this case a dam in order to make a tank.

mṛiga-dvijàn, 'beasts and birds.' **dvi-ja**, 'twice-born,' has curiously different meanings. It is a 'bird,' as being born a second time from the egg (xx 42, &c.): a 'tooth' (xii 66, su-dvij'-ànanà, 'with beautiful teeth and mouth'): lastly it means a member of one of the first three castes (though especially applied to the Brahmans) as being born a second time when he receives the sacred cord: see M. Williams, 'Hindu Wisdom,' p. 246. On receiving the cord the youth is admitted to the privilege of repeating the Vedas, and of performing religious rites which were before forbidden. The word has this sense xii 77, &c. Dvi-jàti has the same meaning, xii 78.

piçàcoragaràkṣasàn, 'fiends, serpents, and Ràkṣasas': for the two last see i 29. The Piçācas resemble the Rākshasas in eating meat indiscriminately—a great abomination, see Manu v 27, &c.: at line 50 a man who eats flesh-meat, 'Piçàca-vat,' is classed with one who forsakes the law. The derivation is unknown: the first part of the word seems to contain the root of 'piçuna,' 'malignant,' PIK, whence πικρός and our 'foe,' Curt. no. 100. (This PIK is perhaps distinct from the root of the same form, whence come ποικίλος and pingo.) Benfey however suggests piça, 'a deer,' and √añc. Piçàci (fem.) occurs xiii 27.

8. **palvalàni**, 'pools,' connected with palu(d)s, and πηλός (mud), Curt. G. E. no. 361.

taḍàgàni, 'ponds': there seem to be other forms—taṭàka and taḍàka. At Manu iv 203 a man is ordered to bathe, 'nadiṣu, devakhàteṣu taḍageṣu (i.e. 'ponds dug by holy persons') sarahsu ca.' At Hit. 689 it is used of a tank.

nirjharàn, 'waterfalls': jhari has the same meaning: and this disposes of the derivation from √jhṛi, 'to grow old.' Benfey connects with √kṣar.

9. **yûthaço**, 'by herds': for the termination comp. ekaika-ças, i 25. Yûtha apparently belongs to √yu.

nandini, from √nand, 'to delight' (v 33 note), at the end of a compound is used for a daughter. Nanda is a common proper name among Hindus to the present day.

pannagân, 'snakes,' app. from pad + na + √ga(m)—a peculiar compound. Again at xiv 8.

10. **tejasâ**, &c., i 8 and 10 notes.

lakṣmyâ, 'good fortune,' generally personified as the wife of Vishṇu; like Çri, i 18. **sthityâ**, v 37. **anveṣati**, part. of anu + √iṣ, 'to go,' iii 7 note.

11. **abibhyat**, imperf. of √bhi, with genitive **kasyacit**, see notes on xii 1, xiii 32. The form is irregular for abibhet.

dârunâm, 'hard,' 'sharp,' 'terrible': it may be from √dṛi, ix 4. **prâpya**, 'having gotten, i.e. as her abode, the terrible wood.' **vyasana**, vii 13 note. **piḍita**, v 2 note.

12. **tanayâ**, 'daughter,' as tanaya is 'a son'; tanayâbhyâm occurs xiii 34 of Damayanti's two children. It is a Vedic word, and means 'continuation,' from √tan, 'to stretch.'

çilâ-talam, see notes on ix 22, ii 28. **âçritâ**, v 15 note.

13. **vyuḍhoraska**, 'broad-chested': for the *-ka*, see page 7, and comp. hrasva-bâhu-ka, xviii 6. vyuḍha is p. p. of vi + √vah (which means 'to marry,' whence vivâha, v 39): it means 'arrayed,' of an army, Bh. Gītā, i 2; hence 'compact,' 'large,' as here. **uras**, see note on uraga, i 29.

14. 'How is it, O hero, that after sacrificing the horse-sacrifice (v 44 note) and others, together with gifts to Brāhmans (comp. kratubhir âpta-dakṣiṇaiḥ, v 44), thou conductest thyself falsely in my case?' **mithyâ** must be the instrumental of an unused noun * mithi from the Vedic √mith, our 'meet,' but always in a hostile sense. It occurs again at xiii 17, mithyâ-vacanam, Hit. 415 mithy'-opacâra, 'pretended service.' **pravartase**, ix 2 dyûtam pravartatâm, see note on vi 4.

15. **mahâ-dyute**, see note on vii 5.

smartum, xi 24 note. **kalyâṇa**, iii 22 note.

16. **vihagair**, 'sky-going' (like kha-ga and kha-gama, i 24): the different form vihaṃga occurs xii 41, see page 6: at xx 1 we have

the locative in khe-cara. Vıha is only found in compounds: but we had vıhâyas at ix 14.

avekṣıtum, 'to consider,' from ava + √iks, 'to look,' i 20 note, which at xxiii 11 is used in the primary sense of 'looked down upon': so Manu vii 10, kâryam so 'veksya, 'he having fully considered the business.' For √ikṣ with parı see xxiii 2; and with upa xxii 5.

17. 'On the one side are the four Vedas, with their An·gas and Upân·gas (iii 12 note), well read (by thee) in their full extent. On the other side assuredly is truth alone," and that is superior even to the Vedas. So in the Mârkandeya Purâṇa, xlvi 9,

> açvamedhasahasraṃ ca satyaṃ ca tulayâ dhrıtam,
> açvamedhasahasrâddha satyam eva vıçışyate,

i.e. when a hundred açvamedhas and truth are weighed in the balance, truth is superior to a hundred açvamedhas. I owe this explanation to Prof. Cowell.

The four Vedas (vi 9 note) together with the Brāhmaṇas and Upanishads (which are often included under the same general name) are regarded as Revelation (Çruti). But besides this there is a large body of tradition (Smṛiti), at the head of which come the "six Vedān·gas, 'limbs for supporting the Veda,' or in other words helps to aid the student in reading, understanding, and applying it to sacrificial rites: they are—(1) Kalpa, 'ceremonial directory,' comprising rules relating to the Vedic ritual, and the whole complicated process of sacrifices...: (2) Çikshā, 'the science of pronunciation': (3) Chandas, 'metre'; (4) Nirukta, 'exposition of difficult Vedic words': (5) Vyākaraṇa, 'grammar': (6) Jyotisha, 'astronomy,' including arithmetic and mathematics, principally in connection with astrology. Of these Vedān·gas (1) and (6) are for employing the Veda at sacrifices, (2) and (3) are for reading it, (4) and (5) for understanding it." 'Ind. Wisdom,' p. 155.

savıstarâḥ, 'with all detail,' comp. vıstareṇa, xii 75. Vıstara is from vı and √strı, to spread, orig. STAR, whence στορέννυμι, sterno, strew: Curt. no. 227.

18. **çatru-ghna,** 'slayer of thy foes': çatru is of doubtful origin; ἐχθρός, which is also isolated, hardly comes near enough in form. Ghna shews the *g* lost in √han, i 20 note: so also does ghâtın in the identical compound amıtra-ghâtınaḥ, xii 33; and vı-gh(a)na, xiii 23.

19. **nâma,** see xi 4 note. **pratıbhâṣase,** viii 4 note.

20. **bhakṣayati**, ix 14 note.

raudro, 'terrible,' formed by vṛiddhi from Rudra, a name of Çiva, 'the roarer,' from √rud, x 20.

vyâttâsyo, 'open-mouthed': vy-âtta is anomalous for vi + â + datta, p. p. of √dâ. **âkṛite**, v 5 note.

araṇya-râṭ, 'forest-king': bases in j, like râj, which are roots without any suffix, generally change *j* to *ṭ* in the nominative, instead of *k* according to rule. M. M. Gr. § 162. M. W. 176 e.

21. **Bhârati** is a name of Sarasvatī, wife of Brahmā; she was identified with Vāch, the goddess of speech, who is Vedic. Sarasvatī in the Veda is only a river goddess (as her name implies), "lauded for the fertilising and purifying power of her waters, and is the bestower of fertility, fatness, and wealth... In later times she is the goddess of speech and learning, inventress of the Sanskrit language and the Devanāgarī letters, and patroness of the arts and sciences." Dowson, s. v. Sarasvatī: where also is given Dr Muir's attempt to account for her connection with speech. Here her name Bhāratī is used in the simple sense of 'speech.'

23. **malinâṃ**, x 6 note.

24. **harinim**, 'a doe,' so called from its colour, the word being from the same root as 'harit.' Comp. Çak. i 10.

pṛithu-locana, 'broad-eyed,' comp. âyata-locana, v 27, &c. Pṛithu is Greek πλατύς, and Lith. platùs, 'broad'—a remarkable agreement. The Latin lătus and lāter are doubtless analogous; but not (st)lātus. See Curt. no. 367 b.

mânayasi, 'honour,' 'pay regard to,' causal of √man—unless it be rather a denominative from mâna, 'honour,' iv 4, whence mâna-da, ib. For the root MAN and its long history see Curt. G. E. no. 429. Mâna in the sense of 'measure' comes from MA (μέ-τρον, &c.), i 15 note.

25. **ekâkini**, 'solitary,' probably for ekaikin, i.e. eka + eka + in.

26. **kula-çil'-opasampanna**, 'of high birth and character,' applied to horses, xix 13: çila occurs xvi 24, tulya-çila-vayo-yuktân, 'endowed with like nature and age.' Kula and çila are frequently joined, and in fact the meanings of the two shade into each other: kula is 'family,' whence the adj. 'kulina' (xvii 12), of good family, or pure blood; kulastri, 'a noble woman,' xviii 8 (comp. 'Ind. Wisdom,' 219 note), and the compound 'kulâcâra,' family observances and customs, comp. Manu ii 34: çila is 'nature,' especially when good, comp. çilavân, xii 46, and then 'conduct,' 'morality,' çila-nidhi, xxiv

37, and so is practically identical with good kulâcâra. Comp. Manu ii 7,

> vedo 'khilo dharmamûlaṃ, smṛtiçîle ca tad-vidâm,
> âcâraiçcaiva sâdhûnâm âtmatuṣṭibhir eva ca,

i.e. the root of dharma is the entire Veda, and the tradition and morality of those who know the Veda, together with the immemorial practices of good men, and self-satisfaction: this last means that in indifferent matters, where there is no revelation, tradition, or established custom, each man is a law to himself. Comp. also i 108, âcâraḥ paramo dharmaḥ, 'immemorial practice is transcendent law'; and the following lines.

câru sarvân-gaçobhana, apparently a badly balanced Dvandva, in which câru (see iii 14) stands alone. For çobhana see iii 25.

27. **çayânam**, middle pres. part. of √ci, i 17 note.

upaviṣṭam, 'sitting down,' the regular meaning of upa + √viç, i 31, ii 3 note.

29. 'Has king Nala been seen by thee meeting him here (iha) in this wood?' I read saṃgatya, the ind. p. p. of saṃ + gam, and so Benfey. M. Williams apparently took it as saṃgatyâ, instr. of saṃgati, 'meeting' in the sense of 'accidentally.' For the construction of saṃgatya with tvayâ, see viii 22 note, and comp. xii 83, sa kaiçcin nikṛti-prajñair...âhûya...jito râjyam.

praṣṭavyo, fut. part. of √prach, xi 31: see M. W. Gr. § 633: M. M. App. no. 115. Note the acc. Nalam, as though it were 'quis mihi rogandus est Nalum?'

30. **paravyûha-vinâçanam**, 'destroyer of a host of foes': for para, see ii 2 note. Vyûha is from vi + √ûh, 'to arrange,' which is doubtless a weakened form of √vah (comp. vyûḍha, xii 13), and has nothing to do with Lat. augeo from UG, iii 21 note.

31. 'Whose sweet voice shall I to-day hear saying "He whom thou seekest, king Nala with lotus-like eye, this is he"?' Ayam sa correspond to 'hic is,' but the Latin would be content with hic, as the Greek with οὗτος: we agree with the Sanskrit. **nibha**, xi 32: **ikṣaṇa**, ix 34 note.

çrimânç, i.e. çrimân (ç inserted before çatur), nom. of çrimat, 'fortunate,' 'illustrious,' a title of respect applied to gods, as Vishṇu and Çiva; also çri is prefixed to the names of gods or distinguished persons, e.g. 'Çri-gaṇeçâya namaḥ,' 'reverence to Gaṇeça,' the opening of the Hitopadeça.

çatur-daṃṣṭro, 'four-tusked': daṃṣṭra is from √daṃç, orig. DAK (the Sanskrit root being weakened and nasalised), whence δάκ-νω, Curt. no. 9. The p. p. daṣṭa and imperf. adaçat occur xiv 12.

hanuḥ, 'jaw' (γένυς, gena, chin, Curt. no. 423). The root may be GHAN, comp. çatru-ghna, xii 18, and amitra-ghâtin, next line.

32. **açan·kitâ,** viii 3 note.

33. **amitra,** from a (negative) and mitra, 'a friend' (comp. amitra-gaṇa-sûdana, xii 126). Mitra is a Vedic god generally found in connection with Varuṇa—but more important in the Persian religion under the form of Mithra. The derivation is uncertain—possibly from √mid, a Vedic root = to cling to: whence the Sanskrit meda, 'fat': which however Curtius connects with μύδος and μυδάω (G. E. no. 479).

34. **kṛipaṇâm,** 'wretched,' xix 5. Kṛipâ = 'pity' occurs xvii 40, kṛipâṃ kuryâd mayi, comp. Hit. 322: the derivative kârpaṇya = 'misery,' Hit. 622. The origin of the word is uncertain: it cannot be akin to ἔλπω, as Bopp suggested, for that word began with a *v*, comp. Latin volup, &c.: the Vedic form of the root is krap, which gives no help.

35. **Nalam,** &c., 'if thou canst not tell of Nala': comp. note on pra + √çaṃs, i 6, iii 16. The simple verb occurs again xiii 53, xxii 16.

khâdaya, 'devour me,' from √khâd: the primary sense seems to be 'to tear in pieces.' Curtius connects it (G. E. no. 284) with κήδω and κῆδος, which would then be used in a metaphorical sense: compare the derivation of ὀδύνη from √ἐδ, and the Horatian 'curae edaces.'

vimocaya, from vi + mocaya, causal of √muc, v 28.

36. **mṛiṣṭa-salilam,** 'with clear water': mṛiṣṭa is p. p. of √mṛij, see v 4 note. **âpagâm,** 'a water goer,' i.e. 'a river,' from ap, 'water,' declined in the plural as âpas. **sâgaraṃgama,** 'goer to the ocean' (sâgara), so samudra-ga, ix 22. For the *m* in the first base see page 6, and compare vihaṃ-ga, xii 41. The accusative of motion to a place is more widely used in Sanskrit than in Greek or Latin: in Latin we can say 'ire domum,' but not 'ire oceanum.' So also in Sanskrit we have the person to whom some one goes in the accusative alone, as vrajâmy enam, xii 31: Damayantîṃ smṛitvâ, xvii 35; mano mama tâṃ gatam, vi 2: comp. ânitâ bândhavân, 'brought to my relations,' xviii 17. For the acc. of the state into which one goes, see note on ix 8. The examples of each of these rather peculiarly Sanskrit uses are not, I think, very numerous: neither should

we expect them to be so: in other languages they have been superseded by the use of other cases, or by more closely defining the accusative by the help of prepositions. But they are interesting relics of the oldest form of syntax, dating from a time when the other cases were still unfixed.

37. 'This sacred mountain-mass, with its many lofty peaks, glittering, sky-touching, many-hued, enchanting the mind, &c.' For **çıla** see ix 22. **uccaya** is a 'heap' from ud + √cı to 'heap' or 'gather,' already referred to at ii 2, v 14. **puṇyam** is generally translated here as 'holy': but it may mean no more than 'goodly'—a sense derived from 'auspicious,' which the P.W. gives as the primary one, regarding 'holy,' 'pure' as derived meanings from 'good,' and connecting the word (after Benfey) with √puṣ, and not √pû, 'to purify.' It occurs as a subst. xv 16, = 'good deed,' 'merit.' **çṛın·ga** is primarily a 'horn' (so Hitop. 181), and so naturally used for a mountain peak; comp. 'Wetterhorn,' 'Schreckhorn,' &c. It is difficult to separate it from çıras, a head (xxiv 17), which must be identical in form with *κέρας*, 'horn': but it seems to mean 'that which goes or is found on the head,' and so the meaning 'horn' belonging to the simple Greek word is perplexing. Curtius suggests (no. 50) that *karas meant at first 'something hard,' from which the meanings 'horn' and 'head' came separately in the separate languages. **ucchṛıtaıḥ** from ud + çṛıta, p. p. of √çṛı, see v 15 note. Observe the use of the sociative here: it is very natural, and just like our own use, 'with its peaks': it gives the origin of the Latin abl. of description: 'mons multis culminibus' might be accurately called a sociative ablative, parallel to the instrumental uses which the ablative also took in Latin. So too 'vir magno corpore,' 'puella minimo naso' are sociatives, and, I think, peculiar Latin developments of the case. The same use occurs xii 53, xvi 8 rûpeṇ' âpratımena, xix 14 daçabhır âvartaıḥ: we had the case used of a person (or rather 'army'—balaıḥ) at ii 11; again at xxvi 2, 34. For the case generally see vi 2 note.

vırâjadbhır, v 3 note. **dıvı·spṛıgbhır**; for √spṛç see note on upasparça, vii 3. Observe that dıvı is used in the locative in the compound—not the base 'dıv': comp. dıvas-patı, and see page 6. The special reason is the unfitness of *v* to combine with the following letter.

naıkavarṇaır, 'not of one colour,' i.e. of many, a *μείωσις* well known in Greek: comp. xii 109.

38. **nàná-dhâtu**, xii 6. **upala**, 'a stone,' doubtless here 'precious stone' (Bopp compares 'opal')—but not necessarily so: at Manu xi 167 it is joined with iron and brass (ayaḥ-kâṃsy'-opalânâm) while 'gems' (maṇı) occurs in the same line. It occurs Çak. i 14.

ketu-bhûtam, 'up-rising like a banner of (or 'above') this mighty forest.' Ketu is from *√kıt the older form of √cıt (v. 2), in the sense of that which makes itself visible or recognisable. In the Veda, Agni is the 'ketu' of the sacrifice, the smoke of which rises as a banner to heaven: see Grassmann, s.v. For **bhûta** at the end of a compound comp. ratna-bhûtâm, ii 23, cıhna-bhûta, xvii 7: in all these the participle is quite redundant. But it is wanted in hâhâ-bhûtam, xvii 31: also in prâñjalır bhûtvâ, v 16: and perhaps çvo-bhûte, 'tomorrow,' xviii 25.

39. **mâtan·ga**, 'elephant,' i.e. matta + an·ga: comp. mada, xiii 7, and i 25 note.

patatrıbhır, 'birds,' i.e. patatra + ın: patatra = πτέρον from √pat, i 22.

samantâd, 'altogether': the ablative (like sâkṣât, i 4 note) of samanta, a B.V., 'having the ends together.' **anunâdıtam**, xii 1 note.

40. **supuṣpaır**, 'with fair flowers.' Puṣpa is from √puṣ, to 'nourish,' 'support,' a Sanskrit secondary of the common root PU, whence putra, puer, πῶλος, foal: Curt. no. 387. Comp. also xii 37, note on puṇya.

41. **çıkharaıs**, 'peaks,' see note on çıkhâ, xi 36.

tâvat, 'so much,' and no more: often so used without any correlative yâvat. We may compare the use of the Greek οὕτως, and our colloquial 'just.' Tâvat = τέως, all the phonetic change being on the side of the Greek, where *v* falls out, final *t* passes into *s*, and there is compensatory change of the length of the vowels: comp. λεώς for λαός. Similarly yâvat = ἕως, Homeric εἷος (or rather ἧος), which is nearer.

pṛıcchâmı...pratı, see note on ii 7.

42. **dıvya-darçana**, 'of divine aspect': darçana from √drıç, i 13.

çaraṇya, adjective formed from çaraṇa, 'refuge' (see v 15), but without the usual vṛıddhı of the first syllable.

43. 'I approach and bow down to thee: **praṇame**, middle pres. of pra + √nam, whence namas, 'reverence,' see iv 1 note. **abhıgamya**, note the form with *m*, which is equally admissible with that in *t* (abhıgatya).

snuṣâṃ, 'daughter-in-law,' shortened from sunu-sā, 'belonging to a son': which is probably the Indo-European form, sunu being preserved in Sanskrit (sûnu), Gothic and Lithuanian. The root is SU, xi 30 note. The agreement of the derivative in the different languages is remarkable: νυός (orig. σνυσός), nurus, Sclav. snŭca, Germ. Schnur. See Curt. no. 444, comp. no. 605.

44. **mahârathaḥ**, ii 11 note. **kṣiti-patis**, ii 20 note.

caturvarṇyasya, &c., 'protector of the four castes' (see i 4 note): the word is not used as an adjective, but rather as a sort of collective noun.

45. **râjasuya**, 'a royal sacrifice,' often joined as here with the açvamedha (e.g. Indr. i 15). It does not appear that 'suya' can be a separate word meaning sacrifice from √su mentioned just above: though it might be derived from the Vedic √su to 'produce,' 'make' (with which the other is ultimately identical): but no such word seems to occur. Benfey divides the word râjasu-ya.

âhartâ, xi 29 note.

añcita, ii 18 note.

46. **anaśuyaka**, 'not a scorner,' formed from √asûya, 'to curse,' which is apparently a denominative from asu, breath, see xi 38: it occurs again 117 and xiv 17 asuyayitvâ, perhaps 'having made cursed,' i.e. punished.

47. **goptâ**, nom. of goptṛ (again at 179), from √gup, to 'protect,' p. p. gupta, xvii 22. Its present base is gopâya, xviii 8 (or gopaya), and it may therefore be plausibly regarded as a denominative verb formed from gopa, a cow-herd, from PA, whence pascor, pabulum, Pales, Πᾶν (i.e. Πάων the shepherd), Curt. no. 350.

48. **çvaçuro**, 'father-in-law' (xxv 2), identical with ἑκυρός, socer-(us), Germ. Schwieger, Scl. svekrŭ, Lith. szészuras (Curt. no. 20)—another most remarkable instance of the persistency of terms of relationship. Sanskrit alone varies from the other languages by its initial *ç* instead of *s*: as there is no apparent derivation to be gained by the change, we must suppose that it is due to the assimilating effect of the following ç. The derivation is doubtless sva + kura (see note on çura, i 3), 'own master,' a complimentary term, like French beau-père.

gṛhitanâmâ, app. 'who has received (rightly) his name,' i.e. rightly called Virasena, 'with a host of heroes.' Gṛhita is p. p. of √grah, i 19. **vikhyâto**, see initial note on the term 'Nalopâkhyâna.' **sma ha** seem fearfully out of place: 'sma' however as we saw (i 12) turns a present verb into a past, and 'ha' (viii 8) was generally found with a perfect: past tense is required here, as Virasena is presumably dead: but there is no verb in the sentence: perhaps 'sma ha' indicate a missing 'ásit': compare ha with anuçástı, next line.

49. **parákramah**, i 5 note. **krama-práptam**, 'obtained (or 'arrived') in due course,' see note on i 11. Krama is properly 'a step,' from √kram (ix 6 note), then like 'gradus' it gets the meaning 'order': so kramena, 'in order,' xvi 31. **samanuçástı**, iii 21 note.

50. **arı-há**, 'foe-slayer,' vii 10 note: like nırjıt'-árı-gana, above 47.

çyámaḥ, 'dark,' used of Damayanti, xvi 10, xvii 6, xviii 11: probably connected with κύανος, Curt. G. E. Vol. II p. 164 (Eng. tr.). Hesychius' Gloss. κυναμα· μελαν(α), Λάκωνες is helpful. Darkness of skin seems a strange reason of compliment in a country where the highest caste (varṇa) was marked by the lightest colour: but it may be 'clear-skinned,' like the Theokritean μελίχλωρος and the Ovidian 'flavus.'

Puṇya-çlokaḥ, 'told of in sacred verse,' acc. to Burnouf, a title commonly given to Nala, but not confined to him. Benfey and the P. W. translate it 'well-famed,' apparently following the Vedic meaning of çloka, 'praise': which is probably connected with √çru, the *l* appearing as in κλέος, &c. Çloka is the regular term for the epic verse of 32 syllables, which we have before us in the 'Nala.'

vágmi, 'eloquent,' from √vac, i 32.

soma-po, 'soma-drinker.' The juice of the soma (afterwards a name of the moon, as at xii 82) was drunk at sacrifices: hence a soma-drinker is a pious man. The soma is the *Asclepias acida*, the juice of which can be fermented. "Its exhilarating qualities were grateful to the priests, and the Gods were represented as being equally fond of it." Dowson, s. v. But the most surprising thing is the position of this plant in the Vedic hymns. "It was raised to the position of a deity and represented to be primeval, all-powerful, healing all diseases, bestower of riches, lord of other Gods, and even identical with the Supreme Being," ib. "The high antiquity of this cultus is attested by the reference to it found in the Persian Avesta; it seems however to have received a new impulse on Indian territory," Whitney. In later times it passed away altogether. For a fuller account, see Dr Muir, 'Sk. Texts,' v 258, &c. He well compares the Euripidean rationale of the worship of Dionysus, esp. Bacchae 298 &c.

μάντις δ' ὁ δαίμων ὅδε· τὸ γὰρ βακχεύσιμον
καὶ τὸ μανιῶδες μαντικὴν πολλὴν ἔχει,
ὅταν γὰρ ὁ θεὸς εἰς τὸ σῶμ' ἔλθῃ πολύς,
λέγειν τὸ μέλλον τοὺς μεμηνότας ποιεῖ.

The effect on health of soma-drinking is not stated: the exhilarating effect being alone dwelt upon. It is mentioned with commendation in Manu, where the use of spirituous liquors is strictly forbidden.

agnimân, 'having the consecrated fire alight' for proper sacrifices, such as the Çráddha, Manu iii 122.

51. **yaṣṭá**, i. e. √yaj + tṛi; as **yoddhá** is √yudh + tṛi. **samyak**, viii 13 note.

praçásitá, 'a ruler,' from √çás.

52. **hinám**, v 24 note. **vyasana**, vii 13 note.

53. **kham ullikhadbhir**, 'touching the sky,' from ud + √likh 'to scratch': perhaps therefore 'cutting the sky' would more nearly represent the idea. The root seems specially Sanskrit: from it come lekha 'a letter,' citra-likh 'a painter,' &c. It has nothing to do with √lih, orig. LIGH, whence λείχω, ligurio, lick, &c. **kha** has occurred before in kha-ga, &c.; the primary meaning is 'hollow,' hence Manu xi 120, kham sanniveçayet kheṣu, 'let him enclose the ether in the cavities of his body' (nose, ears, &c.)—a striking passage in which all nature, material and immaterial, is regarded as existing only in the divine spirit, Átman. Curtius (G. E. Vol. II p. 114, Eng. tr.) allows a Sanskrit hardening of original *gh* into *kh*, whereby kha is brought into connection with χάος, and with √há from orig. GHA, see ix 14 note. Generally words with *kh* in Sanskrit must be carefully separated from apparent congeners which shew χ in Greek.

çṛin·ga-çatair, xii 37 note, where the sociative use of these words was pointed out. It would however be possible to take them instrumentally, the peaks being looked upon as a sort of instrument of vision to the mountain.

54. **gajendravikramo**, 'with the prowess of the king of the elephants': for indra see i 2 note. Vikrama is used in the same sense as parákrama: comp. vikránta = 'brave,' 'a hero,' here and 56. For the passive participle in this active sense, see notes on ii 21 and i 11.

dirgha-báhur, 'long-armed': dirgha must be weakened from * dárgha which = δολιχός, where the iota is auxiliary: Curt. no. 167.

Bâhu is certainly the same as πηχυ-, Curt. no. 176: both languages are irregular here as the Indo-Eur. word began with *bh*.

amarṣaṇa, 'vehement,' see vii 13 note.

55. **vihvalâm**, xi 14 note.

56. Here she breaks off her address to the mountain, which is pathetic though somewhat tedious; and appeals to Nala himself.

satyasandha, 'faithful to thy promise': sandha is from sam + √dhâ. Again at 79.

57. **âtmânam âtmanâ**, vi 12.

kadâ, &c. 'When shall I hear that pleasant deep voice of the king, like to the sound of the storm-cloud, that voice like nectar?' **snigdha** is p. p. of √snih, 'to be damp' or 'oily,' whence sneha 'love,' Hit. 306, but also 'oil': from the same root came νίφα and our 'snow,' see Curt. no. 440. Snigdha may get its meaning either from the literal sense (we speak of an 'oily tone') or from the derived sense of 'love,' comp. Latin amoenus. **gambhira**, 'deep,' also spelt gabhira, is from √gâh to dip, orig. GABH, whence βαθύς &c., by labialism, Curt. no. 635. It is applied at xxi 4 to the sound of Nala's chariot, 'yathâ meghasya nadato gambhiraṃ jalad'-âgame, 'as the sound of a cloud deeply roaring at the coming of the rains.'

svana = sonus, just as sopor is from √svap. But there is no need to attach φωνή here (as Bopp did) for original *σφωνή by a change like that of σφε from sva: it can be more simply connected with φά-τις, φή-μη &c.

58. **vispaṣṭâṃ**, 'clear.' Benfey and the P. W. make it the p. p. of √spaç 'to see' in the sense of 'evident': the transition from sight to sound is the reverse of that of our own word and of Lat. 'clarus.'

59. **âmnâya-sâriṇim**, 'containing the essence of the Vedas,' i.e. as sweet to me: **âmnâya** (from â + √mnâ = "sacred tradition: the Vedas in the aggregate," Dowson. **sâra** is the strength or essence of anything. At xxiv 16 Damayanti's eyes are called kṛṣṇasâra, either 'intensely black' or 'with black pupils.' At Çak. i 10 arrows are called vajrasâra, i.e. having the properties of the thunderbolt, hardness, force, &c. At Hit. 1292 antaḥsâra = 'treasure.'

ṛiddhâm, x 2 note.

'Comfort ye me in my terror, O king, lover of duty.' Perhaps the mountain is still present to her mind as well as the king, and hence the plural âçvâsayata. Or it may be simpler to take it as a plural of respect. **vatsala**, 'fond' (adj.), and 'fondness' (subst.) is a problem. It is commonly connected with vatsa, 'a calf' (vitulus and ἰταλός): the *s* makes it impossible to add vatsala to the last two words, as well as the difficulty of meaning. Comp. dvijâti-jana-vatsala, xii 78. Vâtsalya = 'fondness,' 'tenderness,' Hit. 281.

60. **uttarâm**, 'higher,' 'superior,' and with secondary meaning 'northern.'

61. **ahorâtrân**, 'nights and days,' a Dvandva. Ahas stands in compounds for ahan, and also in inflection before the consonantal terminations. Sometimes we find ahar as aharahaḥ, 'day by day.' See M. M. Gr. §§ 196—8. **tâpasa**, 'an ascetic,' x 19 note. **atulam**, 'unequalled,' xxiv 38, see iv 6 note.

divya-kânana-darçanam, 'with the look of a heavenly grove,' comp. divya-darçana, xii 42.

62. 'Made glorious by ascetics equal to Vasishṭha, Bhṛigu, and Atri'—three of the ten Prajāpatis or progenitors of the human race, given in Manu i 35. Atri also appears at a later time as one of the seven Ṛishis, and as the head of the Lunar race, for which see Dowson s. v. Chandra-vaṃça. Bhṛigu is the son of Manu (i 59), and is appointed by him to promulgate his laws to the assembled Ṛishis. Vasishṭha is a great Vedic Ṛishi, and the author of many of the hymns. He is best known by the stories of his warfare with the great Kshatriya Viçvāmitra: see Dowson.

saṃyatâhârair, 'taking limited food': notes on i 4, and xi 29: **çauca**, vi 10 note.

63. 'Living on water, living on air, furthermore having leaves as their food.' **parṇa** (xx 9) is a wing in Vedic, but also the leaves of the trees regarded as their feathers. Grassmann compares Lith. sparna-s, and so connects the word with SPAR, Curt. no. 389. The Vānaprastha, or Brāhman in the third period of life (see note on ix 22) is allowed by Manu something more than this: at vi 5 he may have 'many sorts of pure food, green herbs, roots, and fruit' (çâka-mûla-phala): but it would seem that special limitations might be practised by each ascetic: and onions, mushrooms, and other nice things are forbidden. But as these hermits are specially 'striving to see the way to Svarga' or Indra's heaven, they require further bodily mortification.

mahâbhâgaiḥ, x 14 note. **mârga**, 'a path,' xiii 10, &c.—from mṛij, v 5: hence the verb mârg (1 cl. and 10), 'to seek,' at 125, xiii 62.

64. 'Clothed in bark and goat-skins'; compare Manu vi 6, vasita carmma ciraṃ vâ, 'let him be clad in a skin or in bark.' **ajina**,

comp. αἰγίς: the αι being due to epenthesis from orig. ag-ı, from √AG, Curt. no. 120.

adhy-uṣıtam, p. p. of adhı + √vas, 'to dwell,' ii 12.

âçrama-maṇḍalam, 'the circle of the hermitage': for âçrama, see ix 22. **maṇḍala** is used here, as in sârtha-maṇḍala, xiii 15 (like tala ii 28, deça v 27, taṭa, and other words) at the end of a compound with the general sense of extension: as we talk of a 'circle of acquaintances' or 'a sphere of usefulness,' without any exact limitation to those figures. Compare âçrama-padam (πέδον) *infra* 67. It is akin to √maṇḍ, xvi 10, 'to adorn,' and maṇḍa, 'an ornament,' which may come from the Vedic √mand, 'to rejoice,' 'delight,' with suffix *-tra*; and this would explain the cerebral. If 'mundus' (as Bopp has it) be akin to maṇḍa, it must come direct from √mand with suffix *-o*.

65. **ȷuṣṭam,** 'frequented by,' p. p. of √ȷuṣ, 'to enjoy,' 'frequent.' It is from GUS (whence γεύομαι, gustus, choose, Curt. G. E. no. 131. It has a further sense (like Lat. colo) 'to observe,' 'follow,' so in Bh. Gītā ii 2, anâryaȷuṣṭa, 'not followed by the good': and the causal ȷoṣaya, ib. iii 26, has the same meaning—ȷoṣayet svakârmânı vıdvân, 'let the wise man carry out his own works.'

çâkhâ-mṛıga, is a 'branch-animal,' or monkey. Çâkhâ occurs xx 11, also praçâkhıkâ. çâkhın = a tree, Çak. i 15.

66. **sukeçi,** 'fair-haired,' v 6 note.

sukucâ, 'with fair bosom': kuca is from √kuc, 'to bend' or 'curve.' **dvıȷa,** xii 7 note.

supratıṣṭhâ, 'famous': from pratı-ṣṭhâ, which means firstly 'firm-standing,' then 'accomplishment' (Çak. iii 73), 'fame.' Compare pratıṣṭhıta, 'famed,' xxii 22. Our phrase 'of good position' is somewhat similar.

svasıtâyatalocanâ, 'with black long eyes.' **a-sıta,** 'not white': so asıtakeçântâ, 'black-haired,' xvi 21.

67. **yoṣıd-ratnam,** 'the pearl of women,' a T. P., or perhaps more accurately a 'K. D. comparativum,' like nara-çârdûla, 'a woman who is in all respects a pearl.' Comp. ii 23 ratna-bhûtâṃ lokasya: and for yoṣıt ii 21. **tapasvıni,** x 19 note.

68. 'After saluting (causal of abhı + √vad, with same sense, and at xxv 2) the hermits she stood bowed down by modesty; and "welcome to thee," thus was she addressed by all those hermits.'

ava-nata, p. p. of √nam, iv 1 note. **vınaya,** from vı + √ni, 'to lead' (see note on ânayya, viii 5), and so 'to train,' 'educate':

compare the similar Latin 'e-duco'; p. p. vinita, 'modest,' xxvi 30. Niti is conduct specially of a king, 'statemanship,' in which sense it constantly occurs in the Hitopadeça. Pra-naya (from the same root) = 'affection,' iv 2, as we speak of 'a leaning towards' a person. **svâgatam**, i.e. su + âgatam, is used as a single word like our 'welcome.' So svâgaten' ârcitas, 'honoured with a welcome,' Indr. 4. 5. **proktâ**, i.e. pra + uktâ.

69. **âsyatâm**, i 11 note, 'let it be sat' (by thee). This use of the passive imperative for a request is exceedingly common in Sanskrit: comp. e.g. viçrâmyatâm, 'let rest be taken,' xxi 27. So a story is commonly introduced by çrûyatâm, 'let it be heard,' e.g. Manu i 4; and constantly in the Hitopadeça.

karavâmahai, comp. iv 1 'kim karavâṇi te.'

70. 'Is there success (kuçalam, viii 14 note) in your austerities here, your sacrificial fires, your duties, your beasts and birds, O blameless holy men, in your special duties and in your conduct?' unless we may take svadharmâcaraṇeṣu not as a Dvandva, but as a T. P. 'in the performance of the special duties' (i.e. of the Vānaprastha): âcaraṇa, however, seems to have the same meaning as âcâra, see xii 26 note. Kuçalam (viii 4 note) is the word to be introduced in the address to a Brāhman: so Manu ii 27,

> Brâhmaṇaṃ kuçalam pṛcchet, Kṣatrabandhum anâmayaṃ,
> Vaiçyaṃ kṣemaṃ, samâgatya, Çûdram ârogyam eva ca,

i.e. 'on meeting him, let him ask a Brāhman, if his devotion prospers; a Kshatriya-person, if he is unhurt; a Vaiçya, if his wealth is secure: a Çûdra, if he enjoys good health,' using the proper term in each case. Indra however (at ii 15) asked Nārada after both his kuçala and his anâmaya. Further nice proprieties to be observed in addressing different people will be found in Manu ii 117—139. **bhagavatâm**, 'the worshipful ones,' is the subjective genitive with tapasi, &c., being used like bhavat as a respectful substitute for the pronoun of the 2nd person: so at 87.

tapasi, see note on paraṃtapa, x 19.

mṛiga-pakṣiṣu seem to be included in the general belongings of the hermits: they are sacred, as may be seen from the first act of the Çakuntalā, where the king Dushyanta nearly commits the sacrilege of shooting a deer belonging to a hermitage. The compound can hardly be taken as 'among your beasts and birds,' comp. deveṣu, &c. i 13, or xxvi 27 râjasu: it would come in awkwardly with the other locatives in a different sense, and the sociative would also have been more naturally used.

71. **sarvatra**, comp. ii 16, ávayoḥ kuçalam sarvatra gatam. The supernatural effect of their religious self-mortification extends to all around them. Compare note on ātman, x 29: the soul is not confined to its own body.

73. **vismayo**, ii 29 note.

samáçvasihi, 2 sing. imperat. of sam + á + √çvas, which inserts *i* irregularly before all the consonantal terminations except *y*: M. W. Gr. § 326. Comp. rodimi, xi 11.

má çucaḥ, 'grieve not': iii 9 note. Çuc-am, çuc-as, &c. is the simpler aorist form (without the augment when used with má), corresponding to the 2nd aorist in Greek, wherein the terminations are attached at once to the unmodified root. There is likewise a fuller form with inserted *s*, corresponding so far to the 1st aorist in Greek. Lastly there is a reduplicated aorist, e.g. adudruvam 'I ran,' corresponding to ἤγαγον and the numerous epic forms. See Schleicher, 'Compendium,' §§ 289 and 292. With this full verb system it might have been expected that Sanskrit would have exhibited the same nice tense-distinctions as the Greek does. But the genius of the language did not lie in this direction: consequently the aorist (which is common in Vedic and is used there in the proper aorist sense, see Delbrück's 'Altindische Tempuslehre') gradually dropped out of the language, and in the Epic is not often found except in this special connection with *má*. We have prádát xxiii 21, abhút i 17, v 9, açakat xxi 30.

In Vedic Sanskrit we find constructions which remind us more of the classical languages. Thus the conjunctive—not the indicative —of the aorist is most commonly found, e.g. má bhuv-a-t, rather than má bhút. So Ṛigv. 1. 25. 12, sa no...ádityaḥ supathá karat, 'may the son of Āditi make our paths straight,' where karat is the conj. of the aorist, or simplest form, of √kṛi. (Yet even in Vedic the indicative (minus the augment) is found, e.g. 1. 38. 5, má vo... jaritá bhúd ajoṣyaḥ, 'never shall your praiser be unwelcome': so M. Müller, Vol. I. p. 65.) We find also the optative aorist (also called the 'benedictive,' see xvii 36 note), e.g. 7. 59. 2, mṛityor mukṣiya má 'mṛitát, 'may I be freed from death not from immortality.'

In later Sanskrit we find the optative with má, e.g. Mahābh. i 6003 má çabdaḥ sukhasuptánám bhrátṛiṇám me bhavet: compare Latin 'ne sit' (for siet). Also (as already said) we have the aorist without the augment. Whether this was from a recollection of the unaugmented conjunctive, or whether the augment was absorbed into the long vowel of mâ, cannot be told.

utâho, 'or' = uta (see ii 25) + âho *ib.*, a doubtful word meaning 'or' at xxi 34. It occurs again, 120, and xix 29, with svid, where see note. The sandhi here is irregular: after indeclinable words like âho, a following ă ought not to be dropped. M. M. Gr. § 47.

75. **viprâ**, 'Brahmans'—but only in a secondary sense. It means in Vedic 'one inspired,' 'a singer,' from √vip 'to quiver,'—then 'wise,' as applied to Gods. Hence it passed into its later sense.

76. **vistareṇa**, 'at length,' xii 17.

abhidhâṣyâmi, 'I will tell,' abhi + √dhâ.

78. **saṃgrâmajit**, 'victor in the battle,' a loc. T. P. Saṃgrâma (xiv 19) is from sam + √grah: for jit, see vii 5.

devatâbhyarcanaparo, 'devoted to the worshipping of the Gods,' see note on cintâpara ii 2: and for arcana see ii 15 note.

dvi-jâti, a B.V. with the same meaning as dvija, 'twice born,' esp. a Brahman, see note on xii 7. So ekajâti is applied to a man of the 4th class, Manu x 4.

jana is redundant, 'the Brahman folk,' like sakhi-jana ii 5.

79. **vaṃçasya**, 'of the stock of Niṣadha': it means first (and in the Veda) 'a bamboo': then it means 'race,' 'lineage,' by the same metaphor as our own: xxvi 9, vaṃçabhojyaṃ râjyam = 'hereditary kingdom.'

astra, 'a weapon,' from √as 'to throw,'—a root which is rare in Sk. and hardly found in other languages: sam-asta occurs xvi 12, vi-ny-as-ya, xxiv 45, and san-ny-âsa, xxv 5. It supplies the worst derivation for ἀστήρ as though that word meant 'the thrower' of light.

80. **daivata**, formed in the common way (by Vṛddhi and suffix -a) from devatâ in the derived sense 'a God' (not 'godhead' which is the first meaning): this also means 'a God.'

81. **viçâlâkṣaḥ**, 'with large eyes.' **viçâla** (of uncertain origin) is 'large'; then 'illustrious,' so Hit. 88, viçâlakulasambhava is 'one who is born of an illustrious family.' At xvi 9 we have viçâlâkṣi applied to Damayanti.

pûrṇendu-vadano, 'with face like the full moon,' see xi 32 note. **indu**, 'the moon,' occurs xvii 7. In the Veda the word is used of the soma-drops.

mukhyânâm, 'chief,' see iv 4: note that it stands second in the compound, like pûrva (i 29 note) and antara.

pâragaḥ, 'one who goes to the "pâra" or opposite bank,' xvi 22: and so in the secondary sense 'bringing to an end,' 'reading,' 'studying': again at xiii 44. Curtius classes it with *πέρα*, and *περαίνω*, (no. 357); at no. 356 he takes the cognate group *πόρος*, porta, experior, fare. All are from PAR 'to carry over' (Sk. pṛi, 3 and 10), distinct in sense from PAR to fill (i 18), Sanskrit pṛi (9). Another pṛi (6 cl. middle, pṛiye), 'to be active,' is closely akin to *πέρνημι*, *πρίαμαι*, &c., Curt. no. 358: paṇa (for parṇa) belongs to this group.

82. **sapatna**, 'an enemy.' A further form—sapatni (fem.)—is Vedic: and Grassmann regards the masc. form as derived from the feminine, which expressed the hostility of rival wives (patni = wife xii 114).

ravi, 'the sun,' Hit. 556, &c. **soma**, xii 50 note. The whole compound is elliptical, prabhâ being required after soma to make up the logical form: comp. the Greek *χαῖται Χαρίτεσσιν ὁμοῖαι.*

nikṛiti-prajñair, 'having knowledge of dishonesty,'—a somewhat peculiar force of ni in composition.

anâryair, 'ignoble': a term first applied to the original Indian peoples—the Dasyus, &c.—who were driven to the hills by the invading Âryas—(a name which occurs often in the Vedic hymns): see 'Ind. Wisdom,' p. 313. It is commonly derived from √ar 'to plough': which seems to me improbable: 'ploughers' is not a title which an early people would be likely to apply to themselves as a mark of honour. The root is more probably AR 'to fit' (whence *ἀρετή* and *ἀρείων*), from which the meaning 'suitable,' 'good,' flows naturally, and is parallel to the Roman 'boni,' and Greek *ἐσθλοί.*

akṛitâtmabhiḥ, 'with intellect unimproved.' Thus in Manu vi 18, the study of the omnipresent spirit (the antarâtman) is said to be hard for the akṛitâtmânaḥ. Akṛita, in the sense 'unworked,' is applied to a field, Manu x 114.

83. **âhûya**, 'having called upon (challenged) him,' to be taken with the instrumentals preceding: see notes on viii 23 and i 22. For the verb see v 1.

parâyaṇaḥ, used like para at the end of a compound, ii 2 note. So xxiii 1, çoka-parâyaṇa.

devane kuçalair, viii 1 and 4 notes.

jihmair, 'crooked' (here morally): in Veda 'oblique.'

84. **avagacchadvam**, from ava + √gam, 'to come down upon,' and so 'to know.'

darçana-lâlasâm, 'with eager desire for the sight.' **lâlasa** is formed by reduplication from √las, 'to play,' orig. LAS (with a secondary Sanskrit laṣ 'to desire'), whence λι-λα-ίομαι, lascivus, lust. The same form occurs xii 124, xiii 1.

86. **raṇa-viçârada**, 'skilled in the fight.' As **raṇa** also means noise, we might seem to have here a parallel to the Homeric βοὴν ἀγαθός. But the Vedic meaning of the word is 'delight' and √raṇ (or ran) is 'to take pleasure'—doubtless akin to √ram: so that 'delight of battle,' has been the transition, and χάρμη is the Greek equivalent—in sense only.

viçârada, 'wise,' 'skilful,' xx 26 saṅkhyâne viçâradam: the derivation is not clear.

kṛitâstram, 'skilled in weapons': 'astrâṃ kṛi' is 'to practise the use of arms.'

87. **bhavet**, for the optative see i 30 note.

88. **yat-kṛite**, 'for whose sake,' ix 19 note. The antecedent to yat is Nalam in the next line.

bhṛiça-dâruṇam, see v 12 note.

89. 'If in some (few) days and nights I shall not see king Nala, I will join myself to happiness by loosing myself from this body.' **ahorâtrair**, for the instrumental see note on divâ (ii 4): for the Dvandva, xii 61. Damayanti neglects the contingency of being born again: at all events she will be one step nearer to final happiness, by getting rid of this present life.

dehasya, 'body,' xvi 18, from √dih, v 11 note. The primary sense would seem to be 'something moulded' (comp. the use of Latin fingo) to receive the soul: which is often called 'dehin' 'the embodied,' e.g. Bh. Gītā, ii 22.

90. 'What good to me is life, apart from the king of men?'—a very idiomatic use of the instrumental, parallel to Latin opus with the ablative, 'what work is there to be done by means of life?' Comp. Bhag. Gītā iii 18 naiva tasya kṛitenârtho nâkṛiteneha kaçcana: literally 'there is not of him any concern whatsoever (or 'business') with a thing done or undone here'; i.e. all things earthly are indifferent to the man who manages life rightly. For **artha** see note on iii 7. Very often the instrumental can be used alone, without any other noun—e.g. Hit. 169 nirujaḥ...kiṃ auṣadaiḥ? 'what has a healthy man to do with medicines?': here we must assume an ellipse, unless we prefer to take auṣadaiḥ as sociative: as we might say in Latin 'quid tibi est mecum?'

ṛite, iv 26 &c., is the locative of ṛita (see xxi 13 note) p. p. of √ṛi, see iv 7.

92. **udarkas**, 'thy coming time,' so udarke 'in the future,' xxi 26. It means first 'breaking up' or 'forth' (Vedic, of wind and song) from *ark, whence √arc and √ṛic 'to stream forth'; with further meanings, for which see note on ii 15: hence also arka 'the sun' xvi 16.

kṣipram, 'quickly' from √kṣip, 'to put into quick motion,' and so 'to throw,' iii 13 note. It can hardly be the Greek κραιπνός as Bopp suggests: that is for κραπ-ινο-ς, and of the same family as καρπ-άλιμος, our 'leap,' and Lat. carpo in the phrase 'carpere viam.'

drakṣyasi, 2 fut. of √dṛiç, the ç passing into orig. *k* before *s*, M. M. Gr. § 125.

93. **ripu-nipâtinam**, 'him who makes his foes to fall.' **ripu** is formed by suffix *u* from Vedic √rip 'to smear,' and varies only by having *r* for *l* from LIP, whence λίπος, λιπαρής, ἀλείφω, &c., Curt. no. 340. Hence the Vedic meaning of ripu is 'a deceiver,' by a very common metaphor: in Plautus we have fuci et fallaciae, os sublinere alicui &c.; and Curtius quotes from this very root λιμφεύειν, ἀπατᾶν, Hesych., and compares Germ. 'anschmieren.'

vigatajvara, 'his fever past away': comp. Macbeth's phrase 'after life's fitful fever he sleeps well.' **jvara** comes from √jvar which is the same as √jval already discussed at xi 35, but while that means 'to blaze,' this is limited to the sense of 'fever,' 'sickness,' and 'pain.' Again at xx 39, xxiv 53.

94. **sarvapâpebhyaḥ**, viii 3 note. **praçâsatam**, 'ruling this city,' iii 21 note. **bhûyaḥ**, viii 14 note.

95. 'The causer of fear in them that hate him.' **dviṣatâm**, pres. part. of √dviṣ (ix 9 note) used for a subst., like amans and a few others in Latin. Here the Sanskrit and Latin alike miss the Greek article.

kalyâṇâbhijanam, 'of noble race': xvi 26 tulyâbhijana. The identical ἐπί-γονο-ς has a different sense.

96. **mahiṣim**, i 7 note.

antarhitâḥ, 'disappeared,' p. p. of antar + √dhâ; there is no Latin *interdo; but inter-eo 'to disappear,' 'perish utterly,' is the corresponding passive. The first *a* of antarhitâḥ coalesces irregularly with the final of tâpasâ (for tâpasâs).

sâgnihotrâçramâs, 'with their fires and hermitages'—a B. V. compound. Agni-hotra is primarily the oblation (hotra) to the consecrated fire, so 'agnihotram...juhuyât,' Manu iv 25: then the sacred fire itself, as v 127, strīṃ dvijātiḥ pūrva-māriṇīṃ dāhayed agnihotreṇa, 'let the twice-born consume with sacred fire the wife who predeceases him.'

97. **āçcaryam**, 'a wonder,' from ā + √car with euphonic ç, i.e. 'a thing to be gone to,' and āçcaryavat, Bh. G. ii 29. Again xxiii 14.

98. **ko 'yaṃ vidhir**, "What hath been this wondrous chance." Dean Milman. Vidhi = 'ereigniss' (event) P. W. See note iv 17.

99. **nagā**, 'non-goers,' here (and apparently 109) 'trees'; elsewhere naga is a mountain (xiii 9) like acala. Agama (xii 103) has the same history.

100. **dhyātvā**, ind. part. of √dhyai orig. dhyā (whence this form and others before terminations beginning with *t* or *s*). See note on sandhyā vii 3. The perf. dadhyau occurs xix 3.

101. **vāṣpasaṃdigdhayā**, 'indistinct through tears': digdha is p. p. of √dih, v 11 note.

açru, 'a tear,' prob. from √ak 'to be sharp': the radical idea being 'pain'—as much as if we followed Grassmann's suggestion that it comes from DAK; he compares δάκ-ρυ and δάκ-νω.

tarum, 'a tree,' prob. from √tar in the sense of 'pressing through,' 'forcing up'—though it must be admitted that the etymology is a little strained. It is difficult to separate it from taruṇa 'tender' or that from Latin teres—both of which Curtius (no. 239) derives from √tar in the sense of 'rubbing' (whence tero, τείρω).

102. **pallava**, 'a shoot.' At Hit. 645 we have pallava-grāhi pāṇḍityam 'superficial (lit. 'twig-picking') learning.'

āpiḍitam, v 2 note. Benfey however takes it as a derivative of āpiḍa (next line) = 'chapleted.'

103. **vanāntare**, vii 2 note.

āpiḍair, 'chaplets,' from ā + piḍ, v 2 note. The primary sense is 'squeezing.'

bhāti, in the primary sense 'shines,' see note on subhāṣitam, viii 4.

parvata-rāṭ, 'mountain-king': the final *j* has passed into *ṭ*, as at 31 and 36.

104. Note the obvious play on the name of the tree, the A-çoka 'no-sorrow.' It is further carried on in vita-çoka (vita = vi + ita), and at 107.

bhayābādham, 'unannoyed by fear,' see note on vyādha, xi 26.

106. **tanu**, 'fine,' 'delicate' (ταναός, tenuis, thin) tanu or tanū is also used for 'the body': comp. xxvi 32 tanū-ruḥ 'hair' (body-grower).

tvacam, from tvac, 'skin'—literally 'covering': there is a Vedic root of the same form.

arditam. See note on vii 17: where the other form àrtta occurs as in 108.

107. For the final sentence see note on i 21.

110. **kandaràn**, 'caves': Benfey ingeniously suggests that it = kam (an older form of kim, see note on ko-vida i 1) and dara from √dṛi 'to burst,' 'split.'

nitambhàn = 'slopes' of mountains: generally it = nates.

111. **prakṛiṣṭam**, 'long' from pra + √kṛis, vii 14. It = pro-tractus.

adhvànam, 'a road,' so adhvam kṣama 'endurance on the road,' xix 12. Bopp's derivation from √at 'mutato t in dh' is just possible.

sàrtham, 'a caravan,' from sa + artha. **saṃkulam**, see note on àkula, iv 18.

112. **uttarantam**, pres. part. of ud + tṛi, 'to cross (or 'to get out of') a stream': see ii 30 note.

prasanna, p. p. of pra + √sad i 8 note.

suçàntatoyàm, &c. 'a river of very calm water, spread out, covered with canes.' **çànta**, p. p. of √çam, see note on v 22: **toya** is a dubious word: **hradinim**, comp. vi 13 note.

vetasa, like vetra, ἰτέα, vitis and our 'withy,' comes from vi 'to bind.'

113. **prodghuṣṭam**, see ii 11 note on ghoṣa. **krauñca** is a curlew: for **kurara** see xi 20.

cakravàka is the red goose: **kùrma** is a turtle: **gràha**, 'the grasper,' is a shark (Benfey) or an alligator: at xi 21 it was used of a serpent. **jhaṣa** is fish. **pulina** and **dvipa** both mean 'island' —the second being from dvi + ap 'water': the first seems to be rather a delta, or sandbank by the side of a river.

115. **unmatta-rùpà**, see viii 1 note.

pàṃçu-dhvasta-çiroruhà, 'having dust scattered on her hair': for pàṃçu see x 6: again at xiii 28. **dhvasta** is p. p. of √dhvaṃs 'to fall to pieces': a simpler Vedic form dhvas seems to be used in the sense of being spread out like dust. At xvi 15 we have vidhvasta-parṇa-kamala 'a lotus with leaves fallen off': paridhvaṃsa = 'ruin' x 9, and Hit. 125 dhvaṃsa-kàrin = 'destroying.' **çiroruha**, 'head-growing' is a good paraphrase for hair; as çirodhara is for the neck.

116. **pradudruvuḥ**, i 25 note. **pracukruçuḥ**, see xi 2 note.

117. **sma** here seems certainly to turn this present among past tenses into a perfect sense: i 12 note.

abhyasúyantı, xii 47 note. **dayám**, see note on dayıta, ii 19.

118. **mṛıgayase**: see x 23 note.

vyathıtá, 'disquieted,' p. p. of √vyath 'to tremble,' xxii 23. It is near in form to √vyadh xi 26: but they are distinct from Vedic time. If **smeha** be for smas ıha, and not for sma ıha (M. W. Glossary) there is a peculiar violation of Sandhi: comp. sm' etı xvii 35.

120. **sur-án.ganá**, 'a woman of the gods,' i. e. an Apsaras, one of the nymphs of Indra's heaven, comp. xxvi 14 mám upasthásyatı...dıvı Çakram ıv' ápsaráḥ: see Dowson, who has abridged Goldstücker's article.

sarvathá, &c., 'in all ways bless us.' **svastı**, i. e. su + √as + tı is properly a feminine noun meaning 'happiness': but it was used as a greeting (i. e. svasty astu) and eventually is used here as though it were an indeclinable word with √kṛı.

121. 'That this caravan may by all means go hence speedily in safety, so order matters, lady, that prosperity may be ours,'—a double final clause after vıdhatsva, for which see v 19 note.

kṣemi, formed from kṣema 'safety,' 'happiness,' but apparently in its first meaning 'a quiet abode' from √kṣı (for which see ii 20 note); so Grassmann, s. v. Compare note on line 70.

çighram, 'quick,' so xv 6, yena çighrá hayá mama bhaveyuḥ.

123. **yuva-sthavıra-bálás**, 'youths and old men (iv 25) and children'—a Dvandva. **yuvan** rejects its final *n* in compounds, like rájan, &c. The word is very parallel to Lat. iuvenis, which however has a further suffix. The Zend keeps orig. *a* in yavan. Curtius (no. 257 note) connects it with √dıv, 'to play,' as Bopp originally did: if so, the Sanskrit and Latin, Gothic and Sclavonic forms would come from the secondary dyu: and the *d* seems to be lost in all the languages.

125. **márgámı**, 'I seek.' See note on márga, xii 63.

aparájıtam, 'unconquered,' a + pará (i 5 note) + √jı.

126. **amıtra-gaṇa-súdana**, comp. xii 33: and for **súdana**, ii 23.

128. **netá**, see note on ánayya, viii 5.

130. 'Manıbhadra, king of the Yakshas,' is supposed to be Kuvera; but at xiii 22, 23 the two are distinct, for Vaıçravaṇa is a patronymic of Kuvera, son of Vıçravas. However that may be, the name has apparently the same meaning as 'Ratna-garbha,' another name of the

god of wealth. He appears here and xiii 22 as the protector of travellers.

prasidatu, 'be propitious,' from pra + √sad (i 8 note): the present base is sida, M. W. Gr. § 270, M. M. App. no. 52.

131. **banijaḥ**, 'merchants': it is corrupted from * paṇij, and a still simpler form paṇi is Vedic, chiefly in the sense of the 'covetous' man, who will not sacrifice to the gods. The root is paṇ (whence paṇa, vii 8); see xxvi 6, and the p. p. paṇita, xxvi 19, 'defeated at play' or (as we say) 'played out.' The root was originally a present base par-ṇa (hence the cerebral), from orig. PAR, whence πέρνημι, πρίαμαι. See note on xii 81.

132. **janapadam**, 'district,' so pura-janapade 'pi ca, 'in town and country,' xxvi 33.

làbhàya, 'for the sake of getting.' The √labh is certainly the same as Gr. √λαβ, but it shews an aspirate, which is also seen in λάφ-υρα and εἴληφα—but these may be special Greek changes. The form lambh is also found, which recalls the Ionic λάμψομαι. In different ways the root is perplexing. It is discussed at length by Curtius, Vol. II. pp. 144—6 (Eng. tr.).

Note the dative of the purpose. It occurs again xxvi 12 arjitaṃ vittam pratipàṇàya: and arthàya is the same (Nalasyàrthàya xiii 42, Ṛituparṇasya...arthàya, xxiii 10). Comp. also xiii 4 niveçàya mano dadhuḥ. But it is not nearly so common here as the locative. In Vedic however it is constantly used, especially of nouns which denote some operation, e.g. piti, 'drinking'—Indraṃ somasya pitaye... havàmahe; and the frequently recurring jivase (= Latin vivere), and dàvana (= Greek δοῦναι) throw valuable light on the origin of the infinitive in those languages, i.e. originally a dative (or locative) expressing the object of an action: so the Homeric ξυνέηκε μάχεσθαι (for the fighting) or βῆ δ' ἰέναι, 'he strode forth to go': comp. the Horatian 'tradam... portare ventis' (for the carrying). There is a further interesting analogy between the Latin supine, which also represents the object of going ('spectatum veniunt') and the Sanskrit infinitive: here 'motion towards' has been the primary idea. It is noteworthy that in classical Sanskrit, where the locative is used to express the object, it is mainly used with verbs which do *not* denote motion, such as √kṛi, √dhà, &c.

2. **kâle bahutithe**, see ix 12 note.

saugandhikam, formed from su-gandha, by Vṛiddhi, and suffix ika (Gr. -ικο, Lat. -ico).

3. **prabhûta-yavas'-endhanam**, 'with abundant grass and fire-wood.' **prabhûta**, p. p. of pra + √bhû = 'large,' 'long,' 'abundant.' **yavasa** is akin to yava, 'barley,' Greek ζεά (perhaps also ἠία, but see note on çasya, xxiv 48), Lith. yava, 'any kind of corn.' Probably the root is yu, 'to bind.' **indhana** is from √indh, orig. IDH, whence αἴθω, &c., aedes, Curt. no. 302.

4. **nirmala**, see note on x 6.

suçitalam, 'very cold,' from çitala, a fuller form of çita, which is p. p. of a Vedic √çyâ, 'to stiffen': hence 'to freeze.' Çitâṃçu, 'cold-rayed' is a name for the moon, xxiv 53.

5. **sammate**, 'with the approval of the conductor, they entered that splendid wood,' sammate, p. p. of sam + √man, being the loc. abs., 'it being approved.' **sârthavâhasya** must be genitive of the agent, like ipsito varanârinâm, i 4. **uttama** is generally 'topmost,' 'best': used here, as sattama, &c., not 'best of all,' but one of the class 'best.'

velâm, &c., 'having reached the evening time.' **velâ** is a 'limit,' 'boundary,' but specially used of time, perhaps at first like καιρός, but then without any apparent sense of limit. At Hit. 362 lagna-velâ = auspicious time; Çak. iii 59 ugratâpâ velâ, 'time of fierce heat.'

paçcimâm, formed from paçca, a Vedic adj. afterwards disused, except in the abl. paçcât = 'behind,' 'afterwards' xviii 18. It there means 'western': as dakṣiṇa (ix 21) meant 'southern.' Pûrva is 'eastern.' So in Manu ii 22,

> â samudrât tu vai pûrvâd, â samudrât tu paçcimât,
> tayor ev' ântaraṃ giryor Âryavarttaṃ vidyur budhâ,.

i.e. 'as far as the eastern ocean, and as far as the western ocean, the country which lies between those two mountains (Himālaya to the north, Vindhya to the south) the learned consider to be Aryavartta (i.e. the home of the Aryas).' A-paçcima xiii 33 = 'that which has no last,' 'extreme': comp. anuttama v 35. M. Williams (Glossary) takes it 'having no end,' apparently therefore = endless. Paçca is formed from pas + ca, which (as in ucca, nica) may be a weakening of √anc. The same stem is seen in Italian pos (Lat. pone for posne, Osc. pos-mos, 'last'), Curt. Gr. Et. Vol. II p. 385 (Eng. tr.).

âsâdya, x 7 note.

6. 'Then at the half-night-time (vii 1 note) voiceless and motionless, at that moment, when the wearied caravan slept, a herd of elephants approached the mountain stream, turbid with the flow of the mada, to get drink.' **niḥçabda-stimita** is a Dvandva. For niḥçabda, see 28 note. Stimita is 'wet,' from √stim, then 'motionless,' perhaps through an intermediate sense 'numb.' In the P. W. however the order of the meanings is reversed.

pariçrânte, see note on âçrama, ix 22.

7. **pâniya**, 'drink,' properly fut. part. pass. from √pâ, whence πῶμα, potus, &c.

mada-prasravaṇa, 'flowing of the mada,' i.e. the juice that exudes from the temples of the elephant, see i 24 note: **prasravaṇa** from √sru, orig. SRU for SAR-U, whence ῥέω, ῥεῦμα, rumen, 'stream,' &c., Curt. no. 517: srotas, 'water,' xvi 14.

8. **grâmya-gajân**, 'tame elephants': grâmya, from grâma, 'a village,' iv 10.

vegena, 'impetuously,' see ix 26 note: for the instrumental, comp. javena, xi 26 note.

jighaṃsanto, 'eager to kill,' pres. part. of desiderative of √han, M. W. Gr. § 654. M. M. App. no. 168.

utkaṭa is 'excessive.' So Hit. 435 aty-utkaṭaiḥ pâpa-puṇyair ihaiva phalam açnute, 'a man reaps even here the fruit of excessive bad and good deeds' (comp. the use of fruor with the instr. ablative). Then it means 'drunken,' 'furious,' as here.

9. 'The impetuosity of those elephants, as they fell unexpectedly upon them, was irresistible, like that of rent peaks falling from the mountain top upon the earth.' â + √pat gives the further idea of nearness and sometimes of surprise. **karin** is an elephant, from kara, 'a hand' (comp. hastin, ii 11); but used absolutely for an elephant's

trunk, below at 12. **duḥsaho** from dus + √sah, see note on utsahate, iv 8.

naga, xii 99 note.

çirṇânâṃ, p. p. of √çṛi, 'to hurt,' or 'break.' It is apparently Gr. √κερ in κείρω, &c., Lat. curtus, Curt. no. 53; with vı, it occurs xiii 17 = 'broken down,' 'trampled on.' Also it is used of fading away, as flowers, e.g. Hit. 625 vıçiryed...vane.

çṛın·gânâm, xii 37 note. **nag'-âgrâd**, xii 99.

'The paths of the rushing elephants were destroyed (i.e. strewn) by the growths of the wood, blocking the path of the lake against the slumbering caravan': so I take this rather difficult passage, making sârtham acc. after mârgaṃ saṃrudhya, like çaraṇaṃ devâñ jagmatur, v 33, jıtvâ râjyaṃ Nalam, vii 5. The simple verb can take a double accusative: see P. W. s. v.

10. **syandatâm**, literally 'streaming,' from √syand. At Çak. i 14 it = 'drip.'

nâgânâm, 'elephants': but 'serpents,' at v 7.

naṣṭâ, from √naç, viii 18.

udbhava is 'birth,' 'origin': so vanodbhava is 'that which has the wood for its origin,' trees, boughs, leaves, &c.

saṃrudhya, from sam + √rudh, iv 10 note.

padmıni, 'abounding in lotuses,' regular synonym for a lake, so xvi 15.

11. 'They crushed it suddenly as it struggled on the earth.' **ceṣṭamânam**, see xi 28 note.

hâhâkâram, 'a cry of lamentation': comp. hâhâ-bhûtam, xvii 31; and hâh'etı muktaḥ çabdaḥ v 28: for muñca, the base of √muc, see M. W. Gr. § 281, M. M. App. no. 107: comp. vında from √vıd, ii 4.

çaraṇârthınaḥ, 'seeking a refuge.' See notes on v 15, and iii 7.

12. **vanagulmâñç**, xi 9: **dhâvanto**, i 26.

nıdr'ândhâ, 'sleep-blind.' **nıdrâ** is from nı + √drâ, 'to sleep': the orig. form must have been DAR, of which √drâ is the nearest exponent: in other languages we find a secondary letter as ἔ-δραθ-ον, dor-m-io; Curt. no. 262. **andha**, 'blind,' is of uncertain origin: Grassmann (s.v.) refers it to the root ADH; whence come andhas, 'herbs,' especially those offered in sacrifice, and a very large family in Greek, mainly nasalised, as ἄνθος, ἀνθέω, ἀν-ήν(ο)θ-ε, &c.: see Curt. no. 304: also Lat. ador. But for all these it suffices that the root meaning should be 'to bloom.' In order to bring andha, 'blind,' under the same root, Grassmann takes an original sense 'to cover.'

dantaıḥ...gajaıḥ: note the instrumental used alike of the agent and of the instrument: and compare line 15.

13. **nıhatoṣṭrâç**, 'with their camels killed,' a curious way of expressing the fact by a B.V. compound. **uṣṭra** can hardly come (as Bopp took it) from √us 'to burn': yet it cannot be easily referred to any of the different roots of the form VAS.

padâtı-jana, 'the foot-going people.' Padâtı (xxvi 2) is very near to ped-it-i: but that must come from √ı, 'to go': this may be from √at, 'to go.'

parasparahatâs, 'slain the one by the other': see note on v 33.

14. 'Uttering dreadful cries they fell on the earth, having climbed up in the trees in their agitation, and fallen upon the rough spots.' There should be no comma after patıtâ, which is to be taken with vıṣameṣu: the ca may either join patıtâ to vṛıkṣeṣv âruhya, or (better) may join the whole line to the preceding one.

âruhya is ind. part. of â + √ruh, see note on âropya viii 19.

saṃrabdhâḥ is from sam + √rabh, see iv 16 note: it occurs again xxvi 3. **vıṣameṣu**, viii 13 note.

15. 'Thus in many ways by fate through the elephants having attacked them, all that prosperous caravan was destroyed.' For âkramya with hastıbhıḥ see note on viii 22, taiḥ sametya. Note the three instrumentals; prakâraır, modal, daıvena, causal, and hastıbhıḥ, instrumental, or perhaps of the agent.

samṛıddham, x 2 note. **sârtha-maṇḍalam**, comp. âçrama-maṇḍala, xii 64.

16. 'And there was a huge cry causing fear in the three worlds': see ii 13 note. **ârâva** is from â + √ru, x 20 note. 'It is a bad fire that has broken out.' Kaṣṭa occurs Hit. 487 = 'difficult,' 'troublesome,' and kaṣṭaṃ alone is a frequent ejaculation. **trâyadhvam**, 2 pers. plur. imp. mid. of √traı, iv 7 note.

17. **râçır** is 'a heap,' 'quantity': so at Hit. 966, payorâçı = 'the sea.' **vıçirṇo**, see note on xiii 9.

gṛıhṇidhvam, 'pick them up: why do ye run away? This property is common: this is no deception of mine.' For the conjugation of √grah, see M. W. Gr. §§ 699 and 359, M. M. App. 157.

sâmânya is formed from sa-mâna, 'like' (sa + √mâ, 'to measure'), and has the same meaning.

draviṇaṃ, see note on dravya, viii 5. **mithyá**, xii 14 note.

18. **abhidhásyámi**, xii 76.

sakátaráḥ, 'cowardly': kátara is 'timid': Benfey (followed by the P.W.) would derive it from katara, 'which of the two.'

19. **saṃkṣaye**, 'destruction,' from √kṣi, ii 12 note.

bubudhe, 'woke up,' as at x 22. **santrasta**, xi 1 note.

20. **vaiçasam**, 'destruction,' through *viçasa from vi + √ças, xi 10 note; again at 35.

21. **saṃsaktavadanáçvásá**, 'with breathing stuck to her mouth,' i.e. with suppressed breathing. **saṃsakta**, p. p. of sam + √sañj, v 9. **vihvalá**, xi 14.

vinirmuktá, 'escaped,' p. p. of vi + nis + √muc, v 28. **avikṣatáḥ**, see note on akṣaya, ii 18.

ye...kecid, 'whoever,' compare yat...kiṃcana, iv 2: perhaps here = 'the few, who,' &c.

22. 'Of what action is this the fruit?' see note on ix 11. 'Surely it must be that Maṇibhadra was not honoured.'

núnam, see note on viii 17.

23. **Váiçravaṇaḥ**, i.e. Kuvera, see note on xii 130. He is properly called 'the lord of the Yakshas.'

na pújá, &c. 'Or has worship not been first offered to the causers of hindrances?' because those who cause can also remove them. Vighna an obstacle (xx 19, vighnaṃ kartum) is from vi + √han (ghan) + a: see note on çatru-ghna, xii 18. Gaṇeça, the elephant-headed son of Çiva, also called Vighneça, and Vighna-hári, is the God especially meant, "He is the God of wisdom and remover of obstacles; hence he is invariably propitiated at the beginning of any important undertaking, and is invoked at the commencement of books." Dowson. He is still one of the most widely worshipped Gods in India: being the domestic household God of all classes.

24. **çakunánám**, from çakuna (n.) 'an omen': at ix 12 çakuna (m.) was 'a bird,' in which sense it occurs in the Vedic hymns. At Manu iv 126 and 130 omens are given: if cattle, or a frog, or a cat or other beast cross the path, reading of the Vedas is to be stopped: and passing over the shadow of images of the Gods, Brāhmans or others is unlucky. But these have nothing to do with birds. Schlegel (note on Bh. G. i 31) quotes from Rámáyaṇa I lxxiv, an apparent case of drawing omens from the cries of birds, 'ghoráḥ sma pakṣiṇo váco vyáharanti samantataḥ': whence Vasishṭha augurs evil. But the same authority says that he knows of no omens drawn from the

flying of birds. I do not find in Manu instructions for the road, such as the caravan here required: at iv 130 there is a general direction that a man must not travel too early or too late, or too near midday, or with an unknown man, or alone, or with Çûdras. M. Williams, 'Ind. Wisdom,' p. 296, gives us one of the indications of the later date of Yājnavalkya's code (as compared with Manu's), that in it "the worship of Gaṇeça as the remover of obstacles is expressly alluded to at I 270, and Graha-yajna or offerings to the planets is directed to be made." The line is apparently to be taken thus: 'Or is this certainly the adverse result of omens?' For **viparitam**, see note on viparyayas viii 15, and for **dhruvam**, vi 11.

grahà, &c. 'But surely the planets were not adverse'—apparently carrying on the force of nûnam. The Grahas are the five principal planets, Mercury, Venus, Mars, Juppiter and Saturn, called respectively Budha, Çukra, Man-gala, Vṛihaspati and Çani.

kim, 'apart from these, what is this that is come upon us?'

25. **jnàtidravyavinàkṛitàḥ**, 'deprived of relations and wealth.' Curtius (G. E. no. 135) takes jnâti from jnâ, 'to know,' in the sense of 'acquaintance,' and so 'relations'—in order to keep the derivatives of √jan and √jnà distinct. Generally no doubt they are distinct; yet in most languages there is a little overlapping. In Greek γνή-σι-ος shews the same primary base (gnâ-ti) as the Sanskrit, and in the same sense: and in Latin we have gna-tus. It seems best to attribute these forms to imperfect differentiation.

vinà-kṛitàḥ, see note on alaṃ-kṛi, i 11.

yàsàvadya, i.e. yà asau adya, 'she who to-day, &c.'

asau (iii 2, xxii 10, 17, xxiii 8) is a rather rare pronoun, used in the nom. sing. masc. and fem.; the bases seem to be a + sa + u: see note on uta ii 25. In the other cases (except the neut. nom. and acc., where the form is adas) the base is amu, i.e. a + ma + u. This restriction of *s* to the masc. and fem. nominative, is parallel to the history of the more common pronoun sa, sà, tad. **hi**, i 29 note; here just like γάρ, 'why, by that woman who, &c.'

26. **vikṛit-àkàrà**, 'disfigured in shape'—not necessarily however meaning more than 'changed': for àkàra, see ii 5 note.

vihità, 'brought about.' See note on v 19. So Hit. 963, sàdhyasiddhir vidhiyate, 'success in the undertaking is obtained.'

màyà, 'deceit,' or 'trick': at Hit. 828, asatyaṃ sàhasam màyà... 'untruthfulness, precipitancy, deceit,' &c. are the special faults of women. Here it seems to mean 'witchcraft,' or something of that sort. In the sense 'illusion,' it expressed the doctrine of the later Vedānta philosophy (now supposed to have been introduced into it from Buddhism), that all the visible world was a mere phantasm, possessing no real existence. This is an interesting parallel to Plato's doctrine, and partially to that of Berkeley.

27. **piçáci**, xii 7 note.

n' átra, &c., 'there is no investigation to be made therein,' i.e. there is no doubt of that: see note on vicára v 15.

28. 'If we could see the evil one, destroyer of the caravan, giver of many a woe, with clods, aye with dust, with grass and with sticks, with our fists, we would assuredly kill her that is the bane of the caravan.'

tṛiṇa, 'grass,' is our 'thorn,' German 'dorn': Curtius (II. p. 108, Eng. tr.) connects *θρόνα*, of which a variant *τρόνα· ἀγάλματα ἢ ῥάμματα ἄνθινα* is preserved by Hesychius.

káṣṭha is 'wood' generally, or logs of wood, it may be the boughs of the fallen trees here. Bopp would connect it with Welsh 'coed.' **muṣṭi** is supposed by Bopp and Benfey to be the same as our 'fist.'

29. **avaçyam**, 'involuntary,' from a + vaç = ἀ-Fεκ, see viii 15: the phrase 'avaçyam eva,' is very common = 'without any choice,' 'of necessity.'

kṛityakám is from kṛityá, which means 'practice' against any person to his hurt: at Manu ix 290, is given the penalty for persons who so practise 'múlakarmaṇi (i.e. with roots)...kṛityásu vividhásu ca.' It is formed from √kṛi, not from √kṛit, 'to cut.'

30. **hritá**, 'ashamed,' p. p. of √hri: of doubtful connection. Bopp connects with our 'rue,' through hreowan (Benfey): if so the Sanskrit translation must have come from k through g and gh, which seems unlikely. Hence hri, 'shame,' Hit. 629, dáridrád dhriyam eti, 'from poverty he comes to shame.'

saṃvigná, see note on udvejate ix 26.

prádravad, &c., 'ran away to the forest,' lit. ran where the forest (is). It somewhat resembles the use of *ὡς* (virtually as a preposition) with *τὸν ἄνδρα* in Greek. But the noun remained in the nominative case: comp. xxiv 6, Nalam praveçayámása yatra tasyáḥ pratiçrayaḥ. There is an antecedent at vii 1, ájagáma tatas tatra, yatra rájá sa Naiṣadhaḥ.

paryadevayat, from pari + √div, 'to lament' (10 cl.—also 1), and so distinguished from div to play (4 cl. base divya): a separate base dev is also assumed for it. The p. p. paridevitam occurs v 22 (where see note), and paridevaná, Bh. G. ii 28. The two senses of √div—'to shine,' and 'to play' (esp. at dice)—may be united in a primary sense 'to throw,' or 'scatter.' But this third sense of 'lamentation,' is not easy to be understood.

31. 'Alas! above me (comp. upari sarveṣám i 2) is the great and terrible wrath of fate': for **saṃrambha**, see note on árabhya, iv 16: the same root occurred xiii 14 in the sense of 'confusion,'—whence came the later idea of passion. Vidhi (iv 17) is 'lot,' 'destiny,' and here personified: 'fatum' has a similar history.

n'ánubadhnáti, &c., 'good luck (viii 4 note) comes not after me.' The verb is from anu + √bandh (9 cl.), which with four others rejects the radical nasal before the inflectional, M. W. Gr. § 362: this is probably a grammatical way of stating the fact that the radical nasal was only an inflectional one made permanent in the other tenses, as in Latin iungo, iunxi, iunctum. But if so, the inflection is Indo-European, for it is extensively found in the derivatives. There are two roots BHANDH, and BHIDH, the second a corruption of BHADH the original of the first: for which, see Curtius (G. E. nos. 326 and 327): the first is seen in bandhu 'relation,' xvi 18, in πενθερός, and our 'band,' the second in πείθω, fidus, foedus, with a metaphorical sense: but the concrete is seen in filum for *fid-lum. In Sanskrit, the simple verb means 'to bind': but with anu, it is 'to hold together,' 'continue,' 'follow,' as here. It is used with ni in the simple sense xvi 8. For p. p. baddha comp. xxvi 16.

32. 'I remember not any sin done to any man whatsoever, even the least.' **açubha**, comp. xxii 14: so we speak of a 'black' or a 'dark' deed. Note the genitive of the object after kṛi. This construction is not uncommon. At xvii 39 we have tasyáḥ prasádaṃ kuru: at xxiii 12 tṛiṇamuṣṭiṃ...savitus taṃ samádadhat, i.e. the genitive with √dhá. So krudh, 'to be angry,' takes a genitive at xviii 11: and √bhi, 'to fear,' at xii 11. See further examples at v 38 note.

aṇu is 'small,' 'minute': also used as a noun for the smallest measure of time: and aṇuka for an atom.

karmaṇá, &c., 'by deed, or thought, or word': probably these are better taken as modal instrumentals with the preceding words, rather than with what follows.

33. 'Surely some great evil done in another (previous) birth is fallen

on me.' See note on antara, vii 2. Many ill deeds in previous lives were punished by bodily defects, unless they were duly expiated: these are given in Manu xi 48 &c., and are curious: thus a drinker of spirits will have black teeth, a slanderer will have bad breath, a stealer of a lamp blindness, and so on. Men who have committed great crimes may be born in lower forms: see Manu xii 54. Thus a slayer of a Brāhman must enter (according to the aggravating circumstances) the body of a dog, a boar, an ass, a camel, a bull, a goat, a sheep, a stag, a bird, or a Chandāla, i.e. the lowest of the low, the offspring of a Çūdra father by a Brāhman woman.

apaçcımám, see note on xiii 5.

34. 'The taking away of husband and kingdom (unless we take bhartṛ-rájya as a T. P. 'the kingdom of my husband'; but it is better taken as a dvandva) and separation from my own folk, sundering from my husband, and loss of my children.'

parájaya is 'victory' or 'defeat of a person,' hence the loss incurred by that person—used with the abl. of the thing lost. **bhartrá saha vıyogas** is a curious oxymoron, 'separation with (instead of 'from') my husband.' The sociative is often used with words expressing separation: so xv 14 tayá vyayujyata: xx 44 vımuktaḥ Kalıná 'freed from Kalı'; xix 14 varjıtál lakṣaṇaır 'free from marks'; xiii 53 bhúṣanaır varjıtam 'without ornaments': so hina at xvi 18 and 20, vıhina at xvii 20. Also the preposition vıná 'without' is so used, as bhúṣanaır vıná xvi 19. The conception of union comes first and is denoted by the sociative—in this case with the addition of saha which seems quite unnecessary: then comes the idea of 'disjunction' expressed in another word.

tanayábhyám, xii 12 note: **vıcyutı**, ix 18 note.

35. **nırnáthatá**, 'the state of being without a protector' (nátha, x 21).

aparedyuḥ, 'the next day,' an adverb, though here it would certainly be more convenient to take it as a loc. with samprápte: it may be taken however 'on the next day, when it (the day) came.' The fact that apare is locative helps the collocation: but dyus is for dıvas, or, perhaps, originally, dıvası.

hata-çıṣṭá, 'left out of the slain,' or perhaps 'having the remainder slain,'—taking it as a B. V. For çıṣṭa see i 30 note. Hataçeṣa, in the same sense, occurs at 44: and the P. W. takes çeṣa as an adj. in this compound; which favours the first explanation.

36. **sakháyam**, from sakhı, which has two bases, sakháy for the

strong cases, and sakhi for the weak ones. The nom. is sakhâ, xiv 8; see M. M. Gr. § 232.

37. **arṇavaḥ**, 'company' at the end of a compound: literally 'sea,' as also the Vedic arṇa: the word seems to run back to √AR 'to go.'

38. **manda-bhâgyâd**, 'ill luck'—a secondary sense from 'unhappiness,' which again arises from the literal meaning 'little merit,' obtained in previous existences. Compare alpa-bhâgya xv 19, and also alpa-puṇya xv 17, which has just the same meaning, i. e. 'bad.' See x 14 note. Manda = 'a fool' at xiii 69, xv 10, and is used adverbially = 'little' at xvi 8: mandaṃ mandam is 'slowly,' 'softly' (Hit. 981), 'gradually' Çak. i 15.

eva = γε: 'by *my* ill luck (and no one's else) this arises.'

prâptavyam, &c. 'Assuredly even on this very day a long misery is to be entered upon by me.'

39. Compare xi 7, where the same idea occurs.

anuçâsanam, 'precept': derived like çâstra from √çâs, iii 21 note.

yad, 'inasmuch as,' or 'because' (quod) as at vi 6, xi 10: the statement being made as an additional confirmation of the rule, and so (in so far as it goes) a proof of it. Yat stands here in the place of yatra xi 7.

40. 'For nothing whatsoever is there here on earth done by men (gen. of agent) contrary to fate.' It might help the argument to take narâṇâm as genitive of the object after kṛtam, like kasyacit in line 32; i.e. 'everything that befalls man is fated.' But it comes to nearly the same thing, inasmuch as a man's actions in a previous life constitute his destiny in the next.

vidyate, ii 4 note.

na ca, &c. 'And nothing evil has been done by me even in the state of infancy, by deed thought or word, that this evil has come upon me.' **yat** here introduces a sort of object clause '*in that* I am suffering, it is not my fault.' So viii 17 na doṣo 'sti Naiṣadhasya mahâtmanaḥ, yat tu me vacanaṃ râjâ n'âbhinandati: if the reading there be right: compare also xvi 20.

Damayantī seems to mean that she has done nothing wrong 'even in infancy' when she could not know the nature of her actions, and so sinned, if at all, involuntarily. But demerit may be accumulated unintentionally. We frequently find that penance is to be done for faults involuntarily committed. For example, many kinds of food are unlawful, and some of these may have been unwittingly taken:

therefore a twice-born man must annually perform a penance 'ajñáta-bhuktı-çuddhy-artham,' 'for the sake of purification of unknown (improper) food' (Manu v 21).

41.   **manye** is often used parenthetically, like Greek οἶμαι, or Lat. credo, reor, &c., to emphasize a statement: so at viii 17, &c.: though it does not often stand first.

42.   'There the Gods were refused (iv 4) by me for the sake of Nala (see notes on iii 7, xii 132): assuredly by their influence (iii 24) I have earned this divorcement.'   **práptavati** is like dṛṣṭavat, i 29.

43.   **evam-ádını**, see iii 5 note.

vılapya, vii 16 note: **pralápa** has the same sense—it also means 'prattling,' from the natural force of pra.

44.   **veda-páragaıḥ**, see xii 81.

candra-lekhá, 'like the autumnal moon-streak,' or as we should say 'sickle.'   **çáradi** is formed from çarad (the season between Varshā 'the rains' and Hemanta 'the cold season').   Comp. xxvi 25, 'live a hundred autumns!' sañjiva çaradaḥ çatam.

45.   **ásádayad**, x 7 note.   **sáyáhne**, xi 12 note.

46.   **amárjıtám**, 'uncleansed,' see v 4 note.

48.   **kutúhalát**, 'from curiosity'; compare i 16, where the meaning was rather 'eagerly.'

49.   **prásáda**, 'palace'—but apparently some raised portion of the building, commanding a view, to which the queen-mother had gone. It is exterior, for the peacocks (xxi 6) are upon it; also Damayantī at xxii 4.   In the P. W. 'a raised place for sitting on or taking a view' is given as the first meaning.   At Manu ii 204 in Haughton's translation the word is rendered 'terrace.'

ánaya, xii 68 note.

50.   **klıçyate**, 'is tormented'—perhaps akin to √kṛç, whence kṛça ii 2.

'Such the form I see, she lightens up my house'—apparently condensed from rúpo yam paçyámı—analogous to the English; comp. perhaps xviii 25, tathá ca gaṇıtaḥ kàlaḥ, sa bhavıṣyatı.   The Latin uses the relative—as 'quae tua virtus, expugnabis,' in Horace.

51.   **várayıtvá**, 'having kept off,' i.e. hindered from coming nearer: see iii 7 note.

52.   **áropya**, viii 19 note.

'Even though thus penetrated (ii 3 note) by sorrow, thou bearest a noble form (iii 12 note): thou shinest as lightning among clouds.' We might compare the Beggar Maid: 'as shines the moon in cloudy skies, she in her poor attire was seen.' The Sanskrit has the advantage in brevity.

53. çaṃsa, xii 35 note.

varȷıtam, 'deprived of,' 'without,' p. p. of the causal of √vṛȷ (see xvi 30) meaning 'to deprive,' 'abandon': so varȷıtâl lakṣaṇaır hinaıḥ 'free from bad marks,' xix 14 and vı-varȷıta *ib.* xiv 9 : â-varȷıta xxiii 15 is 'inclined towards,' 'poured out' (of water). The original form is VARG, whence εἴργω, urgeo, 'wring'; the primitive meaning being according to Curtius (no. 142) 'to press,' according to Benfey 'to bend.' Curtius says "There is a contrast of long standing between this root and no. 153 (ARG, whence ὀρέγω, rego, 'reach') which survives in the English *right* and *wrong*." The one means 'stretched fully out,' straight before one: the other 'pressed' or 'bent' to one side, crooked.

54. 'Though unaccompanied thou shrinkest not from men, thou of immortal beauty.' asahâyâ, see vi 2 note. udvıȷası, from √vıȷ, 'to tremble,' ix 26 : like √bhi and other verbs of fearing, it takes an ablative of the source of alarm.

55. saırandhrim, &c. 'a handmaid, though of noble birth.' The word is derived by Benfey from sira 'a plough' + √dhṛı, so that a farm-servant should be the first meaning—then servant in general. On the other hand the P. W. makes it originally 'valet de chambre' (Kammerdiener). ȷâtı, 'birth,' in the form ȷāt has now supplanted varṇa in the meaning of 'caste'—which is supposed to be a Portuguese word.

bhuȷıṣyâm, &c. 'a servant, living where I will,' i. e. 'independent,' and so contrasted with 'bhuȷıṣyâ'. Kâmaga at xviii 23 has the same meaning.

56. yatrasâyam-pratıçrayâm, 'having my abode where it is evening,' i.e. lying down where she finds herself at evening. yatrasâyam is an Av. B. compound, like yathârham, ii 11 note. pratıçrayo is 'an asylum,' or 'home' in general, from pratı + √çri : again at xxiv 6. asaṃkhyeya, 'not to be counted' (xxi 9), from sam + √khyâ xiv 12. Hence saṃkhyâna 'counting,' xx 7.

nıtyam, 'constantly': nıtya means firstly 'own,' 'belonging to one,' and so 'permanent.' Grassmann derives it from √ni, which is possible. The adverb nıtyaças occurs vi 9, xxvi 14. For acc. after anuvratâ, see ii 27 note.

57. 'I was devoted to the hero, following him like a shadow on the path.' bhaktâ, see v 23 note: châyâ, v 25.

prasan·go...devane, 'attachment to play': for construction see v 22, and comp. pritis tvayi xiii 65. **prasan·ga** is from √sañj, 'to stick,' v 9.

58. **upeyivân**, x 9 note.

59. **kâranântare**, 'on some occasion of a cause,' i.e. some cause or other suggesting the time to do it. In this way of taking the phrase, antara is a noun, see vii 2 note. Benfey takes it apparently as an adj. coming last in the compound, 'for some special cause,' antara meaning first 'other,' then 'peculiar.'

60. **vyasarjayat**, v 27 note.

nagnam, 'naked'—from the same root; which seems to have fallen out in Greek and Latin. As the verb 'to nake' is used by Chaucer ('whi nake ye youre bakkis?'), Prof. Skeat is probably right in supposing that the √NAG meant 'to strip.'

62. **tyaktavân**, p. act. part. of √tyaj, 'to leave,' i 29 note, and ii 17.

anâgasam, 'guiltless,' from âgas, 'offence.' It must be akin to ἄγος, ἐναγής, &c. (Curt. no. 116), though the length of the vowel is not easily explained.

mârgamânâ, xii 63 note.

63. **kamala-garbh-âbham**, 'bright as the calyx of the lotus,' comp. xii 1 note. **âbha** from â + √bhâ, xxi 9.

prâneçvaram, v 31 note. **prakhya**, 'like,' xxi 11, from pra + √khyâ, xvi 8; but it means 'to praise'; and the derived sense of prakhya seems to have come through an intermediate one of 'clear,' transferred from sound to sight: conversely, vispaṣṭa (xii 52) was from sight to sound.

65. **vasasva mayi**, 'dwell in me,' i.e. in my neighbourhood, or under my protection. See v 32 note.

mṛigayiṣyanti, see x 23 note.

66. 'Or perhaps he of himself may come as he wanders hither and thither.' For api see i 31: for the independent use of the optative i 30.

upalapsyase, viii 3 note.

67. 'On an understanding (vii 1 note) I can dwell under thy protection, mother of heroes: I am not to eat broken meat, not to do foot-washing, and not to have converse (viii 4) with men other (than my husband) under any circumstances; if any man ask for my hand, he is to be corrected (iv 10 note), and the fool is to be punished (if he do it) more than once; such is the vow undertaken by me; but for the sake of seeking my husband (iii 7 note) I am to see

Bráhmans. If such is to be the course here, I will dwell (here) without doubt. On other terms than these, dwelling is not at all in my heart.'

68. **ucchiṣṭa**, 'remainders' of food, p. p. of ut + √çiṣ, i 30 note. At Manu v 140 it is ordained that Çūdras are to feed on 'dvijocchiṣṭam' the leavings of the 'twice-born.' **bhuñjiyám**, see ii 4 note: the verb is of the 7th class. **dhávana** is from √dháv, 'to wash' (distinct from √dháv 'to run' at i 26, &c.). Benfey compares our 'dew.' Note the usage of the optative in this passage: it is in no sense dependent: but the indefinite future sense which originally belonged to the mood comes fully out. We have analogies in Latin—an almost exact one in Horace (Od. III iii 57),

> sed bellicosis fata Quiritibus
> *hac lege* dico, *ne* nimium pii
> rebusque fidentes auitis
> tecta *uelint* reparare Troiae,

'on these terms—viz. they are not to wish, &c.'—at any future time. Good examples may also easily be found in old Latin of the independent use of the conjunctive: e.g. in Plautus (Epidicus 582) *Periphanes.* Haec negat se tuam esse matrem. *Fidicina.* Ne fuat, | si non uolt = 'she is not to be, if she doesn't like': or 'I don't want her to be.'

69. **prárthayet**, from pra + arthaya, denominative verb from artha (iii 7; see note on ii 23). **asakṛit**, ix 24.

70. **asaṃçayam**, x 1 note.

71. **ato 'nyathá**, comp. tvad-anyam, i 21 note: and for atas see ix 23 note. **vartate**, vi 40. **kvacit**, like που in Greek, is here simply modal.

72. **diṣṭyá**, instrumental of diṣṭi, 'happiness,' lit. 'with happiness to thee,' so Sáv. vi 23; used as an ejaculation = τύχῃ ἀγαθῇ, or quod tibi felix faustumque sit. 'Good luck to thee with such a vow.' Comp. xxv 10, diṣṭyá sameto dáraiḥ svair bhaván; xxvi 12, diṣṭyá tvayá 'rjitaṃ vittam.

'Having reached equality by age (with thee) let her be thy friend.'

74. **etayá**, &c. 'Together with her take thy pleasure (comp. mudita, v 39) with mind ever undisquieted,' see ix 26, note on udvejate.

75. **upádáya**, 'having taken (á + √dá) near,' or here 'with her': comp. xxv 18, sútam anyam upádáya. At xxiii 16, puṣpány upádáya is 'having taken close to him.'

1. **dávam**, 'a fire,' from √du 'to burn,' distinct from √dah xi 39. It has been raised to δαυ in Greek, whence δεδαυμένος, but generally the *u* is lost as in δέ-δη-α (with compensatory lengthening), δαίω (for δαϝ-ι-ω), δαίς, &c.: see Curt. no. 258.

gahane, xi 26.

2. **çuçráva**, perf. of √çru. **çabdam**, v 28 note; also for çapta (*inf.* 5) and çápa (6).

abhidháva, 'run to me,' see i 26.

3. **má bhair**, 'fear not'—aorist as çucaḥ xii 73; also see note on má, iii 9. But the regular aorist of the verb is abhaiṣam, abhaiṣis, abhaiṣit: so that we should have had má bhaiṣir. See M. M. App. no. 193, M. W. Gr. § 889.

kuṇḍali-kṛitam, 'curled into a ring'—kuṇḍala, see v 5. The final *a* regularly passes into *i* before kṛi.

5. **pralabdho**, 'deceived,' from pra + labh: so pralabdhavya xix 15.

6. **sthávara**, 'fixed,' stationary,' used of guards at their post. Manu ix 266. The root is probably STU, Sanskrit √sthu, whence sthula, &c., Greek στῦλος, and our 'steam,' regarded as a 'pillar,' whether of fire or vapour; so Skeat. It is generally however, derived from √sthá.

kvacit, 'some time or other,' as at xiii 61. In each place a single action is referred to, but the time is not defined.

ito netá, &c. This line shews two peculiarities, which if we were dealing with a classical author would certainly lead to emendation. The first is the position of **hi** which makes no sense with **netá**, and can hardly stand at the beginning of a new sentence. The other is the use of **mokṣyasi** as a passive verb with active terminations. (Mokṣyase would not scan, as the fourth and second syllables from the end of each half line must be short.) This is however found elsewhere in Epic poetry, e.g. adṛçyat, xx 39. Otherwise it would be easy to alter to tvâm...mokṣyati. It would probably be too abrupt to read it so, and take *ito netà hi* parenthetically, 'for he shall lead thee hence': there is a similar parenthesis at lines 20, 21.

7. 'Through his curse I am unable to put one foot before another,' lit. 'to move foot from foot.' As √cal (see v 9 note) is intransitive, padam must be regarded as a contained accusative.

trâtum arhati, see note on iii 7.

8. **sakhâ**, xiii 36 note: **pannagaḥ**, xii 9 note.

laghuç, &c., 'I shall be light to thee, swiftly come and take me.' Laghu, of course, = ἐλαχύ-ς, levis, light, with slight variation of meaning.

9. **an·guṣṭha-mâtrakaḥ**, 'of the size of a thumb,' a B.V. with suffix ka (see page 7), 'having a thumb for his measure.' An·guṣṭha is formed from *an·gu (seen in an·gula 'a finger,' Vedic an·guri) connected with an·ga, iii 13 note. An·guṣṭha-mâtra is the measure of the body in which it was believed that after the funeral sacrifice the soul arose to heaven: see 'Indian Wisdom,' pp. 204—7, 'Hinduism,' p. 65.

10. 'When he had reached a place of clear air, free from the black-pathed (fire), and desired to let the serpent go, Karkoṭaka the serpent spake to him again.' **âkâça** is 'clear air' from √kâç 'to shine,' see xvii 6 note. **vartman** is 'a road' from √vṛt, vi 4 note: the compound is a B.V., 'that which has a black path,' i.e. smoke. **utsraṣṭu** from ud + √sṛj + tu, see v 27; the root appears in the mediate form sraj—comp. v 4, where that form occurs as a noun—from orig. SARG.

11. 'Go, counting (x 29 note) some indefinite number of thy footsteps: thereupon I will assign thee the highest happiness.' This counting steps is a not unfamiliar ceremony: at some marriage rites the bridegroom makes the bride take seven steps to the N.E., each for the obtaining of some particular wish: 'Ind. Wisdom,' p. 199. For the order of the words in the last half line, see iv 3 note.

12. **ârabdham**, iv 16 note. **saṃkhyâtum**, xiii 56 note. **adaçad**, xii 31.

tadrûpam, as tasya daṣṭasya follows, probably means 'that form,'—a K. D.: otherwise we should have taken it as a T. P., 'the form of him.' **antaradhiyata**, 'was concealed' under the cover of his new shape: a rather different sense of the passive of antar + √dhá from that at xii 96, xiv 26, whence it = 'vanish.'

14. **çántvayan**, viii 12 note.

mayá, 'by me thy form has been concealed, with the thought (iti, see i 30 note, and ix 35) "people are not to know thee".' It would doubtless be possible to construe this here as a final cause, 'lest people should know thee,' and na would have the same use as Latin ne. But the construction is exactly parallel (only negative instead of positive) to ix 35 ayam abhipráyas tava 'jñátin vrajed' iti. At that passage there is no particle of purpose (e.g. yathá) corresponding to Latin ut: and it is best here also to take the clause as independent—but appositional. Iti is the indication of that apposition: and just in the same way we cannot doubt that 'ut' in Latin indicated nothing more. Ut (uti, cuti—the oldest form) is formed from the stem *ka*, which was demonstrative before it became relative, just as iti is formed from the demonstrative stem i. Compare xiii 68 note.

15. 'And he (i.e. Kali), on whose account thou art afflicted with great grief (i.e. by thy exile, &c.), he by reason of my poison shall miserably dwell in thee.'

ni-kṛito, see xi 5 note.

16. 'With limbs pervaded by poison, as long as he shall not set thee free, so long shall he dwell in thee.' At xx 30, when Nala has become thoroughly skilful in dice, Kali, apparently driven out by a stronger power, passes from his body, and is himself freed from the poison of Karkoṭaka. Nala remains freed from Kali, but still in his altered form. At xx 35 Kali says that he has dwelt in the body of Nala ever after Damayantī's curse (xi 16), tormented by the poison. We must therefore suppose that the serpent bites Nala at the same moment as Damayantī curses Kali. Kali, of course, has been in Nala ever since Nala's fatal omission (vii 3), and has perverted his reason both in gambling and in his desertion of Damayantī (x 25).

saṃvṛitair gátrair is very nearly an absolute use: though the original sociative sense is still sufficiently apparent: but there is an extension of the 'descriptive' use of the sociative illustrated at xii 37, because the noun does not here describe any permanent property of the person or thing, as it did there in 'the mountain with its lofty peaks.' We have a still clearer absolute use at xvii 11, malen' ápakṛiṣṭena, 'the dirt being washed away': another at xxv 15 sarva-kámaiḥ suvihitaiḥ (contrast xvii 18). In prahṛiṣṭen' ántarátmaná iii

30, xx 42, and prahṛṣṭena manasá xiii 71, xvii 17, the sociative use is stronger than the absolute.

17. 'Thy (bhavatas, gen. of bhavat ii 31 note) deliverance is wrought by me, by cursing in wrath him (Kali), by whom thou blameless and unworthy art afflicted.' **krodhád** is the ablative either of origin or of circumstance, like kutúhalát, i 16 note. **asúyayitvá** (xii 46 note) goes with me.

18. **bhayaṃ daṃṣṭrıbhyaḥ**, see note on pratibhayam xii 1. **çatruto**, 2nd abl. of çatru, 'an enemy,' see vi 4 note: its use, co-ordinate with daṃṣṭrıbyaḥ, shews how fully it was felt to be an ablative. **Brahmarṣıbhyaç**, i 6 note; their power to harm, if they were hostile, was greater than that of any ordinary foe. **prasádád**, comp. prasanno, i 8.

19. **vıṣa-nımittá**, see ix 34 note.

saṃgrámeṣu, xii 78.

çaçvat, 'ever,' 'always.' The history of the word is very uncertain: for Benfey's ingenious identification of it with ἅπας (i.e. sa-çvant = ἁπαντ) is open to objection. Grassmann connects it with a √çaç 'to repeat itself'—distinct from √çaç 'to leap,' whence çaça 'a hare' is supposed to come.

20. **akṣa-naipuṇam**, 'dexterity at dice.' Naipuṇa is from nipuṇa, 'clever'—apparently from some earlier meaning, 'exact,' 'complete,' found at Manu v 61, nipuṇáṃ çuddhim icchatám, 'of those who desire complete purity.' This clause must be taken parenthetically, for Ayodhyám (next line) must depend upon gaccha.

21. **hṛdayam**, 'knowledge,' so at xx 29. Compare the Latin cor, and cordatus. Note the instrumental case used of the exchange—a natural use, the 'knowledge' being the instrument whereby the exchange is made. Hence we may explain the Latin ablative in the same connection as instrumental; and perhaps the Greek genitive (ἀλλάσσειν τί τινος) as the representative of the instr. ablative.

22. **Ikṣváku-kula-jaḥ**, 'born of the race of Ikshwaku,' i.e. the solar race: see Dowson, s.v.

23. **dárais**, 'thy wife,' xxv 10: dára (whence dáraka 'a son,' viii 20) is literally 'a ploughed field,' from √dṛi (ix 4). It is used in the masc. plur. of a wife: it may be called a plural of respect (like vayam xix 15; comp. also xii 59)—a usage due to the desire to avoid the appearance of too great familiarity with any individual person: compare Dolly Winthrop's plurality of Gods in 'Silas Marner.' It is especially ill-bred to talk to a Hindu of his wife.

mâ sma çoke manaḥ kṛthâḥ: here again we have the aorist (of √kṛ in the middle voice) without the augment, see note on xii 73. Note that mâ is followed here by sma, as often. But we cannot infer that sma takes the place of the augment here: see note on i 12.

24. **saṃsmartavyas**, 'I am to be called by thee to mind, and thou art to put on thy garment.'

nivâsayes, causal in the same sense as the simple verb.

25. **pratipatsyase**, vii 5 note.

vâsoyugam, 'a pair of celestial garments,' i.e. garments endowed with supernatural power.

26. **saṃdiçya**, 'having taught,' sam + √diç; at xvi 2 = 'to command': pra + √diç = 'to urge,' xvii 34. For â + √diç, see iv 25.

2. **vâhane yuktaḥ**, compare sârathye bhojane ca vṛta, xxii 12, sûtatve pratiṣṭhitaḥ, *ib.*

3. 'In difficult questions I am to be consulted, and in matters of dexterity.' **artha-kṛcchrâṇi** = rerum difficultates: kṛcchra (vi 13) being used as a substantive. **praṣṭavyo**, fut. part. of √prach xi 31.

anna-saṃskâra; this was one of the gifts of Yama, v 37.

anyair viçeṣataḥ, 'conspicuously with (i.e. amongst) others.' A special example of the 'disjunctive' use, for which see xiii 34 note. Compare abhyadhiko nṛpaiḥ xxi 14.

4. **çilpâni**, 'arts,' 'handicrafts,'—a doubtful word.

yatiṣye, 'I will strive,' from √yat, xvii 29, 34, &c.; possibly as Grassmann thinks, identical with *αἰτέω*, which would then be a limited sense of the general root. Hence yatna i 6, iv 16, &c.

bharasva, 'employ me': comp. bhṛti, viii 25.

5. **bhadraṃ te**, iii 25 note. **çighra**, xii 121. 'On swift chariot-driving my mind is ever especially set.'

6. 'Do thou apply thyself to the business of making my horses swift.' **sa tvam** is a common collocation, parallel perhaps to οὗτος σύ in Greek: comp. xvii 4. **yoga** is taken here in its most general sense, 'business'—in which it is often redundant at the end of a compound, e.g. kathâ-yoga, 'conversation,' Sâv. ii 1. Benfey takes it as 'mode' (whereby, &c.), quoting Manu ix 330, mânayogâṃç ca jâniyât tulya-yogâṃç ca, 'let him know the different ways of measuring and weighing': the word could be taken there in either sense; indeed they do not greatly differ. **âtiṣṭha**, comp. xviii 24, âsthâsyati.

vetanam, 'thy wages be a hundred hundreds' of kârṣâpanas, probably, the modern Bengal kāhan, equivalent to the rupee. See Manu viii 131—136. For the form vetana, see note on geha xvii 16.

7.   **upasthásyatas**, 2 dual 2 fut. of upa + √sthā, comp. viii 25, and iii 1 note : also upatiṣṭhatı, below at 10.

9.   **sáyaṃ sáyam**, 'evening by evening,' xi 12 note.

jagáda from √gad, 'to speak,' 'recite' : probably (as Benfey suggests) the same as our 'quoth,' for which see Skeat, Lex.—but not akin to βάζω the root of which must have ended in a guttural.

10.   **mandasya**, xiii 10 note.

11.   **nıcáyáṃ**, 'on a night,' loc. of nıçā (xvi 14), either from nı + √çi 'to lie,' or from √naç 'to hurt' (viii 18 note); comp. nakta and nox.

12.   **áyuṣman**, 'long-lived,' xvi 29, a common address of honour : it comes from áyus, with suffix -mat ; the first meaning of áyus (also áyu, sb. and adj., Vedic) was 'activity,' 'energy' : it is probably from √ı, 'to go.' Then it means 'length of life.' Curtius suggests that it = áıvas, by change of the vowel and semivowel ; and so is parallel to αἰών and aeuom : see no. 585 note.

13.   'To a certain man of little wit there belonged a highly honoured wife : his speech was very infirm.' **adṛḍhataram** is comparative of a + dṛıḍha 'firm ' (vi 10) : the comparative is used just as in Greek or Latin ' more infirm than it should be.' Comp. árttatara xiii 64.

14.   **tayá...vyayujyata**, see note on xiii 34.

bhramatı, 'wanders,' see note on sambhránta iii 15 : it occurs again with an accusative of extension xvi 30; as also vı-bhramat xv 16.

15.   **dıvá-rátram** may be considered as an Av. B. compound of an irregular kind, as dıvá is a case and not a base.   At ii 4 we had naktam...dıvá, separately.

atandrıtaḥ, 'unwearied,' xvii 46, xx 36, from tandrá, 'weariness,' xxiv 53.   There is a Vedic √tand, 'to weary.'

gáyatı, from √gaı, base gáya (whence gáyamánáḥ xxiv 27) really from a simpler form √gá.   It is possible that this verb may be identical with √gá a Vedic form = √gam, so that the original meaning should be 'to go to,' or 'address' some one with song: the acc. of the person with a simple verb of going is quite admissible.   Curtius suggests (II p. 84, Eng. tr.) that Latin vates is from this root, the v being parasitic, and having expelled the guttural, as in (g)uenio, &c.

16.   **anusaṃsmaran**, 'called to mind repeatedly,' see notes on xi 24, and (for **bhúyas**) viii 14.

17.   **alpa-puṇyena**, 'bad,' properly 'of little merit,' see xii 37, also note on manda-bhágya xiii 38.

duṣkaraṃ yadı jivatı, 'she scarcely lives,' lit. 'it is hardly done if she lives': comp. xvi 20 and the use of the German schwerlich.

18. 'Alone, young, without knowledge of the roads, unfit for such treatment.' **a-tathâ-ucıtâ** = non-sic-idonea: √uc is 'to be accustomed,' see ii 30, note on okas, 'a house'; so ucıtâ...maṃsyasya, 'accustomed to the food.' Hence the secondary sense 'fit for,' 'worthy of,' which it has here, and perhaps xvi 16, though there the primary sense would do.

19. **çvâpada**, xi 18 note. **alpabhâgyena**, comp. alpapuṇyena, above l. 17, and see note on x 14.

mârıṣa, 'venerable,' one of the usual addresses to Yudhishṭhira. It is a theatrical term, applied to the leading actor.

20. **ajñâta-vâsam**, 'an unknown living,' contained acc. after **nyavasad**.

1. 'When Nala had thus his kingdom rent from him, and was gone together with his wife into the state of a servant.' **preşya**, fut. part. of pra + eṣaya causal of √iṣ, iii 7, &c. = 'one who is to be sent,' 'a servant'; again at xvii 33, xxi 28. Hence preṣyatâ, 'slavery.'

prasthâpayâmâsa, xvii 23, causal of pra + √sthâ, 'to set forth,' xii 1, &c.

kân.kṣayâ, ii 23.

2. **saṃdideça**, xiv 26 note.

puṣkalam, 'much,' also 'good.' It is from √puṣ, 'to nourish,' whence puṣpa, 'a flower,' xii 40, perhaps also puṇya, xii 37; see notes. The second half of the word probably shews a double suffix *ka* + *la* (also *ra* in the word puṣkara 'a blue lotus flower'—and many other meanings). The different senses of the word are developed naturally.

3. 'I will give a thousand kine to the man of you who shall bring here the two.' **yo vas** = ὅστις ὑμῶν (or rather ἐξ ὑμῶν), but in Greek the relative clause should rather have preceded; and so, I think, also in Sanskrit, where there is no antecedent expressed.

agrahârân, a royal grant of lands to Brāhmans—the technical word. Agra is 'best,' 'topmost,' 'first' (hence ekâgra xix 37, and agre, 'in front of,' xxiii 21): comp. the Greek ἀκροθίνια, a somewhat parallel word. The agrahâra-grâma, or endowed village, the exclusive residence of Brāhmans, is common in India at the present day.

grâmam, iv 10 note. **sammitam**, 'of the same measure,' 'as large as': p. p. of sam + √mâ: comp. buddhi-sammita, xxv 9.

4. 'And if they cannot be brought here, Damayantī, or Nala even, if it be but known (where they are) I will give ten hundred kine, great wealth.' As the gift is the same in either case, we must suppose that the second offer is a second thought, on the assumption

that to know where they are is as good as having got them. **na ced** = non si, but meaning 'si non': the negative regularly precedes xxvi 8, &c. **ced** (xvii 29, xviii 16, &c.) = ca + id: ca is 'and' and so the use is identical with the Middle-English 'an' (i.e. and) in the sense of 'if': it is Vedic, e.g. Indraç ca mṛḍayâti no, na naḥ paçcâd agham naçat, 'an Indra have mercy on us, ill will not hurt us afterwards.'

This is a very curious transition from co-ordination to subordination of clauses, apparently effected by putting the clause which begins with the connecting particle in the first place, instead of its natural position at the end: in this way emphasis is thrown upon it, and it is understood to be the condition of the event mentioned in the other clause. Compare note on xix 31. That emphasis is then further increased by adding **id** to **ca**. This particle often stands alone in the hymns and emphasises the preceding word: it is supposed to be the demonstrative base i, and in fact to be identical with Latin id: the use is a curious one: it may have been originally added on to pronouns only: there is always a tendency in them to accumulation of different bases, comp. a-gha-m, &c.: then it may have passed on to other words.

The parallel Vedic form ned, i.e. na + id, is used not with conditional, but in final, clauses.

Sometimes the ca is found even when the relative pronoun is used: e.g. xx 36 ye ca tvâm kirtayiṣyanti. This looks very like οἵ κε: but κε goes with κεν, and that with old Sanskrit kam.

çakyâv ânetum, for construction, see vii 10 note.

5. **jñâta-mâtre**, see ix 10 note.

6. **cinvanto**, 'seeking,' pres. p. of √ci, which although of the same class (5) as √ci mentioned ii 2 note, is probably distinct from it: perhaps the original form was SKI, as Grassmann suggests, with the sense of 'seeing,' 'appearing'; and so with a case it got the sense of 'looking after' a thing, 'searching.' He would connect with it our 'shine'; which is probable: but it is hardly likely that σκιά or Lat. scio have anything to do with it. The latter is connected by Curtius (no. 456) with κείω (for *σκειω) to split; he compares the different derived uses of German scheiden.

purarâṣṭrâṇi, 'cities and kingdoms,' seems to be an acc. of extension, like xxiv 23, dûtâç caranti pṛthivim, with a verb implying motion.

vâ stands before its word, as at xix 8, satyaṃ vâ 'satyam: it almost always follows like Latin ve: the Greek ἤ however, which seems to be the same word, precedes. According to the native view, the corresponding vá is elided.

8. **puṇyáha-vácane,** v 1 note.

mandam, used adverbially, see xiii 33. 'Her with her beauty (see xii 37 note) peerless (before) little to be praised (now), like the brightness of the sun entangled (lit. 'bound' xiii 31) by a net of mist, her, when he had seen,' &c. **pra + √khyá** = 'to tell forth,' 'praise,' comp. note on prakhya xiii 63. Dhúmajála might also be rendered 'a mass of mist,' for jála has both meanings, but the first seems to suit with nibaddha.

vibhávasoḥ, from vibhávasu (vibhá + vasu, P. W.) which in Vedic was used as an adj. = 'bright': then it was used as a name of fire, then (as here) the sun.

9. **viçála,** xii 81 note. **adhikam,** 'exceedingly,' used as an adverb with malinám, see xi 16 note.

tarkayámása, see v 12 note. **upapádayan,** 'effecting (the result) by virtue of certain reasons.' **káraṇa** (comp. 27, xxiii 3) is the usual word for a 'cause,' or 'reason': comp. Hit. 1194 bhaya-káraṇam, 'cause for fear.' We had the ablative used as a preposition at iv 4 tava káraṇát. The 'causes' which lead to Sudeva's conclusion are stated with Hindū fulness in the following speech.

10. 'As is that woman seen by me before, of such form is this woman.' The use of the same pronoun (iyam) in each clause seems strange to those who are accustomed to the distinctness given by 'hic' and 'ille,' οὗτος and ἐκεῖνος.

kṛitártho, 'having my object attained,' xviii 21: see note on iii 7.

11. **nibha,** 'like,' see note on svastha, ii 1. **çyámám,** xii 50.

cáru-vṛitta-payodharám, comp. xi 32, pina-çroṇi-payodhará: and for cáru see iii 14. Vṛitta is the p. p. of √vṛit (vi 4 note) with a secondary sense, 'round.'

kurvantím, &c., 'making by her brightness the world free from darkness.' **vitimira** from vi + timira, 'dark,' connected with tamas, 'darkness': the root is TAM, 'to be stunned,' whence probably tenebrae, for teme-b(e)ra by change of nasal, and our 'dim': perhaps also támra xxvi 17, 'copper-coloured,' 'dark.' See Curt. Vol. II. p. 162 (Eng. tr.).

12. **Ratim,** the wife of Kámadeva. The genitive Manmathasya recalls Vergil's 'Hectoris Andromache.'

samasta, 'whole,' p. p. of sam + √as, 'to throw,' so parallel in sense to cunctus (co-iunctus). For the root see note on astra, 'a weapon,' xii 79.

13.   'Uptorn as it were from the waters of Vidarbha by this cruelty of fate, with limbs stained by dirt and mire, like a lotus uptorn.' uddhṛıtâm, p. p. of ud + √hṛı. The repetition of this word shews that something is wrong : but whether uddhṛıtâm in the first half of the line has superseded some other word, or whether the whole passage is a cento, cannot be determined in the absence of any canon.

14.   'Like night at the full moon, when the moon has been devoured by Râhu.' paurṇamâsim is an adj. formed by vṛıddhı from pûrṇa-mâsa, 'the full of the moon.' Nıçâ-kara, 'night maker,' is a name for the moon as Dına-kara is for the sun.   Râhu is the dragon who causes eclipses by swallowing the moon.   For the legend of his animosity to the sun and moon, see Dowson, s.v. Râhu and Ketu, the dragon's head and tail also appear in the list of nine planets. grasta, iv 9 note.

çuṣkasrotâm, 'like a river whose waters are dried up.' çuṣka is from √çuṣ, 'to be dry.'   If the ç has arisen by assimilation from original *s*, we may compare αὖος for saus-os and our 'sere,' perhaps Latin siccus, see Curt. no. 600 b.   srota is used at the end of a compound for the base srotas, 'water,' from √sru, see xiii 6 note.

15.   vıdhvasta, see xii 115 note.   The compound is a B. V. 'Like a lake when the lotus has its leaves fallen off, whence the birds have been scared away (xi 1 note), disturbed by the trunk of the elephant, and disquieted.' parâmṛıṣṭa, from parâ + √mṛıç, see notes on i 5, and vii 13: literally it is 'stroked the wrong way.'

16.   ratnagarbhagṛıh-ocıtâm, 'fit for (or 'accustomed to,' see xv 18 note) a house full of jewels.'   garbha is that which contains any-thing and is commonly used of the womb : also the embryo see i 19 note : at xiii 63 it stood for the calyx of the lotus.   At Çak. i 14 the hollow of a tree in which parrots live is called çuka-garbha-koṭara.

arkeṇa, 'by the sun,' see note on arcayıtvâ ii 15.

17.   audarya, 'dignity,' 'nobleness,' formed from udâra, see i 4. amaṇḍıtâm, see xii 64 note. vyomnı, 'in the sky,' from vyoman—a word of doubtful origin. Bopp's suggestion that it is from vı-dyoman from √dyu is the best. In the P. W. it is suggested that it may be from vı + √vâ 'to weave,' apparently in the sense of the 'cloud-woven.'

18.   **hinȧm**, see v 24 note.

bandhujana, 'kinsfolk,' xvii 24; also bȧndhava, ib., and sam-bandhın xxv 14: see note on xiii 31, for √bandh.

deham, &c. 'Supporting her body (i.e. enduring life, comp. xviii 9—and for deha see xii 89) by her desire to see her husband.'

19.   'A husband truly is a woman's highest ornament, all other ornaments apart (see notes on xiii 34 and vi 2): for forsaken by him, though bright, she is bright no more.' **rahıta**, from √rah, see note on rahas, i 18.

20.   'It is with exceeding difficulty that Nala reft of her endures life and sinks not from grief.'

duṣkaraṃ kurute yad is like duṣkaraṃ (astı) yadı, xv 17: for yad so used see xiii 41.

avasidatı, comp. ix 26 sidanty an-gȧnı sarvaçaḥ.

21.   **çatapatra**, 'the hundred-leaved,' a name of the lotus.

çatapatr'-ȧyata, 'lotus-long' is a K. D., like ghana-çyȧma 'cloud-black' or our 'clay-cold,' &c.

22.   'When indeed shall the bright one pass to the other shore of sorrow': see note on pȧraga, xii 81.

Rohıṇi was the daughter of Daksha, and wife of the moon: see Dowson, s. v. Soma.

23.   **medınim**, xi 39.

24.   **abhıjana**, xii 95.

25.   **yuktam**, 'fit,' used with the infinitive, like çakta or çakya, vii 10 note.   Literally 'it is fit to console by me the wife of this incomparable valorous and truthful (king).' The acc. (which the so-called infinitive is) seems to depend on the verbal sense in yuktam; it is not therefore strictly analogous to such uses as καλὸν δρᾶν in Greek.   It is tempting to regard the whole sentence except yuktam as the subject of astı understood, and yuktam the predicate; in which case we should have a close analogy to the Greek use of the infinitive.   But this, I think, is foreign to Sanskrit usage.

26.   **ȧçvȧsayȧmı**, present instead of future, to express immediate action—a rather common use in Sanskrit; comp. xix 18.

dhyȧna-tatparȧm, 'sunk in thought.' The meaning is nowise different from dhyȧna-para ii 3.   But tat-para means firstly 'having that prominent,' 'intent upon that' and so simply 'intent on': and it is used, as here, after another base, just like para; or absolutely, as at xxi 15.

27. **vimṛiçya**, 'having considered,' or 'come to a conclusion about her,' see vii 13 note.

29. **âyuṣmantau**, 'the long-lived ones' (xv 12) i.e. the royal family.

30. **bandhuvargâs**, 'thy relations,' literally 'relative-classes': varga is from √vṛij 'to exclude,' see note on xiii 53: so it means that which is separated from the rest, a class of things: then it is used for a number or mass of things: and at the end of a compound it is often redundant as here.

gatasattvâ, 'with their being gone,' 'lifeless,' 'powerless.' Sattva is the essence of a thing. It sometimes is used at the end of a compound, e.g. xxiv 53 harṣa-vivṛiddha-sattva, lit. 'with increased essence of joy,' i.e. with increased joy, simply.

âsate, 3 pl. of √âs: the termination is ate (not ante) in the 2, 3, 5, 7, 8, 9 classes.

bhramanti mahim, 'wander (over) the earth,' see iii 15 note: the verb takes the accusative of extension as at xv 16.

31. **krameṇa**, 'in order,' xii 49 note: for the instrumental see v 26: and tattvena, below l. 38.

33. **ekânte**, 'alone,' loc. of ekânta, used adverbially. The **anta** seems redundant: comp. vṛittânta iv 23.

34. **janitryâḥ**, genitive with √kath 'to tell': so xxiii 5 tad âkhyeyaṃ tvayâ mama: xviii 13 râjñaç caiva nivedaya: xvi 38 mam' âcakṣva: and generally for the genitive after a verb see v 38 note.

vettha (like veda xix 30) a contracted form of the perfect of √vid—used like the parallel Greek οἶδα in a present sense. The full form would be viveditha. See M. W. G. § 308 a: M. M. App. no. 172. 'By meeting with the Brâhman thou knowest (or 'mayest know) her, if thou think well.' Or the first two words might (perhaps better) go with the preceding clause.

yadi manyase is a common formula of politeness: so ix 3, xix 2, &c.

37. **vâma-locanâ**, 'beautiful-eyed.' Vâma (Vedic) is 'dear,' 'worthy,' and as a sb. 'well-being'—probably from √van 'to solicit,' whence perhaps Lat. venus, veneror &c.: but the root has several meanings; or rather, perhaps several different roots have run into the same form.

evaṃ gatâ sati: sati redundant, as in ajñâyamânâ sati xvii 18, apakṛite sati xi 5. Comp. xii 25.

38. **ácakṣva**, viii 5 note. The verb has this peculiarity in the present base, that in conjugation it drops the *k* before all consonantal terminations except those beginning with *m* or *v*. Hence the 3 sing. ácaṣṭe in the next line: M. W. Gr. § 321.

39. **yathátatham**, here used as a noun, not adverbially: see iii 2 note.

3. **na prâjñâyata,** 'was not known.' Pra + jñâ implies full, clear knowledge about him, although not seen: see iii 1 note. Vijñâ and abhijñâ would mean to 'distinguish' or to 'recognise' him when seen.

4. **te vayam** (1 pers.) and **sâ iyam** (3 pers.) shew the same use of the double demonstrative as sa tvam xv 6. It is a further illustration of the tendency to accumulate pronominal bases, already alluded to at xvi 4, of which Latin gives us further examples in egomet, tutemet &c. The more these 'deiktic' (and not very definitive) syllables can be heaped together, the clearer the sense is supposed to be.

âsâditâ, x 7 note.

5. 'For like her (i.e. the woman at thy court) in beauty, woman is there none' (vidyate, see ii 4). Therefore she is Damayantī, the most beautiful woman in the world. Then comes the reason of her beauty—the mole. 'For there between the eyebrows of this dark woman is a beautiful congenital mole, like a lotus, seen by me, although become (almost) hidden, for it is covered by the dirt upon her, like the moon concealed by a cloud.'

bhruvor madhye, comp. sakhi-madhye i 12.

6. **san·kâço,** 'like' from √kâç 'to shine,' whence âkâça 'sky,' 'clear air,' xiv 10, xix 24, sakâça 'presence,' i 21, xxiv 2, &c., and prakâça 'bright,' comp. xxvi 37.

channo, from √chad, see note on châyâ v 25: comp. pracchâdana 'covering,' line 10.

7. 'This mark, fashioned by the Creator for the sake of (i.e. to exhibit) his power, like the streak of the moon when opaque at the first day of change, shews no excessive brightness.'

cihna is 'a mark' or 'sign': **bhûto** is redundant, like ketu bhûtam xii 38, where see note.

vibhûti, 'pre-eminent power,' comp. vibhu, applied to the Gods ii 15 &c.

dhâtṛi, 'the Creator,' i.e. Brahmā who holds this place in the later Hindu trinity: the other two being Vishṇu the Preserver, and Çiva the Destroyer. It is not perhaps remarkable that of these three, Brahmā receives little or no worship, and Çiva, on the whole, the largest share.

vinirmitaḥ, p. p. of vi + nis + √mâ; an irregular change seen in sthita from √sthâ, hita from √dhâ.

pratipat is the first day of the moon's increase or decrease—but especially the former.

kaluṣa is 'turbid,' 'dirty': Benfey compares kalan-ka and kalmaṣa, in both of which the notion of stain or dirt is found: probably the first part of each word is akin to κελ-αινός and caligo; also, if the root was originally SKAL (Curt. G. E. no. 46), to squalor &c.

indor, see xii 81.

8. **vapur**, iii 12 note. **samâcitam**, 'covered,' p. p. of sam + â + √ci 'to order,' see v 15, note on viniçcitya.

asaṃskṛitam, 'even although unadorned, it shines distinctly, like gold.'

vyaktam is p. p. of vi + √añj 'to smear,' whence añjana 'anointing': Lat. unguo. But the word has the further meaning of 'making bright by smearing': and so the part. = 'distinct,' 'clear': used adverbially at xxvi 14.

9. 'Here has been seen by me the girl with that form, marked out by that mole, as concealed flame by the heat.'

sûcitâ, see v 25.

nibhṛito, from ni + √bhṛi, 'borne down,' and so 'hidden.' It commonly means 'humble.' At Hit. 385 nibhṛitam brûte = 'speaks in a whisper.'

uṣmaṇâ, from √us, 'to burn.'

10. **çodhayâmâsa**, perfect of causal of √çudh, see note on viii 18. It is used here in the simplest sense = 'cleansed.'

11. **malen' âpakṛiṣṭena**, see xiv 16 note.

vyabhre nabhasi, 'in the sky free from cloud'; see ii 30 note.

12. **pariṣvajya**, 'having embraced her with tears,' xxiii 24, and sasvaje xxiv 44: from √svañj, pres. base svaja: the Vedic form is svaj.

muhûrtam, x 26 note.

13. **utsṛjya**, ix 5, utsṛjya bhūṣaṇāni, 'having stripped off his ornaments': here 'shedding (tears).'

çanakaiḥ, iv 18.

bhaginyâḥ, 'of my sister.' As derived from bhaga it is apparently a title of compliment.

14. **sute**, dual nom. of sutá.

15. 'She was given (in marriage) to king Bhima': the genitive here admits of an easy explanation 'given to be of Bhima,' i.e. so as to belong to Bhima: comp. Manmathasya Rati, xvi 12.

16. **geham**, 'house,' a corruption of gṛha: so perhaps, as Benfey suggests, vetana xv 6 of vartana (through *vṛtana), and medini of mṛdini, xi 39.

'As thy father's house to thee, so is mine (i.e. at thy disposal): and as my command (over all things) so also is thine.' Comp. x 1 note.

18. **sati**, see xvi 27 note. 'Even when unknown I have dwelt at ease in thy house (v 32) well provided with all objects of desire (=sarvakâmaiḥ suvihitaiḥ, abs. instr. xxv 15) ever protected by thee.'

19. **sukhât sukhataro**, 'more happy than happiness,' i.e. most happy: or, more simply, 'happier than happy,' i.e. my lot at home shall be happier even than this with thee. For the abl. of comparison, see xi 16 note.

na saṃçayaḥ, x 1 note.

viproṣitâm, 'exiled,' = vi + pra + uṣita, ix 10. **anujñâtum**, see iii 1 note.

20. **nitau**, viii 5 note.

kathaṃ nu, 'how (forsaken) indeed (are they)?'—a parenthetic question, or practically, an ejaculation.

21. **yânam âdiça**, 'give order for a carriage': for **yâna**, see vii 9: see also iv 25.

22. **vâḍham**, 'well.' It also means 'much.' Benfey would connect it with bahu (vahu).

guptâm, see note on goptṛ, xii 47.

anumate, 'with the assent of,' p. p. of anu + √man: comp. sammate sârthavâhasya, xiii 5.

23. **prâsthâpayad**, xvi 1 note.

naravâhinâ, 'having men as bearers,' a B. V. compound. For vâhin, see viii 22.

anna-pâna-paricchadâm, 'having with her food, drink and necessaries for travelling.'

parıcchada, is properly 'a covering,' from √chad, above line 6. At Manu viii 405, pumâṃsaç c' âparıcchadâḥ is used of 'men with little luggage,' who pay small toll at a ferry. At Sâv. iii 16, parıcchada seems to mean 'a surrounding,' i.e. attendants: and there is no reason why it should not have that meaning here: compare parıvâra xxvi 1.

26. **vıdhınâ**, 'with highest ceremony'; see note on iv 17.

27. **dravıṇena**, viii 5 note.

28. **vyuṣṭâ**, 'having dwelt,' irregular participle of vı + √vas, for vyuṣıta, comp. vıproṣıta l. 19. The vı has no force here. But in vıvâsa, 'dwelling separate,' xix 6, the *vı* has its full force.

rajanim, 'for a night.' Rajani is probably 'the dark-coloured': √rañj is 'to colour,' see note on anurâga, v 22.

29. 'Strive for the bringing hither of that heroic Nala.' **ânayana** from â + √nî, xii 68: for the locative, see note on iii 6. **yata**, see xv 4.

30. **apıhıtâ**, 'covered,' from √dhâ with apı—rarely used as a prefix.

uttaram, 'answer,' a secondary meaning of the word, which is literally 'above': see xii 60: either in the sense of a thing put upon another, or from another derived sense 'later.' In Hit. 381, it means 'discussion'—kım anen' ottareṇa? 'what is the good of this debate?'

31. **hâhâ-bhûtam**, 'full of lamentation,' a curious compound: hâhâ-kâra, xiii 11, was natural enough.

33. 'Casting aside bashfulness, she has herself said, &c.' For **lajjâ**, see iii 18 note.

preṣyâḥ, xvi 1 note.

34. **pradeçıto**, see xiv 16. **vaçavartınaḥ**, viii 15.

35. **Damayantiṃ sṛıtvâ**, see xii 36 note: for the verb sṛı, see xi 26.

sm' etı, apparently for smas ıtı, like sm' eha, xii 118, which is perhaps for smas ıha.

36. **brûyâsta**, 'ye are to say': 2 pres. plur. of the so-called 'benedictive' tense of √brû. It is really the aorist of the optative: to which tense (or mood) it bears a close analogy (see M. M. Gr. § 385): but it shews the *s* of the 'sigmatic' aorist, between the *yâ* of the optative and the terminations. The opt. aor. is regularly used in curses in Greek—διαρραγείης, ἐξόλοιο, &c.

saṃsatsu, 'assemblies,' from sam + √sad: comp. consessus.

37. **kıtava**, 'gamester,' 'cheat': hence kaıtava, 'play,' xxvi 10.

vipine, 'in the forest,' a doubtful word.

38. **yathâ samâdiṣṭâ**, 'as ordered by thee': we should rather have expected an Av. B.—yathâsamâdiṣṭam.

tathâ 'ste, i.e. tathâ âste, from √âs 'to sit,' i 11.

tvat-pratikṣini, 'waiting for thee': pratikṣin is from pratikṣâ, 'expectation,' from prati + √ikṣ, i 20.

39. **prasâdaṃ kuru...tasyâḥ**, for construction see xiii 32.

40. 'And thus a further thing is to be said (not 'thus and more,' which would be 'evamâdini') that he may have mercy upon me.' See xii 34 note.

vâyunâ, 'for the fire fanned by the wind burns the forest.' That is, the fire is already in Nala's heart, and this is to be excited by the wind of the Brâhman's speech.

dhûyamâno, pres. part. of √dhû, 'to shake,' orig. DHU whence θύω, fumus, dust: see Curt. G. E. no. 320.

pâvakaḥ is literally the 'purifier,' from √pû: probably πῦρ and 'fire' are akin: see Curt. no. 385.

41. 'Yes (hi inceptive like γάρ), a wife is to be supported, is to be protected by a husband ever. Whence comes it that both these duties have been violated by thee who knowest all duty?'

ubhaya is a secondary from ubha, with the same meaning, xvii 25. The original form is ambha, whence ἄμφω and ambo, see Curt. no. 401.

tava, genitive of agent after naṣṭam, see i 4 note.

42. **khyâtaḥ**, 'told of as,' 'famed for being,' comp. prakhyâyamânena xvi 8.

sânukroço, 'compassionate': anu-kroça is 'after-crying,' i.e. 'crying for a person,' from √kruç, xi 2.

madbhâgya-saṃkṣayât, 'through my ill fate,' lit. through the destruction of my fortune: see note on x 14.

43. **ânṛiçaṃsyam**, 'mildness,' 'mercy,' formed by vṛiddhi and suffix *ya* from a-nṛi-çaṃsa—for which see xi 10 note. 'Mercy is the highest duty, from *thee* I have heard this.'

45. **tad**, &c., 'thou must receive that speech of his and report it to me.' **âdâya** goes with the instrumental tvayâ understood. See note on i 22. **âvedyam**, with the same sense as nivedaya i 32.

46. 'And that he may not know that you are speaking by my command, and know of your coming again (to me), ye must provide for this without delay.' The final clause precedes the main one, as at xii 107, yathâ viçokâ gaccheyâm, açokanâga, tat kuru; and xii

121, xviii 16. It is the commonest order in Greek: and I think also in Sanskrit: in this poem the instances are about evenly balanced: the dependent clause follows, i 21, v 21, xv 6, xvii 40, xviii 20: in the two cases where the future is used, not the conjunctive, (i 21, xviii 20), the clause follows. Compare note on i 20.

atandrıtaıḥ, see xv 15 note.

47. 'Whether he be rich (x 2 note) or whether he be poor, or if he be desirous of wealth, I must know his intention.' **adhana** and **arthakáma** are not necessarily identical: he may be poor, yet want nothing. **cıkirṣıtam**, p. p. of cıkirṣa, desiderative of √kṛı.

48. **vyasanınam**, formed with suffix *-ın* from vyasana, vii 13 note: comp. balın, i 1, vádın, i 3, &c.

49. **ghoṣán**, 'settlements of herdsmen': there is no obvious connection with ghoṣa, 'a noise,' ii 11, &c.

adhıjagmur, 'found him': this is not a usual sense of adhı + gam, derived from that of 'attaining to.' It often means 'to study,' e.g. Hit. 89.

50. **çrávayáñcakṛıre**, 3 pers. plu. perf. middle of çrávaya, causal of √çru. It is a rarer form than that with √as: but seems more natural to a grammatical mind.

irıtam, 'uttered,' p. p. of √ir 'to make to go'—practically a causal of √ṛı; see note on v 29. The verb has first a general meaning; then it is specialised, like our own verb, 'to utter.'

1. **dirghasya kâlasya**, a rare genitive of time, which recalls the Greek θέρους, νυκτός, ἠοῦς (Il. viii 525), or even more exactly ἥξοντα βαιοῦ, κοὐχὶ μυρίου, χρόνου (Soph. O. C. 397). But there is no assurance that the two usages have been reached by the same path. Neither on the other hand may we attribute them both to the original sense of connection which the genitive expressed. The old theory that the genitives in Greek were remnants of a genitive absolute, where the participle has been lost, will hardly serve.

2. **Naiṣadham mṛigayânena**, for the acc. see ii 27 note: the instrumental is like dautyen' âgatya iv 15.

3. **çrâvitas**, 'was made to hear thy speech.'

4. **pâriṣadaḥ**, 'belonging to the assembly' (pariṣad—comp. saṃsad xvii 36).

5. **vijane**, 'privately,' loc. of vijana (xi 1, &c.) used adverbially.

6. **hrasva**, 'short': it is 'low' or 'narrow' at xxiii 9. The derivation is uncertain: but it is not likely to have anything to do with χερείων (Benfey): that is doubtless formed from χέρης, 'well in hand,' 'subject,' Curt. G. E. no. 189. For the compound, comp. vyûḍh'-oras-ka, xii 13.

kuçalo, 'skilled in rapid driving (vii 9 note) and a skilful cook for eating.' **miṣṭa** is p. p. of √miṣ, 'to sprinkle,' and means any dainty dish. **bhojane** is the loc. of the purpose, iii 6 note.

8. **vaiṣamyam**, viii 13 note. **gopâyanti**, see xii 47, note on goptṛi. **âtmânam âtmanâ**, vi 12, xii 57: as the verb is plural here, we see that the phrase had become conventional.

jitasvargâḥ, 'winning heaven, without doubt': see note on Indraloka ii 13.

9. **krudhyanti**, 'are angry,' from √krudh (4th cl.) whence the infin. kroddhum xviii 10, and krodha, 'anger,' vi 5. It may be a secondary root of KRU, 'to be hard,' for which see Curt. no. 77: the Latin

crudus comes from the simple root most probably: crudelis might come from either.

cáritra-kavacát, 'by the armour of their good conduct'—a K. D. comparative. **cáritra** is firstly 'observance,' formed from caritra, which is itself derived from √car (see v 9 note on cacála) which has derived senses parallel to that of colo, cultus, &c. in Latin, and θεηπολός in Greek: it then gets the general sense of 'conduct.' Caritra is 'ancient usage,' like ácára, see xii 26, note on çila: then (like its derivative) it = 'conduct.'

práṇán dhárayanti, 'maintain their life.' The inverted práṇá dharisyanti, 'life shall hold out,' occurred at v 32. This phrase with the causal is analogous to deham dhárayatim (xvi 18 and 20).

varastriyaḥ, comp. varanári, i 4.

10. **viṣamasthena**, viii 13. **múḍhena**, vi 12 note.

paribhraṣṭa, vi 15 note.

yat...na...arhati: see note on vi 6: this clause must be carried back to the main verb dhárayanti in the preceding line. They endure, inasmuch as Damayanti is not overcome by passion—one instance of the general rule: compare xiii 39, n'ápráptakálo mriyate ...yad n' áham adya...duḥkhitá (mriye).

11. **práṇa-yátrám**, 'maintenance of life.' Yátrá, 'going,' has many derived senses. Like this phrase, we have çarira-yátrá, Bh. G. iii 8. In Manu iv 3, it is used absolutely in the same sense, yátrá-mátra-prasiddhy-artham, 'for the sake of obtaining mere maintenance' (uictus).

çakunair, ix 12.

pariprepsoḥ, 'seeking all round to get,' gen. of pari + pra + ipsu, see iii 5, note on didṛkṣu.

ádhibhir, 'anxieties,' from á + √dhyai 'to think,' xii 100. **çyámá**, xii 50 note.

12. **vyasanáplutam**, 'drenched in misfortune': for á-pluta see note on iv 13.

13. **çrutvá**, &c. 'When thou hast heard thou art the authority.' Comp. pramáṇam tu bhavantas, iv 31.

15. 'This matter is not to be communicated to Bhima.' Here we have the locative with a verb of telling as at i 31, 32, ii 6, iii 9, viii 21, xxii 13: though we had the genitive in line 13, and in the passages quoted at xvi 34.

niyokṣye, 'I will give a charge to Sudeva.' ni + √yuj is to 'command': often 'to appoint to an office,' so Hit. 1272, káryádhikàri na dhanàdhikàre niyoktavyaḥ, 'a manager of the executive is not to be appointed to the management of the treasury': and niyogin is 'a minister' or 'functionary.'

16. **pratipadyeta**, 'may learn,' see vii 5 note.

prayattavyam, xv 4.

17. 'As I was swiftly brought to my relations (for acc. see note on xii 36) by means of Sudeva, with that same luck let Sudeva go quickly at once, &c.' **man·gala** as an adj. = 'lucky,' and as a noun (n.) 'prosperity,' comp. sa-man·gala, line 21: it is also (m.) the name of the planet which we call Mars, see note on graha xiii 24.

18. **paçcàt**, 'afterwards,' see note on paçcima xiii 5.

19. **arcayàmàsa**, ii 15 note.

bhùyo, viii 14 note.

20. **yat...sameṣyàmi**, 'that I may meet': for the future, rather than the optative, see note on i 21. The clause yathà...kariṣyati is of course parenthetic, 'as no other than thou will ever do.'

21. **àçirvàdaiḥ**, 'blessings.' àçis is from à + √çàs, iii 21 note.

kṛitàrthaḥ, xvi 10, having attained his object, i.e. 'satisfied': compare xvi 10.

23. **Ṛituparṇam vaco brùhi**, comp. vàcam vyàjahàra Nalam i 20.

kàmagaḥ, 'meeting him as one that goes by chance,' or 'of his own free will': in the first case it means going without any settled purpose: in the other, going without being sent by anybody. Cf. xiii 55 kàmavàsini, applied to Damayantī wandering in the wood.

24. **àsthàsyati**, 'will enter upon,' 'hold,' compare xv 6 àtiṣṭha 'apply thyself to,' iv 4 viṣam àsthàsye, xix 23 javam àsthàya, xx 16 yatnam samàsthitaḥ.

25. 'And so is the time reckoned, it will be held to-morrow': the relative particle which should correspond to tathà is omitted; comp. xiii 50 note.

çvo-bhùte, 'when to-morrow has appeared': for **bhùta** see note on xii 38. It seems to be sufficient if one member of the compound have the locative ending: as in aparedyus xiii 35. **çvas** is certainly very near to Latin cras, and Vaniçek connects them, p. 99: but the change of sound is unexplained.

sambhàvaniyas, fut. part. pass. of sam + √bhàvaya, causal of √bhù. The verb means 'to cause to be together,' i.e. to meet: and means further 'to do honour to,' 'pay one's respects to'—perhaps with that sense here: comp. Megh. 28: Çak. i 20 (p. 26 ed. Williams). The p. p. sambhàvita = 'adequate,' Çak. i 34 (ib. p. 56): 'honoured,' 'highly esteemed,' Bh. G. ii 34, sambhâvitasya c' âkirtir maraṇâd atiricyate, 'in the case of the man in high repute, dishonour is worse than death.'

26. **sûryodaye**, 'at the rising of the sun.' **sûrya** is one of the commonest names for the sun: it is from √svar 'to be bright'—sometimes used alone for 'heaven,' sometimes in a compound as svar-ga. From the same root Curtius derives sura 'a god': but see note on ii 13: *σέλας*, *σελήνη* and *Σείριος* are doubtless from it: also Latin serenus: see G. E. no. 663.

na hi, &c., 'for the hero Nala is unknown, whether he lives or no,' an instance of oblique interrogation, with the indicative as we should expect. Compare xix 8 yad atra satyaṃ, vâ 'satyaṃ, gatvâ vetsyâmi, 'what herein is true or untrue, I will go and know': xx 14, ahaṃ hi nâbhijânâmi, bhaved evaṃ, na veti ca, 'I don't know whether it is or no'—one of the best instances of a dependent clause in this poem, yet the dependence is not specially denoted by the mood: we can see the looser joining in xxii 3, atra me mahati çan-khâ, bhaved eṣa Nalo nṛpaḥ 'here I have great doubt, whether this is king Nala'; here it would be more literal to translate bhavet as a deliberative conjunctive 'will this be Nala?' Again at xix 33 in a sentence similarly expressing doubt and deliberation we have pramâṇât parihinas tu bhaved, iti matir mama 'such is my thought'—where the independence of the conjunctive bhavet is complete.

1. **çàntvayaṅ çlakṣṇayá vácà**, see notes on viii 12 and v 5.

2. **ekáhnà**, 'in one day': the instrumental used of time like divà ii 4, &c.

3. **vyadiryata**, ix 4 note. **pradadhyau**, 3 sing. perf. of pra + √dhyai, xii 100.

4. 'Could Damayantī speak thus? Could she do it infatuated (vi 12 note) by sorrow? Or will it be on my account that this great plan has been devised?' **upáyas**, see iv 19.

There are sixteen exx. in this poem of the optative used absolutely—to ask a question: v 12 (bis), ix 27, x 10 and 17, xii 87, xix 4 (ter), 27, 28, 29, xxi 33, xxii 13, xxiv 11 and 22. Of these, twelve are in the 3rd person, one in the 1st, none in the 2nd: in exact agreement with Greek and Latin, e.g. *τίς κατάσχοι*; Soph. Ant. 605, *καὶ τί, φιλός, ῥέξαιμι*; Theok. xxvii 24: and this is more evident in the parallel use of the conjunctive, which is more common, as *τί πάθω*; ε 465 *τί νύ μοι μήκιστα γένηται*; ε 299, but *not τί γένῃ*; in Latin 'quid faciam' and 'quid faciat.'

Often it does not much matter whether the sentence be regarded as a question, or a doubtful statement: e.g. in xxi 33 Várṣṇeyena bhaven núnaṃ vidhyá s' aiv' opaçikṣita?: this though called a question only differs from viii 6 api no bhágadheyaṃ syát, in the difference of the particles, and yet neither of them is specially interrogative.

In the passages referred to, the event is generally future, sometimes quite indefinite. In this passage alone is the event a past one. This fact is important for the enquiry into the original meaning of the 'optative.' The very great predominance of the future time seems strongly in favour of my view that the primary meaning of the mood was future action conceived of indefinitely, much as in the conjunctive: developing into 'indefinite possibility' without regard to time (as in vaded here = 'that she should speak!'—the mere possibility of the thing whether past, present or future), and lastly into 'wish.' This theory is opposed to Delbrück's: he regards 'wish' as primary, then 'will,' and lastly 'indefinite possibility': and still more opposed to that of Kühner, who sees the origin of the mood in a 'conception of something past.'

5. **nṛiçaṃsam**, 'wicked,' see xi 10 note. A second marriage was regarded as disgraceful, see Manu v 161: but that such marriages were not unusual is plain from the fact that widows re-married have a special title (parapurvà, i.e. wife of another before), Manu v 163. The feeling about a second marriage is shewn in the well-known lines Manu ix 47 (given in Sàv. ii 26),

sakṛid aṃço nipatati, sakṛit kanyà pradiyate,
sakṛid àha 'dadàni' iti: triṇy etàni satàṃ sakṛit:

'once for all an inheritance descends; once for all a girl is given in marriage; once for all a man says "I am to give": these three are done once for all by the good.' A good woman after her husband's death is to devote herself to Brahmacarya (pious austerity—lit. the course of the young student); by this she reaches heaven (svargaṃ gacchati) even though childless.

'Surely a wicked thing the virtuous daughter of Vidarbha is desirous of doing (comp. ix 31 tyaktukàmas) in her wretchedness, misused by me vile and evil-minded.'

kṣudreṇa, see xi 36 note. **kṛipaṇà**, xii 34 note.

6. 'Woman's nature in this world is fickle: and my faults are grievous. It may even be so: she may be doing it, when her friendship (for me) has been lost through separation.'

loke, comp. lokeṣu i 10. **calo**, from √cal, see v 9 note.

vivàsàd, see xvii 28. Others take gatasauhṛidà 'bereft of friends,' as though suhṛid had been used: but this would not describe Damayantī's condition in her father's house.

7. **saṃvignà** (see ix 26 note), 'disquieted by her grief for me': it is not so well taken 'by my grief,' like tava doṣas, 'thy fault,' iv 9.

nairàçyàt, 'in despair,' abl. of cause: formed from nir-àça, 'hopeless.' Àçà is 'desire,' 'hope,' comp. àçis, xviii 21: hence bhagnàça, 'spes fractas habens,' Hit. 351.

sàpatyà, 'especially as she has children': apa-tya = 'off-spring': the -tya is suffix as in Greek νη-πυ-τιο, &c.

8. **niçcayam**, 'certainty,' see v 22 note: it may be either acc. after vetsyàmi, or used adverbially.

9. **niçcitya**, v 15 note.

10. **pratijânâmi**, iii 1 note.

11. **açva-çâlâm**, 'stable': hence çâlâ-stha, xxi 6, rathaçâlâ, xxi 29. Çâlâ is 'a hall': prob. from KAL, whence καλιά, cella, domi-cil-ium: Curt. no. 30: our word is apparently the same.

12. **tvaryamâṇo**, pres. part. pass. of √tvar, v 2 note.

jijñâsamâno, pres. part. of jijñâsa, desiderative of √jñâ.

13. **samarthân**, iii 7 note. **adhvani**, &c., 'powerful on the road'; see notes on xii 111, and iii 8.

tejo-bala, iv 26 note. **kulaçila**, xii 26.

14. 'Free from bad marks': see notes on v 24, xiii 34 and 53. **varjitân** changes final *n* into *l* before lakṣanair, M. W. Gr. § 56. M. M. § 75. But the *l* is nasal, and is written in Sanskrit with the arddha-candra (half-moon) mark (◡) over it.

pṛithu-prothân, 'broad-nosed.'

çuddhân, p. p. of √çudh, 'pure,' 'white': here = 'faultless.'

âvartair, 'curls of the horse's hair,' apparently on six different parts of the horse's body, see line 17. These were good marks. The case is the descriptive sociative or instrumental, see xii 37 note.

Sindhujân, 'born in Sindh.' Sindhu seems to have been the name of the river Indus before it was applied to the country along its banks. Hence the Greeks derived their term 'Ινδοί, dropping the *s*, whence our India.

vâta-raṃhasaḥ, 'wind-speed.' For vâta, see x 21: raṃhas is from √raṃh: a doubtful Vedic root: it possibly may be connected with laghu (ἐλαχυ, &c.), which has another form raghu: if so *h* is from *gh* and the vowel has been nasalised. Benfey would add τρέχω, in which case the orig. root would be TRAGH: this is very doubtful.

15. **kopa**, 'anger,' so vi 14: from √kup, 'to be in motion, or agitation,' p. p. kupita, xxvi 17. It is interesting because it appears with a very different sense in Lat. cupio: the orig. form is KVAP, Greek καπνός and Lith. kvapa-s, 'breath': see Curt. G. E. Vol. I, p. 144 (Eng. tr.): so that the history of the word is nearly that of θυμός. We have already noticed the difference in meaning between Sansk. harṣa and Lat. horror, from the same primary root hars, 'to be rough.' Probably it is due to difference of climate: what is pleasant in one country is unpleasant in another. Similarly tāpa, 'heat,' came in India to mean 'pain,' or 'misery.' I owe this suggestion to Prof. Cowell.

kim idam, 'what is this desired (by you) to do?' unless, taking the simpler sense of prárthaya, we construe 'what is this the thing which you were asked to do?'

pralabdhavyá, see xiv 5.

16. **mahad-adhvánam**, 'a great way'—an unusual exception to the rule that mahat becomes mahá in compounds, except Tat-purushas: this is of course a K. D.: but by rule it should mean, 'the road of the great': comp. mahad-áçraya, 'recourse to the great,' Hit. 1699. Note the acc. with gantavyam: it is a contained accusative; yet, so far as it is an acc., the construction is parallel to the rarer Greek form, e.g. νέοις ζηλωτέον τοὺς γέροντας, which was probably (as Madvig suggests) modelled upon intransitive usages, like ἐπιχειρητέον τῷ ἔργῳ. 'How are we to go a great journey with horses like those?'—sociative instr.

17. 'One on the forehead, two on the head, two and two on side and under-side (? flank), two are to be discerned on the breast, and one too on the back.' **párçva** is from parçu, 'a rib': the root therefore is PARK, but no derivatives appear in the other languages: πλευρόν is too far phonetically.

vakṣas, 'the breast,' may come from √vakṣ (Greek √αυξ, see G. E. no. 583) in the sense of that which expands itself in breathing: so Grassmann. Benfey would assume an older pakṣas, and connect with Latin pectus. **prayáṇa** is commonly 'a journey,' (comp. prayáta xx 2): hence apparently 'the back' through the sense of extension.

18. **yojayámi**, present, of future action, comp. xvi 26.

20. **java**, viii 19 note.

21. **samárohat**, see note on áropya viii 19.

jánubhis, 'with their knees'—γόνυ, genu, knee, Curt. no. 137.

23. **raçmibhis**, 'reins,' (xx 15) also used of the rays of the sun, &c.; Grassmann takes 'rope' to be the primary meaning, afterwards transferred to the sun's rays, like arrows, rays (radii) and other similar objects. Benfey compares laqueus, but that is better referred with il-lic-io, &c. to VRAK (ϝελκ, &c.). The word might come from RAG (rego and ὀρέγω).

samudyamya, from sam + ud + √yam, i 4. It is 'to pull up,' and so may mean either to stop, or to get the horses in hand with the reins before starting, which is the meaning here.

iyeṣa, perf. of √iṣ, 'to wish,' i 1: M. M. App. no. 118.

ásthāya, 'having entered upon speed,' or 'attained speed,' like yogam átiṣṭha, xv 6: see note on xviii 24.

24. **codyamânâ**, 'urged on,' from √cud: the connection of the word is doubtful by reason of the numerous possibilities: the most obvious identification is with Gr. σπεύδω (if we may suppose labialism in that peculiar word which apparently corresponds to Lat. studium, and so presents a fresh difficulty): we must then compare (with Benfey) A. S. sceotan our 'shoot'; and assume an original SKUD. In Vedic time, acc. to Grassmann, there are two radical significations, 'to put into quick motion,' and 'to sharpen,' the latter will come from the first through the sense of 'whetting': he would therefore assume an original KV, not SK, for the root.

âkâçam, 'to the sky,' see note on saṃkâça, xvii 6.

mohayann (the double *n* before the following *i*), pres. part. of mohaya, 'to stupefy,' 'infatuate,' 'bewilder,' see vi 12, note on mûḍha. The participle is left undeclined, as at viii 12, Bhaimi çântvayan (for çântvayanti): but the licence is unusual.

26. **hayajñatâm**, 'the horse-knowing-ness,' formed from hayajña, with suffix tâ, like preṣyatâ, xvi 1.

27. Mātali was the charioteer of Indra: Cālihotra (next line), though apparently a god, unknown to fame: he is not given by Dowson.

tallakṣaṇam, 'the mark or sign of him' (Mâtali).

29. **utâho**, see note on xii 73. **svid**, 'surely,' with âho at xxi 34: it is for su + id, like ced for ca + id, xvi 4. We might compare the German 'wohl,' used in the same manner, and our 'it may well be.'

âyâta, i.e. âyâtas, p. p. of a + √yâ: the p. p. of verbs of motion (ita from √i, &c.) are at first surprising in Sanskrit.

30. **atha vâ**, 'or then'—literally 'then or'—used to introduce a new idea. 'Well, Vâhuka has as much knowledge as Nala, for I see the skill equal of Vâhuka and Nala. Furthermore (**api ca**, see note on i 31) here is the age equal of Vâhuka and Nala. If this be not heroic Nala, it will be one who has his knowledge.' For the future **bhaviṣyati**, see note on iii 17. The connection of the two clauses is curious, and is the converse of the Vedic usage pointed out at xvi 4. The first clause has no particle; the second has ca. 'This (is) not Nala, and it will be, &c.' is the relic of a still older form of parataxis. So in Epic Greek we find τε in the apodosis: e.g. ὅς κε θεοῖς ἐπιπείθηται, μάλα τ' ἔκλυον αὐτοῦ. Further even in classical time, we find a protasis in which there is no formal relative particle, e.g. Eur. Medea, 386, καὶ δὴ τεθνᾶσι, τίς με δέξεται πόλις; But here καὶ δὴ doubtless is just as plain as εἰ when found with the perfect, which is the regular tense in this connection. In Latin the

nearest parallel is in phrases like Horace's (Odes IV iv 65), merses profundo, pulcrior evenit. But there too the conjunctive is a sign of the construction, which is not found here—where indeed there is no verb at all.

The logic of the passage (which is an interesting specimen of Hindū ratiocination) is impeded by this line; which is not (as might seem at first reading) the conclusion of the argument: that does not come till line 34. We have had the two reasons given above—like knowledge, like age. Then we might have gone on at once to the counter argument—unlike form. But the first argument is repeated in a slightly different form: and in the following line is the general consideration that there is no reason why it should not be Nala, because (hi) great ones do go about the earth in concealment: this is really applicable to all the arguments, not to one only: but it is not unnaturally put here in close connection with the one which is most prominent in Vārṣṇeya's mind—that derived from Nala's skill. Redundance is frequent in Hindu reasoning: it is found even in the form of the syllogism, of which the following is the well-known type (see 'Ind. Wisdom,' p. 72): 'the hill is fiery; for it smokes: whatever smokes is fiery: this hill smokes: therefore this hill is fiery.' M. Williams is right in saying that although the repetition seems clumsy, yet the form has its advantage, when regarded as a rhetorical statement of an argument.

32. **pracchannás**, see note on chāyā v 25.

daivena, as an adj. taken with **vidhiná**, 'divine command,' 'destiny.'

rúpataḥ, 'on the side of their form': hence the ablative—'looked at *from* that side'. See note on vi 4.

33. 'But there will be a division of my mind (i.e. doubt), with reference to his deformity of limb: "he will be destitute of certain proof", such is my thought.' That is to say the deformity prevents the absolute conviction which his skill and equality in age would otherwise bring: there is no τεκμήριον (to which pramāṇa corresponds), no certain evidence, only σημεῖα. Still in the end he sets the deformity aside, and concludes that the two are identical.

bheda is from √bhid, Lat. findo.

vairúpyatá, from vairūpya + tā; and vairūpya is from vi + rūpa.

pramáṇát, see iv 23 note: for the ablative see note on prahāsyati xxvi 24.

34. 'The proof from age—that is identical (or rather it should have been "the age is identical"); but on the score of form there is contrariety.' Perhaps however we might take pramáṇam here in the earlier sense of 'measurement.' 'Their measure of age is the same: but on the score of form there is change (for the worse, in Váhuka)': for viparyaya (in this sense) see note on viii 15.

Nalam, 'in the end I deem Nala to be Váhuka.' The change of form is more probable than that two men should have so great skill.

36. **mumude**, see note on v 39.

37. **aikágryam**, 'intentness,' from ekágra, 'intent on one thing': see note on agrahára xvi 3.

tathá, 'moreover,' 'and,' see iii 4 note.

utsáham, 'power,' 'energy,' from ud + √sah + a: the verb occurs iii 8, where see note.

saṃgrahaṇam, comp. xxi 5 saṃgṛhita: 'and that management of horses which he possesses.' This is the reading of the Bombay edition: saṃgrahaṇe, which appears in Prof. M. Williams' and Prof. Jarrett's texts is a misprint of the Calcutta edition.

mudam, 'joy,' from √mud without any suffix used as a feminine noun.

avápa, perf. of ava + √áp.

1. **khecaraḥ**, 'goer in the sky,' i.e. bird, comp. khagama i 24 &c. The locative is used in the place of the base, see page 6. The acc. was found in vihamga xii 41. The alliteration in khecaraḥ khe carann iva, 'sky goer, going in the sky,' is not strong.

2. **uttariyam**, 'upper garment,' from uttara, xvii 30, &c. **adho** exactly = ἔνθεν.

bhraṣṭam, 'fallen,' see note on vi 15.

3. **paṭe**, probably as Benfey suggests = patre, 'woven cloth' and then 'a garment.'

4. **nigṛhṇiṣva**, 'pull in,' from ni + √grah (9th class) i 19: comp. saṃgrahaṇa xix 37.

yàvad, 'meanwhile let Vārṣṇeya bring me back my robe': the use of the relative with the imperative seems at first sight strange: but it is nòt impossible to regard it as condensed for 'remain what time he is to bring—and do bring it.'

5. **samatikrànto**, 'passed beyond (i.e. left behind) a yojana': here the participle is used as a passive—not (as often) an active, e.g. ii 21. A yojana is variously reckoned at five or nine miles: the smaller amount is a more than sufficient exaggeration. On the insatiable appetite for the marvellous shewn in these poems see M. Williams' 'Ind. Wisdom,' p. 432. In the Mahābhārata, "full as it is of geographical, chronological and historical details, few assertious can be trusted. Time is measured by millions of years; space by millions of miles: and if a battle has to be described, nothing is thought of it unless millions of soldiers, elephants and horses are brought into the field." Of a piece with this is the bad taste (as it seems to us) of giving numerous arms and several heads, not merely to monsters (for here the Greeks are alike to blame), but even to Gods. Thus Brahmā appears with four heads and four arms: Vishṇu and Çiva with four arms apiece, and Çiva with five faces.

áhartuṃ çakyate, see note on vii 10 for construction: it is as though we could say 'it is not can-ned (by any one) to take it up,' i.e. no one can take it up: for **áhartum** xi 29.

6. **ásasáda**, x 7 note.

7. **mam' ápi**, emphatic, '*my* skill in counting' (as yours in driving). But, as the exhibition of the one spoils the other, the introduction of it here is awkward. **saṅ·khyáne**, xiii 56 note.

8. **pariniṣṭhá**, 'complete accomplishment': niṣṭhá from ni + √sthá is 'a basis,' 'settlement.' So at Bh. G. iii 3 we have the dvividhá niṣṭhá of knowledge and works.

9. **parṇáni**, xii 63.

ekam adhikaṃ çatam, 'a hundred with one over': the more obvious form of the phrase would be ekádhikam, M. M. Gr. p. 220; M. W. § 206. Adhika is 'exceeding'; so abhyadhika xi 16, xxi 14: and is regularly used thus in numeration, as also is úna, signifying 'less,' M. W. Gr. 207; so line 11 pañc'-onaṃ çatam = 100 – 5 = 95. At xxi 25 adhikaṃ çatam = 'a hundred and more.'

10. **pañcakoṭyo**, 'fifty millions': koṭi (f.) = ten millions, commonly a 'krore'.

11. **pracinuhi**, 'gather,' v 15 note. **praçákhikáḥ**, 'twigs', from çákha, 'a branch,' xii 65: it is the technical term for a recension of the Vedic text, belonging to a special Caraṇa or 'school'.

phala-sahasre, &c., 'two thousand fruits and a hundred less five,' i.e. 2095.

12. **avastbápya**, 'having stayed' (causal): avasthita, p. p. of the simple verb, occurs vii 15.

parokṣam, i.e. paras + akṣam, 'beyond sight,' 'invisible': hence (next line) **parokṣatá**, 'obscurity.' For paras compare pará, i 5 note.

katthase, 'thou boastest,' from √katth, apparently connected with √kath, 'to tell,' and kathá 'a tale' (xxi 23).

13. **çátayitvá**, 'having felled': çátaya is causal of √çad for which çiya (pass. of √çi i 17) is used in the first four tenses: it is no doubt = Lat. cad-o: but Bopp's ingenious identification of çátaya with caedo cannot be right: the diphthong shews that we must connect caedo with √skid 'to cut' (whence scindo σχίζω, &c.).

gaṇite, x 29 note.

14. **ahaṃ hi**, &c., see note on xviii 26.

15. **paçyatas te**, gen. absolute: comp. vii 8.

vájinám, 'of the horses': vájin is from vája a very common

Vedic word which, from an original sense of 'activity' or 'swiftness,' has developed many meanings—among them, battle, an offering to the Gods, and wealth; vájin is the strong and swift, and used of a battle horse, a hero, a sacrificer, &c.

16. **vilambitum**, 'to stay,' see viii 3 note on upalabhya. Ava + √lamb = 'rest upon,' Hit. 119.

param, &c. 'intent upon a great undertaking': for samásthitaḥ see xviii 24.

17. **pratikṣasva**, 'wait,' from prati + √ikṣ i 20.

Várṣṇeya-sárathiḥ, a B. V. compound, 'with Várṣṇeya for charioteer': comp. xv 8 saha-Várṣṇeya-Jivalaḥ.

19. **vighnam**, see xiii 23 note.

20. 'If thou shalt shew the sun to me after going to Vidarbha to-day,' i.e. if we shall arrive at Vidarbha before night.

22. **akáma**, 'as one unwilling')(sakáma 'one who has attained his desire.'

samádiṣṭam, iv 25 note.

23. **avatirya**, ii 30 note.

túrṇam, 'quickly,' p. p. of √tvar, M. M. Gr. § 432, as also tvarita (line 26) and see note on v 2. It might be referred to the Vedic form √tur—or √túr.

24. 'Having counted, the fruits are so many as said (by thee).' Note the very loose construction of gaṇayitvá: there is no mayá to which it can be referred: it rather resembles the so-called 'nominativus pendens' construction. See i 22 note.

25. **atyadbhutam**, see note on adbhuta i 24: adbhutatama occurs xxiii 13.

26. **tvarito gamane**, 'eager for the going,' see note on viii 1.

viçáradam, xii 86 note.

27. **dehi mama**, 'give me': v 38 note.

28. **kárya-gauravát**, 'by reason of the gravity of his business.' Gaurava is formed by vṛiddhi from guru (gravis, βαρύς). In the sense of 'venerable' (comp. vir pietate gravis) the term is applied to the father who performs the proper ceremonies on the birth of a child, Manu ii 142, while the religious teacher, who girds the pupil with the cord which gives him second birth is called ácárya (ib. ii 140): and at 146 we find that

utpádaka-brahmadátror gariyán brahmadaḥ pitá,

'of the natural and of the spiritual father, the giver of sacred knowledge is more venerable' (gariyas is the comparative of guru). Guru sometimes governs a genitive, e.g. Hit. 348 sarvasy' ábhyágato guru, 'a guest is everyone's superior,' comp. ib. 529.

lobhád, see note on lubdhaka xi 34.

hṛıdayam, see xiv 21 note.

29. **nıkṣepo**, 'compensation,' literally 'deposit' or 'pledge,' comp. nıkṣıpya viii 20, xxii 14; and note on ákṣıpantim iii 13.

30. **tikṣṇam**, 'sharp,' 'acute,' from √tıj, see note on tejas iv 26.

udvaman, 'vomiting up,' √vam (ἐμέω, vomo).

31. **çápágnıḥ**, 'that fire-curse,' i.e. curse which was just like a fire: comp. naraçárdúla, &c.

karṣıto, see vii 14 note.

anátmaván = non sui compos: 'out of his mind.'

32. **aıcchat**, imperf. of ıṣ 'to wish,' see note on ıṣṭa, i 1.

35. **avasaṃ tvayı**, see v 32 note.

suduḥkham, a curious collocation of su (εὖ) and duḥ (δυσ-). But su has often only an intensive force, as in sukumára, suvarcas &c.

36. **ye ca**, see note on xvi 4. **kirtayıṣyantı**, fut. of √kṛit (10th cl.), really a denominative from kirtı 'renown,' which is from √kṛi 'to scatter' iv 18. **atandrıtáḥ**, xv 15 note.

37. 'The fear that is born from me shall never be theirs, if thou shalt not curse me when tormented by fear I have supplicated thee': i.e. 'they shall not have occasion to fear me.'

39. **adṛıçyat**, another example of the passive voice with active terminations, like mokṣyası xiv 6. Doubtless it is assisted by the analogy of the 4th class verbs, which form the present base with ya.

gata-jvara, 'his affliction gone,' see xii 93 note.

41. **javanaır**, 'speedy,' from java viii 19 note.

apraçastaḥ, 'untold of,' i.e. accurst: compare Vergil's 'illaudati Busiridis aras' (Georg. iii 5). 'But the Vıbhitak became accurst by the entrance of Kalı.' **saṃçraya** is from sam + √çri v 15 note.

43. **Vıdarbhábhımukho**, 'with his face set toward Vıdarbha.'

44. 'Freed from Kalı (see xiii 34 note), dispossessed of his form only': for **mátra** so used in composition, see ix 10 note. Kali is ejected from him, but he still remains the misshapen Vāhuka. See note on xiv 16.

2.   nàdayan, 'making to resound,' see xii 1 note on nadi.
savıdıço, 'with the intermediate points.' Dıç has the same
meaning as deça 'region,' but the primary meaning 'direction' is
retained by it.   So the whole phrase means 'all the (main) quarters
with the intermediate points.'

3.   Naláçvàs, i.e. the horses brought by Vàrṣṇeya, at the end of
the 8th canto. sannıdhau, v 31 note.

4.   gambhiram, comp. xii 57 note. jalada, 'a cloud' is a 'water-
giver,' iv 4 note.

5.   Nalena, &c., 'as before, when the horses (xx 15) of Nala were
driven by Nala,' comp. san.grahaṇa xix 37.

6.   'And the peacocks on the palace roof (see xiii 49 note) and the
elephants in their stalls (xix 11 note) &c.'
çıkhın, 'having a çıkhà' or 'crest,' xi 36.
vàraṇa (which comes from √vṛ and also means 'armour') is 'an
elephant' probably from their use as 'a covering' in battle.

7.   pranedur, perf. of pra + √nad, like mene from √man (line 6 :
see note on nıpetuḥ i 23).   'With necks uplifted they clamoured, as
restless at the roaring of the rain-cloud'—or perhaps megha-nàde
may go more closely with utsuka 'longing for the rain.'   This the
peacocks are observed to do.   Comp. Indr. iii 4 açaniç ca mahànàdà
megha-barhıṇa-lakṣaṇàḥ, 'Indra's thunderbolts, with mighty roar,
marked by clouds and peacocks (barhıṇa).'

8.   medınim, xi 39 note.
àhlàdayate, 'makes to rejoice,' causal of à + √hlàd = Gr. χλαδ,
and probably also our 'glad.'   Curtius (no. 186) rejects it because of
the irregularity of the final dental.   But Grimm's law is not nearly
so sure at the end of a word as it is at the beginning.

9.   candràbhavaktram, 'moon-faced' : for àbha see xiii 63.
asan.khyeya, xiii 56 note.

10. **bâhvor**, dual gen. of bâhu. **antaram**, see vii 2 note.

sukha-sparçam, 'whose touch is happiness': sparça from √spṛç, vii 3.

11. 'This very day I will enter the fire with its colour like gold': i.e. I will destroy myself.

câmikara is said to be from camikara 'a mine': and that should come from *cama and a √cam: which does occur, but only in the sense of rinsing the mouth: see note on vii 3.

prakhyam, see xiii 63. **Hutâçanam**, see iv 9.

12. **vikrânta**, xii 54: also **vikrama.**

13. **anṛitam**, 'untrue' = an + ṛita p. p. of √ṛi, iv 7, see Curt. G. E. no. 488. It has lost its participial sense and means only 'true' or 'truth.' Curtius thinks that the primary meaning of AR is 'to fit,' and that verb can be used transitively or intransitively: this meaning suits very well to the numerous derivations in Greek, ἀραρίσκω, ἄρθρον, ἄρτιος, ἀριθμός, ἀρετή, &c., Latin artus, arma, &c., and others in other languages. But it seems to me not to explain the Sanskrit words, e.g. √ṛi in the sense of 'going'. Grassmann takes the first meaning 'to put into motion'—then 'to bring through motion into position,' 'to fit in.' This seems somewhat artificial.

apakâratâm, 'an injurious action,' from apakâra, which generally means 'injury': comp. Hitop. 1047, dviṣatam apakâra-kâraṇât, 'for the sake of injuring enemies.' But it must be regarded here as an adjective, meaning 'injurious'; otherwise it could not go with the suffix -tâ.

paryuṣitam, p. p. of pari + √vas, 'to live,' 'that which has dwelt round (a night),' and so is 'stale': at Manu iv 211, çuktam paryuṣitaṃ caiva, 'that which is turned acid and that which is kept over night,' is forbidden to be eaten by a Brahman. Here perhaps 'a profitless speech.'

svaireṣu, 'even in matters unimportant,' lit. in matters depending on one's own free will, comp. svairavrittâ, xxiv 24, where there is no rule laid down, and each man must decide for himself, according to âtmatuṣṭi, 'self-satisfaction'—Manu ii 7, quoted above at xii 26.

14. **abhyadhiko**, 'as a giver conspicuous among kings': compare for construction, anyair viçeṣataḥ, xv 3; and for adhika, see xi 16, note.

raho, &c., 'not following ignoble practices in secret.' **rahas**, see i 18 note: **anica**, 'not low,' xi 2, note on uccaiḥ. Nicaga is used of a stream.

klivavad, 'like a mean man'; kliva or kliba is 'a eunuch.'

15. **tat-paràyà**, 'intent,' 'devoted'—here used alone: at xvi 26, it is at the end of a compound. **vınàkṛıtam**, i 11 note.

16. **vılapamànà**, vii 17 note.

17. **kakṣàyàm**, see iv 25 note.

19. **rath'-opasthàt**, 'from the seat of the car'; **upastha** (upa + √sthà) is the 'lap,' often in Vedic.

20. **akasmàt**, 'without a cause,' 'suddenly,' 'unexpectedly.' Kasmàt is 'why,' and so akasmàt is literally 'without a why.'

strimantram, compare xviii 16: it is really Damayantī's plan. **sma**, i 12 note.

22. **satya-paràkrama**, compare the name Ἐτεο-κλέης (satya-kravas).

24. **bhavantam abhıvàdakaḥ**, 'to greet your majesty': formed from abhıvàda, 'salutation': for acc. after a subst. or adj., see ii 27 note.

25. 'The (true) cause of his coming 100 yojanas and more, past many villages (see ix 21 note)—he has not really attained.' That is to say, he had some motive for coming, but he has not been able to carry it out. In this way adhı + √gam has its proper sense 'to attain to a thing': comp. xvii 49. The line is generally taken as though the verb meant 'to arrive': in which case the first half line must be in apposition with yathàtatham, which there means 'as so (said by him),' a rather different sense from that which it commonly has (e.g. at iii 2) 'truly,' i.e. so as it actually is.

26. **vınırdıṣṭam**, 'assigned': nıs + √dıç = 'to point to,' and vı seems only to intensify the meaning: which the simple root has at line 28, dıṣṭaṃ veçma.

paççàd udarke, 'afterwards in the future,' see note on xii 92.

27. **vyasarȷayat**, 'dismissed him,' see note on v 27.

vıçràmyatàm, 'let rest be taken,' the usual passive of politeness, not naming the person, see xii 69 note: for √çram see note on àçrama ix 22.

klànto, 'wearied,' see note on klama, ix 28.

28. **ràȷa-preṣyaır**, see xvi 1.

29. **rathaçàlàm**, xix 11 note.

30. **upacarya**, from upa + √car, 'to minister to,' or 'tend': but at xxiii 8, upacàra seems only to mean 'conduct,' 'practice': compare Latin ministerium. Anu with √car has the same meaning, comp. anucara, 'service,' Hit. 312: compare also parıcàrıkà viii 4.

çàstrataḥ, 'according to rule'; see note on √çàs, iii 21.

32. **nısvana** = svana. **Nalasya**, &c., 'it was great as that of Nala, and yet I see not Nala.'

33. **na ca** = neque, as at x 17.

upaçıkṣıtá, 'learnt,' from upa + çıkṣ, desiderative of √çak (i 18) literally 'to wish to be able.' Hence çıkṣá, 'learning.'

34. **áhosvıd**, 'or belike': for áho, comp. utáho xii 73; for svıd xix 29 note.

35. **tarkayıtvá**, see v 12 note: it regularly describes a process of reasoning.

anveṣane, locative of purpose, iii 6 note.

2. **mṛidu-pûrvam**, 'gently,' lit. 'with soft front,' see note on xi 34. **samâhitâ**, i 6 note.

pṛicchethâḥ, note the optative used in a request = ἔροιο ἄν: again twice in line 4. The 2 pers. opt. is rarely so found alone in Greek: καὶ νῦν εἴ τί που ἔστι, πίθοιό μοι, δ 192: see Delbrück ('Conj. und Opt.' p. 197).

3. **çan·kâ bhaved**, 'doubt whether he be,' see note on xviii 26.

yathâ, 'as is (i.e. so extreme is) the delight of my mind, and the tranquillity of my heart.' **tuṣṭi** is from √tuṣ, 'to be glad,' i 7 note. **nirvṛitiḥ** is from nis + √vṛi, whence the p. p. nirvṛita xxvi 33, Hit. 1030. It means apparently at first, 'freedom from constraint.'

5. **upaikṣata**, 'looked on,' apparently: but the usual sense of upa + √ikṣ is 'to neglect': so Hit. 1037, upekṣâṃ karoṣi, comp. Megh. 8. We can say 'to look over' a thing in two quite opposite senses.

sâdhu, v 29 note.

7. **kadâ**, 'when did ye set forth?' Keçinī knows where they come from: therefore she asks the time of their journey: for this depends upon the rate of driving: and the driving may indicate Nala.

8. **bhavitâ çva**, 'it will be to-morrow': this is the speech of the Brahman.

9. **yâyibhiḥ**, 'able to go,' from √yâ: the second *y* is euphonic.

10. **samâhitam**, 'entrusted to thee,' with the loc. tvayi: a more concrete force of the participle than at xxii 2.

11. **pradrute**, 'when Nala was runned away' literally: see ii 21 note. For √dru, see i 25.

12. **pratiṣṭhitaḥ**, see note on pratiṣṭhâ xii 66. **sûtatve**, 'charioteership'—the suffix *tva* used like *tâ* which would be less euphonic here.

vṛitaḥ, 'selected by Ṛituparṇa for driving and for preparing food': see iii 6 note.

13. katham, &c., 'and how has it been told to thee by him (Vârṣṇeya)?' Here we have the regular locative (tvayi) with a verb of telling, comp. i 31, xviii 15, &c., and not the genitive as below line 21, xviii 13, &c.

14. açubha-karmaṇaḥ, comp. açubhaṃ kṛitam, xiii 32.

15. gûḍhaç, p. p. of √guh, 'to cover,' 'conceal': see note on guhâ, v 7.

naṣṭa-rûpo, x 29 note.

16. yâ ca, 'and that in him which is next to it,' i.e. to self. anantara is a B. V. 'that which has no between': and with tad it makes a T. P. compound. This next to self (âtman) is apparently buddhi, the second principle in the Sān-khya list, standing before ahaṃkara or consciousness.

na hi, 'for Nala tells not at any time the marks which distinguish him': so hayajñasya lin-gâni, xxiii 6; and compare note on v 13. çaṃsati, xii 35, and i 16 notes.

17. yo 'sau, see xiii 25 note. 'He, the Brahman, that went first to Ayodhyâ (went) saying over again and again these words of the lady.' gatavân, like dṛiṣṭavat i 29.

18-20 =xvii 37—39.

22. 'That reply which was given to him by thee when thou hadst heard that (word) from him, that the princess of Vidarbha desires to hear again from thee.' çrutvâ goes with tvayâ, see note on viii 22, and tasya is governed by dattam, as v 38, xx 27, &c.

23. vyathitam, see xii 118.

24. sandigdhayâ, v 11 note.

25-29 =xviii 8—12.

30. soḍhum, inf. of √sah, 'to hold in,' 'restrain,' iii 8 note; M. W. Gr. § 611 a, M. M. App. no. 93. açakat, aor. of √çak, i 18: M. W. Gr. § 679, M. M. App. no. 144, see note on çucaḥ, xii 73.

31. vikâram, 'change,' here mental, and so 'emotion,' again at xxiii 26; comp. vikṛita xiii 26; and see note on âkâra, ii 5.

1. **parâyaṇâ**, see xii 82 note. **çan·kamânâ**, iv 12.

2. **parikṣâm**, 'make examination of Vâhuka,' with the locative: at xix 11 we had pariksâm açvânâm cakre: the participle parikṣita occurs xxiv 3.

caritâni, 'his doings' or as we might say 'his goings on': see vi 8 note.

3. **yadâ kiṃcid**, 'whensoever any,' see notes on iv 2.

kâraṇam usually means 'a cause' or 'instrument'; it is here used for Nala's conduct as that which gives a cause for inference respecting him, like nimittam at line 5: and comp. xvi 9 kâraṇair upapâdayan, and 27.

tatra, 'observing there the conduct of him as he goes on—': we must carry on lakṣaya from the previous line to complete the sentence. **saṃceṣṭamânasya** and **viceṣṭitam** are from the same √ceṣṭ 'to move' (in the first instance) 'violently,' but that force has disappeared in ordinary use: ceṣṭita and ceṣṭâ are used in the same general sense at line 18: see note on nirviceṣṭam xi 28.

4. 'And not even fire must be given to him, by way of hindrance,' i.e. he is not to be helped by giving fire to him: this is an extraordinary method of expressing the mere absence of help as a positive hindrance: but I see no other way to take the words: and even so the instrumental pratibandhena seems hardly parallel to dautyen' âgatya (iv 15) and the like.

yâcate, 'water is not to be given by thee in haste to him if he asks for it.' Water, grass and earth to sit on are the things which, according to Manu iii 101, are never to be refused by any one however poor: comp. iv 29 where roots and fruit are added. Fire and water are to be withheld here to test Vâhuka. If he be Nala, they will come at his call, according to the gifts of Agni and Varuṇa, v 36 and 37. √yâc is 'to ask': hence yâcñâ 'begging,' Hit. 626:

and comp. 1033 yácate káryakále yaḥ, sa kımbhṛıtyaḥ, 'he who begs at working-time is a bad servant.' It is parallel to ζητέω: but probably the final consonant of the root in each language is an independent determinative letter: the primary root will be yá, which in Greek takes the form ζη (i.e. dyá), whence δίζη-μαι: see Curt. G. E. Vol. 2, p. 262 (Eng. tr.). The same instinctive feeling that even enemies have a claim to the common necessaries of life is embodied in the Roman proverb given in Plautus, Trin. 679, 'datur ignis tametsi ab inimico petas': compare also Rud. 438, 'cur tu aquam gravare quam hostis hosti commodat.'

5. **nımıttam**, see ix 34 note.

ákhyeyam mama, comp. xvi 34. **apı** may here have the primary sense 'further,' see i 31.

6. **nıçamya**, 'having perceived,' see v 22 note.

7. **dıvyamánuṣam**, 'divine and human,' a Dvandva, and not to be taken as though one excluded the other. Part of Vāhuka's conduct is human, part superhuman.

8. **dṛıḍhaṃ**, 'very much,' used adverbially: dṛıḍha is 'fast,' the p. p. of a Vedic √dṛıṃh, 'to be or to make fast.' It occurred in the compound dṛıḍha-vrata vi 10.

çucy-upacáro, 'holy,' from çuci 'pure' iv 18, &c. orig. 'white,' 'clear'; and upacára 'practice,' see xxi 30.

9. 'Having reached a low entrance, he bends not his head at all (iv 1 note): the entrance seeing him on the moment of his approach rises up conveniently.' **yathásan·gam** is an Av. B. from san·ga, 'meeting,' 'joining': Benfey explains it 'so as to be adapted,' which is rather the meaning of **yathá-sukham**, which again he translates 'willingly': but sukha means 'happiness,' 'pleasure,' and so here 'convenience.'

hrasvam, meant 'short' in hrasva-báhuka xviii 6: here 'low.'

10. **arthåya**, comp. xiii 42 Nalasy' árthåya.

bhojaniyam, 'food,' fut. part. of √bhuj ii 4.

máṃsam, 'flesh' (general), while **páçavam** (formed from paçu = pecus, vieh) is flesh of cattle.

11. **prakṣálana**, 'cleansing,' 'purification,' see xi 29 note: and comp. 23 prakṣálya mukham.

upakalpıtáḥ, 'prepared for use,' causal of upa + √kḷıp 'to be fit': comp. pra-kalpıta xxv 7.

te, &c., 'the vessels, when looked upon (xii 16 note) by him, became then full,' by virtue of Varuṇa's gift, v 37.

12. **tṛṇa-muṣṭiṃ** (xiii 28), 'having taken up a handful of grass he held it up to the sun: then blazed forth (xi 35) in it suddenly (v 28) the fire.' **Havya-váhanaḥ**, 'sacrifice-carrier,' i.e. fire: see iii 4 note on Agni: havya is the fut. part. of √hu iv 9. The presence of fire is Agni's gift.

14. **áçcaryam**, 'marvel,' xii 97. **yad** = quod vi 6.

15. **chandena**, 'on the desire': from √chand 'to please,' primarily 'to appear,' and so 'appear good to,' compare δοκεῖν. Chandas in late Vedic is 'a hymn,' and in still later times = 'metre.' Svacchanda = 'one's own will,' like sponte sua, e.g. Hit. 367, svacchandavanajáta 'growing spontaneously in a wood.' Benfey would connect the root with spondeo. **vahati**, 'flows,' used intransitively.

ávarjitam, 'turned towards him,' or 'turned down,' 'poured out,' see xiii 53 note. **drutam**, 'quickly,' p. p. of √dru 'to run,' i 25.

16. **upádáya**, xiii 74 note. **hastábhyám**, ii 11 note on hastin.

páṇibhyám, 'with his hand,' xxiv 14: it is certainly akin to παλάμη and palma, the ṇ shewing a lost r equivalent to the l of the other languages. The radical idea is probably 'flatness' (seen in ἐπιπολή and palam). See Curt. G. E. nos. 345 and 354. The commoner derivation is from PAR 'to fill.'

17. **hṛṣitáni**, 'fresh,' lit. 'bristling,' see i 24 note on hṛṣṭa.

18. **abhisúcitam**, v 25 note.

20. **mahánasác chṛitam**, for mahánasát çṛitam, 'taking from the kitchen meat cooked by Váhuka.' **pramattasya**, 'negligent,' 'inobservant,' p. p. of pra + √mad, i 24 note on pramadá. **çṛitam** is not from √çṛi 'to go,' but from √çrá 'to cook,' for which Benfey and Bopp give a considerable list of parallels in other languages, e.g. κλίβανος, καρπός, cremo, harvest, ripe: but though the 2nd, 4th and 5th of these are doubtless akin, yet they come from a root KARP which may be a secondary of KRA, but may also have nothing to do with it, for Latin carpo does not seem to agree in sense. Curtius (no. 52) allows of only κέραμος 'terra coctilis,' and κέρνος 'a dish,' which seem fairly certain.

21. **agre**, 'in front of,' see note on agráhara xvi 3: agratas is the same xxiv 14.

atyuṣṇam, 'exceedingly hot': uṣṇa from √uṣ 'to burn.'

22. **ucitá**, 'accustomed to the food prepared by Nala.' See note on xv 18. **siddhasya**, p. p. either of √sidh or of √sádh 'to accomplish,' whence sádhu v 29 &c.: either verb is common in Sanskrit,

but hardly clear in other languages, unless they be akin to √sad, which is unlikely. Sâdhaya (10th cl.) may be regarded as an irregular causal of sidh (4th cl.) which has the force of 'evenire.' Siddha also = 'perfectus,' one who has liberated himself from all passion : so Bh. G. x 26.

prâçya, 'having tested,' from √aç, see note on Hutâça iv 9.

prâkroçad, xi 2 note.

23. **vaiklavyam**, 'commotion,' from viklava 'confused,' of uncertain origin. Benfey suggests √klam.

prakṣâlya, &c., 'having cleansed her mouth with water': comp. Manu v 145 where a Brahman is required 'after sleeping, sneezing, eating, spitting, or telling untruths,' to rinse his mouth.

mithunam, 'her pair of children': v 38 note.

24. **pariṣvajya**, xvii 12.

an.kam ânayat, 'set upon his knees,' lit. 'led into his lap,' from â + √ni xii 68. In the same sense an-kam âropayâmâsa is used Indr. ii 21. **an.ka** (which also means 'a hook' and 'a mark,' comp. Çak. i 13 and 24) is ἀγκών, ὄγκος, uncus, angle, the primary idea of all being something bent, see Curt. G. E. no. 1.

25. **samâsâdya**, 'having gotten,' intensified from âsâdya x 7 &c.

susvaram, 'loudly,' *su* being intensive, as in su-sadriçam 'just like,' line 27, su-alpa xxv 13, suduṣkaram xv 4, suduḥkha xx 35 where see note.

26. **vikâram**, xxii 31 note: again at xxiv 1.

27. **utsṛiṣṭavân**, v 27 note.

28. 'If thou meet me often, people will suspect thee of fault.' Here √çan-k (viii 3 note) is used with the ablative: at xxiv 26 it has the instrumental.

deçâtithayo, 'strangers in the land'; atithi = 'a guest,' connected by Benfey with √at 'to go.' A curious derivation of the word is given Manu iii 102,

> ekarâtraṃ tu nivasann atithir Brâhmaṇaḥ smṛitaḥ :
> anityaṃ hi sthito yasmât, tasmâd atithir ucyate,

i.e. a Brâhman who tarries but for one night is called 'atithi,' because remaining not in perpetuity he is called a-tithi ('not a lunar day,' v 1 note).

2. **bhûyaḥ**, viii 14 note.

sakâçam, 'sent into the presence of her mother.' Sakâçe (from kâç xvii 6) occurred i 21.

3. **ekaḥ**, 'one *only* doubt'—the common use of the word.

4. 'Let him be made to enter here, mother, or do thou permit me to go to him,' literally 'think right to dismiss me': see iii 1 note on pratijñâya: 'whether known or unknown of my father, let it be decided': for saṃvidhiyatâm see v 19 note.

5. **abhiprâyam**, ix 35 note. **anvajânât**, 'allowed,' iii 1, the meaning being a shade different from that in the last line.

6. **Nalam**, 'caused Nala to be brought into her chamber': see xiii 56, and for the use of **yatra** see xiii 30.

8. **tivra**, xi 13 note.

9. **kâṣâya**, 'dark reddish brown': it is the colour worn by ascetics, &c., in the woods. So at Sāv. iii 18, Sāvitrī strips off her ornaments and jagṛhe valkalâny eva vastraṃ kâṣâyam eva ca, i.e. 'dark robes and a brown dress.' At Mahābh. iii 15805 Duryodhana says to Karṇa,

> kinnu syâd adhikaṃ tasmâd, yad ahaṃ Drupadâtmajâm
> Draupadiṃ, Karṇa, paçyeyaṃ kâṣâyavasanâṃ vane?

i.e. 'what could be better than this, that I should see Draupadī wearing the ascetic dress in the wood?' Kâṣâyavâsas (applied to Buddhists) is found in Yâjñavalkya i 272: M. Williams, 'Ind. Wisdom,' p. 296.

jaṭilâ, adjective formed from jaṭâ 'matted hair,' whence Dhûrjaṭi (Hit. 1) and Jaṭâdhara names of Çiva who wears it as the great ascetic: see Dowson. At Manu vi 6 the Vânaprastha is ordered 'jaṭâç ca nibhṛyân nityam.'

mala-paṅkini, 'covered with mud and dirt'; formed with

suffix *in* from the Dvandva mala-pan-ka. For mala see x 6 note: pan-ka occurs Hit. 173 &c.

10. **nâma**, see xi 4 note.

vipine, xvii 27.

11. **anâgasam**, xiii 62 note. **ṛite**, iv 26 note.

12. **aparâddham**, 'injury done to him,' p. p. of apa + √râdh v 20 note. The noun aparâdha with the same sense occurs xxv 11, 13.

bâlyâd, 'from folly,' a noun formed from bâla 'a child' by suffix *ya*.

13. **apahâya** goes with **mayâ**, 'he who was aforetime openly (sâkṣâd 'face to face' i 4) chosen by me to the rejection of Gods, how could he forsake me &c.?'

putriṇim, 'the mother of his children,' from putra + suffix *-in*.

14. **agnau**, 'in presence of the sacred fire': for a description of a marriage ceremony taken from the Āçvalâyana Gṛihya Sûtras (I. vii) see M. Williams, 'Ind. Wisdom,' p. 199.

pâṇiṃ gṛihitvâ, 'having taken my hand,' a regular part of the ceremony.

agratas, xxiii 21.

bhaviṣyâmi, i.e. tâvat tvayi bhaviṣyâmi, Nala's promise at v 32.

pratiçrutya, iv 16 and note on saṃçrutya iii 9.

16. **kṛiṣṇa-sârâbhyâm**, 'black,' see note on sâriṇi xii 59.

raktântâbhyâm, 'with red corners': for rakta see note v 22.

17. 'That my kingdom was lost (viii 18 note on vinaçet), 'twas not I that did it: that was done by Kali, trembler; and also that I forsook thee.' **bhiru** is from √bhi xii 1.

18. **kṛicchreṇa**, vi 12 note. **vanasthayâ**, 'dwelling in the wood,' see note on svastha ii 1.

19. **âhitaḥ**, here in the concrete sense (something like ad-ditus), not abstract as at i 6 &c.

20. **vyavasâyena**, 'energy,' 'resolution'; so Sâv. iv 6: from vi + ava + √so (class 4); pres. base sya, and nearly always with ava and some other preposition.

antena...bhavitavyam, 'here is to be the end of our sorrow': lit. 'it is to be *with* this end,' a very idiomatic Sanskrit use of the instrumental with the passive participle of √bhû: comp. Hit. 1176 tasya prâṇino balen' âpi sumahatâ bhavitavyam, i.e. 'that creature will be of very great strength.' It arises from the fondness of the language for the passive construction: i.e. tvayâ gantavyam, 'thou must go,' is preferred to 'gaccha' or the like: and so even in the verb bhû, tvayá bhavitavyam stands for bhaviṣyasi: and here antena bhavitavyam = anto bhaviṣyati: and the predicate ayam 'this will be the end' passes into anena. For other exx. see M. W. Gr. § 905 a.

21. **vipula-çroṇi**, see notes on vi 6 and xi 32.

prayojanam, 'business,' see note on prayujya v 16.

24. **svairavṛttá**, 'having become her own mistress,' see note on svaireṣu xxi 13.

anurúpam, 'conformable,' 'suited to': so Hit. 1062 sattvánurúpam phalam 'fruits suited to one's nature,' comp. Çak. i 22.

26. **doṣeṇa pariçan·kitum**, comp. notes on viii 3 and xxiii 28.

27. **gáyamána**, see note on xv 15. **gáthábhir**, from the same √gai is 'a song' or 'verse': it is analogous to the Latin use of carmen and cano.

diço daça, 'the ten quarters': we had eight only at xxi 2 savidiço diçaḥ, four primary and four intermediate. But here the zenith and the nadir are included: as they are in the division into six, which is more common.

29. 'When speech had been duly (sámyak, see note on viii 13) made by him, and reply likewise received, this device was perceived by me, for thy recovery.'

31. **spṛiçeyam**, 'I will touch' (at any time—the original indefinite future sense of the tense) 'as not even in my thought do I go on any evil way.' This is practically an oath: 'as I am innocent, I am ready to do that which would bring down punishment on me, if guilty,' for √spṛiç see xi 3 note. Touching the feet seems to be a formality in taking an oath to a superior. At Manu viii 114 a witness on great occasions is to hold fire, or dive under water or touch the head of his children and his wife. Compare Juv. xiv 219 Cereris tangens aramque *pedemque.*

32. 'Here moveth in this earth witnessing all creatures the ever-moving (wind)—may he let loose my life, if I tread the path of evil.' For √muc see v 28 note.

33. 'Likewise the sun continually traverses the universe above.' **tigmáṃçu** is the 'hot-rayed,' as the moon is çitáṃçu 'the cold-rayed,' below line 53: tigma is primarily 'sharp' from √tij, see note on tejas iv 26: aṃçu is probably from AK 'to be sharp': the same word in Vedic means the soma-plant. Compare also aṃçumat 'the rayed one,' i.e. the sun, v 43. **pareṇa** is 'beyond' and here 'above': comp. ataḥ param ix 23.

34. 'The moon goes in the midst of all living creatures like a witness.'

antaç stands for antar and takes a genitive as though antare had been used. **candramas** is a fuller name for candra the moon, here and at xvii 6. The last syllable is akin to √mā 'to measure.'

35. **trailokyam**, see ii 13 note on loka. Sun, moon and wind are well selected as the most sure natural witnesses. Çītā in the Rāmāyaṇa, when similarly misdoubted by her husband Rāma, enters the fire as an ordeal to prove her innocence: and she is of course miraculously preserved.

36. **antarikṣād**, see i 20 note.

37. **çila-nidhiḥ**, 'the treasure of her virtue': for çila see note on xii 26: for nidhi note on vidhi iv 17.

sphito, 'large,' properly, 'swollen,' is p. p. of √sphāy (1st cl.) 'to swell,' a root for which we may fairly assume an older form √spa, the final *y* being formative and the *ph* due to the *s*. This √spa *may* be akin to the Greek √σπα in σπάω, σπασμός, &c.: for which see Curt. no. 354: he connects it (as Benfey also does) with the fuller form √span, seen in σπάνις, also probably in πένης, πόνος &c., in penuria, and our 'spin'—the radical signification being 'to draw' or 'urge on.' But the connection of meaning with √sphāy is not too clear.

parivatsarān, 'three complete years.' Pari has an intensive force here as in pari-ṣodaçaiḥ, xxvi 2, paripluta (l. 46) &c.: it is as we might say 'a year round.' The simplest form of the word is vatsa, which has the same root, though not the same suffix, as Fέτ-ος and vet-us: for which see Curt. no. 210.

38. **atulo**, xii 61 note.

na hy, &c.: no man will be able to drive a hundred yojanas except Nala: but Vāhuka has driven a hundred yojanas: therefore Vāhuka is Nala; and Nala has been discovered by his so driving: therefore Damayantī's plan was for Nala's sake. Hence the conjunction *hi*.

40. **puṣpa-vṛiṣṭiḥ**, 'a flower-rain': for vṛiṣṭi see note on varṣa vii 3. This is a common sign of divine approbation. A picture of such a shower falling on Çītā's head may be seen in Moor's 'Hindu Pantheon,' p. 120, plate XXXIV.

devadundubhayo, 'the kettledrums of heaven': so Indr. ii 11. **nedur**, perf. of √nad xii 1. This is a further attestation of Damayantī's innocence.

vavau, perf. of √vā 'to blow,' x 21, like dadau from √dā &c., i 8 &c.

41. adbhutatamam, 'this greatest miracle,' see note on adbhuta i 24.

Damayantyáṃ vïçan·kâm, 'lack of trust *in* Damayantï': for the case see v 22 note.

vyapàkarṣad, 'he tore' or 'swept away,' from vi + apa + √kṛṣ, vii 14.

42. vastram, the 'divyaṃ vàso-yugaṃ' of xiv 25, given by Karkoṭaka. araıaḥ = virajàṃsı iv 8.
     lebhe, perf. of √labh viii 4. vapuḥ, iii 12.

43. pràkroçad, xi 2.
     álın·gya, 'embracing' from à + √lın·g, which hardly occurs except thus compounded with à. It is certainly connected with lın·ga v 14.

44. sasvaıe, xvii 12. yathàvat, 'duly,' 'properly,' vi 8.
     pratyanandata, viii 7.

45. 'Having laid her face down on his very breast' (i 29 note on uraga), sva being used here in the sense 'self,' 'very,' like αὐτός, see i 15 note. vınyasya, from vı + nı + √as 'to throw,' see xii 79. san-ny-àsa is a thing laid down, i.e. 'a stake,' at xxvi 5.

46. dıgdha, p. p. of √dıh, v 11 note on sandeha.

48. kṛıta-çaucam, 'after he is duly purified.' It looks a somewhat pointed allusion to Nala's original sin. But this purification is to be done always immediately on rising. See Manu iv 93, quoted above at vii 3, and this (joined with kalyam 'at daybreak,' in the next half line) shews that Bhïma is only politely saying that he will see Nala as soon as possible next morning. For çauca see vi 10 note. The adv. kalyam is apparently the neuter of kalya 'whole' 'sound' (καλός) whence kalyàṇa iii 22, where see note. It probably means the time when the twilight has become complete—the perfect day.

     draṣṭá, fut. of √dṛç. It is the 3rd sing. used for the 1st person draṣṭàsmı. But as the first person is only the verbal noun with asmı, the licence here amounts to no more than leaving that asmı out.

49. purátanam, 'ancient,' 'of old days,' used like antiquus. The suffix is the same as in crastinus, diutinus, &c.: hardly the same as protenus (Benfey).

     vıcarıtam, 'wandering,' comp. i 19, and vi 8 note. ùṣatur, 2 dual perf. of √vas.

50. parasparasukhaıṣınau, 'eager for each other's happiness': eṣın is from √ıṣ, i 1.

51. **varṣe**, vii 3 note. **su-siddhártho**, comp. kṛitártha, xvi 10: for siddha, see xxiii 22.

52. **ápyáyitá**, 'increased,' 'refreshed' (something like the use of Latin 'auctus'), p. p. of the causal of √pyai, a fuller form of √pi: see note on pina, v 5. 'Refreshed like the earth that has gotten rain when its fruits are half grown.' **çasya**, 'fruit,' 'corn,' would seem to be the fut. part. of √çaṃs, 'to praise': it is also written sasya (e.g. Manu, iv 26), and if (as the P. W. asserts) that is the true form, it may be compared with ἤια (as Benfey does) just as well as yava (xiii 3) can. In the P. W. the word is referred to a rare root sas, 'to slumber,' also 'to be inactive,' 'rot,' which would be a somewhat fanciful etymon.

toya, hence toyádhára, 'a reservoir,' Çak. i 14.

53. **vyapaniya**, from vi + apa + √ni, 'having dispelled.' **tandrám**, xv 15. **çánta-jvará**, 'her sorrow soothed,' xii 98 note. **sattva**, xvi 30 note.

çitáṃçuná, 'like the night when the moon (xiii 4) is up.'

It will be observed that the metre changes in this last line. Instead of the ordinary Çloka or Anuṣṭubh, we have a variety of the Triṣṭubh, in which the half line consists of eleven syllables instead of eight. The scansion is as follows:

– – ⏑ – – | ⏑ ⏑ – ⏑ – – || – – ⏑ – – | ⏑ ⏑ – ⏑ – – ||
⏑ – ⏑ – – | ⏑ ⏑ – ⏑ – – || – – ⏑ – – | ⏑ ⏑ – ⏑ – ⏑ ||

When the first syllable is long, the line is called Indra-vajrā: when short, Upendra-vajrā. The effect is very nearly that of four Sapphic lines: the difference being that the second syllable is long and the third short: so that the general effect down to the caesura is iambic instead of being trochaic.

For the ordinary anuṣṭubh metre, see M. W. Gr. § 935. The type may be given here:

⏓ ⏓ ⏓ ⏓ ⏑ – – ⏓ || ⏓ ⏓ ⏓ ⏓ ⏑ – ⏑ ⏓ ||

or (more rarely)

⏓ ⏓ ⏓ ⏓ ⏑ ⏑ ⏑ ⏓ || ⏓ ⏓ ⏓ ⏓ ⏑ – ⏑ ⏓ ||

1. **kále**, 'at the proper time' = ἐν καιρῷ; absolute, as at ii 18, çastreṇa nidhanaṃ kále ye gacchanty aparáṅ-mukháḥ.

2. **prayataḥ**, 'humble,' p. p. of pra + √yam, a compound which generally means 'to give,' e.g. Hit. 1224, from the primary idea of 'holding forth,' comp. Latin promo, with which prayam is probably identical, though Bopp took it for Lat. premo: but the short vowel is against this: prayata therefore = promptus, but with a different abstract sense: it has often the same meaning as niyata and saṃyata i.e. 'self-restrained,' e.g. Manu ii 222.

çvaçuram, xii 48 note. **abhivádayámása**, xii 68 note.

vavande, 'saluted,' perf. of √vand (1st cl.) which is apparently only √vad nasalised: but as in iungo, fingo, &c., the nasal has got from the present base into the perfect.

4. **arhaṇám**, 'respect,' from √arh, see iii 7 note.

paricaryám, 'he fitly expressed in return his own service to Bhīma.' Paricaryá (see note on paricárika viii 4) means 'service,' in the same conventional sense as when we say, 'my service to you.'

6. 'They made the city bright with banners, flags, and garlands; the highways, rich with delicate flowers, were watered and adorned.' **patáká**, is probably from √pat, 'to sink.' **dhvaja** (of which the older form was dhvaj) is perhaps from √dhú, xvii 40. **málinam**, see ii 11 note.

siktáḥ, p. p. of √sic, 'to moisten,' orig. √SIK, whence probably ἰκ-μάς, see Curt. no. 246.

áḍhyáh, see v 38 note.

7. **puṣpabhan·gaḥ**. The general sense of this line seems to require for this word the sense generally given 'flower-bending': i.e. at every door of the city-people festoons of flowers were prepared. But √bhañj means 'to break,'—not 'to bend,' and bhan·ga is 'breaking.' Hence Benfey (after the Indian commentator who para-

phrases by 'sammarda') translates 'trampling on flowers,' as though
the flowers were strewn in the street. This must be taken, though
it hardly fits in with the rest of the line.

prakalpıtaḥ, from pra + causal of √klıp, xxiii 11.

àyatanànı, 'abodes,' à + √yat = to rest upon, Megh. 16 : so
'resting place' is the first idea.

8.   jahṛıṣe, perf. of √hṛıṣ, i 24.
9.   ànàyya, 'causing to be brought' (μεταπεμψάμενος), see viii 5
note.

kṣamayàmàsa, 'asked his pardon,' causal of √kṣam, 'to be
content,' or 'endure,' iii 8, and inf. 12 kṣantum.

sa ca, 'and he (Rıtuparṇa) craved pardon of Nala with reasons
commensurate with good sense,' i.e. with sensible reasons or excuses.

10.   dıṣṭyà, see xiii 72. 'Happily is thy majesty met with thy own
queen.' dàraıḥ, see xiv 23.
11.   aparàdham, 'offence'; compare the p. p. aparàddham, xxiv 12.
12.   'If either intentionally or even without intention any things
whatsoever that should not be done were done by me, deign to
excuse these.' buddhı-pùrvàṇı = 'with knowledge before,' 'pre-
meditated,' see notes on i 14 and xi 34. abuddhyà is instr. of
abuddhı, 'that which is not knowledge,' 'lack of understanding.'
13.   kṛıte 'pı, 'even though offence had been given, there were no
wrath on my part, for I must excuse thee.'
14.   sambandhi, 'relation,' xvi 18 note.

ata ùrdhvam, 'henceforward,' comp. ix 23, ataḥ param: ùrdhvà
is firstly 'high,' and is perhaps the same as ὀρθός, which shews signs
of an initial F : and the Sanskrit ù may be due to original va, as in
√ùh = VAH: see note on ùhını, i 4. But in that case, 'arduus' and
the Celtic 'ard,' which Bopp connects with this word, must be
distinct.

prıtım àhartum : it would seem that we might render this
either 'to give me (thy) friendship,' or 'to take friendship from
me': but probably the former is right, for à + √hrı when meaning 'to
take,' generally implies violence, as in àhṛıtya, xxvi 7 : though
àhartum (xx 5) means only to 'take up,' or 'get back.' The sense 'to
give' is certainly found, e.g. at Manu ii 245, where a student is to
make an offering according to his means to his Guru (çaktyà gurvar-
tham àharet): from this and from the use of àhartṛı, 'an offerer of
sacrifices' (xii 45), we can see how the two contrary meanings arose
from the primary notion of 'carrying up,' either to a place to make

15

an offering (and so simply 'to give'), or picking a thing up, and carrying it off for oneself.

15. **suvihitaiḥ**, see xiv 16 note. **uṣitas**, ix 10.

16. 'And this knowledge of horses that is in me, belongs to thee': **tiṣṭhati** here and xx 29 (like -stha at the end of a compound, ii 1 note) has lost its primary sense and is simply *est*. Quite literally the words would mean 'stands in me as thine.'

upákartum, 'to deliver over to thee,' upa + á + √kṛi: upa + √kṛi, 'to minister to' (e.g. Hit. 1047), is parallel. This exchange of horse-knowledge and dice-knowledge took place apparently at xx 30: in fact it is not until Nala has got perfect skill in dice that Kali leaves him. We have here therefore either a slip of memory, or this giving is regarded as the confirmation of a less regular proceeding. Perhaps it does not much increase the difficulty of understanding what is in itself unintelligible.

17. **vidhi-dṛiṣṭena**, 'approved by rule,' dṛiṣṭa having got the secondary sense of 'seen and approved,' like 'visé'—parallel to our 'audited.'

karmaṇá, 'action,' 'ceremonial,'—here practically 'etiquette.'

18. **upádáya**, xiii 74.

1. **àmantrya,** 'having taken leave of,' see vi 5 note.

alpa-parıvàro, 'with small attendance,' or 'surrounding' (to give the root-sense more nearly): inf. 21 sa-parıvàro.

2. **dantıbhıḥ,** 'with elephants full sixteen'; for 'the tusked-beast,' comp. kàrın, xiii 9, and hastın, ii 11: parı in parıṣodaçaıḥ has the same force as in parı-vatsara, xxiv 37. Note the irregular plural instead of ṣo-daçabhıḥ, as though the base were daça, not daçan.

pañcàçadbhır, 50, here declined in the plural, from pañcàçat, which is properly indeclinable.

padàtıbhıḥ, xiii 13 note.

3. **kampayann,** 'making earth tremble,' causal of √kamp, 'to tremble': so vı + √kamp, Bh. G. ii 31, na vıkampıtum arhası: anu + kamp = to pity, Çak. p. 112 (ed. M. Williams): i.e. to be shaken in mind in following up a thing. It is very tempting to identify the word with κάμπ-τω: but there is no satisfactory connection between the ideas 'bending' and 'shaking': though κάμπη, 'a caterpillar,' and kapanà, 'a worm,' which must be connected (as by Curt. no. 31 *b*), perhaps point to a primary sense of 'wriggling,' which might unite the two.

susaṃrabdhas, 'in great wrath,' xiii 14 note.

tarasà, 'speedily': taras must come from √tṛi, see ii 30: it can have nothing to do with √tvar, v 2.

4. **vıttam,** see ii 4, 'much wealth has been won by me.' **arjıtam,** p. p. of √arj, 'to earn' (comp. Hit. 495, and arjana, 761), which is identified by Curtius (no. 153) with ὀρέγω and rego, as though the primary sense had been to 'stretch out to,' and so 'acquire,' like German erlangen. This does not seem to me certain: erlangen would not have got its meaning without the prefix, and there is no such prefix in the Sanskrit verb.

5. **vıdyate,** ii 4 note.

sannyásas, 'stake,' from sam + ni + √as 'to throw': see xxiv 45, note on vinyasya.

6. **niçcitá**, 'my mind is made up,' from nis + √ci, ii 2 note.

paṇena, &c., 'let us play a single game, so please you, for our lives.' Note the 'cognate instrumental' with paṇávahe. The nearest parallels in this poem are at v 44, xii 14, xxvi 37, where açvamedhena, or some such word, is used with the verb yaj, 'to sacrifice.' Compare also the instrumental with verbs of going, note on ix 14.

bhadram, see note on iii 25.

práṇayos, genitive of the stake—that about which, or in connection with which, the game goes on: see note on hiranyasya dyútam, vii 9.

7. 'After a victory, and taking away (xxv 14) another's property, whether it be kingdom or whether it be money, a counter-game must be allowed; this is called an imperative duty.'

For pratipáṇaḥ, see ix 2 note. Observe yadi vá used without a verb: it is the same with sive in Latin.

8. 'And if thou wishest (v 36) not for this game, let the battle-game go on; let either thou or I have satisfaction by the duel.' **dvairathena** is formed by vriddhi from dvi-ratha, 'two-chariot,' and is properly an adj. requiring yuddha. **çántis** is from √çam, v 22, it means 'tranquillity,' 'ease of mind,' and answers very closely to our term, given in my translation.

9. 'This hereditary kingdom is to be sought anyhow, by any device whatsoever: this is the rule of the aged.' **vaṃçabhojyam** is from vaṃça 'a stock,' see xii 79, and bhojya fut. part. of √bhuj 'to eat,' so 'to enjoy,' see note on bhoga, ii 4. **arthitavyam**, from arthaya denominative of artha, iii 7. **yathátathá**, not like yathátatham, 'fitly,' i.e. 'in that way in which he ought,' but rather 'in that way in which he can,' 'in which way (of all possible ways), in that way.' **yena kena**, iv 2 note.

vṛiddhánám, see note on abhivardhate, viii 14.

10. 'Determine at once, Puṣkara, on one or other of these two things': compare çoke manaḥ kṛi, xiv 23: 'on dice-playing for (lit. with) a stake, or let the bow be bent for battle.' **akṣavatyáṃ** (which is properly an adj. from akṣa-vat) is in apposition with ekatare in the previous line. **kaitava** (which is formed from kitava, xvii 37) is 'a stake.'

námyatám, imperative passive of námaya the causal of √nam, iv 1 note.

11. **dhruvam**, 'thinking his own victory sure': see vi 11 note.

12. **dıṣṭyâ**, xiii 72. Here it seems to mean 'I am delighted to hear that you have gotten wealth.'

pratıpâṇâya, dative of purpose, xii 132 note.

duṣkaram, &c., 'the difficult business of Damayantī has come to an end': kṣaya in this sense must come from √kṣı, 'to destroy,' ii 18, not √kṣı, to build, whence kṣıtı. Note how kṣayaṃ gata is equivalent to a passive, comp. ii 7 note. In the P. W. duṣkaraṃ karma is translated 'die schwere Zeit der Leiden.' It seems to me to suit the passage better to make Puṣkara rejoice at having in anticipation already got Damayantī.

13. **dhṛıyase**, passive of √dhṛı, 'to hold,' meaning 'thou livest,' 'art held in life,' comp. Manu iii 220, dhṛıyamâṇe pıtarı, 'while a father is alive.'

sadâro, 'with thy wife,' xiv 23.

14. **vyaktam** (xvii 8), 'shall wait on me manifestly.' **upasthâsyatı**, viii 25.

nıtyaço, vi 9, note on xiii 56. **pratikṣe**, 'look out for thee.'

15. 'I take no pleasure by reason of play with folk that are not friends': note the sociative instrumental, following upon a noun: comp. mıtreṇa saṃlâpaḥ, Hit. 248.

16. **kṛıtakṛıtyo**, 'one who has done what was to be done,' i.e. successful, contented. Hence the derivative at Manu iv 17, sâ hy asya kṛıtakṛıtyatâ, 'this is his happiness.' Compare also kṛıtârtha, xvi 10.

abaddha, 'foolish,' lit. 'unbound,' 'unrestrained,' from a (*neg.*) + baddha, p. p. of √bandh, xiii 31.

pralâpınaḥ, 'babbling,' 'chattering,' from √lap, vii 16.

17. **ıyeṣa**, perf. of √ıṣ, i 1. M. W. Gr. § 370, M. M. App. no. 18: the reduplicated *ı* becomes *ıy* before *e*.

çıras, see note on çṛın-ga xii 37.

khaḍgena, see x 18. **kupıto**, see xix 15 note on kopa.

'Smiling, with eyes copper-coloured with wrath.' **smayan**, from √smı, ii 29. **tâmra**, see note on vıtımıra xvi 11. **roṣa**, xi 35 note.

18. **vyâhârase**, 'talk,' here with the implication of 'idly,' but not generally, see i 20 note.

19. 'Together with all the collections of his jewels and treasures, and with his very life, was he won in play.' **koça**, see x 18 note. **nıcaya** is from nı + √cı, ii 2: the cases here are of course sociative, see vi 2 note.

20. 'Mine is all this kingdom undisturbed, its foes destroyed.' **vyagra** is 'disquieted,' also 'actively engaged,' probably from agra xvi 3, though the history of the word is not quite clear.

kaṇṭaka is a 'thorn,' and so metaphorically an enemy: it cannot come from the root of *κεντέω*, as Bopp suggested, because of the cerebral *ṇṭ*: but it may be from KART, the original form of √kṛt (x 16) nasalised.

21. **apasada**, 'degraded,' from apa + √sad: often used irregularly at the end of a K. D. compound, instead of the beginning, perhaps on the same principle as nara-çārdūla &c., to denote the utterly degraded state.

vikṣitum, simply 'to behold,' from vi + ikṣ (i 20): for the infinitive with çakya see note on vii 10.

tasyās seems to go with **dāsatvam**: so far from her being thy servant, 'thou thyself with all thy following art come into slavery *to her*.' **dāsa**, comp. dāsi i 11, like δοῦλος (which is supposed to be from δοσυλο-ς, but this is doubtful, see Curt. no. 264 note), must have meant originally a foeman captured in war; for its older Vedic sense is a foeman (human or spiritual); comp. dasyu which is connected by M. Müller with δήιος.

23. 'I will not put upon thee in any wise the fault committed by another': i.e. Kali is really to blame, Puṣkara being only Kali's instrument.

avasṛjāmi, 'I remit to thee thy life,' v 27 note.

24. 'Moreover I grant thy own inheritance in all its fulness,' i.e. undiminished: or we might take **saṃbhāra** in the sense of 'wealth,' 'together with all thy wealth': it does not make much difference. The word is literally 'massing together' and so 'completeness' and then 'wealth'—something like 'opes.'

aṃço, 'inheritance' (to be carefully distinguished from aṃsa, ὦμος a shoulder), is from √aç, 'to get' (cl. 5), iv 9. See Grassmann's article on the root: he thinks that the older form was aṃç, as shown by this aṃça and the old perf. ānaṃça, which corresponds most strikingly with ἤνεγκα: διηνεκής, ποδηνεκής, &c. also obtain a satisfactory explanation from this reduplicated root. Curtius discusses the forms (G. E. no. 424) under √νεκ (whence naçāmi—with same sense—nanciscor &c.): whether there were at first two distinct roots, 'ank' and 'nank,' as Curtius thinks, or whether NAK and ANK were merely phonetic varieties, possible where a nasal is concerned, and so AK (aç) was a weakened form of the latter, seems to me uncertain.

vitarámi, from vi + √tṛi, ii 30: lit. 'I cross away'—from which the regular sense 'to grant' is not clearly deducible.

mama pritis tvayi, 'my affection for (lit. 'in') thee (see v 22 note), and further, my friendship shall not at any time depart from thee.' **tvatto**, the ablative used here with pra + √há, to fail or be lacking: √há generally is transitive, and has an accusative: the participle has an ablative xix 33, pramáṇát parihinas. Boetlingk and Roth suggest prahásyate.

25. **çaradaḥ**, 'live thou a hundred years': for çaradaḥ see vii 3 note on varṣa; and xiii 44.

26. **preṣayámása**, see iii 7 note: with the double acc. bhrátaram and √svapuram.

28. **akṣayyá**, 'imperishable,' from a and kṣayya from √kṣi, see note on akṣayas ii 18: the form ksayya is rare.

varṣáyutam, 'ten thousand years.' **ayuta** seems to have been at first 'unlimited,' from a + yuta, p. p. of √yu—but afterwards confined to this special number.

adhiṣṭhánam, used both of 'government' and the 'city' which a person governs: our 'province' has a similar duplicity of meaning, though the history of the word is quite different. Either sense will do here.

30. **vinitaiḥ**, xii 68 note on vinaya.

paricárakaiḥ, viii 4 note.

31. **anámayam**, ii 15 note.

32. **paura-jánapadáç**, 'the towns-people and the country-folk': formed from pura and janapada, which occur next line: for janapada see xii 132.

samprahṛiṣṭa-tanúruháḥ, 'with hair erect' (from joy), comp. note on hṛista i 24: **tanúruh** is the body-grower, from tanú, see xii 106 note, and ruha from √ruh viii 19.

sámátya-pramukháḥ, 'with the counsellors first,' i.e. at their head: unless the meaning be 'with the chief counsellors'; but in this case the natural order of the compound is inverted. For amátya see viii 5.

33. 'Happy are we to-day both in the city and in the fields, come to pay homage again to thee, like the Gods to Indra.' **sma**, intensive, but not with the verb. **nirvṛita** means 'tranquil,' 'at rest,' see note on nirvṛiti xxii 3. **upásitum**, from √as, comp. paryupásat i 11.

Çata-kratu, 'he of the hundred sacrifices,' is a name of Indra. It has been already mentioned, ii 14 note, that the Gods themselves perform sacrifices and undergo austerities, with the view of attaining unlimited power and the highest spiritual knowledge.

34. **praçânte**, v 22.

mahotsave, 'the great festival': utsava is from ud + √su, but the connection is not clear.

35. **amey'-âtmâ**, 'of mighty (lit. unmeasurable) soul': ameya is from a + meya, fut. part. of √mâ.

36. **Nandane**, the garden of Indra in Svarga.

37. **prakâçatâm**, 'having gained renown': it is from prakâça, 'clear,' 'bright,' 'open,' from √kâç, see note on san-kâça xvii 6.

Jambu-dvipe, "one of the seven islands or continents of which the world is made up. The great mountain Meru stands in its centre, and Bhārata-varṣa or India is its best part," Dowson. Observe the usual exaggeration of tone. Nala's kingdom need hardly have been larger than India.

râjasu, 'among the kings,' comp. i 13: it is the least common use of the locative in this poem.

ije, perf. of √yaj, 'he sacrificed.' We may picture to ourselves some Brāhman editor giving the final touch to all Nala's glory, in the âpta-dakṣiṇaiḥ (v 44) of this (unnecessary) line.

INDEX I.

INDEX II.

kârya ii 7
√kâç xvii 5
kâṣṭha xiii 28
kitava xvii 37
kirti xx 36
√kup xix 15
kumâra iii 13
kula xii 26
kuçala viii 4, xii 70
√kṛi i 6
√kṛi with alam i 11
√kṛit x 16
kṛite ix 19
kṛityâ xiii 29
kṛitsna ii 16
kṛipâ xii 34
kṛiça ii 2
kṛiṣ vii 14
kṛiṣṇavartman xiv 10
√kṝ iv 18
√kḷip ii 28
ketu xii 38
kovida i 1
koṣa x 18
√kra v 44
kratu v 44
√krand xi 20
√kram ix 6
√krudh xviii 9
√kruç xi 2
√klam ix 28
√kliç xiii 50
kṣaṇa ii 3
√kṣam iii 8
√kṣal xi 29
√kṣi (build) ii 20
√kṣi (destroy) ii 18
√kṣip iii 13
kṣipra xii 92
kṣudra xi 35
√kṣudh ix 11
kṣema xii 121

kh

kha xii 53
khaga i 24
khaḍga x 18
√khâd xii 35
√khyâ init.

g

gaṇa ii 6, x 29
√gad xiv 9
Gandharva i 29
√gam i 6
— (with adhi) xvii 49
gambhira xii 57
√gar (eat) xi 21
garbha i 19, xvi 16
gâtra v 9
√gâh vi 13
√gup xii 47
guru xx 28
√guh v 7
geha xvii 16
√gai xv 15
√gras iv 9
√grah i 19
graha xiii 24
grâma iv 10
√glai xi 25

gh

√ghad ii 11
√ghuṣ ii 11
ghoṣa xvii 49

c

√cakṣ viii 5
√cam xxi 11, vii 3
√car xviii 9
carita vi 8
√cal v 9
câru iii 14
√ci (arrange) ii 2, v 15

√sûd ii 23
Sûrya xviii 26
√sṛ xi 26
√sṛj v 27
√sṛp i 25
√sev x 23
√so xxiv 20
soma xii 48
√stambh ii 30
√stṛ xii 17
√stim xiii 6
sthavira iv 20
√sthâ (with â) xviii 23
sthâvara xiv 7
snigdha xii 57
snuṣa xii 43
√spṛç vii 3
√sphây xxiv 37
sma i 12
√smi ii 29
√smṛ xi 24
√svañj xvii 12
svana xii 57
√svap x 6
svayam i 15, viii 3
svayamvara ii 8
√svar xviii 26
svarga ii 13
√svastha ii 1
svid xix 29
svaira xxi 13

h

ha viii 8
√han i 20, ii 18
hanu xii 31
harṣa i 24, xix 9
√has iii 14
hasta ii 11
hastin ii 11
√hâ ix 14
hi i 29, ix 6
hita i 6
hina v 24
√hṛ i 20
— with â xi 29
hṛcchaya i 17
hṛd i 17
√hṛṣ i 24
√hu iv 9
hotra xii 96
hrasva xviii 6
√hri xiii 30
√hve v 1

CAMBRIDGE: PRINTED BY C. J. CLAY, M.A. AT THE UNIVERSITY PRESS.

UNIVERSITY PRESS, CAMBRIDGE,
December, 1880.

CATALOGUE OF

WORKS

PUBLISHED FOR THE SYNDICS

OF THE

Cambridge University Press.

London:
CAMBRIDGE WAREHOUSE, 17 PATERNOSTER ROW.

Cambridge: DEIGHTON, BELL, AND CO.
Leipzig: F. A. BROCKHAUS.

1000
11/12/80

PUBLICATIONS OF

The Cambridge University Press.

THE HOLY SCRIPTURES, &c.

THE CAMBRIDGE PARAGRAPH BIBLE

of the Authorized English Version, with the Text Revised by a Collation of its Early and other Principal Editions, the Use of the Italic Type made uniform, the Marginal References remodelled, and a Critical Introduction prefixed, by the Rev. F. H. SCRIVENER, M.A., LL.D., Editor of the Greek Testament, Codex Augiensis, &c., and one of the Revisers of the Authorized Version. Crown Quarto, cloth, gilt, 21*s.*

From the *Times.*

"Students of the Bible should be particularly grateful to (the Cambridge University Press) for having produced, with the able assistance of Dr Scrivener, a complete critical edition of the Authorized Version of the English Bible, an edition such as, to use the words of the Editor, 'would have been executed long ago had this version been nothing more than the greatest and best known of English classics.' Falling at a time when the formal revision of this version has been undertaken by a distinguished company of scholars and divines, the publication of this edition must be considered most opportune."

From the *Athenæum.*

"Apart from its religious importance, the English Bible has the glory, which but few sister versions indeed can claim, of being the chief classic of the language, of having, in conjunction with Shakspeare, and in an immeasurable degree more than he, fixed the language beyond any possibility of important change. Thus the recent contributions to the literature of the subject, by such workers as Mr Francis Fry and Canon Westcott, appeal to a wide range of sympathies; and to these may now be added Dr Scrivener, well known for his labours in the cause of the Greek Testament criticism, who has brought out, for the Syndics of the Cambridge University Press, an edition of the English Bible, according to the text of 1611, revised by a comparison with later issues on principles stated by him in his Introduction. Here he enters at length into the history of the chief editions of the version, and of such features as the marginal notes, the use of italic type, and the changes of orthography, as well as into the most interesting question as to the original texts from which our translation is produced."

From the *Methodist Recorder.*

"This noble quarto of over 1300 pages is in every respect worthy of editor and publishers alike. The name of the Cambridge University Press is guarantee enough for its perfection in outward form, the name of the editor is equal guarantee for the worth and accuracy of its contents. Without question, it is the best Paragraph Bible ever published, and its reduced price of a guinea brings it within reach of a large number of students. . But the volume is much more than a Paragraph Bible. It is an attempt, and a successful attempt, to give a critical edition of the Authorised English Version, not (let it be marked) a revision, but an exact reproduction of the original Authorised Version, as published in 1611, minus patent mistakes. This is doubly necessary at a time when the version is about to undergo revision. . . To all who at this season seek a suitable volume for presentation to ministers or teachers we earnestly commend this work."

From the *London Quarterly Review.*

"The work is worthy in every respect of the editor's fame, and of the Cambridge University Press. The noble English Version, to which our country and religion owe so much, was probably never presented before in so perfect a form."

THE CAMBRIDGE PARAGRAPH BIBLE.

STUDENT'S EDITION, on *good writing paper,* with one column of print and wide margin to each page for MS. notes. This edition will be found of great use to those who are engaged in the task of Biblical criticism. Two Vols. Crown Quarto, cloth, gilt, 31*s.* 6*d.*

London: Cambridge Warehouse, 17 *Paternoster Row.*

THE LECTIONARY BIBLE, WITH APOCRYPHA,

divided into Sections adapted to the Calendar and Tables of Lessons of 1871. Crown Octavo, cloth, 3*s*. 6*d*.

BREVIARIUM AD USUM INSIGNIS ECCLESIAE SARUM.

Fasciculus II. In quo continentur PSALTERIUM, cum ordinario Officii totius hebdomadae juxta Horas Canonicas, et proprio Completorii, LATINIA, COMMUNE SANCTORUM, ORDINARIUM MISSAE CUM CANONE ET XIII MISSIS, &c. &c. juxta Editionem maximam pro CLAUDIO CHEVALLON ET FRANCISCO REGNAULT A.D. MDXXXI. in Alma Parisiorum Academia impressam: labore ac studio FRANCISCI PROCTER, A.M., ET CHRISTOPHORI WORDSWORTH, A.M. Demy Octavo, cloth. 12*s*.

FASCICULUS I. *In the Press.*

"Not only experts in liturgiology, but all persons interested in the history of the Anglican Book of Common Prayer, will be grateful to the Syndicate of the Cambridge University Press for forwarding the publication of the volume which bears the above title, and which has recently appeared under their auspices. . . When the present work is complete in three volumes, of which we have here the first instalment, it will be accessible, as the Sarum Missal is now, thanks to the labours of Mr G. H. Forbes, to every one interested in the subject-matter with which it is connected."—*Notes and Queries.*

"We have here the first instalment of the celebrated Sarum Breviary, of which no entire edition has hitherto been printed since the year 1557. . . Of the valuable explanatory notes, as well as the learned introduction to this volume, we can only speak in terms of the very highest commendation."—*The Examiner.*

GREEK AND ENGLISH TESTAMENT,

in parallel Columns on the same page. Edited by J. SCHOLEFIELD, M.A. late Regius Professor of Greek in the University. Small Octavo. New Edition, with the Marginal References as arranged and revised by Dr SCRIVENER. Cloth, red edges. 7*s*. 6*d*.

GREEK AND ENGLISH TESTAMENT,

THE STUDENT'S EDITION of the above, on *large writing paper*. 4to. cloth. 12*s*.

GREEK TESTAMENT,

ex editione Stephani tertia, 1550. Small Octavo. 3*s*. 6*d*.

THE GOSPEL ACCORDING TO ST MATTHEW

in Anglo-Saxon and Northumbrian Versions, synoptically arranged: with Collations of the best Manuscripts. By J. M. KEMBLE, M.A. and Archdeacon HARDWICK. Demy Quarto. 10*s*.

THE GOSPEL ACCORDING TO ST MARK

in Anglo-Saxon and Northumbrian Versions synoptically arranged: with Collations exhibiting all the Readings of all the MSS. Edited by the Rev. Professor SKEAT, M.A. late Fellow of Christ's College, and author of a MŒSO-GOTHIC Dictionary. Demy Quarto. 10*s*.

THE GOSPEL ACCORDING TO ST LUKE,

uniform with the preceding, edited by the Rev. Professor SKEAT. Demy Quarto. 10*s*.

THE GOSPEL ACCORDING TO ST JOHN,

uniform with the preceding, by the same Editor. Demy Quarto. 10*s*.

"*The Gospel according to St John, in Anglo-Saxon and Northumbrian Versions:* Edited for the Syndics of the University Press, by the Rev. Walter W. Skeat, M.A., Elrington and Bosworth Professor of Anglo-Saxon in the University of Cambridge, completes an undertaking designed and commenced by that distinguished scholar, J. M. Kemble, some forty years ago. He was not himself permitted to execute his scheme; he died before it was completed for St Matthew. The edition of that Gospel was finished by Mr., subsequently Archdeacon, Hardwick. The remaining Gospels have had the good fortune to be edited by Professor Skeat, whose competency and zeal have left nothing undone to prove himself equal to his reputation, and to produce a work of the highest value to the student of Anglo-Saxon. The design was indeed worthy of its author. It is difficult to exaggerate the value of such a set of parallel texts. . . . Of the particular volume now before us, we can only say it is worthy of its two predecessors. We repeat that the service rendered to the study of Anglo-Saxon by this Synoptic collection cannot easily be overstated."—*Contemporary Review.*

THE POINTED PRAYER BOOK,

being the Book of Common Prayer with the Psalter or Psalms of David, pointed as they are to be sung or said in Churches. Royal 24mo. Cloth, 1*s*. 6*d*.

The same in square 32mo, cloth, 6*d*.

"The 'Pointed Prayer Book' deserves mention for the new and ingenious system on which the pointing has been marked, and still more for the terseness and clearness of the directions given for using it."—*Times.*

THE CAMBRIDGE PSALTER,

for the use of Choirs and Organists. Specially adapted for Congregations in which the "Cambridge Pointed Prayer Book" is used. Demy 8vo. cloth extra, 3*s*. 6*d*. Cloth limp, cut flush, 2*s*. 6*d*.

THE PARAGRAPH PSALTER,

arranged for the use of Choirs by BROOKE FOSS WESTCOTT, D.D., Canon of Peterborough, and Regius Professor of Divinity in the University of Cambridge. Fcap. 4to., 5*s*.

THE MISSING FRAGMENT OF THE LATIN TRANSLATION OF THE FOURTH BOOK OF EZRA,

discovered, and edited with an Introduction and Notes, and a facsimile of the MS., by ROBERT L. BENSLY, M.A., Sub-Librarian of the University Library, and Reader in Hebrew, Gonville and Caius College, Cambridge. Demy Quarto. Cloth, 10*s*.

"Edited with true scholarly completeness."—*Westminster Review.*

"Wer sich je mit dem 4 Buche Esra eingehender beschäftigt hat, wird durch die obige, in jeder Beziehung musterhafte Publication in freudiges Erstaunen versetzt werden."—*Theologische Literaturzeitung.*

"It has been said of this book that it has added a new chapter to the Bible, and, startling as the statement may at first sight appear, it is no exaggeration of the actual fact, if by the Bible we understand that of the larger size which contains the Apocrypha, and if the Second Book of Esdras can be fairly called a part of the Apocrypha."—*Saturday Review.*

THEOLOGY—(ANCIENT).

SAYINGS OF THE JEWISH FATHERS,

comprising Pirqe Aboth and Pereq R. Meir in Hebrew and English, with Critical and Illustrative Notes. By CHARLES TAYLOR, M.A. Fellow and Divinity Lecturer of St John's College, Cambridge, and Honorary Fellow of King's College, London. Demy 8vo. cloth. 10*s*.

"It is peculiarly incumbent on those who look to Jerome or Origen for their theology or exegesis to learn something of their Jewish predecessors. The New Testament abounds with sayings which remarkably coincide with, or closely resemble, those of the Jewish Fathers; and these latter probably would furnish more satisfactory and frequent illustrations of its text than the Old Testament." —*Saturday Review*.

"The 'Masseketh Aboth' stands at the head of Hebrew non-canonical writings. It is of ancient date, claiming to contain the dicta of teachers who flourished from B.C. 200 to the same year of our era. The precise time of its compilation in its present form is, of course, in doubt. Mr Taylor's explanatory and illustrative commentary is very full and satisfactory."—*Spectator*.

"If we mistake not, this is the first precise translation into the English language accompanied by scholarly notes, of any portion of the Talmud. In other words, it is the first instance of that most valuable and neglected portion of Jewish literature being treated in the same way as a Greek classic in an ordinary critical edition... The Talmudic books, which have been so strangely neglected, we foresee will be the most important aids of the future for the proper understanding of the Bible... The *Sayings of the Jewish Fathers* may claim to be scholarly, and, moreover, of a scholarship unusually thorough and finished."—*Dublin University Magazine*.

"A careful and thorough edition which does credit to English scholarship, of a short treatise from the Mishna, containing a series of sentences or maxims ascribed mostly to Jewish teachers immediately preceding, or immediately following the Christian era..." —*Contemporary Review*.

THEODORE OF MOPSUESTIA'S COMMENTARY ON THE MINOR EPISTLES OF S. PAUL.

The Latin Version with the Greek Fragments, edited from the MSS. with Notes and an Introduction, by H. B. SWETE, D.D., Rector of Ashdon, Essex, and late Fellow of Gonville and Caius College, Cambridge. In Two Volumes. Vol. I., containing the Introduction, with Facsimiles of the MSS., and the Commentary upon Galatians—Colossians. Demy Octavo. 12*s*.

"One result of this disappearance of the works of Diodorus, which his Arian opponents did their utmost to destroy, is to render more conspicuous the figure of Theodore. From the point of view of scientific exegesis there is no figure in all antiquity more interesting."—*The Expositor*.

"In dem oben verzeichneten Buche liegt uns die erste Hälfte einer vollständigen, ebenso sorgfältig gearbeiteten wie schön ausgestatteten Ausgabe des Commentars mit ausführlichen Prolegomena und reichhaltigen kritischen und erläuternden Anmerkungen vor."—*Literarisches Centralblatt*.

"Eine sehr sorgfältige Arbeit. Nichts ist dem Verfasser entgangen, auch nicht die in deutscher Sprache geschriebenen Specialschriften über die Antiochener. Druck und Ausstattung sind, wie man das bei der englischen Literatur gewöhnt ist, elegant und musterhaft."—*Literarische Rundschau*.

"It is the result of thorough, careful, and patient investigation of all the points bearing on the subject, and the results are presented with admirable good sense and modesty. Mr Swete has prepared himself for his task by a serious study of the literature and history which are connected with it; and he has produced a volume of high value to the student, not merely of the theology of the fourth and fifth centuries, but of the effect of this theology on the later developments of doctrine and methods of interpretation, in the ages immediately following, and in the middle ages."—*Guardian*.

"Auf Grund dieser Quellen ist der Text bei Swete mit musterhafter Akribie hergestellt. Aber auch sonst hat der Herausgeber mit unermüdlichem Fleisse und eingehendster Sachkenntniss sein Werk mit allen denjenigen Zugaben ausgerüstet, welche bei einer solchen Text-Ausgabe nur irgend erwartet werden können. . . . Von den drei Haupthandschriften . . . sind vortreffliche photographische Facsimile's beigegeben, wie überhaupt das ganze Werk von der *University Press* zu Cambridge mit bekannter Eleganz ausgestattet ist."—*Theologische Literaturzeitung*.

VOLUME II. *In the Press.*

SANCTI IRENÆI EPISCOPI LUGDUNENSIS

libros quinque adversus Hæreses, versione Latina cum Codicibus Claromontano ac Arundeliano denuo collata, præmissa de placitis Gnosticorum prolusione, fragmenta necnon Græce, Syriace, Armeniace, commentatione perpetua et indicibus variis edidit W. WIGAN HARVEY, S.T.B. Collegii Regalis olim Socius. 2 Vols. Demy Octavo. 18*s.*

M. MINUCII FELICIS OCTAVIUS.

The text newly revised from the original MS., with an English Commentary, Analysis, Introduction, and Copious Indices. Edited by H. A. HOLDEN, LL.D. Head Master of Ipswich School, late Fellow of Trinity College, Cambridge. Crown Octavo. 7*s.* 6*d.*

THEOPHILI EPISCOPI ANTIOCHENSIS LIBRI TRES AD AUTOLYCUM

edidit, Prolegomenis Versione Notulis Indicibus instruxit GULIELMUS GILSON HUMPHRY, S.T.B. Collegii Sanctiss. Trin. apud Cantabrigienses quondam Socius. Post Octavo. 5*s.*

THEOPHYLACTI IN EVANGELIUM S. MATTHÆI COMMENTARIUS,

edited by W. G. HUMPHRY, B.D. Prebendary of St Paul's, late Fellow of Trinity College. Demy Octavo. 7*s.* 6*d.*

TERTULLIANUS DE CORONA MILITIS, DE SPECTACULIS, DE IDOLOLATRIA,

with Analysis and English Notes, by GEORGE CURREY, D.D. Preacher at the Charter House, late Fellow and Tutor of St John's College. Crown Octavo. 5*s.*

THEOLOGY—(ENGLISH).

WORKS OF ISAAC BARROW,

compared with the Original MSS., enlarged with Materials hitherto unpublished. A new Edition, by A. NAPIER, M.A. of Trinity College, Vicar of Holkham, Norfolk. 9 Vols. Demy Octavo. £3. 3*s.*

TREATISE OF THE POPE'S SUPREMACY,

and a Discourse concerning the Unity of the Church, by ISAAC BARROW. Demy Octavo. 7*s.* 6*d.*

PEARSON'S EXPOSITION OF THE CREED,

edited by TEMPLE CHEVALLIER, B.D. late Fellow and Tutor of St Catharine's College, Cambridge. New Edition. [*In the Press.*

AN ANALYSIS OF THE EXPOSITION OF THE CREED

written by the Right Rev. JOHN PEARSON, D.D. late Lord Bishop of Chester, by W. H. MILL, D.D. late Regius Professor of Hebrew in the University of Cambridge. Demy Octavo, cloth. 5*s.*

WHEATLY ON THE COMMON PRAYER,

edited by G. E. CORRIE, D.D. Master of Jesus College, Examining Chaplain to the late Lord Bishop of Ely. Demy Octavo. 7*s*. 6*d*.

CÆSAR MORGAN'S INVESTIGATION OF THE TRINITY OF PLATO,

and of Philo Judæus, and of the effects which an attachment to their writings had upon the principles and reasonings of the Fathers of the Christian Church. Revised by H. A. HOLDEN, LL.D. Head Master of Ipswich School, late Fellow of Trinity College, Cambridge. Crown Octavo. 4*s*.

TWO FORMS OF PRAYER OF THE TIME OF QUEEN ELIZABETH.

Now First Reprinted. Demy Octavo. 6*d*.

"From 'Collections and Notes' 1867—1876, by W. Carew Hazlitt (p. 340), we learn that—'A very remarkable volume, in the original vellum cover, and containing 25 Forms of Prayer of the reign of Elizabeth, each with the autograph of Humphrey Dyson, has lately fallen into the hands of my friend Mr H. Pyne. It is mentioned specially in the Preface to the Parker Society's volume of Occasional Forms of Prayer, but it had been lost sight of for 200 years.' By the kindness of the present possessor of this valuable volume, containing in all 25 distinct publications, I am enabled to reprint in the following pages the two Forms of Prayer supposed to have been lost."—*Extract from the* PREFACE.

SELECT DISCOURSES,

by JOHN SMITH, late Fellow of Queens' College, Cambridge. Edited by H. G. WILLIAMS, B.D. late Professor of Arabic. Royal Octavo. 7*s*. 6*d*.

"The 'Select Discourses' of John Smith, collected and published from his papers after his death, are, in my opinion, much the most considerable work left to us by this Cambridge School [the Cambridge Platonists]. They have a right to a place in English literary history."—Mr MATTHEW ARNOLD, in the *Contemporary Review*.

"Of all the products of the Cambridge School, the 'Select Discourses' are perhaps the highest, as they are the most accessible and the most widely appreciated...and indeed no spiritually thoughtful mind can read them unmoved. They carry us so directly into an atmosphere of divine philosophy, luminous with the richest lights of meditative genius... He was one of those rare thinkers in whom largeness of view, and depth, and wealth of poetic and speculative insight, only served to evoke more fully the religious spirit, and while he drew the mould of his thought from Plotinus, he vivified the substance of it from St Paul."—Principal TULLOCH, *Rational Theology in England in the 17th Century*.

"We may instance Mr Henry Griffin Williams's revised edition of Mr John Smith's 'Select Discourses,' which have won Mr Matthew Arnold's admiration, as an example of worthy work for an University Press to undertake."—*Times*.

THE HOMILIES,

with Various Readings, and the Quotations from the Fathers given at length in the Original Languages. Edited by G. E. CORRIE, D.D. Master of Jesus College. Demy Octavo. 7*s*. 6*d*.

DE OBLIGATIONE CONSCIENTIÆ PRÆLECTIONES

decem Oxonii in Schola Theologica habitæ a ROBERTO SANDERSON, SS. Theologiæ ibidem Professore Regio. With English Notes, including an abridged Translation, by W. WHEWELL, D.D. late Master of Trinity College. Demy Octavo. 7*s*. 6*d*.

ARCHBISHOP USHER'S ANSWER TO A JESUIT,

with other Tracts on Popery. Edited by J. SCHOLEFIELD, M.A. late Regius Professor of Greek in the University. Demy Octavo. *7s. 6d.*

WILSON'S ILLUSTRATION OF THE METHOD

of explaining the New Testament, by the early opinions of Jews and Christians concerning Christ. Edited by T. TURTON, D.D. late Lord Bishop of Ely. Demy Octavo. *5s.*

LECTURES ON DIVINITY

delivered in the University of Cambridge, by JOHN HEY, D.D. Third Edition, revised by T. TURTON, D.D. late Lord Bishop of Ely. 2 vols. Demy Octavo. *15s.*

ARABIC AND SANSKRIT.

POEMS OF BEHÁ ED DÍN ZOHEIR OF EGYPT.

With a Metrical Translation, Notes and Introduction, by E. H. PALMER, M.A., Barrister-at-Law of the Middle Temple, Lord Almoner's Professor of Arabic and Fellow of St John's College in the University of Cambridge. 3 vols. Crown Quarto.

Vol. I. The ARABIC TEXT. *10s. 6d.*; Cloth extra, *15s.*

Vol. II. ENGLISH TRANSLATION. *10s. 6d.*; Cloth extra, *15s.*

"Professor Palmer's activity in advancing Arabic scholarship has formerly shown itself in the production of his excellent Arabic Grammar, and his Descriptive Catalogue of Arabic MSS. in the Library of Trinity College, Cambridge. He has now produced an admirable text, which illustrates in a remarkable manner the flexibility and graces of the language he loves so well, and of which he seems to be perfect master.... The Syndicate of Cambridge University must not pass without the recognition of their liberality in bringing out, in a worthy form, so important an Arabic text. It is not the first time that Oriental scholarship has thus been wisely subsidised by Cambridge."—*Indian Mail.*

"It is impossible to quote this edition without an expression of admiration for the perfection to which Arabic typography has been brought in England in this magnificent Oriental work, the production of which redounds to the imperishable credit of the University of Cambridge. It may be pronounced one of the most beautiful Oriental books that have ever been printed in Europe: and the learning of the Editor worthily rivals the technical get-up of the creations of the soul of one of the most tasteful poets of Islâm, the study of which will contribute not a little to save honour of the poetry of the Arabs."—MYTHOLOGY AMONG THE HEBREWS (*Engl. Transl.*), p. 194.

For ease and facility, for variety of metre, for imitation, either designed or unconscious, of the style of several of our own poets, these versions deserve high praise. .... We have no hesitation in saying that in both Prof. Palmer has made an addition to Oriental literature for which scholars should be grateful; and that, while his knowledge of Arabic is a sufficient guarantee for his mastery of the original, his English compositions are distinguished by versatility, command of language, rhythmical cadence, and, as we have remarked, by not unskilful imitations of the styles of several of our own favourite poets, living and dead."—*Saturday Review.*

"This sumptuous edition of the poems of Behá-ed-dín Zoheir is a very welcome addition to the small series of Eastern poets accessible to readers who are not Orientalists. ... In all there is that exquisite finish of which Arabic poetry is susceptible in so rare a degree. The form is almost always beautiful, be the thought what it may. But this, of course, can only be fully appreciated by Orientalists. And this brings us to the translation. It is excellently well done. Mr Palmer has tried to imitate the fall of the original in his selection of the English metre for the various pieces, and thus contrives to convey a faint idea of the graceful flow of the Arabic. ..... Altogether the inside of the book is worthy of the beautiful arabesque binding that rejoices the eye of the lover of Arab art."—*Academy.*

NALOPÀKHYÀNAM, OR, THE TALE OF NALA;

containing the Sanskrit Text in Roman Characters, followed by a Vocabulary in which each word is placed under its root, with references to derived words in Cognate Languages, and a sketch of Sanskrit Grammar. By the Rev. THOMAS JARRETT, M.A. Trinity College, Regius Professor of Hebrew, late Professor of Arabic, and formerly Fellow of St Catharine's College, Cambridge. Demy Octavo. 10*s.*

NOTES ON THE TALE OF NALA,

by J. PEILE, M.A. Fellow and Tutor of Christ's College. [*In the Press.*

GREEK AND LATIN CLASSICS, &c. (See also pp. 20—23.)

A SELECTION OF GREEK INSCRIPTIONS,

With Introductions and Annotations by E. S. ROBERTS, M.A. Fellow and Tutor of Caius College. [*Preparing.*

THE AGAMEMNON OF AESCHYLUS.

With a Translation in English Rhythm, and Notes Critical and Explanatory. By BENJAMIN HALL KENNEDY, D.D., Regius Professor of Greek. Crown Octavo, cloth. 6*s.*

"One of the best editions of the masterpiece of Greek tragedy."—*Athenæum.*

"By numberless other like happy and weighty helps to a coherent and consistent text and interpretation, Dr Kennedy has approved himself a guide to Aeschylus of certainly peerless calibre."—*Contemp. Rev.*

"It is needless to multiply proofs of the value of this volume alike to the poetical translator, the critical scholar, and the ethical student. We must be contented to thank Professor Kennedy for his admirable execution of a great undertaking."—*Sat. Rev.*

"Let me say that I think it a most admirable piece of the highest criticism. . . . I like your Preface extremely; it is just to the point."—Professor PALEY.

"Professor Kennedy has conferred a boon on all teachers of the Greek classics, by causing the substance of his lectures at Cambridge on the Agamemnon of Æschylus to be published...This edition of the Agamemnon is one which no classical master should be without."—*Examiner.*

THE THEÆTETUS OF PLATO by the same Author.

[*In the Press.*

ARISTOTLE.—ΠΕΡΙ ΔΙΚΑΙΟΣΥΝΗΣ.

THE FIFTH BOOK OF THE NICOMACHEAN ETHICS OF ARISTOTLE. Edited by HENRY JACKSON, M.A., Fellow of Trinity College, Cambridge. Demy Octavo, cloth. 6*s.*

"It is not too much to say that some of the points he discusses have never had so much light thrown upon them before. . . . Scholars will hope that this is not the only portion of the Aristotelian writings which he is likely to edit."—*Athenæum.*

PRIVATE ORATIONS OF DEMOSTHENES,

with Introductions and English Notes, by F. A. PALEY, M.A. Editor of Aeschylus, etc. and J. E. SANDYS, M.A. Fellow and Tutor of St John's College, and Public Orator in the University of Cambridge.

PART I. Contra Phormionem, Lacritum, Pantaenetum, Boeotum de Nomine, Boeotum de Dote, Dionysodorum. Crown Octavo, cloth. *6s.*

"Mr Paley's scholarship is sound and accurate, his experience of editing wide, and if he is content to devote his learning and abilities to the production of such manuals as these, they will be received with gratitude throughout the higher schools of the country. Mr Sandys is deeply read in the German literature which bears upon his author, and the elucidation of matters of daily life, in the delineation of which Demosthenes is so rich, obtains full justice at his hands. .... We hope this edition may lead the way to a more general study of these speeches in schools than has hitherto been possible.—*Academy.*

PART II. Pro Phormione, Contra Stephanum I. II.; Nicostratum, Cononem, Calliclem. *7s. 6d.*

"To give even a brief sketch of these speeches [*Pro Phormione* and *Contra Stephanum*] would be incompatible with our limits, though we can hardly conceive a task more useful to the classical or professional scholar than to make one for himself. .... It is a great boon to those who set themselves to unravel the thread of arguments pro and con to have the aid of Mr Sandys's excellent running commentary .... and no one can say that he is ever deficient in the needful help which enables us to form a sound estimate of the rights of the case. ...... It is long since we have come upon a work evincing more pains, scholarship, and varied research and illustration than Mr Sandys's contribution to the 'Private Orations of Demosthenes'."—*Sat. Rev.*

"...... the edition reflects credit on Cambridge scholarship, and ought to be extensively used."—*Athenæum.*

PINDAR.

OLYMPIAN AND PYTHIAN ODES. With Notes Explanatory and Critical, Introductions and Introductory Essays. Edited by C. A. M. FENNELL, M.A., late Fellow of Jesus College. Crown Octavo, cloth. *9s.*

"Mr Fennell deserves the thanks of all classical students for his careful and scholarly edition of the Olympian and Pythian odes. He brings to his task the necessary enthusiasm for his author, great industry, a sound judgment, and, in particular, copious and minute learning in comparative philology. To his qualifications in this last respect every page bears witness."—*Athenæum.*

"Considered simply as a contribution to the study and criticism of Pindar, Mr Fennell's edition is a work of great merit. But it has a wider interest, as exemplifying the change which has come over the methods and aims of Cambridge scholarship within the last ten or twelve years. ... The short introductions and arguments to the Odes, which for so discursive an author as Pindar are all but a necessity, are both careful and acute... Altogether, this edition is a welcome and wholesome sign of the vitality and development of Cambridge scholarship, and we are glad to see that it is to be continued."—*Saturday Review.*

"There are many reasons why Mr C. A. M. Fennell's edition of 'Pindar's Olympian and Pythian Odes;' should not go unnoticed, even though our space forbids doing it full justice; as a helpful complement and often corrective of preceding editions, both in its insight into comparative philology, its critical acumen, and its general sobriety of editing. In etymology especially the volume marks a generation later than Donaldson's, though holding in respect his brilliant authority. . . Most helpful, too, is the introductory essay on Pindar's style and dialect, while the chronological sequence of the Odes (pp. xxxi.—xxxii.), and the 'Metrical Schemes,' which immediately precede the text and commentary, leave nothing to be desiderated."—*Contemporary Review.*

THE NEMEAN AND ISTHMIAN ODES. [*Preparing.*

THE BACCHAE OF EURIPIDES.

with Introduction, Critical Notes, and Archæological Illustrations, by J. E. SANDYS, M.A., Fellow and Tutor of St John's College, Cambridge, and Public Orator. Crown Octavo, cloth. 10s. 6d.

"Of the present edition of the *Bacchæ* by Mr Sandys we may safely say that never before has a Greek play, in England at least, had fuller justice done to its criticism, interpretation, and archæological illustration, whether for the young student or the more advanced scholar. The Cambridge Public Orator may be said to have taken the lead in issuing a complete edition of a Greek play, which is destined perhaps to gain redoubled favour now that the study of ancient monuments has been applied to its illustration."—*Saturday Review.*

"The whole of this preliminary matter is of a valuable and most of it of an interesting kind, but of a kind hitherto seldom met with in editions of the classics prepared for the use of students. Still more rare is it to find the author of a class-book making so large a use as Mr Sandys makes of ancient art to illustrate the text of Euripides, and conversely using the text to so large an extent to illustrate ancient art. This is a distinctive characteristic of the work, and one which adds greatly to its value. Thirty-two beautifully executed wood engravings of ancient artistic productions, all of which, as well as others not included in the selection, are briefly but intelligibly described, lend an additional interest to this portion of the book. A careful examination of Mr Sandys' emendations and of the reasons given in support of them must satisfy every scholar that this department of the work has been judiciously and ingeniously managed. The explanatory notes are a mine rich in the results of careful study, varied learning and accurate research."—*The Scotsman.*

"This charming edition of the *Bacchæ* ought certainly to become the favourite edition of a play which, by a pretty wide consensus of critical opinion, is held to be in the front rank of the greatest works of Euripides. ...Mr Sandys has done well by his poet and by his University. He has given a most welcome gift to scholars both at home and abroad. The illustrations are aptly chosen and delicately executed, and the *apparatus criticus*, in the way both of notes and indices is very complete."—*Notes and Queries.*

ARISTOTLE.

THE RHETORIC. With a Commentary by the late E. M. COPE, Fellow of Trinity College, Cambridge, revised and edited by J. E. SANDYS, M.A., Fellow and Tutor of St John's College, Cambridge, and Public Orator. With a biographical Memoir by H. A. J. MUNRO, M.A. Three Volumes, Demy Octavo. £1. 11s. 6d.

"This work is in many ways creditable to the University of Cambridge. The solid and extensive erudition of Mr Cope himself bears none the less speaking evidence to the value of the tradition which he continued, if it is not equally accompanied by those qualities of speculative originality and independent judgment which belong more to the individual writer than to his school. And while it must ever be regretted that a work so laborious should not have received the last touches of its author, the warmest admiration is due to Mr Sandys, for the manly, unselfish, and unflinching spirit in which he has performed his most difficult and delicate task. If an English student wishes to have a full conception of what is contained in the *Rhetoric* of Aristotle, to Mr Cope's edition he must go."—*Academy.*

"Mr Sandys has performed his arduous duties with marked ability and admirable tact. ...Besides the revision of Mr Cope's material already referred to in his own words, Mr Sandys has thrown in many useful notes; none more useful than those that bring the Commentary up to the latest scholarship by reference to important works that have appeared since Mr Cope's illness put a period to his labours. When the original Commentary stops abruptly three chapters before the end of the third book, Mr Sandys carefully supplies the deficiency, following Mr Cope's general plan and the slightest available indications of his intended treatment. In Appendices he has reprinted from classical journals several articles of Mr Cope's; and, what is better, he has given the best of the late Mr Shilleto's 'Adversaria.' In every part of his work—revising, supplementing, and completing—he has done exceedingly well."—*Examiner.*

"A careful examination of the work shows that the high expectations of classical students will not be disappointed. Mr Cope's 'wide and minute acquaintance with all the Aristotelian writings,' to which Mr Sandys justly bears testimony, his thorough knowledge of the important contributions of modern German scholars, his ripe and accurate scholarship, and above all, that sound judgment and never-failing good sense which are the crowning merit of our best English editions of the Classics, all combine to make this one of the most valuable additions to the knowledge of Greek literature which we have had for many years."—*Spectator.*

"Von der Rhetorik ist eine neue Ausgabe mit sehr ausführlichem Commentar erschienen. Derselbe enthält viel schätzbares.... Der Herausgeber verdient für seine mühevolle Arbeit unseren lebhaften Dank."—*Susemihl in Bursian's Jahresbericht.*

PLATO'S PHÆDO,

literally translated, by the late E. M. COPE, Fellow of Trinity College, Cambridge. Demy Octavo. 5*s.*

P. VERGILI MARONIS OPERA

cum Prolegomenis et Commentario Critico pro Syndicis Preli Academici edidit BENJAMIN HALL KENNEDY, S.T.P., Graecae Linguae Professor Regius. Extra Fcap. Octavo, cloth. 5*s.*

M. TULLII CICERONIS DE NATURA DEORUM

Libri Tres, with Introduction and Commentary by JOSEPH B. MAYOR, M.A., Professor of Classical Literature at King's College, London, formerly Fellow and Tutor of St John's College, Cambridge, together with a new collation of several of the English MSS. by J. H. SWAINSON, M.A., formerly Fellow of Trinity Coll., Cambridge. Vol. I. Demy 8vo. 10*s.* 6*d.*

M. T. CICERONIS DE OFFICIIS LIBRI TRES,

with Marginal Analysis, an English Commentary, and copious Indices, by H. A. HOLDEN, LL.D. Head Master of Ipswich School, late Fellow of Trinity College, Cambridge, Classical Examiner to the University of London. **Third Edition.** Revised and considerably enlarged. Crown Octavo. 9*s.*

"Dr Holden truly states that 'Text, Analysis, and Commentary in this third edition have been again subjected to a thorough revision.' It is now certainly the best edition extant. A sufficient apparatus of various readings is placed under the text, and a very careful summary in the margin. The Introduction (after Heine) and notes leave nothing to be desired in point of fulness, accuracy, and neatness; the typographical execution will satisfy the most fastidious eye. A careful index of twenty-four pages makes it easy to use the book as a storehouse of information on points of grammar, history, and philosophy. . . . This edition of the Offices, Mr Reid's Academics, Lælius, and Cato, with the forthcoming editions of the *De Finibus* and the *De Natura Deorum* will do much to maintain tho study of Cicero's philosophy in Roger Ascham's university."—*Notes and Queries.*

MATHEMATICS, PHYSICAL SCIENCE, &c.

MATHEMATICAL AND PHYSICAL PAPERS.

By Sir W. THOMSON, LL.D., D.C.L., F.R.S., Professor of Natural Philosophy, in the University of Glasgow. Collected from different Scientific Periodicals from May 1841, to the present time. [*In the Press.*

THE ELECTRICAL RESEARCHES OF THE HONOURABLE HENRY CAVENDISH, F.R.S.

Written between 1771 and 1781, Edited from the original manuscripts in the possession of the Duke of Devonshire, K. G., by J. CLERK MAXWELL, F.R.S. Demy 8vo. cloth. 18*s.*

"This work, which derives a melancholy interest from the lamented death of the editor following so closely upon its publication, is a valuable addition to the history of electrical research.... The papers themselves are most carefully reproduced, with fac-similes of the author's sketches of experimental apparatus. . . . Every department of editorial duty appears to have been most conscientiously performed; and it must have been no small satisfaction to Prof. Maxwell to see this goodly volume completed before his life's work was done."—*Athenæum.*

"Few men have made such important discoveries in such different branches of Natural Philosophy as Cavendish. . . The book before us shews that he was in addition the discoverer of some of the most important of the laws of electricity."—*Cambridge Review.*

A TREATISE ON NATURAL PHILOSOPHY.

By Sir W. THOMSON, LL.D., D.C.L., F.R.S., Professor of Natural Philosophy in the University of Glasgow, and P. G. TAIT, M.A., Professor of Natural Philosophy in the University of Edinburgh. Vol. I. Part I. 16*s*.

Part II. *In the Press.*

"In this, the second edition, we notice a large amount of new matter, the importance of which is such that any opinion which we could form within the time at our disposal would be utterly inadequate."—*Nature.*

MATHEMATICAL AND PHYSICAL PAPERS,

By GEORGE GABRIEL STOKES, M.A., D.C.L., LL.D., F.R.S., Fellow of Pembroke College, and Lucasian Professor of Mathematics in the University of Cambridge. Reprinted from the Original Journals and Transactions, with Additional Notes by the Author. Vol. I. Demy Octavo, cloth. 15*s*.

VOL. II. *In the Press.*

ELEMENTS OF NATURAL PHILOSOPHY.

By Professors Sir W. THOMSON and P. G. TAIT. Part I. 8vo. cloth, *Second Edition.* 9*s*.

"This work is designed especially for the use of schools and junior classes in the Universities, the mathematical methods being limited almost without exception to those of the most elementary geometry, algebra, and trigonometry. Tiros in Natural Philosophy cannot be better directed than by being told to give their diligent attention to an intelligent digestion of the contents of this excellent *vade mecum.*"—*Iron.*

A TREATISE ON THE THEORY OF DETERMINANTS, AND THEIR APPLICATIONS IN ANALYSIS AND GEOMETRY,

by ROBERT FORSYTH SCOTT, M.A., of St John's College, Cambridge. Demy 8vo. 12*s*.

HYDRODYNAMICS,

A Treatise on the Mathematical Theory of the Motion of Fluids, by HORACE LAMB, M.A., formerly Fellow of Trinity College, Cambridge; Professor of Mathematics in the University of Adelaide. Demy 8vo. 12*s*.

THE ANALYTICAL THEORY OF HEAT,

By JOSEPH FOURIER. Translated, with Notes, by A. FREEMAN, M.A. Fellow of St John's College, Cambridge. Demy Octavo. 16*s*.

"Fourier's treatise is one of the very few scientific books which can never be rendered antiquated by the progress of science. It is not only the first and the greatest book on the physical subject of the conduction of Heat, but in every Chapter new views are opened up into vast fields of mathematical speculation."

"Whatever text-books may be written, giving, perhaps, more succinct proofs of Fourier's different equations, Fourier himself will in all time coming retain his unique prerogative of being the guide of his reader into regions inaccessible to meaner men, however expert."—*Extract from letter of Professor Clerk Maxwell.*

"It is time that Fourier's masterpiece, *The Analytical Theory of Heat*, translated by Mr Alex. Freeman, should be introduced to those English students of Mathematics who do not follow with freedom a treatise in any language but their own. It is a model of mathematical reasoning applied to physical phenomena, and is remarkable for the ingenuity of the analytical process employed by the author."—*Contemporary Review*, October, 1878.

"There cannot be two opinions as to the value and importance of the *Théorie de la Chaleur.* It has been called 'an exquisite mathematical poem,' not once but many times, independently, by mathematicians of different schools. Many of the very greatest of modern mathematicians regard it, justly, as the key which first opened to them the treasure-house of mathematical physics. It is still *the* text-book of Heat Conduction, and there seems little present prospect of its being superseded, though it is already more than half a century old."—*Nature.*

AN ELEMENTARY TREATISE ON QUATERNIONS,

By P. G. TAIT, M.A., Professor of Natural Philosophy in the University of Edinburgh. *Second Edition.* Demy 8vo. 14*s*.

COUNTERPOINT.

A Practical Course of Study, by Professor G. A. MACFARREN, M.A., Mus. Doc. Second Edition, revised. Demy Quarto, cloth. 7*s*. 6*d*.

A CATALOGUE OF AUSTRALIAN FOSSILS

(including Tasmania and the Island of Timor), Stratigraphically and Zoologically arranged, by ROBERT ETHERIDGE, Jun., F.G.S., Acting Palæontologist, H.M. Geol. Survey of Scotland, (formerly Assistant-Geologist, Geol. Survey of Victoria). Demy Octavo, cloth, 10*s*. 6*d*.

"The work is arranged with great clearness, and contains a full list of the books and papers consulted by the author, and an index to the genera."—*Saturday Review*.

ILLUSTRATIONS OF COMPARATIVE ANATOMY, VERTEBRATE AND INVERTEBRATE,

for the Use of Students in the Museum of Zoology and Comparative Anatomy. Second Edition. Demy Octavo, cloth, 2*s*. 6*d*.

A SYNOPSIS OF THE CLASSIFICATION OF THE BRITISH PALÆOZOIC ROCKS,

by the Rev. ADAM SEDGWICK, M.A., F.R.S., and FREDERICK M^cCOY, F.G.S. One vol., Royal Quarto, Plates, £1. 1*s*.

A CATALOGUE OF THE COLLECTION OF CAMBRIAN AND SILURIAN FOSSILS

contained in the Geological Museum of the University of Cambridge, by J. W. SALTER, F.G.S. With a Portrait of PROFESSOR SEDGWICK. Royal Quarto, cloth, 7*s*. 6*d*.

CATALOGUE OF OSTEOLOGICAL SPECIMENS

contained in the Anatomical Museum of the University of Cambridge. Demy Octavo. 2*s*. 6*d*.

THE MATHEMATICAL WORKS OF ISAAC BARROW, D.D.

Edited by W. WHEWELL, D.D. Demy Octavo. 7*s*. 6*d*.

ASTRONOMICAL OBSERVATIONS

made at the Observatory of Cambridge by the Rev. JAMES CHALLIS, M.A., F.R.S., F.R.A.S., Plumian Professor of Astronomy and Experimental Philosophy in the University of Cambridge, and Fellow of Trinity College. For various Years, from 1846 to 1860.

ASTRONOMICAL OBSERVATIONS

from 1861 to 1865. Vol. XXI. Royal 4to. cloth. 15*s*.

LAW.

AN ANALYSIS OF CRIMINAL LIABILITY.

By E. C. CLARK, LL.D., Regius Professor of Civil Law in the University of Cambridge, also of Lincoln's Inn, Barrister at Law. Crown 8vo. cloth, 7*s*. 6*d*.

A SELECTION OF THE STATE TRIALS.

By J. W. WILLIS-BUND, M.A., LL.B., Barrister-at-Law, Professor of Constitutional Law and History, University College, London. Vol. I. Trials for Treason (1327—1660). Crown 8vo. cloth, 18*s*.

"A great and good service has been done to all students of history, and especially to those of them who look to it in a legal aspect, by Prof. J. W. Willis-Bund in the publication of a *Selection of Cases from the State Trials*. . . . Professor Willis-Bund has been very careful to give such selections from the State Trials as will best illustrate those points in what may be called the growth of the Law of Treason which he wishes to bring clearly under the notice of the student, and the result is, that there is not a page in the book which has not its own lesson. . . . . In all respects, so far as we have been able to test it, this book is admirably done."—*Scotsman*.

"Mr Willis-Bund has edited 'A Selection of Cases from the State Trials' which is likely to form a very valuable addition to the standard literature. . . There can be no doubt, therefore, of the interest that can be found in the State trials. But they are large and unwieldy, and it is impossible for the general reader to come across them. Mr Willis-Bund has therefore done good service in making a selection that is in the first volume reduced to a commodious form."—*The Examiner*.

"Every one engaged, either in teaching or in historical inquiry, must have felt the want of such a book, taken from the unwieldy volumes of the State Trials."—*Contemporary Review*.

"This work is a very useful contribution to that important branch of the constitutional history of England which is concerned with the growth and development of the law of treason, as it may be gathered from trials before the ordinary courts. The author has very wisely distinguished these cases from those of impeachment for treason before Parliament, which he proposes to treat in a future volume under the general head 'Proceedings in Parliament.'"—*The Academy*.

This is a work of such obvious utility that the only wonder is that no one should have undertaken it before.... In many respects therefore, although the trials are more or less abridged, this is for the ordinary student's purpose not only a more handy, but a more useful work than Howell's."—*Saturday Review*.

"Within the boards of this useful and handy book the student will find everything he can desire in the way of lists of cases given at length or referred to, and the statutes bearing on the text arranged chronologically. The work of selecting from Howell's bulky series of volumes has been done with much judgment, merely curious cases being excluded, and all included so treated as to illustrate some important point of constitutional law."—*Glasgow Herald*.

"Mr Willis-Bund gives a *résumé* of each case as it comes, only quoting from the reports where the words of the original are important in themselves, and very often stating the point decided in his own words. By following this method he is able to introduce extraneous matter which does not strictly belong to the case in hand, such as Acts of Parliament, and in that way to make his book both more intelligible and more interesting. In the several trials which we have read he has done his work very well. The book should be very interesting to the historical student. . . . From what we have seen of this book we have great pleasure in recommending it."—*Guardian*.

"Mr Bund's object is not the romance, but the constitutional and legal bearings of that great series of *causes célèbres* which is unfortunately not within easy reach of readers not happy enough to possess valuable libraries. . . . Of the importance of this subject, or of the want of a book of this kind, referring not vaguely but precisely to the grounds of constitutional doctrines, both of past and present times, no reader of history can feel any doubt."—*Daily News*.

Vol. II. *In the Press*.

THE FRAGMENTS OF THE PERPETUAL EDICT OF SALVIUS JULIANUS,

collected, arranged, and annotated by BRYAN WALKER, M.A. LL.D., Law Lecturer of St John's College, and late Fellow of Corpus Christi College, Cambridge. Crown 8vo., Cloth, Price 6*s*.

"This is one of the latest, we believe quite the latest, of the contributions made to legal scholarship by that revived study of the Roman Law at Cambridge which is now so marked a feature in the industrial life of the University. . . . In the present book we have the fruits of the same kind of thorough and well-ordered study which was brought to bear upon the notes to the Commentaries and the Institutes . . . Hitherto the Edict has been almost inaccessible to the ordinary English student, and such a student will be interested as well as perhaps surprised to find how abundantly the extant fragments illustrate and clear up points which have attracted his attention in the Commentaries, or the Institutes, or the Digest."—*Law Times*.

THE COMMENTARIES OF GAIUS AND RULES OF ULPIAN. (New Edition, revised and enlarged.)

With a Translation and Notes, by J. T. ABDY, LL.D., Judge of County Courts, late Regius Professor of Laws in the University of Cambridge, and BRYAN WALKER, M.A., LL.D., Law Lecturer of St John's College, Cambridge, formerly Law Student of Trinity Hall and Chancellor's Medallist for Legal Studies. Crown Octavo, 16*s*.

"As scholars and as editors Messrs Abdy and Walker have done their work well. . . . . . For one thing the editors deserve special commendation. They have presented Gaius to the reader with few notes and those merely by way of reference or necessary explanation. Thus the Roman jurist is allowed to speak for himself, and the reader feels that he is really studying Roman law in the original, and not a fanciful representation of it."—*Athenæum*.

THE INSTITUTES OF JUSTINIAN,

translated with Notes by J. T. ABDY, LL.D., Judge of County Courts, late Regius Professor of Laws in the University of Cambridge, and formerly Fellow of Trinity Hall; and BRYAN WALKER, M.A., LL.D., Law Lecturer of St John's College, Cambridge; late Fellow and Lecturer of Corpus Christi College; and formerly Law Student of Trinity Hall. Crown Octavo, 16*s*.

"We welcome here a valuable contribution to the study of jurisprudence. The text of the *Institutes* is occasionally perplexing, even to practised scholars, whose knowledge of classical models does not always avail them in dealing with the technicalities of legal phraseology. Nor can the ordinary dictionaries be expected to furnish all the help that is wanted. This translation will then be of great use. To the ordinary student, whose attention is distracted from the subject-matter by the difficulty of struggling through the language in which it is contained, it will be almost indispensable."—*Spectator*.

"The notes are learned and carefully compiled, and this edition will be found useful to students."—*Law Times*.

"Dr Abdy and Dr Walker have produced a book which is both elegant and useful."—*Athenæum*.

SELECTED TITLES FROM THE DIGEST,

annotated by B. WALKER, M.A., LL.D. Part I. Mandati vel Contra. Digest XVII. I. Crown 8vo., Cloth, 5*s*.

"This small volume is published as an experiment. The author proposes to publish an annotated edition and translation of several books of the Digest if this one is received with favour. We are pleased to be able to say that Mr Walker deserves credit for the way in which he has performed the task undertaken. The translation, as might be expected, is scholarly." *Law Times*.

Part II. De Adquirendo rerum dominio and De Adquirenda vel amittenda possessione. Digest XLI. I & II. Crown Octavo, Cloth. 6*s*.

Part III. *In the Press.*

GROTIUS DE JURE BELLI ET PACIS,

with the Notes of Barbeyrac and others; accompanied by an abridged Translation of the Text, by W. WHEWELL, D.D. late Master of Trinity College. 3 Vols. Demy Octavo, 12*s*. The translation separate, 6*s*.

HISTORY.

LIFE AND TIMES OF STEIN, OR GERMANY AND PRUSSIA IN THE NAPOLEONIC AGE,

by J. R. SEELEY, M.A., Regius Professor of Modern History in the University of Cambridge, with Portraits and Maps. 3 Vols. Demy 8vo. 48*s.*

"If we could conceive anything similar to a protective system in the intellectual department, we might perhaps look forward to a time when our historians would raise the cry of protection for native industry. Of the unquestionably greatest German men of modern history—I speak of Frederick the Great, Goethe and Stein—the first two found long since in Carlyle and Lewes biographers who have undoubtedly driven their German competitors out of the field. And now in the year just past Professor Seeley of Cambridge has presented us with a biography of Stein which, though it modestly declines competition with German works and disowns the presumption of teaching us Germans our own history, yet casts into the shade by its brilliant superiority all that we have ourselves hitherto written about Stein.... In five long chapters Seeley expounds the legislative and administrative reforms, the emancipation of the person and the soil, the beginnings of free administration and free trade, in short the foundation of modern Prussia, with more exhaustive thoroughness, with more penetrating insight, than any one had done before."—*Deutsche Rundschau.*

"Dr Busch's volume has made people think and talk even more than usual of Prince Bismarck, and Professor Seeley's very learned work on Stein will turn attention to an earlier and an almost equally eminent German statesman. . . . . . . It is soothing to the national self-respect to find a few Englishmen, such as the late Mr Lewes and Professor Seeley, doing for German as well as English readers what many German scholars have done for us."—*Times.*

"In a notice of this kind scant justice can be done to a work like the one before us; no short *résumé* can give even the most meagre notion of the contents of these volumes, which contain no page that is superfluous, and none that is uninteresting. . . . . To understand the Germany of to-day one must study the Germany of many yesterdays, and now that study has been made easy by this work, to which no one can hesitate to assign a very high place among those recent histories which have aimed at original research."—*Athenæum.*

"The book before us fills an important gap in English—nay, European—historical literature, and bridges over the history of Prussia from the time of Frederick the Great to the days of Kaiser Wilhelm. It thus gives the reader standing ground whence he may regard contemporary events in Germany in their proper historic light. . . . . We congratulate Cambridge and her Professor of History on the appearance of such a noteworthy production. And we may add that it is something upon which we may congratulate England that on the especial field of the Germans, history, on the history of their own country, by the use of their own literary weapons, an Englishman has produced a history of Germany in the Napoleonic age far superior to any that exists in German."—*Examiner.*

THE UNIVERSITY OF CAMBRIDGE FROM THE EARLIEST TIMES TO THE ROYAL INJUNCTIONS OF 1535,

by JAMES BASS MULLINGER, M.A. Demy 8vo. cloth (734 pp.), 12*s.*

"We trust Mr Mullinger will yet continue his history and bring it down to our own day."—*Academy.*

"He has brought together a mass of instructive details respecting the rise and progress, not only of his own University, but of all the principal Universities of the Middle Ages...... We hope some day that he may continue his labours, and give us a history of the University during the troublous times of the Reformation and the Civil War."—*Athenæum.*

"Mr Mullinger's work is one of great learning and research, which can hardly fail to become a standard book of reference on the subject.... We can most strongly recommend this book to our readers."—*Spectator.*

VOL. II. *In the Press.*

HISTORY OF THE COLLEGE OF ST JOHN THE EVANGELIST,

by THOMAS BAKER, B.D., Ejected Fellow. Edited by JOHN E. B. MAYOR, M.A., Fellow of St John's. Two Vols. Demy 8vo. 24*s*.

"To antiquaries the book will be a source of almost inexhaustible amusement, by historians it will be found a work of considerable service on questions respecting our social progress in past times; and the care and thoroughness with which Mr Mayor has discharged his editorial functions are creditable to his learning and industry."—*Athenæum.*

"The work displays very wide reading, and it will be of great use to members of the college and of the university, and, perhaps, of still greater use to students of English history, ecclesiastical, political, social, literary and academical, who have hitherto had to be content with 'Dyer.'"—*Academy.*

"It may be thought that the history of a college cannot be particularly attractive. The two volumes before us, however, have something more than a mere special interest for those who have been in any way connected with St John's College, Cambridge; they contain much which will be read with pleasure by a far wider circle... The index with which Mr Mayor has furnished this useful work leaves nothing to be desired."—*Spectator.*

HISTORY OF NEPĀL,

translated by MUNSHĪ SHEW SHUNKER SINGH and PANDIT SHRĪ GUNĀNAND; edited with an Introductory Sketch of the Country and People by Dr D. WRIGHT, late Residency Surgeon at Kāṭhmāṇḍū, and with facsimiles of native drawings, and portraits of Sir JUNG BAHĀDUR, the KING OF NEPĀL, &c. Super-royal 8vo. Price 21*s*.

"The Cambridge University Press have done well in publishing this work. Such translations are valuable not only to the historian but also to the ethnologist;......Dr Wright's Introduction is based on personal inquiry and observation, is written intelligently and candidly, and adds much to the value of the volume. The coloured lithographic plates are interesting."—*Nature.*

"The history has appeared at a very opportune moment...The volume...is beautifully printed, and supplied with portraits of Sir Jung Bahadoor and others, and with excellent coloured sketches illustrating Nepaulese architecture and religion."—*Examiner.*

"Von nicht geringem Werthe dagegen sind die Beigaben, welche Wright als 'Appendix' hinter der 'history' folgen lässt, Aufzählungen nämlich der in Nepâl üblichen Musik-Instrumente, Ackergeräthe, Münzen, Gewichte, Zeittheilung, sodann ein kurzes Vocabular in Parbatiyâ und Newârî, einige Newârî songs mit Interlinear-Uebersetzung, eine Königsliste, und, last not least, ein Verzeichniss der von ihm mitgebrachten Sanskrit-Mss., welche jetzt in der Universitäts-Bibliothek in Cambridge deponirt sind."—A. WEBER, *Literaturzeitung*, Jahrgang 1877, Nr. 26.

THE ARCHITECTURAL HISTORY OF THE UNIVERSITY AND COLLEGES OF CAMBRIDGE,

By the late Professor WILLIS, M.A. With numerous Maps, Plans, and Illustrations. Continued to the present time, and edited by JOHN WILLIS CLARK, M.A., formerly Fellow of Trinity College, Cambridge. [*In the Press.*

SCHOLAE ACADEMICAE:

Some Account of the Studies at the English Universities in the Eighteenth Century. By CHRISTOPHER WORDSWORTH, M.A., Fellow of Peterhouse; Author of "Social Life at the English Universities in the Eighteenth Century." Demy octavo, cloth, 15*s*.

"The general object of Mr Wordsworth's book is sufficiently apparent from its title. He has collected a great quantity of minute and curious information about the working of Cambridge institutions in the last century, with an occasional comparison of the corresponding state of things at Oxford. It is of course impossible that a book of this kind should be altogether entertaining as literature. To a great extent it is purely a book of reference, and as such it will be of permanent value for the historical knowledge of English education and learning."—*Saturday Review*.

"In the work before us, which is strictly what it professes to be, an account of university studies, we obtain authentic information upon the course and changes of philosophical thought in this country, upon the general estimation of letters, upon the relations of doctrine and science, upon the range and thoroughness of education, and we may add, upon the catlike tenacity of life of ancient forms.... The particulars Mr Wordsworth gives us in his excellent arrangement are most varied, interesting, and instructive. Among the matters touched upon are Libraries, Lectures, the Tripos, the Trivium, the Senate House, the Schools, text-books, subjects of study, foreign opinions, interior life. We learn even of the various University periodicals that have had their day. And last, but not least, we are given in an appendix a highly interesting series of private letters from a Cambridge student to John Strype, giving a vivid idea of life as an undergraduate and afterwards, as the writer became a graduate and a fellow."—*University Magazine*.

"Only those who have engaged in like labours will be able fully to appreciate the sustained industry and conscientious accuracy discernible in every page. . . . Of the whole volume it may be said that it is a genuine service rendered to the study of University history, and that the habits of thought of any writer educated at either seat of learning in the last century will, in many cases, be far better understood after a consideration of the materials here collected."—*Academy*.

MISCELLANEOUS.

LECTURES ON TEACHING,

Delivered in the University of Cambridge in the Lent Term, 1880.
By J. G. FITCH, Her Majesty's Inspector of Schools.
Crown 8vo. cloth, 6*s*.

STATUTA ACADEMIÆ CANTABRIGIENSIS.

Demy Octavo. 2*s*. sewed.

ORDINATIONES ACADEMIÆ CANTABRIGIENSIS

Demy Octavo, cloth. 3*s*. 6*d*.

TRUSTS, STATUTES AND DIRECTIONS affecting

(1) The Professorships of the University. (2) The Scholarships and Prizes. (3) Other Gifts and Endowments. Demy 8vo. 5*s*.

COMPENDIUM OF UNIVERSITY REGULATIONS,

for the use of persons in Statu Pupillari. Demy Octavo. 6*d*.

London: Cambridge Warehouse, 17 *Paternoster Row*.

CATALOGUE OF THE HEBREW MANUSCRIPTS preserved in the University Library, Cambridge. By Dr S. M. SCHILLER-SZINESSY. Volume I. containing Section I. *The Holy Scriptures;* Section II. *Commentaries on the Bible.* Demy Octavo. 9*s.*

A CATALOGUE OF THE MANUSCRIPTS preserved in the Library of the University of Cambridge. Demy Octavo. 5 Vols. 10*s.* each.

INDEX TO THE CATALOGUE. Demy Octavo. 10*s.*

A CATALOGUE OF ADVERSARIA and printed books containing MS. notes, preserved in the Library of the University of Cambridge. 3*s.* 6*d.*

THE ILLUMINATED MANUSCRIPTS IN THE LIBRARY OF THE FITZWILLIAM MUSEUM, Catalogued with Descriptions, and an Introduction, by WILLIAM GEORGE SEARLE, M.A., late Fellow of Queens' College, and Vicar of Hockington, Cambridgeshire. Demy Octavo. 7*s.* 6*d.*

A CHRONOLOGICAL LIST OF THE GRACES, Documents, and other Papers in the University Registry which concern the University Library. Demy Octavo. 2*s.* 6*d.*

CATALOGUS BIBLIOTHECÆ BURCKHARDTIANÆ. Demy Quarto. 5*s.*

The Cambridge Bible for Schools.

GENERAL EDITOR: J. J. S. PEROWNE, D.D., DEAN OF PETERBOROUGH.

THE want of an Annotated Edition of the BIBLE, in handy portions, suitable for School use, has long been felt.

In order to provide Text-books for School and Examination purposes, the CAMBRIDGE UNIVERSITY PRESS has arranged to publish the several books of the BIBLE in separate portions at a moderate price, with introductions and explanatory notes.

The Very Reverend J. J. S. PEROWNE, D.D., Dean of Peterborough, has undertaken the general editorial supervision of the work, and will be assisted by a staff of eminent coadjutors. Some of the books have already been undertaken by the following gentlemen:

Rev. A. CARR, M.A., *Assistant Master at Wellington College.*
Rev. T. K. CHEYNE, *Fellow of Balliol College, Oxford.*
Rev. S. COX, *Nottingham.*
Rev. A. B. DAVIDSON, D.D., *Professor of Hebrew, Edinburgh.*
Rev. F. W. FARRAR, D.D., *Canon of Westminster.*
Rev. A. E. HUMPHREYS, M.A., *Fellow of Trinity College, Cambridge.*
Rev. A. F. KIRKPATRICK, M.A., *Fellow of Trinity College.*
Rev. J. J. LIAS, M.A., *late Professor at St David's College, Lampeter.*
Rev. J. R. LUMBY, D.D., *Norrisian Professor of Divinity.*
Rev. G. F. MACLEAR, D.D., *Warden of St Augustine's Coll., Canterbury.*
Rev. H. C. G. MOULE, M.A., *Fellow of Trinity College.*
Rev. W. F. MOULTON, D.D., *Head Master of the Leys School, Cambridge.*
Rev. E. H. PEROWNE, D.D., *Master of Corpus Christi College, Cambridge, Examining Chaplain to the Bishop of St Asaph.*
The Ven. T. T. PEROWNE, M.A., *Archdeacon of Norwich.*
Rev. A. PLUMMER, M.A., *Master of University College, Durham.*
Rev. E. H. PLUMPTRE, D.D., *Professor of Biblical Exegesis, King's College, London.*
Rev. W. SANDAY, M.A., *Principal of Bishop Hatfield Hall, Durham.*
Rev. W. SIMCOX, M.A., *Rector of Weyhill, Hants.*
Rev. ROBERTSON SMITH, M.A., *Professor of Hebrew, Aberdeen.*
Rev. A. W. STREANE, M.A., *Fellow of Corpus Christi Coll., Cambridge.*
The Ven. H. W. WATKINS, M.A., *Archdeacon of Northumberland.*
Rev. G. H. WHITAKER, M.A., *Fellow of St John's College, Cambridge.*
Rev. C. WORDSWORTH, M.A., *Rector of Glaston, Rutland.*

THE CAMBRIDGE BIBLE FOR SCHOOLS.—*Continued.*

Now Ready. Cloth, Extra Fcap. 8vo.

THE BOOK OF JOSHUA. Edited by Rev. G. F. MACLEAR, D.D. With 2 Maps. 2*s.* 6*d.*

THE FIRST BOOK OF SAMUEL. By the Rev. A. F. KIRKPATRICK, M.A. 3*s.* 6*d.*

THE BOOK OF JEREMIAH. By the Rev. A. W. STREANE, M.A. 4*s.* 6*d.*

THE BOOK OF JONAH. By Archdn. PEROWNE. 1*s.* 6*d.*

THE GOSPEL ACCORDING TO ST MATTHEW. Edited by the Rev. A. CARR, M.A. With 2 Maps. 2*s.* 6*d.*

THE GOSPEL ACCORDING TO ST MARK. Edited by the Rev. G. F. MACLEAR, D.D. (with 2 Maps). 2*s.* 6*d.*

THE GOSPEL ACCORDING TO ST LUKE. By the Rev. F. W. FARRAR, D.D. (With 4 Maps.) 4*s.* 6*d.*

THE GOSPEL ACCORDING TO ST JOHN. By the Rev. A. PLUMMER, M.A. With Four Maps. 4*s.* 6*d.*

THE ACTS OF THE APOSTLES. By the Rev. Professor LUMBY, D.D. Part I. Chaps. I—XIV. With 2 Maps. 2*s.* 6*d.*

PART II. *Preparing.*

THE EPISTLE TO THE ROMANS. By the Rev. H. C. G. MOULE, M.A. 3*s.* 6*d.*

THE FIRST EPISTLE TO THE CORINTHIANS. By the Rev. Professor LIAS, M.A. With a Map and Plan. 2*s.*

THE SECOND EPISTLE TO THE CORINTHIANS. By the Rev. Professor LIAS, M.A. 2*s.*

THE GENERAL EPISTLE OF ST JAMES. By the Rev. Professor PLUMPTRE, D.D. 1*s.* 6*d.*

THE EPISTLES OF ST PETER AND ST JUDE. By the Rev. Professor PLUMPTRE, D.D. 2*s.* 6*d.*

THE CAMBRIDGE BIBLE FOR SCHOOLS.—*Continued.*

Preparing.

THE SECOND BOOK OF SAMUEL. By the Rev. A. F. KIRKPATRICK, M.A.

THE BOOKS OF HAGGAI AND ZECHARIAH. By Archdeacon PEROWNE.

THE BOOK OF ECCLESIASTES. By the Rev. Professor PLUMPTRE.

In Preparation.

THE CAMBRIDGE GREEK TESTAMENT,

FOR SCHOOLS AND COLLEGES,

with a Revised Text, based on the most recent critical authorities, and English Notes, prepared under the direction of the General Editor,

THE VERY REVEREND J. J. S. PEROWNE, D.D.,
DEAN OF PETERBOROUGH.

THE GOSPEL ACCORDING TO ST MATTHEW. By the Rev. A. CARR, M.A. [*Nearly ready.*

The books will be published separately, as in the "Cambridge Bible for Schools."

THE PITT PRESS SERIES.

I. GREEK.

THE ANABASIS OF XENOPHON, BOOK VII. With a Map and English Notes by ALFRED PRETOR, M.A., Fellow of St Catharine's College, Cambridge; Editor of *Persius* and *Cicero ad Atticum* Book I. *Price 2s. 6d.*

"In Mr Pretor's edition of the Anabasis the text of Kühner has been followed in the main, while the exhaustive and admirable notes of the great German editor have been largely utilised. These notes deal with the minutest as well as the most important difficulties in construction, and all questions of history, antiquity, and geography are briefly but very effectually elucidated."—*The Examiner.*

BOOKS I. III. IV. & V. By the same Editor. 2*s.* each.

BOOKS II. and VI. By the same Editor. *Price 2s. 6d.* each.

"Mr Pretor's 'Anabasis of Xenophon, Book IV.' displays a union of accurate Cambridge scholarship, with experience of what is required by learners gained in examining middle-class schools. The text is large and clearly printed, and the notes explain all difficulties. . . . Mr Pretor's notes seem to be all that could be wished as regards grammar, geography, and other matters."—*The Academy.*

"Another Greek text, designed it would seem for students preparing for the local examinations, is 'Xenophon's Anabasis,' Book II., with English Notes, by Alfred Pretor, M.A. The editor has exercised his usual discrimination in utilising the text and notes of Kuhner, with the occasional assistance of the best hints of Schneider, Vollbrecht and Macmichael on critical matters, and of Mr R. W. Taylor on points of history and geography. . . When Mr Pretor commits himself to Commentator's work, he is eminently helpful. . . Had we to introduce a young Greek scholar to Xenophon, we should esteem ourselves fortunate in having Pretor's text-book as our chart and guide."—*Contemporary Review.*

AGESILAUS OF XENOPHON. The Text revised with Critical and Explanatory Notes, Introduction, Analysis, and Indices. By H. HAILSTONE, M.A., late Scholar of Peterhouse, Cambridge, Editor of Xenophon's Hellenics, etc. Cloth. 2*s.* 6*d.*

ARISTOPHANES—RANAE. With English Notes and Introduction by W. C. GREEN, M.A., Assistant Master at Rugby School. Cloth. 3*s.* 6*d.*

ARISTOPHANES—AVES. By the same Editor. *New Edition.* Cloth. 3*s.* 6*d.*

"The notes to both plays are excellent. Much has been done in these two volumes to render the study of Aristophanes a real treat to a boy instead of a drudgery, by helping him to understand the fun and to express it in his mother tongue."—*The Examiner.*

EURIPIDES. HERCULES FURENS. With Introductions, Notes and Analysis. By J. T. HUTCHINSON, M.A., Christ's College, and A. GRAY, M.A., Fellow of Jesus College. Cloth, 2*s.*

"Messrs Hutchinson and Gray have produced a careful and useful edition."—*Saturday Review.*

THE HERACLEIDÆ OF EURIPIDES, with Introduction and Critical Notes by E. A. BECK, M.A., Fellow of Trinity Hall. [*In the Press.*

LUCIANI SOMNIUM CHARON PISCATOR ET DE LUCTU, with English Notes by W. E. HEITLAND, M.A., Fellow of St John's College, Cambridge. New Edition, with Appendix. 3*s.* 6*d.*

II. LATIN.

M. T. CICERONIS DE AMICITIA. Edited by J. S. REID, M.L., Fellow of Gonville and Caius College, Cambridge. *Price* 3*s.*

"Mr Reid has decidedly attained his aim, namely, 'a thorough examination of the Latinity of the dialogue.'..... The revision of the text is most valuable, and comprehends sundry acute corrections.... This volume, like Mr Reid's other editions, is a solid gain to the scholarship of the country."—*Athenæum.*

"A more distinct gain to scholarship is Mr Reid's able and thorough edition of the *De Amicitiâ* of Cicero, a work of which, whether we regard the exhaustive introduction or the instructive and most suggestive commentary, it would be difficult to speak too highly. . . . When we come to the commentary, we are only amazed by its fulness in proportion to its bulk. Nothing is overlooked which can tend to enlarge the learner's general knowledge of Ciceronian Latin or to elucidate the text."—*Saturday Review.*

M. T. CICERONIS CATO MAJOR DE SENECTUTE. Edited by J. S. REID, M.L. *Price* 3*s.* 6*d.*

"The notes are excellent and scholarlike, adapted for the upper forms of public schools, and likely to be useful even to more advanced students."—*Guardian.*

M. T. CICERONIS ORATIO PRO ARCHIA POETA. Edited by J. S. REID, M.L. *Price* 1*s.* 6*d.*

"It is an admirable specimen of careful editing. An Introduction tells us everything we could wish to know about Archias, about Cicero's connexion with him, about the merits of the trial, and the genuineness of the speech. The text is well and carefully printed. The notes are clear and scholar-like.... No boy can master this little volume without feeling that he has advanced a long step in scholarship."—*The Academy.*

M. T. CICERONIS PRO L. CORNELIO BALBO ORATIO. Edited by J. S. REID, M.L. Fellow of Caius College, Cambridge. *Price* 1*s.* 6*d.*

"We are bound to recognize the pains devoted in the annotation of these two orations to the minute and thorough study of their Latinity, both in the ordinary notes and in the textual appendices."—*Saturday Review.*

M. T. CICERONIS PRO CN. PLANCIO ORATIO. Edited by H. A. HOLDEN, LL.D., Head Master of Ipswich School. [*In the Press.*

QUINTUS CURTIUS. A Portion of the History. (ALEXANDER IN INDIA.) By W. E. HEITLAND, M.A., Fellow and Lecturer of St John's College, Cambridge, and T. E. RAVEN, B.A., Assistant Master in Sherborne School. *Price* 3*s.* 6*d.*

"Equally commendable as a genuine addition to the existing stock of school-books is *Alexander in India*, a compilation from the eighth and ninth books of Q. Curtius, edited for the Pitt Press by Messrs Heitland and Raven.... The work of Curtius has merits of its own, which, in former generations, made it a favourite with English scholars, and which still make it a popular text-book in Continental schools...... The reputation of Mr Heitland is a sufficient guarantee for the scholarship of the notes, which are ample without being excessive, and the book is well furnished with all that is needful in the nature of maps, indexes, and appendices." —*Academy.*

P. OVIDII NASONIS FASTORUM LIBER VI. With a Plan of Rome and Notes by A. SIDGWICK, M.A. Tutor of Corpus Christi College, Oxford. *Price 1s. 6d.*

"Mr Sidgwick's editing of the Sixth Book of Ovid's *Fasti* furnishes a careful and serviceable volume for average students. It eschews 'construes' which supersede the use of the dictionary, but gives full explanation of grammatical usages and historical and mythical allusions, besides illustrating peculiarities of style, true and false derivations, and the more remarkable variations of the text."—*Saturday Review.*

"It is eminently good and useful. . . . The Introductiou is singularly clear on the astronomy of Ovid, which is properly shown to be ignorant and confused; there is an excellent little map of Rome, giving just the places mentioned in the text and no more; the notes are evidently written by a practical schoolmaster."—*The Academy.*

GAI IULI CAESARIS DE BELLO GALLICO COMMENT. I. II. With English Notes and Map by A. G. PESKETT, M.A., Fellow of Magdalene College, Cambridge, Editor of Caesar De Bello Gallico, VII. *Price 2s. 6d.*

GAI IULI CAESARIS DE BELLO GALLICO COMMENTARIUS SEPTIMUS. With two Plans and English Notes by A. G. PESKETT, M.A. Fellow of Magdalene College, Cambridge. *Price 2s.*

"In an unusually succinct introduction he gives all the preliminary and collateral information that is likely to be useful to a young student; and, wherever we have examined his notes, we have found them eminently practical and satisfying. . . The book may well be recommended for careful study in school or college."—*Saturday Review.*

"The notes are scholarly, short, and a real help to the most elementary beginners in Latin prose."—*The Examiner.*

BOOKS IV. AND V. by the same Editor. *Price 2s.*

BEDA'S ECCLESIASTICAL HISTORY, BOOKS III., IV., the Text from the very ancient MS. in the Cambridge University Library, collated with six other MSS. Edited, with a life from the German of EBERT, and with Notes, &c. by J. E. B. MAYOR, M.A., Professor of Latin, and J. R. LUMBY, D.D., Norrisian Professor of Divinity. *Price 7s. 6d.*

"To young students of English History the illustrative notes will be of great service, while the study of the texts will be a good introduction to Mediæval Latin."—*The Nonconformist.*

"In Bede's works Englishmen can go back to *origines* of their history, unequalled for form and matter by any modern European nation. Prof. Mayor has done good service in rendering a part of Bede's greatest work accessible to those who can read Latin with ease. He has adorned this edition of the third and fourth books of the "Ecclesiastical History" with that amazing erudition for which he is unrivalled among Englishmen and rarely equalled by Germans. And however interesting and valuable the text may be, we can certainly apply to his notes the expression, *La sauce vaut mieux que le poisson.* They are literally crammed with interesting information about early English life. For though ecclesiastical in name, Bede's history treats of all parts of the national life, since the Church had points of contact with all."—*Examiner.*

P. VERGILI MARONIS AENEIDOS LIBER VII. Edited with Notes by A. SIDGWICK, M.A. Tutor of Corpus Christi College, Oxford. Cloth. *1s. 6d.*

London: Cambridge Warehouse, 17 Paternoster Row.

BOOKS VI., VIII., X., XI., XII. by the same Editor. 1*s*. 6*d*. each.

"Mr Arthur Sidgwick's 'Vergil, Aeneid, Book XII.' is worthy of his reputation, and is distinguished by the same acuteness and accuracy of knowledge, appreciation of a boy's difficulties and ingenuity and resource in meeting them, which we have on other occasions had reason to praise in these pages."—*The Academy.*

"As masterly in its clearly divided preface and appendices as in the sound and independent character of its annotations. . . . There is a great deal more in the notes than mere compilation and suggestion. . . . No difficulty is left unnoticed or unhandled."—*Saturday Review.*

BOOKS VII. VIII. in one volume *Price* 3*s*.

BOOKS X., XI., XII. in one volume. *Price* 3*s*. 6*d*.

M. T. CICERONIS ORATIO PRO L. MURENA, with English Introduction and Notes. By W. E. HEITLAND, M.A., Fellow and Classical Lecturer of St John's College, Cambridge. **Second Edition, carefully revised.** Small 8vo. *Price* 3*s*.

"Those students are to be deemed fortunate who have to read Cicero's lively and brilliant oration for L. Murena with Mr Heitland's handy edition, which may be pronounced 'four-square' in point of equipment, and which has, not without good reason, attained the honours of a second edition."—*Saturday Review.*

M. T. CICERONIS IN Q. CAECILIUM DIVINATIO ET IN C. VERREM ACTIO PRIMA. With Introduction and Notes by W. E. HEITLAND, M.A., and HERBERT COWIE, M.A., Fellows of St John's College, Cambridge. Cloth, extra fcp. 8vo. *Price* 3*s*.

M. T. CICERONIS IN GAIUM VERREM ACTIO PRIMA. With Introduction and Notes. By H. COWIE, M.A., Fellow of St John's College, Cambridge. *Price* 1*s*. 6*d*.

M. T. CICERONIS ORATIO PRO T. A. MILONE, with a Translation of Asconius' Introduction, Marginal Analysis and English Notes. Edited by the Rev. JOHN SMYTH PURTON, B.D., late President and Tutor of St Catharine's College. Cloth, small crown 8vo. *Price* 2*s*. 6*d*.

"The editorial work is excellently done."—*The Academy.*

M. ANNAEI LUCANI PHARSALIAE LIBER PRIMUS, edited with English Introduction and Notes by W. E. HEITLAND, M.A. and C. E. HASKINS, M.A., Fellows and Lecturers of St John's College, Cambridge. *Price* 1*s*. 6*d*.

"A careful and scholarlike production."—*Times.*

"In nice parallels of Lucan from Latin poets and from Shakspeare, Mr Haskins and Mr Heitland deserve praise."—*Saturday Review.*

III. FRENCH.

LAZARE HOCHE—PAR ÉMILE DE BONNECHOSE. With Three Maps, Introduction and Commentary, by C. COLBECK, M.A., late Fellow of Trinity College, Cambridge; Assistant Master at Harrow School. *Price 2s.*

HISTOIRE DU SIÈCLE DE LOUIS XIV PAR VOLTAIRE. Chaps. I.—XIII. Edited with Notes Philological and Historical, Biographical and Geographical Indices, etc. by GUSTAVE MASSON, B.A. Univ. Gallic., Officier d'Académie, Assistant Master of Harrow School, and G. W. PROTHERO, M.A., Fellow and Tutor of King's College, Cambridge. 2*s.* 6*d.*

"Messrs Masson and Prothero have, to judge from the first part of their work, performed with much discretion and care the task of editing Voltaire's *Siècle de Louis XIV* for the 'Pitt Press Series.' Besides the usual kind of notes, the editors have in this case, influenced by Voltaire's 'summary way of treating much of the history,' given a good deal of historical information, in which they have, we think, done well. At the beginning of the book will be found excellent and succinct accounts of the constitution of the French army and Parliament at the period treated of."—*Saturday Review.*

HISTOIRE DU SIÈCLE DE LOUIS XIV PAR VOLTAIRE. Chaps. XIV.—XXIV. With Three Maps of the Period, Notes Philological and Historical, Biographical and Geographical Indices, by G. MASSON, B.A. Univ. Gallic., Assistant Master of Harrow School, and G. W. PROTHERO, M.A., Fellow and Tutor of King's College, Cambridge. *Price 2s. 6d.*

LE VERRE D'EAU. A Comedy, by SCRIBE. With a Biographical Memoir, and Grammatical, Literary and Historical Notes. By C. COLBECK, M.A., late Fellow of Trinity College, Cambridge; Assistant Master at Harrow School. *Price 2s.*

"It may be national prejudice, but we consider this edition far superior to any of the series which hitherto have been edited exclusively by foreigners. Mr Colbeck seems better to understand the wants and difficulties of an English boy. The etymological notes especially are admirable. . . . The historical notes and introduction are a piece of thorough honest work."—*Journal of Education.*

M. DARU, par M. C. A. SAINTE-BEUVE, (Causeries du Lundi, Vol. IX.). With Biographical Sketch of the Author, and Notes Philological and Historical. By GUSTAVE MASSON. 2*s.*

LA SUITE DU MENTEUR. A Comedy in Five Acts, by P. CORNEILLE. Edited with Fontenelle's Memoir of the Author, Voltaire's Critical Remarks, and Notes Philological and Historical. By GUSTAVE MASSON. *Price 2s.*

LA JEUNE SIBÉRIENNE. LE LÉPREUX DE LA CITÉ D'AOSTE. Tales by COUNT XAVIER DE MAISTRE. With Biographical Notice, Critical Appreciations, and Notes. By GUSTAVE MASSON. *Price 2s.*

LE DIRECTOIRE. (Considérations sur la Révolution Française. Troisième et quatrième parties.) Par MADAME LA BARONNE DE STAËL-HOLSTEIN. With a Critical Notice of the Author, a Chronological Table, and Notes Historical and Philological. By G. MASSON. *Price 2s.*

"Prussia under Frederick the Great, and France under the Directory, bring us face to face respectively with periods of history which it is right should be known thoroughly, and which are well treated in the Pitt Press volumes. The latter in particular, an extract from the world-known work of Madame de Staël on the French Revolution, is beyond all praise for the excellence both of its style and of its matter."—*Times.*

DIX ANNEES D'ÉXIL. LIVRE II. CHAPITRES 1—8. Par MADAME LA BARONNE DE STAËL-HOLSTEIN. With a Biographical Sketch of the Author, a Selection of Poetical Fragments by Madame de Staël's Contemporaries, and Notes Historical and Philological. By GUSTAVE MASSON. *Price 2s.*

"The choice made by M. Masson of the second book of the *Memoirs* of Madame de Staël appears specially felicitous. . . . This is likely to be one of the most favoured of M. Masson's editions, and deservedly so."—*Academy.*

FRÉDÉGONDE ET BRUNEHAUT. A Tragedy in Five Acts, by N. LEMERCIER. Edited with Notes, Genealogical and Chronological Tables, a Critical Introduction and a Biographical Notice. By GUSTAVE MASSON. *Price 2s.*

LE VIEUX CÉLIBATAIRE. A Comedy, by COLLIN D'HARLEVILLE. With a Biographical Memoir, and Grammatical, Literary and Historical Notes. By the same Editor. *Price 2s.*

"M. Masson is doing good work in introducing learners to some of the less-known French play-writers. The arguments are admirably clear, and the notes are not too abundant."—*Academy.*

LA MÉTROMANIE, A Comedy, by PIRON, with a Biographical Memoir, and Grammatical, Literary and Historical Notes. By the same Editor. *Price 2s.*

LASCARIS, OU LES GRECS DU XVE. SIÈCLE, Nouvelle Historique, par A. F. VILLEMAIN, with a Biographical Sketch of the Author, a Selection of Poems on Greece, and Notes Historical and Philological. By the same Editor. *Price 2s.*

IV. GERMAN.

ZOPF UND SCHWERT. Lustspiel in fünf Aufzügen von KARL GUTZKOW. With a Biographical Introduction and English Notes. By H. J. WOLSTENHOLME, B.A. (Lond.), Professor of German Bedford College, London, Lecturer in German, Newnham College, Cambridge. *Price 3s. 6d.*

Goethe's Knabenjahre. (1749—1759.) GOETHE'S BOYHOOD: being the First Three Books of his Autobiography. Arranged and Annotated by WILHELM WAGNER, Ph. D., late Professor at the Johanneum, Hamburg. *Price 2s.*

HAUFF. DAS WIRTHSHAUS IM SPESSART. Edited by A. SCHLOTTMANN, Ph. D., Assistant Master at Uppingham School. *Price 3s. 6d.*

"It is admirably edited, and we note with pleasure that Dr Schlottmann in his explanation always brings out the kinship of the English and German languages by reference to earlier or modern English and German forms as the case may be. The notes are valuable, and tell the student exactly what he will want to know, a merit by no means common."—*Examiner.*

"As the work abounds in the idiomatic expressions and phrases that are characteristic of modern German, there are few books that can be read with greater advantage by the English student who desires to acquire a thorough knowledge of conversational German. The notes, without being cumbersome, leave no real difficulty unexplained."—*School Guardian.*

DER OBERHOF. A Tale of Westphalian Life, by KARL IMMERMANN. With a Life of Immermann and English Notes, by WILHELM WAGNER, Ph.D., late Professor at the Johanneum, Hamburg. *Price 3s.*

A BOOK OF GERMAN DACTYLIC POETRY. Arranged and Annotated by the same Editor. *Price 3s.*

Der erste Kreuzzug (THE FIRST CRUSADE), by FRIEDRICH VON RAUMER. Condensed from the Author's 'History of the Hohenstaufen', with a life of RAUMER, two Plans and English Notes. By the same Editor. *Price 2s.*

"Certainly no more interesting book could be made the subject of examinations. The story of the First Crusade has an undying interest. The notes are, on the whole, good."—*Educational Times.*

A BOOK OF BALLADS ON GERMAN HISTORY. Arranged and Annotated by the same Editor. *Price 2s.*

"It carries the reader rapidly through some of the most important incidents connected with the German race and name, from the invasion of Italy by the Visigoths under their King Alaric, down to the Franco-German War and the installation of the present Emperor. The notes supply very well the connecting links between the successive periods, and exhibit in its various phases of growth and progress, or the reverse, the vast unwieldy mass which constitutes modern Germany."—*Times.*

DER STAAT FRIEDRICHS DES GROSSEN. By G. FREYTAG. With Notes. By the same Editor. *Price 2s.*

"Prussia under Frederick the Great, and France under the Directory, bring us face to face respectively with periods of history which it is right should be known thoroughly, and which are well treated in the Pitt Press volumes."—*Times.*

"Freytag's historical sketches and essays are too well known in England to need any commendation, and the present essay is one of his best. Herr Wagner has made good use of Carlyle's great work in illustration of his author."—*Journal of Education.*

GOETHE'S HERMANN AND DOROTHEA. With an Introduction and Notes. By the same Editor. *Price* 3*s*.

"The notes are among the best that we know, with the reservation that they are often too abundant."—*Academy*.

Das Jahr 1813 (THE YEAR 1813), by F. KOHLRAUSCH. With English Notes. By the same Editor. *Price* 2*s*.

V. ENGLISH.

LOCKE ON EDUCATION. With Introduction and Notes by the Rev. R. H. QUICK, M.A. *Price* 3*s*. 6*d*.

"Mr Quick has made the study of educational matters and the lives of educational reformers a speciality. He has given us an edition of Locke which leaves little to be desired. In addition to an introduction, biographical and critical, and numerous notes, there are two appendices containing Locke's scheme of working schools, and Locke's other writings on education. The passages in Locke bearing upon the physical training of children are annotated in harmony with modern science by Dr J. F. Payne. The book forms one of the Pitt Press Series, and its general get up is worthy of the University Press."—*The Schoolmaster*.

"The work before us leaves nothing to be desired. It is of convenient form and reasonable price, accurately printed, and accompanied by notes which are admirable. There is no teacher too young to find this book interesting; there is no teacher too old to find it profitable."—*The School Bulletin, New York*.

THE TWO NOBLE KINSMEN, edited with Introduction and Notes by the Rev. Professor SKEAT, M.A., formerly Fellow of Christ's College, Cambridge. *Price* 3*s*. 6*d*.

"This edition of a play that is well worth study, for more reasons than one, by so careful a scholar as Mr Skeat, deserves a hearty welcome."—*Athenæum*.

"Mr Skeat is a conscientious editor, and has left no difficulty unexplained."—*Times*.

BACON'S HISTORY OF THE REIGN OF KING HENRY VII. With Notes by the Rev. J. RAWSON LUMBY, D.D., Norrisian Professor of Divinity; Fellow of St Catharine's College. 3*s*.

SIR THOMAS MORE'S UTOPIA. With Notes by the Rev. J. RAWSON LUMBY, D.D., Norrisian Professor of Divinity; Fellow of St Catharine's College, Cambridge. *Price* 3*s*. 6*d*.

"To enthusiasts in history matters, who are not content with mere facts, but like to pursue their investigations behind the scenes, as it were, Professor Rawson Lumby has in the work now before us produced a most acceptable contribution to the now constantly increasing store of illustrative reading."—*The Cambridge Review*.

"To Dr Lumby we must give praise unqualified and unstinted. He has done his work admirably. . . . . Every student of history, every politician, every social reformer, every one interested in literary curiosities, every lover of English should buy and carefully read Dr Lumby's edition of the 'Utopia.' We are afraid to say more lest we should be thought extravagant, and our recommendation accordingly lose part of its force."—*The Teacher*.

"It was originally written in Latin and does not find a place on ordinary bookshelves. A very great boon has therefore been conferred on the general English reader by the managers of the *Pitt Press Series*, in the issue of a convenient little volume of *More's Utopia* not in the original Latin, but in the quaint *English Translation thereof made by Raphe Robynson*, which adds a linguistic interest to the intrinsic merit of the work. . . . All this has been edited in a most complete and scholarly fashion by Dr J. R. Lumby, the Norrisian Professor of Divinity, whose name alone is a sufficient warrant for its accuracy. It is a real addition to the modern stock of classical English literature."—*Guardian*.

SIR THOMAS MORE'S LIFE OF RICHARD III. With Notes, &c., by Professor LUMBY. [*Nearly ready*.

[*Other Volumes are in preparation*.]

CAMBRIDGE: PRINTED BY C. J. CLAY, M.A., AT THE UNIVERSITY PRESS.

www.ingramcontent.com/pod-product-compliance
Lightning Source LLC
Chambersburg PA
CBHW021049030726
47496CB00006B/1752
9783337074067